"AN ENGROSSING THRILLER . . . A
GRITTY, GRIPPING WALK ON THE WILD
SIDE OF THE SUNBELT."
—*Kirkus Reviews*

"SUSPENSE WITH A REAL TWIST.
HIGHLY RECOMMENDED."
—*Library Journal*

"INTENSE. THOUGHT-PROVOKING."
—*Booklist*

SACRIFICE

MITCHELL SMITH

AN ONYX BOOK

ONYX
Published by the Penguin Group
Penguin Putnam Inc., 375 Hudson Street,
New York, New York 10014, U.S.A.
Penguin Books Ltd, 27 Wrights Lane,
London W8 5TZ, England
Penguin Books Australia Ltd, Ringwood,
Victoria, Australia
Penguin Books Canada Ltd, 10 Alcorn Avenue,
Toronto, Ontario, Canada M4V 3B2
Penguin Books (N.Z.) Ltd, 182–190 Wairau Road,
Auckland 10, New Zealand

Penguin Books Ltd, Registered Offices:
Harmondsworth, Middlesex, England

Published by Onyx, an imprint of Dutton Signet,
a member of Penguin Putnam Inc.
Previously published in a Dutton edition.

First Onyx Printing, December, 1997
10 9 8 7 6 5 4 3 2 1

PUBLISHER'S NOTE
This is a work of fiction. Names, characters, places, and incidents either are the
product of the author's imagination or are used fictitiously, and any resemblance to
actual persons, living or dead, events, or locales is entirely coincidental.

To Linda

Past all possibilities, a seraph goes walking,
Though never soaked by storms of wind or rain.
It hears our every voice, but does no talking,
And feels each loss and wounding, but no pain.
It ambles, moves along, though never at a run,
And is warmed, not burned, by the reddest sun.

—Michael Barzelai, *Coriolis*
The Madrona Press
San Francisco, 1963

Prologue

The basement offices of Trans-Con Company—40 Collins Street, Everard, Michigan—were painted a painful white, walls and low ceiling, and kept cool with air-conditioning and the even temperature of earth beyond its yard-thick concrete walls. Chilly, even under Pierce's ski mask. —His was blue; Freddy's green; Charlie Cooke's snow white.

Four men lay along the basement wall. They lay on their faces, strapped at wrists and ankles with packing tape. Even in their gray express-company uniforms, their mothers would have recognized them by the backs of their necks, seen so often at late-night looks into their boyhood bedrooms, as they lay defenselessly asleep.

One man, the nearest, was bleeding from the right ear. Charlie Cooke had hit him with his gun. Bad practice. Bad for the gun, a complicated European automatic. A quick spatter of that blood had flicked back to stitch along Cooke's white knit mask just over his left eye.

Tyler Pierce and the two others were waiting for a clerk to make up his mind.

Pierce watched the clerk, young, plump, and pale in his shirt-sleeves, his cheeks dotted with acne. The clerk stared back at two masked faces—Cooke was turned to watch the taped men.

There was a small narrow gray block taped to the

office's four-inch-thick green armor glass. A detonator was stuck into the end of the block.

Pierce raised his voice to be heard through the office's talk grille. "You have less than three minutes. Then it goes off, and the glass comes in and slices you up. Then we come in and get what we came for."

"And if the glass don't get you, I'll get you," Cooke said, without turning his head. "For being such a fuckin' asshole."

". . . A couple of minutes, now," Pierce said.

There was always a surprise. And this time, this job, the clerk had been the surprise. . . . Pierce and the other two had come in a green Trans-Con armored van—the real item, stolen off the company's lot over the border in Indiana at six o'clock that evening, then driven to Everard to arrive at this branch's back lot, at the steel bay doors, seventy seconds before the regular night delivery was scheduled in.

The Trans-Con duty officer had been careless about that seventy seconds. He'd raised the big door—and they were in, had taken the officer in his booth, and had raised the door again as the scheduled van came rolling along right behind them and dead on time.

The armored-van guards had felt at home in the Trans-Con bay, had seen the officer smiling in his booth—Charlie Cooke out of sight on the floor beside him, his pistol muzzle shoved up into the smiler's crotch.

When the three-man crew left the van, Pierce and Freddy had come out of the office to meet them. There was no shooting, no trouble, except for Cooke's hitting the company duty officer with his pistol.

The trouble was afterward. The clerk had been in the can—wasn't even supposed to be in the building after five—had come out, seen it happening, got to the office and locked himself in. Freddy had almost caught him, but not quite.

Freddy could have killed the clerk as he ran. But he hadn't. . . .

"It's going to go!" Pierce said, and he and Freddy and Charlie Cooke headed for cover in the corridor. —But the clerk suddenly began to shout and make faces on the other side of his green armor glass. He scrambled to the office's steel door and slid its three bolts back.

Pierce trotted over, reached up and eased the detonator out of the Simvex, and tossed it down the room. It hit the far concrete wall and didn't go off. Then, on the floor, it did—with a ringing crack, like a .22 in one of the old carny shooting galleries.

Then Freddy was in the office, talking to the clerk . . . putting him on the floor. The getting into the installation had been done. Taking the armored-van shipment had been done. —And now they were in the office and had the outgoing, already packed and stacked. Thank God for the Simvex. Worth all the trouble, every fucking dime. —The whole thing such a great effort, though. It seemed to Pierce like swimming through cold water in a dream. Swimming through that water with something coming nearer, something able to swim very well.

Odd, when it was going so smoothly, so perfectly, that he should be worried. Scared, was a more honest way to put it. *I'm too old for this.* . . .

Seven years in the Kansas pen had been too many years. Nothing to do but read every damn book in the library. . . . The years, or the books, had made a difference after all, even for the Iceman.

Then two years planning this job, planning it to *work*—and getting Freddy in from California, Charlie Cooke from Detroit. Planning something so big, that had to be perfect—and wasn't over yet.

And all for pride, not really for the money at all. Pride—the sin for which the angels fell. Aging bank robbers, too. —See? I'm *not* too old. See? Those seven years inside *didn't* make me less than I was.

A fool, and other men brought into his folly.

Freddy wheeled out the dolly. A heavy-duty four-tire dolly, loaded creaking with five small metal boxes. Wheeled it out and across the room and on into the loading-dock corridor. Cooke went after him. Pierce stopped to check the men on the floor. They were fine . . . they were being very good. Quickly checked the clerk—on the office floor and taped, no button or phone in reach. He was being good. . . .

Pierce went out into the long corridor as Cooke was coming back to look for him. When he saw Pierce, Cooke turned and started back again. —Past him, Pierce could see Freddy wheel the dolly out the door at the end of the corridor, into the loading bay.

Cooke was hurrying. They were all hurrying. Hurrying through cold water.

Then, just as Cooke went past the bottom of the building stairwell, there were sudden one-two blasts—explosions so bitter, cracking off the concrete walls, that Pierce thought for an instant the Simvex had gone off for no reason. Then there were two more, and it was shooting.

Charlie Cooke jumped once and yelled "Ow . . . *ow!*" as the shots slammed and rang off concrete, and Pierce saw very clearly Cooke's coveralls twitch at his side as a round went in.

Cooke turned and shot back, fired up the stairs once, and his automatic jammed.

There was more gunfire from up there, and Charlie Cooke seemed to shrug, dropped his pistol, and started away down the hall as if he'd had enough, was tired of that terrific noise.

There was no way Pierce could walk past the bottom of those stairs. Wouldn't make it running, either.

He saw Cooke going away down the corridor, staggering, swaying as if he were on a boat. Freddy's green ski mask was staring back from the loading bay door. Everything slow-motion.

Pierce drew his revolver and walked to the foot of the stairs. He saw a young black man looking down at him through the narrow round steel bars of an armored gate on the first landing.

The young man was in the company's uniform, and stepped back a little to clear his pistol—a Glock, it looked like—and aimed at Pierce through the bars and shot at him and missed. Pierce didn't know where the slug went, didn't hear it in all the noise.

He lifted the Smith & Wesson, sighted up the stairs, and fired one shot and didn't see where that one went, either. Fired another, and deaf from gunfire, barely heard the bullet clang off one of the slender steel bars. The young man jumped back, scared. But he came to the gate again and raised his pistol and Pierce knew this round would hit him, so he hurried a little and shot the man between two bars centering his belly.

It was so close and such a personal thing it was as if he'd shanked the guy, or kicked him—and the young man sagged and sagged and fainted down along the bars and ended sitting there with his face resting against them. The Glock had fallen through the gate, down onto the first step below the landing.

Pierce saw the man's face . . . his eyes alongside a bright steel bar—brown eyes, looking sleepy, gazing away. Pierce felt that the Smith & Wesson wanted to finish him, put another round into him for making so much goddam noise to start with. The big .45 was warm in Pierce's hand, as if it had come to life. The hall was full of echoes, drifts of gunsmoke.

Pierce felt as tired as the young man, and couldn't think what to do. He sure wasn't going to shoot him again. They were both worn out in just a few seconds. . . .

Freddy came running and yelled at him, got him moving.

It was only when they were loaded and in the second armored van and out into darkness, out into the warm night and rolling on the road heading for the drive-away—an old bakery delivery truck—that Pierce felt really there. It was hard to remember getting that heavy office dolly up a ramp and in . . . getting Charlie Cooke in, too.

Yodel-sirens were coming their way. They had three minutes to reach the drive-away; then two minutes to load it and move. They had no more time than that.

Charlie, his ski mask off, was talking through a tiny squirting red fountain that bubbled up in his mouth no matter what he did. "Our share," he said. It was like listening to a goldfish talk. Pierce crouched in the truck bed among the shifting metal boxes and listened, held Cooke's hand.

". . . Where'd that motherfucker come from?" Cooke said.

"Upstairs. Maybe going for overtime."

"Did . . . kill him?"

"I hit him hard." Pierce thought Charlie would rather look at a face than a ski mask, and took his off. When he did that, he saw his hands were shaking, a faint tremor, like an old man's.

"That motherfucker," Cooke said, pretty clearly, and tried to cough away what wouldn't cough away. Pierce felt warm spatter across his face. "Give Connie mine . . . or I'm . . . comin' out of the ground after you."

"She gets your cut," Pierce said, and thought Cooke nodded, but he was only dying and began to kick out, trying to breathe, kicking the metal boxes so they thumped and softly rang to no rhythm.

He did that only a little while.

Chapter 1

The Bureau had transferred Ted Gottfried to Jefferson City as agent in charge four years before, and he'd found to his—and Angela's—surprise, that he liked the town. The kids liked the town, liked school here. But the Missouri summers were not very pleasant, hot and humid. This summer was hot already; he'd sweated his shirt just walking from the parking lot into the building.

The morning, for Agents Gottfried and George Hildebrandt, was being taken up with two armed robbers—one a young man named Collins, a bank robber by courtesy, since he'd only tried that big step up from 7-Elevens once, and it hadn't worked out for him. Collins, just paroled last month, was waiting in the outer office.

Now, a classier specimen of thief was sitting across from Gottfried's desk. Tyler Pierce, first felon up today.

Gottfried had interviewed Pierce before, his name—then as now—having come up on the computer under *Robbers / Armed / Major Felonies / Presently at Liberty*. Two years ago, they'd discussed a series of fairly brutal holdups in Arkansas and across the line up into Missouri. Gottfried had discussed them, Pierce had had little to say. It had seemed then that those crimes had not been Pierce's sort of thing, and so it proved.

Now, the Iceman was back in Jefferson City, having been invited to drive up from Dowland—and was sitting relaxed on the other side of Gottfried's desk, listening to questions concerning the Michigan job, in which a guard had been shot and almost three million dollars in U. S. gold eagles stolen. Much more, it seemed, Pierce's sort of thing—or would have been a few years ago. Now, Pierce didn't seem interested.

He sat at ease in an armless chair, his long legs crossed, dressed like a farmer or construction worker come to town—tan zipper jacket, pressed chinos, lace-up low boots. Red Wings they looked like to Gottfried—a little expensive for the average workingman.

Tyler Pierce looked like a farmer, a big man, very tall, slightly stooped. Rawboned and weather-burned, with a farmer's large, heavy-knuckled hands. There was a little gray in his hair—probably, Gottfried thought, earned in those seven years in the Kansas pen.

Looked like a farmer except for his eyes, amber-brown eyes that didn't shift politely, that stared directly back like a big dog's left to guard in the bed of a parked pickup. Eyes that said, "You leave me alone and I'll leave you alone. Otherwise, you're going to have a problem."

"Tyler, you're not being helpful," Gottfried said.

"Ted, I don't know anything about it, and it's not my business." Pierce used the agents' first names the same way they used his. It annoyed them. "My business is roofing—and this today is costing me a job." Pierce's voice was an even baritone, a younger man's voice.

"I understand that," Gottfried said, and saw Hildebrandt busy taking notes over there as if this were really vital stuff, as if it weren't being taped on the desk machine in plain sight. "I understand that, but we have a man shot and a very major robbery up there—which case believe me will be cleared—and if you have any information on that crime and you do not cooperate, you may stand in jeopardy as accessory after the fact."

Pierce just looked at him.

"That guard, that Robbins, that was shot up there is going to live—"

"Glad to hear it. I saw on TV he was shot."

"—going to live in a wheelchair the rest of his life."

"That's hard," Pierce said, and looked at his watch.

"And you wouldn't have any idea who might have been up for a job that big? No people that got talked about when you were inside? No old friends dropped you a line about some bad boys coming along up North?" A question *pro forma*, for Hildebrandt's notebook and the tape. No answer expected.

"Listen," Pierce said, "I need to be getting back to work," and stood up to go.

"Where do you think you're going?" Hildebrandt sounding surprised.

"Wherever I damn please," Pierce said, leaned over Gottfried's desk and held out his hand to shake. He had an extraordinarily powerful grip, and Gottfried felt it in the restraint, the gentleness with which Pierce held his hand, then let it go.

Pierce nodded to Hildebrandt, turned and walked out of the room, a lengthy unhurried stride. He closed the office door quietly behind him.

"There's a goddam wise-ass." Hildebrandt upset at the lack of respect shown federal agents used to a great deal of respect—fear—from people they dealt with.

"Well," Gottfried said, "our man Pierce was a major bandit, and he comes from people that go back a long way with the Bureau. A long way with law enforcement in the Midwest since way before the Bureau. Pierce is related to some of the Youngers . . . and I believe his grandfather was married to a Nelson. Those kind of people. It must be something in the Clay County water."

"So, do we forget him?"

"Well, George, he's got a solid alibi—which I think I can get Lotts to check out for us, save you a drive. Pierce has an alibi; he's not a young hot-rock anymore, and he's been a good citizen for two, almost three years. . . . But just the same, we'll keep him in mind." Gottfried stood up behind his desk to stretch. He was a short man, and wide; his suits never looked good on him. "You know how our boy there got nailed for that Wichita job? Did his time in Kansas?"

"I haven't read the summary on that."

"Well, Pierce went into the First National over there almost ten years ago, and took that bank for about three hundred and forty thousand. Then, when they were coming out, two local laws started shooting in the parking lot and put down one of his people, man named Mulhune. Pierce, who was already in the getaway and gone, turned right around and came back for his man— who was dying, by the way." Gottfried popped the cassette from the tape recorder, dropped it into his top left desk drawer. "Pierce was carrying Mulhune out on his back when another officer showed and hit him with a load of buckshot and knocked him down."

"Busy day in Wichita."

"You bet. —Let me ask you a question, George. Pierce today, did he strike you as a small-time roofing contractor?"

"Yes . . . no."

"Why not?"

"He acts like . . . a more important person than that."

"There's hope for you yet, George. —Now, let's have the next thief in."

Pierce stopped at Donna's Donuts for two raspberry jellies, then drove his pickup east out of Jefferson City, driving not too fast or too slow, listening to a country-western music station—a girl singer, with all that backup they used now. Guitar and a little group wasn't good enough for them. . . . Pierce's truck was a big Ford 250, red-and-white. He'd bought it brand new the year before—tape deck, air, and all—and was going to be paying on it for quite a while.

Just this side of Loose Creek, he took Highway 63 south and stayed on it past Westphalia and the turnoff to Rich Fountain. There was a dirt farm road past Freeburg, and he steered the Ford left onto that for a few yards, under the shade of four tall trees, and parked.

He climbed out of the truck, took his zipper jacket off and tossed it onto the seat. Then he took a dented Backwoods cigar from his workshirt pocket, lit it, and stood leaning against the nearest tree, an old cottonwood, smoking. His father had smoked Old Golds; Pierce hadn't seen those cigarettes in a long time.

He said aloud, "Damn if it isn't going to be all right. . . ." and stood looking out over a wide hayfield—a hundred-acre field at least, all bright greens and yellows under the summer sun. He saw himself strolling out of that FBI office, just strolling out. . . . He felt good about that, very good about finally succeeding in his profession, no matter what people thought about it—and it did have plenty of bad, it was true. Scaring people, using force to take money that was definitely not his to take. . . . The oldest professions were the toughest to succeed in: whoring, soldiering, and robbery. The oldest and hardest, though other, later professions had their nastiness: look at the lawyers.

There was no question he'd succeeded in a difficult and dangerous profession where most people failed. Succeeded after paying very heavy dues . . .

Considerable satisfaction there—only not as much as he'd thought there'd be. It was as if he'd waited too long for this big a score, and now it wasn't what it might have been. Or maybe he wasn't as easy to please now—as if armed robbery was more a young man's pleasure, and could never be the same as it used to be, no matter how much money he took. Never be the same as those days . . . those days when he'd walked into banks like God Almighty, and Ed Sonnenberg and Peter Mulhune right there with him. People never even thought of giving them a fight except that last time in Kansas. Except for that one time, people used to just fold up like umbrellas and lie down on the floor. . . .

Two blackbirds came shifting through the heated air over the hay. They kited this way and that way, rose higher, then lit nearby on a telephone wire along the road.

"I have more than eight hundred and ninety thousand dollars in new one-ounce gold coins," Pierce said to the blackbirds, as if saying so out loud would make it more certain that twelve years of armed robbery and trouble—and seven years of worse than trouble inside in Kansas—had come to a profit at last.

Profit if a hundred-thousand-dollar alibi—still to be paid for—held up. And if Freddy kept his mouth shut out in California; which Freddy would. Profit if Charlie Cooke's sister kept *her* mouth shut, which she likely would. Appeared to be as tough as Charlie, and smarter. . . .

Seemed to Pierce the gold was a sort of reply to that Kansas pen, its sour screws and the prison psychologist's condescending bullshit. "You have a very high IQ and you've taken advantage of your situation to become one of the few people who really use our library here. We feel, Tyler, that now you have the maturity . . ." and so forth and so forth.

Really saying, "Oh, you're too good for that. Too good to be taking money from banks with a *gun*." And right behind there was "We've got you down, and our foot on the back of your neck. You crawl—or we'll kick."

He'd done the Michigan thing for the money, for sure—but also to show they hadn't taken it out of him. Kid stuff, probably. Wasn't much people did wasn't kid stuff, come right down to it. Didn't do for anybody to look too hard at why they did things. . . .

A car came down the blacktop—a Buick, dark blue—and went on by. The man, an elderly man, had turned his head for a moment to look at Pierce, standing in the shade.

The blackbirds were restless now, sitting on the telephone wire. They shuffled and shifted to one side, then the other. Seemed to be a pattern for all live things: to be a little uneasy with wherever they were.

Pierce stubbed his cigar carefully out on the tree trunk, then waded a few yards off into the hay, bent to handle the stalks. . . . Dry. It had been a dry early summer. Hard on the farmers, as it had been hard on his father years ago. —Hard on his grandfather and great-grandfather too, no doubt. Before that, it had been Quantrill and highway robbery and killing, as far as Pierces were concerned.

And now pretty much come back to that with him. No use saying it hadn't. First few days down from Michigan, he'd walked around a couple of feet off the ground with nearly three million taken and split three ways. Such success and good luck. . . . Of course, not good luck for Charlie Cooke—teeth pulled, fingertips clipped, and buried eight feet deep in Teshowa State Park. Not good luck for that young guard, either, a cripple the rest of his life.

"Would have been kinder to kill him," Pierce said to the blackbirds, and they flew.

He walked to another tree, glanced at the empty road for privacy—and unzipped and peed. Then he zipped up, walked to his truck and climbed in, backed it to the two-lane, and drove south.

Pierce suddenly recalled—no connection he could think of, except the Buick that had driven by—suddenly recalled the first thing he'd taken from anybody. That had been a General Motors car too, a Pontiac four-door. He'd been seventeen years old, and he'd hot-wired it in Bentonville, Arkansas, and just made off with it. Had this thing in his head that he'd sort of earned it by taking it. . . . Pierce supposed something like that was still in his head, or had been.

Two tractors passed him coming the other way—pulling no equipment, must have left their combines in the fields. . . . Both those tractors green John Deeres. Funny how some farmers liked all their machines one color, all green or all red or whatever. Young farmers liked to buy equipment that way; old farmers knew better. . . . And all of them going down. Be no family farms at all in fifty, sixty years. With steady payments and unsteady income, there was only one way that kind of operation could go. Down. —There'd be armed robbers in business long after the family farm was just something in a book.

South, the summer sky was the color of cheap brass plate, and it was hot enough almost for tornado weather. But the clouds were missing—those low, even black clouds pressing down. Person who'd seen that kind of sky, breathed in that dead still air—that waiting-for-something air—never forgot it.

Pierce tried for some music on the radio—got three stations playing rock, and tried again, punched the numbers down until he heard some country-western, or what passed for it these days. . . . That was one of the things that had changed while he was inside; just those seven years had made a difference, and he'd heard it changing. Radios playing new country echoing down the cell block, that music so close to pop you couldn't have told the difference, if they hadn't been singing about trucks.

Just one of the things that had changed . . . In the joint, everything changed except the joint.

And time to be wary, now; time to be careful. Slow and easy. Slow and easy was the way. That much gold, that much money, was like a too-big steak dinner in one of those places where they said if you can eat our sixty-four-ounce steak and all the fixings, it's free.

The $890,000 in gold was like that steak. Generous and grand, and hard to swallow. Swallowing the gold was going to be riskier than taking it had been; FBI and police across the country would be waiting to hear about some people trying to digest that golden steak. . . .

The sky was getting lighter now, down the road to Dowland—less of that nasty color in it. High pillow-white clouds looked to be drifting in from the west and showing no storm weather after all, not even rain. Bad news for the farmers; they would have been looking up, every now and then, while they worked. Hoping . . .

Pierce came into town on Center Street, went four blocks along there and turned up Chestnut to Emma Brice's house, a big handsome white Victorian set on a large lot. Her great-grandfather had built it when he owned the county's two feed stores.

Emma had rented her second-floor-back apartment to Pierce when he first came to town, and hadn't cared where he'd been in Kansas, or what he'd done. She was a very fat old woman with her hair in close curls and dyed light blue, and usually rested on her wide porch in her rocking chair with a little white wicker table beside her for her romance novels and pitcher of squeezed limeade.

Sometimes, when people stopped on the sidewalk to talk with her, Emma—wearing a sizable flowered dress, her bare thick pale legs ending in fat baby feet stuffed into flap-heel slippers—would commence to rock back and forth surprisingly far, would tilt way back, then deeply forward . . . then way back again, so several times when Pierce was talking to her, he expected Emma to rock back all the way and over into a somersault, revealing major panties and her massive butt. . . .

She was out on the porch as he drove up, and waved her paperback book at him, so Pierce stopped the truck in the side drive and rolled down his window.

"Your telephone's been ringin' and ringin', Mr. Pierce." She was rocking, but not extremely.

He called, "Thank you," waved, and drove on through to the backyard. Emma had once laid out a big garden there, but now only a remnant of giant sunflowers bordered the yard. She'd had Pierce fill the turned earth in, gravel the space, and set old railroad ties to keep the pebbles from drifting.

"I never liked gardening, Mr. Pierce—and now, thank God, I'm old enough and fat enough so I don't have to do it. . . ."

He parked, got out—had to reach back in the seat for his jacket—then went up the outside staircase. On the first landing, only a few steps up, Richard groaned as Pierce went by.

"Don't tell me," Pierce said, went up the second flight and unlocked his apartment door. He stepped into shadowy cool and felt, as he felt each time he came home, pleasure at the two small rooms and kitchenette. Pleasure at his privacy—even out of the Kansas pen now almost three years.

The small rooms were very neat, with no pictures on the walls, and furnished from garage sales. Carolyn had found him his couch at a garage sale; it was dark orange, and didn't match anything else, but it was comfortable. She'd found the outdoor set he used as a dining table, too. The set was green-painted wrought iron, dinged a little, but okay.

Pierce stood in his living room and smelled the apartment's air. He'd thought maybe the sheriff's people would come by, just to check. But no one had been in the place. It was their smell that told you if screws had turned your house. Even if they were careful to put everything back the way it had been, there was that slightly different smell left behind.

He went to his refrigerator and took out a beer—Miller's Draft—turned off the top, and stood slowly sipping it. It was surprising how long the pleasures of freedom lasted—and now, of course, he'd risked them again. Forever, this time, if they caught up to him and he let them take him in.

And how strange it was to have come out of prison, where screws and officers had run his life, given him orders every day as if he was a dog. ... strange to come out of there and start right away planning the Michigan job, and all to get a heap of gold that was already doing the same thing—giving him orders. Orders he damned well had to jump to. ...

First order from all that money, those gold coins: *Keep your mouth shut.*

Second order: *Forget. Forget you ever thought of that robbery, worked it up for two years; forget you were in Michigan last weekend; forget Freddy and Charlie Cooke. Forget that boy you shot. Forget it all.*

Third order: *Spend the next year or two dirt-poor and fixing roofs.* ... Gold says, *"Put me somewhere safe, then don't touch me."*

So, for that length of time, and starting now— already started in that FBI office—he would have to obey the gold. It seemed, looking back on it, that bandits often wound up taking orders from whatever it was they stole. ...

And this would mean two or three years waiting, leaving the gold alone. It would mean working for another year in Dowland—just a small-time roofer with a record—working up on people's roofs all summer, and all the next winter too, in cold and wet. Then maybe a move out of state and *another* year mending roofs.

Mending roofs, and drifting. He'd be drifting away from anyone's interest or attention. And he'd have to say goodbye to the people in Dowland ... to Carolyn. Orders from the money, from his gold.

And finally, after that long time playing possum— there'd be Chicago, and new ID right down the line. Costly new ID referring back to some poor infant died more than forty years ago. New everything: birth certificate, Social Security, Army discharge, driver's license.

And after all that—with enough patience, enough care, enough luck—maybe a little cottage on a hillside in the Caribbean, just like in the travel magazines. Sitting out on his deck, sipping a rum-and-whatever in hot sun and a cool sea breeze, to watch the big sailing yachts come sliding in from the blue to anchor.

Have to be a *little* cottage—owner not being really rich, as rich people go. But safe there, and lucky . . . lucky, but with no Carolyn.

Pierce put the bottle in the trash under his kitchenette sink, then went outside and down the staircase to the bottom landing. Richard, lying spraddled there on his piece of old green carpet, heaved himself halfway up and looked over his shoulder, his round ugly head as big as a man's.

"You ever think of lying out under a tree in the yard, Richard? Ever think of doing that?"

Richard—a brindle English bulldog, and very old—only grinned wide from a frosted mask of folds and wrinkles, his pop eyes rolling.

Almost a year ago, Richard had become paralyzed in his hindquarters—and despite Emma's efforts with the town vet, and a holistic healer in Independence, and having Dowland's best chiropractor, Louis Moss, adjust a canine spine under protest, the paralysis proved permanent.

Emma had kept Richard in the house at first, but he'd been unhappy, so she had her nephew, Bud, come from across the street every morning to carry the bulldog to his old spot on the back-stair landing. And there Richard lay through the day with his beef jerky sticks and water bowl, looking out over the yard he'd ruled for eleven years.

In the evening, Emma's nephew came back across the street, picked Richard up—not an easy thing to do—helped him pee and poop in the sunflower beds, then carried him into the house for the night.

Occasionally, though, Richard was caught short and needed to pee early. He would then lie on his carpet scrap and groan until someone strong enough came to help him.

"You sure you have to go?"

Richard looked up, troubled.

"All right." Pierce stooped, gripped Richard under the armpits and hauled him gently up to hug his barrel body, then heaved him up and lugged him down the steps, back legs dangling.

In the yard, Pierce shifted his hold, and cradling the bulldog like some catastrophically ugly baby, carried him over to the sunflower border. Richard looked fat and should have been fat, since eating was his occupation, but ancestors bred to fight bulls determined that what favorites he ate—Velveeta cheese, country sausage, and Whitman's Sampler candy—turned as if by magic into massive muscle, so sized about two cubic feet, he weighed ninety pounds.

Pierce hefted him to the sunflower bed, then bent with a grunt to set him down on his rear in the greenery. Richard, sitting leaning back against Pierce's legs for support, looked up at him, apparently embarrassed.

"It's okay," Pierce bent to hold the dog's forepaws, keep him balanced upright. "Don't worry about it."

Richard groaned and, propped uneasily up, peed an old man's feeble intermittent stream out onto stems and leaves and shadows. The sunflowers, taller than Pierce, nodded above them, green and gold.

Chapter 2

"Oh, slow . . . slow . . . slow."

Carolyn was a small woman, and slow to heat, so it was a while before she could accommodate him, before she oiled enough, lay back and brought her legs up as if she were having a baby, and said, "Oh, Christ, go ahead. Go ahead."

And once, when they'd just been seeing each other a little while, and that night he'd been at her and at her, fucking—desperate about something—she'd said, "Kill me," as she came. And after that, she cried. She only said it that one time, and only cried that one time, and Pierce never knew why and wasn't about to ask, either.

Now she lay beneath him, all spraddled and open. Pierce, as he was in her, saw her face so pale in near darkness, and felt her insides warm and slippery, gripping at him . . . felt her outside, skin smooth and soft, just sweating slightly so all her odors rose off her like fine cooking. Biscuits, seafood, and salt.

Carolyn was small and slight, and four years younger than Pierce. She was assistant librarian and also did hair at Snip N' Style, part-time. She'd been married, and was divorced from a man who was the Ford dealership sales manager—and who, in fact, had gotten Pierce a good buy on his truck.

Carolyn was almost plain—not ugly, but not pretty either; people said she was nice looking. She had an angular foxy face and long light-brown hair, pale-blue eyes, and thin, freckled arms and legs. She had freckles all over.

"I hate them," she'd said, when she first let Pierce see her naked. "I look like some stupid little hick, and they ruined my life. If you were a woman you'd understand, so don't tell me they're cute or something like that."

"I do understand," Pierce had said from the bed. "They're pretty bad. You look like you have the measles."

For whatever reason, Carolyn had liked his saying that that Sunday afternoon, and had come back to bed right away. "I went to church this morning," she'd said, "and here I am in bed with a convicted felon with a record."

Pierce hadn't had to tell her about robbing banks and so forth, and the Kansas pen. She and the whole town already knew about it. Not all that much to talk about in a small farm town, and he'd been a well-known bandit, years ago.

Didn't seem to trouble anybody in Dowland, now. The minister of Carolyn's church—who seemed to be pretty light in his loafers—had stopped Pierce on the street, said, "You are a big fellow," and had spoken to him about Responsibility, referring to him and Carolyn. And also said, "Don't be too shy to come and see me with a problem. Problems are my business. And as far as robbing people goes, there are so-called respectable men in this county make a mere bank robber look sick. . . ."

Dowland people had treated him pretty well. He'd robbed no banks in Missouri, never had any trouble in the state—and no trouble in town in his two years here, not even a fistfight. Pierce supposed they figured him too grown-up now, for trouble. Man with some gray in his hair . . . They seemed to like him well enough, gave him roofing jobs around the county. Small jobs.

Carolyn, usually so silent, hard to get to say anything

in daytime except about the library and her part-time beauty business, always turned into a big talker in bed at night.

It amused Pierce from the first; he enjoyed it—and, like now, would lie in the dark resting from screwing, and listen to her voice as if it were music. Country-western.

"Were they nasty to you up there, Tyler?"

"No. Those federal people are always polite. They don't have to be nasty."

"Surely they know you didn't have anything to do with it. Didn't you tell them you were out at Getchel's all last weekend?"

"Yes, I did."

"Well, they ought to leave you alone—bothering you with something like that, happened way up north, you didn't have anything to do with."

"Yes, they should."

"What did those people get in Michigan—three million dollars?"

"Supposed to be almost."

"Almost three million dollars ... I don't know, Tyler; maybe you retired too soon." And she reached over and began to tickle him. Pierce'd never known he was ticklish, until Carolyn had started doing that.

"Cut it *out*."

"No, I won't. Listen—they aren't going to keep bothering you, are they?"

"No. They think I'm past doing jobs like that."

"Well, you are."

"That's right. I'm getting old. . . ."

"Forty isn't old."

"No, but forty-two is."

"You're not forty-two."

"Yes, I am. August twenty-third."

"Well, forty-two *is* old. . . ."

The phone rang, and Pierce got up on his elbow and reached over Carolyn to pick it up.

"Hello."

"Tyler?"

And just from that one long-distance word, Pierce recognized his wife's voice. Ex-wife. And he hadn't heard Margaret's voice in nine years. Nine years and then some.

"What is it, Margaret?"

"Tyler, is Lisa up there visiting you?"

"No. You know I told her not to come up just yet."

"Are you sure she's not visiting you? Are you lying about our daughter? Are you lying to me?"

"No."

"Margaret?" Carolyn whispering.

"Could she be on her way up there to see you?"

"Margaret—Lisa's not up here, and I haven't heard she was coming up here. Now, what's this all about?"

"Well, she left her job and nobody knows where she is."

"I thought she was engaged to be married. She wrote me she was engaged." So strange to be having this conversation with Margaret, as if nothing had gone so wrong between them. As if all those years . . . as if they'd just stepped over all those years and were having this conversation.

"That's right, and Jason said they didn't have an argument last few days or anything. He's worried sick."

"What happened? How long has this been?"

"Nothing happened! She just walked out on her job, which is a civil-service state job, and you don't just walk out without a word. And that was two days ago, and she hasn't called me or Carl. And she hasn't called Jason, either."

"Well, she's a grown young woman. Maybe she just wanted some alone time. Think things out."

"That your wife?" Carolyn whispering, and poking him in the side.

" 'Think things out'! What in the world are you

talking about, Tyler? Lisa is the happiest person in the world! She's crazy about Jason, and she always liked Carl just fine."

"Have you had a fight with her?"

"No, I have not had a fight with her that was serious at all, and thank you very much for being no help." And hung up.

"Was that your wife?"

"Yes."

"I didn't know you two were . . . you know, in contact anymore."

"We aren't. Our girl's gone off for a couple of days, and Margaret's worried about that."

"Isn't Lisa getting married?"

"She's supposed to be getting married down there."

"Well, you know, Tyler, sometimes women . . . sometimes a girl going to get married, that big a step, sometimes they have to get away, just for a little while."

"That's what I think."

". . . You still love her?"

"My daughter?"

"No, I know you love your daughter, Tyler. I mean your wife."

"Ex-wife."

"I mean her."

"No, I don't love Margaret," Pierce said. "Not anymore."

The sheriff went out to the Getchels' himself. It was a chore just that little bit too important for a deputy to handle. Richard Lotts had been Dowland County sheriff for fourteen years, and people who'd believed a fat old man couldn't be a tough old man had learned different in that time. It was a long drive out to the Getchels' place, and the sheriff had had a big lunch; he had to keep the air-conditioning on high to stay alert, driving.

Truman Getchel, retired from being a major pig farmer in the county, had left the operation to his son, Marcus—not, it was felt, the best move he could have made. It was thought Marcus would be running that farm into the ground pretty presto. He wasn't a steady boy, was unlikely to keep ahead of feed prices.

Now, Truman and Jerrie lived retired in an old house on a four-acre plot sectioned out of the big place. It was treed acreage, and looked very nice and shady under the summer sun. —Looked welcoming as Sheriff Lotts turned in to a long graveled drive. Flowers had been planted along the sides of the driveway.

The Getchels had a nice house here—had belonged to Bergmeir, before Truman bought him out. A nice house, and a barn out back . . . They'd been working on the barn. Ladders out there. Lumber and scraps, and a pad with shingle bundles stacked on it.

Sheriff Lotts pulled in alongside the house, parked, climbed out of the cruiser and stood leaning against it, listening to the engine tick.

Truman Getchel came out of the barn and trudged up the yard. He was wearing overalls and rubber boots and looked his age every bit, a weathered little onion of a man. Sheriff Lotts supposed his son was worrying him, losing money trying to deal with that hog operation. Big companies were pushing the small hoggers pretty hard. . . . Lotts, watching Truman come to him, also noticed a window curtain stir at the side of the house, and saw Jerrie Getchel's shadow peeking from the kitchen.

Getchel came tromping up to the car, his boots looking too big for him. "What can I do for you, Sheriff?"

"How's that barn coming along, Truman?"

"It's a damn mess, and I should have pulled the son of a gun down. Costing way too much to fix up."

"Thought you were retired, Truman."

"Well, I am. But you always got need of a barn."

"Now that's true," the sheriff said. "Barn, or a big garage."

"So, what can I do for you, Sheriff? You want some cold soda? Want a Coke?"

"Who is it you got doing your roof out there?"

"Roof? Uh . . . that's Pierce. He's okay doing the work, but he's not real quick."

"How long is it taking him, get that done?"

"It wouldn't take him so damn long if he'd work weekdays. Now, I wish I got somebody else. If I was still fit for it, I'd go up there and get the damn thing done myself."

It seemed to Sheriff Lotts that Truman looked harassed for a retired man. Probably troubled by getting too old to run his place . . . having to pass that on. Getting old was no pleasure.

"So, what can I do for you, Sheriff?"

"Pierce just comes out weekends?"

"Comes out and stays over. Three meals a day, too. Man just works weekends; says it's too much of a trip in and out to town to be doing every day. Says it would cost him other jobs." Truman turned to look back over his shoulder at his barn, as if something might have changed there in the last few minutes. "Is there a problem with him or something? I know he was in jail once. . . ."

"Came out here the last couple weekends?"

"Last *three* weekends. He had to new-rafter the whole south-side roof under there. I mean—you talk about a mess! And do you see Marcus over here giving us a hand? Like hell you do."

"Pierce was out here last weekend?"

"He was, and he eats a damn big breakfast, lunch, and dinner, I'll tell you that. Sleeps upstairs."

"Came out Saturday?"

"Friday. A three-day weekend at fifteen dollars every hour he put in working."

"Came out Friday evening?"

"Afternoon. Now, what the hell is this all about?"

"Ate a big dinner Friday, did he? What did you folks have?"

Getchel raised his voice. "Jerrie! . . . *Oh*, Jerrie!"

The kitchen window slid up. "What? . . . What is it?"

"Sheriff wants to know what that Tyler Pierce had for dinner, Friday."

"What he had for dinner?"

"That's right. Friday."

"I don't know. . . ."

"She'll come up with it." Getchel smiled as they waited, seemed fond of his wife.

". . . Truman, we had . . . we had chipped beef on toast."

"Chipped beef," Getchel said. "—Wasn't what we called it in the army."

"—Chipped beef and sweet potatoes. And he ate two of those sweet potatoes."

"There you go," Getchel said. "Now, Sheriff, what's this all about? Has he done something or what?"

"Good luck with that barn," Lotts said.

"I'm going to need more money than luck. Man isn't through with that damn roof yet."

Sheriff Lotts reached out to shake Getchel's hand. Getchel's hand wasn't a farmer's hand anymore; no strength to it. Lotts raised his voice. "—Goodbye, Mrs. Getchel! Sorry to have troubled you!" Then he opened the cruiser's door and climbed in, looking forward to air-conditioning.

Truman Getchel watched the sheriff back carefully down the drive, cautious to avoid the borders of daffodils. The sheriff backed out to the road, turned, and drove away.

Truman trudged across the yard to the back door,

went up the steps and into the kitchen and the odor of baking meat loaf.

"You did just perfect, honey bun," he said.

Mickey was a strong fat boy with his hair in a wheat-colored ponytail. He had Corps tattoos on his arms, though the Corps had let him go after a year due to severe hay fever. Almost twenty-one, round-faced, with pale gray eyes always squinted in bright sunlight, Mickey had limitations as a helper; he couldn't handle laying out a fancy shingle pattern, got confused and forgot where he was in the rows. But he had a great advantage roofing—two advantages—he was a worker, happy to nail rather than staple, and he didn't mind heights and heat.

The Bettses' shed was simple, one-tab gray architectural shingles with an easy every-other-one pattern to nail. The shed was big, though—really a high-peak two-car garage, definitely a full day's work, counting taking the old roof off. And midmorning, it was hot on the roof already.

There was only a ten-, twelve-foot fall onto grass—provided you didn't go off the driveway end—and the pitch wasn't steep enough for tacked boards. Wasn't much of a trick to staying on a roof, anyway. Even high roofs with church pitches to them. —Pierce had learned after only two short falls, had learned from reading a book about mountain climbing. What you did, was make the roof a friend and lean into him. While you were with the roof, you weren't going to be going off the roof. . . .

They'd parked Mickey's rolling-wreck stake-bed GMC below on the blacktop drive, and were stripping the old shingles and tar paper and tossing them down. Mickey used a roofing hatchet to do that work; Pierce a different tool he'd found at United Hardware—a two-foot bar with a curved flat pry-leaf at the end.

He didn't know what the tool was supposed to be

for—hadn't wanted to look like a fool asking the hard-ware people—but it did the job on old shingles, lifted them right up and off.

The thick, cracked asphalt shingles and ragged tar paper were already soft with heat. Sunshine hit that material and soaked in, then came right back up off it, so Pierce felt the sun on his face and on his back at the same time. By afternoon, it would be like working on an oven grill, with the broiler flames on low and steady. —First year he'd done it, fresh out of the Kansas pen, Pierce had had to stop once or twice and vomit over the edge of the roof he was working on. He'd felt the summer heat was going to kill him.

Old Widdermeir had thought that was the funniest thing he'd ever seen—this ex-con, this tough gunman barfing over the edge of the Church of Our Savior's roof. "Hey, hardcase," Widdermeir had said to him, "get down and get yourself a damn hat, and drink a quart of cold water down there—then get your ass back up and get to work." Widdermeir'd run a hard school for roofers—hadn't paid much, either.

For Pierce, winters hadn't been as bad—poor roofing weather, anyway. Tacky fiberglass shingles they made now couldn't take much hammering in cold weather; just crack on you and fall apart. Similar to some people now.

And of course, he hadn't planned on doing roofing for the rest of his life. Hadn't planned on doing that at all. . . . And now, by God, he wouldn't.

"Mr. Pierce . . ." Mrs. Betts calling from down in the yard.

"Yes, ma'am?" Pierce thought it was probably the shingle pattern. People always worried a roofer was going to screw that up.

"Telephone call for you. In the house."

"Okay. Thank you." And what fool would be calling him at a customer's house . . . ? Pierce stood up and walked to the ladder, swung around onto it, and climbed down.

Mrs. Betts was standing in her back doorway. "Right through into the family room, Mr. Pierce. Phone's beside the door."

"Sorry to bother you."

"It's no bother, Mr. Pierce."

". . . Hello?"

"Say, Tyler? It's Ray." Ray Younger—a second cousin and almost Pierce's age. Ray was partners in a truck repair outside Joplin, and Tyler'd seen him only a couple of times since getting out.

"What is it, Ray? What are you calling here for? I'm working."

"I got where you was workin' from that librarian lady you brought over to visit that time. She said you was over at the Frank Bettses' house and I looked 'em up."

"What is it, Ray?" Pierce felt a little short of breath, waiting.

"Bad news, boy. Real bad news, Tyler."

Pierce said nothing. He heard Mrs. Betts close the refrigerator in the kitchen. Getting them some iced tea for up on that roof.

"—Tyler? Well, it's Lisa. I am just so sorry; so sorry I can't tell you. . . . Lisa's gone, Tyler. Your girl's dead. Carl called up from Florida and just told me. Said he tried to call you."

Pierce said nothing. He could hear Mrs. Betts pouring tea in the kitchen, ice clinking in the glasses.

"Tyler? Tyler, did you hear me?"

"Yes," Pierce said. "I heard you."

Refrigerator door again. Putting the ice trays away.

". . . found her in her Jeep out in that state park she was rangerin' down there. Oh, Tyler, I just don't know how to say it. . . ."

"Go on."

"That crazy son of a bitch had cut her throat, Tyler.

He cut her real bad. He cut off her . . . breasts, Tyler."
Ray Younger had never said anything but "tits" in his
life, before this. It touched Pierce, in the midst of
everything, that Ray had chosen a gentler word.

"Why would anybody do that?" Pierce said, though
he didn't care. It was just something to say.

"Why? Because the fucker is a *crazy* man, that's
why, Tyler! Your girl's been killed by that Sweetwater
nut down there. She was wearin' her ranger uniform,
and that's why he kills those ladies. He kills ladies got
a uniform on!"

"That's right," Pierce said. "That's right. I read
about him. . . ."

"Four years he's killed five ladies. And now your
Lisa. Oh, Tyler . . . I just can't tell you. Eula can't
come to the phone. She's just sick about it. Just sick
somebody would do your girl that way."

"Thank you for calling me, Ray. I appreciate your
calling me," Pierce said. He hung up the phone and
stood looking out the Bettses' dining-room window.
He supposed they were right to use the Pabco twenty-
year shingles on their shed. Color matched the house
shingles. . . .

"What's the matter?" Mrs. Betts said. She was
standing in the hall with the tea tray, looking at him.
"Mr. Pierce . . . ?"

Pierce walked past her and went on out of the
house. The sun was bright outside, seemed brighter
than before. It came flashing down through the tree
leaves like mirrors, so bright it hurt his eyes.

He felt stranger than after the robbery, set apart
from ordinary things so they didn't look real to him. A
man who had succeeded in his profession. . . . He
walked down the street to get farther from the house
and that phone.

Behind him, he could hear Martha Betts out in her
backyard, calling her husband. *"Frank . . . Frank,
something has happened. . . ."*

Pierce felt much better walking under the trees, just going down the street. Two blocks farther on, then five over. First these two blocks, then those five blocks over to Emma's house.

He walked along, glad no one was near him. It troubled him, as he went, when people came past on the sidewalk or drove by. He supposed they were looking at him because he was still wearing his tool belt.

He got to Emma's house after what seemed a long time—was relieved she wasn't on her porch—and went on around to the back and up the outside stairs. Richard murmured to him as he went by. Pierce remembered he'd left his truck at the Bettses', went on up, and unlocked his apartment door.

He closed the door behind him, left the lights off, and went to lie down on the couch. He lay with his eyes closed, and imagined he was still in his cell, still in his cell with years to go before he got out. If that was so, he wouldn't have gone up to Michigan, wouldn't have taken all that money.

It seemed to him that that robbery of gold had weighted one side of a balance down, and now—so soon after—Lisa had been taken to level that balance up. It had happened swift as judgment.

Pierce lay with his eyes closed, and imagined himself years back and still in prison, expecting a letter from her.

. . . He'd gone in when she was twelve years old. A twelve-year-old little girl who'd loved him as if he was something special, off all the time on selling trips for farm machinery. And that was a lie.

Robbing banks was what he was doing—and selling machinery sometimes. . . .

And then he was shot and caught in Kansas—not such a smart guy, such a famous robber then—and Margaret had said in the courthouse hallway, "Well, that tears it for me, Tyler," and walked away. When she did that, Lisa had stayed and come and hugged him, handcuffs and all, crying. . . . His daughter in a white dress with blue flowers. Still had her braces then, too.

Last time he saw her was right then.

And every single month for seven years, Lisa had written him a letter. Every single month, and an extra at Christmas. Ninety-one letters, regular as clockwork. —And nothing ever from Margaret, except the divorce papers.

A young girl's letters, about her friends and school—and Tarleton, her cocker spaniel.

Then an older girl's letters. First mention of boys she liked—and Tarleton gone, hit by a car in the street.

After a few years, five or six, they were letters from a young woman—shyer telling him some things, bolder telling him others. But like all the rest, full of love. Each month, Lisa's letters had made the Kansas prison bearable for him. There was nothing happened in there so bad, her letters couldn't show him what was better.

He'd written back to her every time, telling her he loved her, and never saying anything against Margaret—and her divorcing him and marrying a man named Hubbard down in Florida. He gave her what advice he dared to give, advice about boys and so forth—and he wrote about Kansas, and did his best to make the place seem only strict, where basically decent men paid for having been foolish. He never wrote her how it was.

. . . When she was eighteen, Lisa'd written to ask to come over and visit him. Pierce had answered no. He'd been afraid that when she saw the place, saw what it was really like, she'd think he must be rotten-bad after all, to have been sent there.

And when he was out, and free, she'd asked again— asked him in one of the phone calls they'd made back and forth, just talking away like two kids—she'd asked if she could come up from Florida to see him. And Pierce had said, "I love you, Lisa. You're the world to me, sugar. But I'm still learning how to get along outside. Let me come see you. I'll come down in a year or so. I'll come see you, and we'll have ourselves a time. . . ."

That's what he'd said to her. He hadn't wanted her to visit him while he was planning the Michigan job, driving up to Springfield, weekends, to call Freddy on a pay phone, working out this and that. Keeping in touch with Cooke, who was not easy to keep in touch with . . . setting up meetings. . . .

He hadn't wanted Lisa within a mile of any of that. As if it would put some kind of dirt on her. . . .

And now, that chance of seeing her was gone. All chances were gone. . . .

Carolyn came to his door after a while. Pierce had heard her step coming up the stairs, then she stood at the door and knocked softly. Knocked again.

"Tyler? . . . Tyler, I heard from your cousin Ray what happened, and I went over to the Bettses' and Martha said you just walked out of the house. Tyler? . . . Will you let me in?"

Pierce went to the door and opened it a little. Carolyn was standing out there in her dress and sweater and high heels from the library; they kept the library very cool. "Honey," Pierce said, "would you do me a favor? Would you just go on now, and let me be for a while?"

Carolyn looked up at him. She appeared to have been crying. "Oh, I am so damn sorry for you to lose your girl this way. It's just—it's just unbearable. . . . Tyler, I want you to have something to eat. You fix something for your supper."

"I will."

"I'll come see you tomorrow. Oh—and Mickey brought your truck over. It's in the driveway—he didn't want to bother you."

"Okay," Pierce said, and she turned and went down the stairs. Pierce heard her stop and say something to Richard, then she went on into the yard.

Pierce closed his door and went back to sit at the little round dining table. He had all the letters there out of the shoe boxes, and most of them still to read.

His phone rang early in the morning. Two o'clock, two-thirty in the morning.

Pierce got up from the table and answered it.

"Tyler—oh God oh God oh God."

"Hello, Margaret."

"Oh, you know what's happened? You know what's happened? Do you . . . ?"

"Margy, Roy called him." Carl Hubbard in the background.

"Tyler, you have to do something."

"I will."

"You have to do something. Oh, my God. Oh . . . my *God!*"

"Margy—"

"You shut up, Carl! You just shut up, you nothing! Tyler . . . Tyler, you have to *do* something!"

"I will, Margaret."

"I always loved you—oh, please do something. My little girl . . . my little girl . . ."

It was a hard voice to listen to. It sounded as though she was singing a slow song.

"Tyler?" Carl on the phone. *"Now wait, sugar,—no no, let me talk to him.* Tyler, this is really awful. Our doctor had to come all the way out here and give her a shot. It's just awful. She and Lisa had a fight last time they saw each other—just a disagreement."

"She hated me . . . !" Sung away from the phone, up the scale and down again. *"The last time she hated me and thought I was terrible. . . ."*

"When is the funeral, Carl?"

"Friday."

"I'll be down," Pierce said, and hung up.

* * *

At six in the morning, Pierce dressed in clean blue jeans, blue work shirt, tan windbreaker and Red Wing boots. He packed his duffel bag, dumped the milk out of his refrigerator into the sink, then left the apartment and locked the door behind him. Still cool, damp from the night, the backyard was barely lit by dawn. A few morning glories, open early, lay white in their green vines along the lot's picket fence.

Richard was still in the house, sleeping, his patch of worn carpet lying empty on the lower landing beside his white-china water bowl.

Pierce walked across the yard to the old garden shed, slid the plank door open and reached in for the shovel. He closed the shed door, went around the side of the house to the drive, and set the shovel quietly into the pickup's bed. He put his duffel bag on the front seat, pushed over to the passenger side. Mickey had left the truck's keys in the sun visor.

Well out of town on 63 North, Pierce drove with sunrise on his right, and noticed that Mickey had filled the truck's tank before bringing it over; tank had been just off empty. A good boy . . .

And considering the truck—and having left it parked up in Jefferson City in the federal lot, talking to those FBI people—Pierce slowed, then pulled off onto the highway's right shoulder.

He got out, took his zipper jacket off, then knelt and looked along under the back bumper. Went to all fours and crawled under, checking the wheel wells and axle housings. Then he backed out, stood up, and went around to do the same at the front.

He checked under there very carefully, but found no small telltale or transmitter. No tiny follow-along or locator tucked away . . . Appeared they didn't think him worth that sort of effort, these days.

Pierce left his jacket off; the day was warming fast. He climbed in, started the truck and swung back on the road. He had a way to go, driving farther north, to Teshowa State Park. Then a few feet down, digging.

Pierce and Freddy had dug Cooke's grave by light of a crooked moon. Dug it deep beneath a stand of the park's live oaks, chopping tangles of roots away as they worked. —Cooke lying wrapped in a blanket, waiting. Freddy'd been at him before, slicing off his fingertips, flipping those little pieces away in the night.

Pierce, with pliers, had already taken Cooke's teeth.

He and Freddy had dug for almost two hours—rich men working very hard—and then rolled Charlie Cooke in deep.

While Freddy stayed to finish, Pierce, carrying his shovel, had gone to the delivery truck in privacy and taken his gold out—an already-split one third. They'd transferred their coins from the express company's strongboxes to heavy-duty fiberglass ammo cases. Pierce's 2,200 gold eagles filled one almost to the top.

He'd lugged that case—very heavy, more than a hundred pounds—lugged it away into a darkening night, the moon sliding down, and buried it almost as deep as Charlie Cooke, but under a very heavy stone lifted away, and the earth dug out beneath that.

The stone had been the fourth in an irregular row edging an old creek bed with poplars above. The poplar's bark had still held the last of moonlight when Pierce was finished. . . .

Now, in bright afternoon, the trees and stones seemed smaller where the creek had run many years ago—fifty, a hundred years ago, its bed now almost filled with foliage.

Pierce had driven slowly through the park, then turned out onto an access road with no other car in sight . . . driving slowly through a sun-hazed afternoon. He'd turned off a second time, into an overgrown dell, followed a fading graveled track, and pulled up. Then he'd gotten out, taken the shovel from the truck bed, and hiked a couple of hundred yards up a long, treed slope. Charlie Cooke lay not far away, through a wooded section.

Sweating, after what seemed to him a very long time digging, the shovel's worn edge ringing softly off small rocks as he worked, Pierce felt the tool at last strike something different, and knelt in the dirt to get to his gold with his hands.

. . . The ammo case fit in one side of the pickup's big double toolbox, bolted across the front of its bed. The ammo case fit in there under tar rags and black-smeared tubes of roofing caulk, some sample shingles, and an old bucket with a sludge of asphalt patch half filling it, and some spilled to run down its sides.

There was a padlock hanging from the hasp to lock the toolbox lid. Pierce took the lock off and put it in the truck's glove compartment. —The toolbox left unlocked, the truck left unlocked when he stopped for food, or a cup of coffee. An honest truck, with nothing to hide . . .

Pierce backed to the access road, and turned on it to drive south, the way he'd come. South, but on past Poplar Bluff and Malden, on into the corner of Tennessee. And south from there.

Chapter 3

Louisiana was warm as steam. Pierce felt the heat pressing on the truck's windows, the air-conditioning laboring to keep ahead of it as he drove Interstate 10.

Pierce had never been down here before, never seen such flat wet country—and smelling very bad past Baton Rouge with fumes from refineries and so forth. There'd been a pretty stretch, too, the highway running over a few miles of cypress marsh with moss hung in the trees . . . and some big white wading birds flocking. Maybe egrets. Whole place looked to have just heaved up from the sea.

The downtown city showed ahead in a haze of late-morning heat . . . and soon New Orleans began to rise on either side as he drove in, careful in swift shifting morning traffic. Didn't want an accident, even a fender bender. This traffic a damn sight heavier than in Dowland, Missouri. . . .

He was headed for Metairie, and almost missed the exit—had to swing over pretty sudden to make it. Car behind him didn't care for that, gave him a long toot as he cut it off, held the pickup's steering wheel hard right, and went pretty fast along a ramp and onto the Causeway Boulevard.

Odd—almost three years out on the street, and driving every day, and he still wasn't quite comfortable running a car or truck. Seven years not doing it had taken away some skill, or confidence. He could drive,

drive as well as most, but he had to think what he was doing. . . .

Staying to the left, now, staying to the left and looking for DuMaine. DuMaine Avenue. Half a mile or so, the traffic going pretty fast, and Pierce thought he saw the sign—and then was sure just after the damn exit went by and there he was, rolling along lost in the middle of a city he didn't know from Adam.

"Son of a bitch . . . " He took the next exit—something "odelette"—and went damn near flying off the highway and down into a street, the big pickup jouncing and bouncing over some poorly mended potholes . . . and rolled along that street and got to one with an American name at least. Millway. —Took a left on that at the light, and drove back up Millway along some streetcar tracks with a bunch of drivers even worse than he was. Passed Orange, then Persimmon. New Orleans did smell better than Baton Rouge . . . gas fumes from the traffic, but there was an ocean kind of smell in there, too. Salty smell. Maybe the Gulf down there.

Place de Something, and the traffic thinning out. More a warehouse district over here . . . Then, another block along, DuMaine.

Pierce didn't know to go right or left on DuMaine, didn't know which way the numbers ran, so he tried going right, saw the numbers running his way . . . and fourteen blocks later—running with the most contrary drivers he'd ever seen—found Bailey Storage on the corner of Beauvallet and Charteris. Neighborhood of warehouses, machine shops, bars and so forth. Art galleries mixed in there, too; looked like art galleries, anyway, from the signs they had out front.

Pierce took the right turn at Bailey Storage—two big four-story red-brick buildings sitting on either side of a paved loading area. Company's name was on each building.

Pierce turned left into their lot, and drove past three

canary-yellow Isusu trucks with *Bailey Storage* painted
along their sides. The brick buildings extended back a
long way. Lots of storage. . . . He parked in a row of
cars and pickups along the right side of the lot, got out,
and walked past two loading bays—black men, in gray
coveralls with *Bailey* on the back, were unloading furniture from another one of the yellow trucks.

There was a glass door labeled "Office" farther
down, and Pierce walked in to a bell sounding as the
door opened, then closed behind him. A black woman
and white woman, both middle-aged, both in slacks
and tucked-in blouses, looked up from their desks, and
the white woman said, "Can we help you?"

"I'd like to see Mr. Bailey."

"Mr. Mathew Bailey or Mr. Rodney Bailey?" The
woman had an odd accent. She sounded like a tough
Chicago Irishwoman pretending to be a Southerner.

"Mathew Bailey."

"And does this concern moving, or storage?"

"Some personal business."

The black woman got up and came to the counter.
"And may I ask your name, sir?" She sounded just the
same as the white lady had.

"Wilkens," Pierce said. "You can tell Mr. Bailey I'm
a friend of Pat Simcoe's. Kansas City."

"All right, I'll do that, Mr. Wilkens, if you care to
wait. Why don't you have a seat over there. An' we
have some *Field & Stream*s and *Newsweek*s to read."

"Thank you." Pierce went and sat in a ladder-back
chair against the wall, picked up a *Field & Stream*, and
read about muskies. . . . There was no doubt the man
who wrote about it had done it. He had that fish down,
and didn't go on about plastic worms. It was spoons,
straight and simple. Spoons and early morning . . .

". . . Mr. Wilkens." The white woman.

Pierce looked up from the beginning of an article
about bass boats, and saw a fat black man in a gray
checked suit smiling at him from the office's inner door.

"Mr. Wilkens?" the fat man said, and held out his hand to shake as Pierce got up and went to him. "—I'm Rodney Bailey. Come on in." He led Pierce down a hall to an elevator door. "—And how's Pat doing? An engaging rascal." The fat man didn't talk black. He sounded like an educated white man.

"Doing life," Pierce said.

"Isn't that sad?" the fat man said. "Real bad luck, because there's not much harm in Pat."

"No, not much," Pierce said, and the elevator door slid open. The fat man gestured him in and followed, leaving not much room. It was a small elevator—for people, not storage goods.

The fat man, Rodney, faced Pierce as the elevator rose. "Had lunch?"

"No."

"Good, you can eat with us. Like pickle sandwiches?"

"With peanut butter and mayo, yes I do."

"Man after my own heart," Rodney said. "Oh, and how do you spell your name again?"

"P-i-e-r-c-e."

"Ah, I misheard it, downstairs. First name?"

"Tyler."

"Um-*hmmm*." The elevator stopped and Rodney stepped out, said, "Okay, Donny," to someone, and stood aside for Pierce.

There was another man standing in the hall when Pierce came out of the elevator—a very tall white man in the company's gray coveralls. He held his right hand behind him, by his back pocket, and watched Pierce as if he didn't like his looks. Kept watching as Pierce followed Rodney down a corridor full of light from windows along its left side. Top-floor corridor . . .

There was a second man standing along the hall—a black man—who watched Pierce as he came and went past. This man had a shotgun leaning against the wall beside him. Ithaca twelve-gauge, it seemed to be.

Rodney led to the last door along the corridor, knocked on it, and stood smiling at Pierce, waiting.

"Come."

Rodney opened the door for Pierce, and followed him into a large sunny corner office. An elderly black man in a blue suit like a banker's was sitting at a wide, polished desk, going through some papers.

"Daddy," Rodney said, "let me introduce Mr. Tyler Pierce to you. Mr. Pierce has mentioned Pat Simcoe."

The old man put his papers down and looked at Pierce. . . . Rodney's father had been handsome once, but his face had fallen with age into wrinkles, a finely wrinkled black mask with a white mustache. His eyes were a dusty black, with almost no white showing.

"I'm Mathew Bailey, Mr. Pierce." Like his son, he sounded like an educated man. A college man.

"Tyler Pierce." Pierce held out his hand, and the old man reached over his desk to shake it. Soft, cool grip. . . .

"Sit down, please. —Have you had lunch?"

"No sir, I haven't."

"Going to have pickle sandwiches with us, Daddy." Rodney was still standing, smiling at them both.

"Well, I consider that a sign of good judgment on your part, Mr. Pierce. —First, however, I have to say that Pat Simcoe is not quite a sufficient reference. Can you help us out with someone else?"

". . . Todd. Frank Todd. And Barry Price, in Chicago."

"Mr. Todd, we don't know. Mr. Price, we do. Are you acquainted with Barry's cousin?"

"Only cousin I know he had, was killed in San Diego about eight or nine years ago."

"Oh, that's right. A shame, really tragic for Barry."

"Barry killed him, Mr. Bailey."

"Why, of course—that's what I meant. That sort of trouble in a family . . ." The old man sat silent then, looking at Pierce as if something about Pierce's face interested him.

"—And Paul Cipriano in St. Louis."

"Oh, yes?" Mr. Bailey said, looked over at his son, and Rodney left the room. "—You're a friend of Mr. Cipriano's."

"No. But he knows me. He's met me."

"Well . . ." The old man leaned back in his swivel chair, turned it slightly to look out a tall window. The office windows were old-fashioned casements, open in the heat. A breeze was coming through, warm. —Mr. Bailey sighed.

"Every time Rodney persuades me to close my windows and start that damn air-conditioning, it is certain sure I'll take a cold. It is the most unnatural thing you can imagine, chilling the air that way, cutting all the moisture out of it. Certain to cause a cold. . . ."

"It affects some people that way," Pierce said.

". . . Been to New Orleans before, Mr. Pierce?"

"No, I haven't. I've wanted to visit."

"Well, there's the tourist city, and there's the real city. And the real city is quite small—everybody knows everybody, everybody knows *about* everybody, and they live and let live. Only civilized city in the country, in my opinion."

"I understand it's special."

"It is; it is. Wonderful food, of course—but you'll be eating very plain food with us. A family-style lunch. A gumbo. Our pickle sandwiches. Hot pecan pie."

"Sounds very good."

"*Is* good, Mr. Pierce," the old man said, then sat silent, looking out the window.

Pierce sat watching out the window with him, as if they both found relaxation in the sky's hazed light blue, the high banners of cloud blown in from the Gulf.

After a while the office door opened, and Rodney Bailey came in pushing a wheeled cart with platters of food and a pitcher of iced tea on it. "Lunchtime!" he said and reached back to close the door behind him. "And I have a message for you, Mr. Pierce, from Murray Green, an associate of Mr. Cipriano's—a friend, I believe, and his attorney. The counselor says, 'How they hanging?' "

"Rodney," his father said, and turned from the window. "—Stop talking and start serving."

... Though Rodney was young and fat, he was not the eater his father was. Old Mathew chewed through the lunch as if he'd been starving. And all three of them together—Pierce hadn't eaten since a Jack in the Box off the highway the night before—the three of them finished bowls of crawfish gumbo, six white-bread peanut butter and sliced dill pickle sandwiches with mayonnaise (really Blue Bonnet salad dressing, according to Rodney), and most of a lard-crust hot pie made with pecans and boiled-down sorghum syrup.

It was different food, but still the same kind of food Pierce had had at his grandmother's when he was a small boy, and it brought those memories back to him. Of that kind of rich food, and company, and the heat.

"Well—well, now!" The old man, full and finished, leaned way back in his swivel chair, smiling, and seemed to Pierce to have been energized by lunch. "Well now, let's talk some business."

"I'm ready," Pierce said. "But first, I'd like to know who baked that pie."

Mathew Bailey seemed pleased by the question. "My wife baked that pie, Mr. Pierce."

"Then you're a lucky man, sir."

"I've known that for a long time, but I thank you. . . . Mr. Pierce, let me tell you what we do here. What we offer. As you apparently have heard from this one and that one—we are bankers in a sense, really transfer agents. Bankers to those who find lawful institutions too confining, too ready to reveal their customers' private business to any government sneak who inquires.

We assist you to the services of a very private—an absolutely private—bank. And we do that while maintaining a profitable public business in the moving-and-storage line."

"I see."

"Now, of course, as bankers we are criminals, and therefore we have to charge a fairly high service fee— which is a one-time ten percent of all monies deposited. Now, you might well ask what you get for that amount. . . ."

"What do I get for that amount?"

"First, and most important, you receive a lack of curiosity. We do not consider it our business how you earned your money. . . . And second, you get a numbered account in a Cayman Islands bank—Surety Island Savings—an account out of the reach of the United States government or any other government but that of the islands. And their interest, of course, is to maintain that secrecy in order to hold their international deposits."

"And a guarantee, Mr. Bailey? Insurance?"

"As to the Cayman bank—your guarantee is their vital self-interest in maintaining their deposits and protecting them. . . . As to us, as transfer agents while the money is in our hands, your insurance is the same as our many other depositors'." The old man smiled. "— Your money's insurance is my life, my son's life, and our families' lives—and let me assure you that many of our clients would not hesitate an instant in claiming that insurance."

". . . Okay."

"—Now, in the Cayman bank, your account will be identified *only* by number, a letter of the alphabet, and the month and year of deposit, which will be this month, this year. Only by those, and not by name. That is absolute. If you forget your number and/or date of deposit, or allow anyone else access to that information, you can kiss your money goodbye. You clear on that?"

"Yes."

"If you decide to go ahead with us, the bank will offer you only three point five percent on your money—just enough to stay even with current U.S. inflation. They will, if you contact them—using your number and deposit month and year—offer the services that any bank might in estate work, disbursement of funds, trusts and so forth. The charges for those services will be high, but not unreasonable."

Pierce sat thinking about it, watching the old man as the old man watched him. It all sounded sensible . . . but he thought about it carefully, nonetheless. In any such setup, trouble of some sort was bound to come— probably had already come several times. In the city, the Baileys would have made arrangements to cover themselves with the police and politicians. None trustworthy.

Once deposited on the island, the gold—the money gotten for it—should be safe enough. Any problem would come before that. "How long for you to make the transfer, Mr. Bailey?"

"Three days . . . sometimes four."

"And you hold yourself personally responsible during that time?"

"Yes, I do. You can check with the Cayman bank in five days, Mr. Pierce. If the deposit is not confirmed, we will return the full amount to you immediately."

"You don't forsee any difficulties?"

"No. None at all. There have been a few problems in the past, and those've been handled to our clients' satisfaction. —Tell you the truth, we couldn't afford to get cute in these matters, Mr. Pierce. That would turn into World War Three very quickly." The old man had a pleasant smile.

Pierce sat awhile longer, considering. . . . Mathew Bailey waited with him, relaxed behind his fine desk.

The day had grown hotter; the sky through the tall open windows had turned a paler blue, almost blue-white with heat.

"We have a deal," Pierce said, and got up to shake the old man's hand.

Rodney Bailey had insisted Pierce stop at Jackson Square before leaving the city. "Tourist stuff—but Tyler, you just cannot leave us without at least having a plate of *beignets* and a cup of chicory *café au lait*. Next time, you stay longer and I'll show you the city. We'll have the stuffed quail at Emeril's, goat cheesecake for dessert, and go on the town from there. New Orleans is even more nicely nasty than Miami. I guarantee you'll enjoy yourself."

This invitation had been offered inside a ramped loading dock in the Baileys' south building, the wide metal door pulled rumbling down and locked shut.

Rodney and his father, come down to watch the unpacking and make their count, had been very pleased by new-minted gold. They hadn't commented on where it might have come from, and were amused that Pierce had brought his treasure with him directly, and had kept it in an unlocked truck toolbox all those miles from Missouri. "I see you are a risk-taker, Mr. Pierce," the old man had said. "A calculating risk-taker."

"I try," Pierce had said—and thinking that these people could, after all that talk about banking, just shoot him through the head and take the gold for themselves, he strolled to where a slender young Hispanic with a wispy mustache and goatee stood guard with a Remington shotgun, looked past him and said, "What's he doing here?"—and when the young man glanced that way, had reached out and snatched the shotgun from him, slipped its safety, and strolled back to watch his gold being counted.

The young man and a second guard hadn't cared for his doing that—there was a trick to it; you had to lift whatever it was up just a little before you jerked it away—but the Baileys had thought it was funny. "Pleasure dealing with a grown-up," old Mathew had said. "You'd be amazed the fools come in here, show no prudence whatsoever."

They'd counted the coins—slice-tested and weighed a dozen at random—and told Pierce they made the sum $897,211.46, at the morning's London fixing of the price of gold.

They'd set their ten percent aside right there, then provided him five thousand in cash, walking-around money.

. . . Pierce sat out on the pavilion of the Café du Monde, watching the street entertainers in Jackson Square, mime actors and sidewalk artists, fortune-tellers, and tourists taking each other's pictures. He watched all that, and the pigeons—and tried to like chicory coffee. The *beignets*, though, were really good. A sort of puffed-up brown cruller, dusted with fine sugar. Carolyn would enjoy all this . . . enjoy a trip down to New Orleans.

After a while, Pierce finished the coffee so as not to waste it, finished the last of the *beignets*. He left a tip on the table, picked up his box of pralines—bought at a little store off the square—and walked back down to public parking through an afternoon heat that seemed to rise up out of the pavement.

He repeated his bank number as he walked, to make sure it was in his memory for good. The old man had whispered it to him twice, asked him to whisper it back twice: 020-635-4117-D. That number, and this month and year.

Though murmuring his number to himself, Pierce stayed attentive, noticed who was walking near him . . . driving past. It would still be to the Baileys' profit to have him shot on the street, as if some passing hoodlum had tried for his wallet.

And if father and son *were* occasional hijackers,

they'd need to deal with him before he was out of town—and able, in case of disappointment calling the Cayman Islands, to pick his time to deal with them.

So he watched out as he walked to the truck, unlocked it, and climbed in. The cab was an oven hot enough to raise a layer cake, but Pierce closed and locked his door, started the engine and backed the pickup . . . then drove on out of the lot before he lowered the windows to get in some slightly cooler breeze to ease the air-conditioner.

He drove up Rue Pleasance, checking the rearview mirrors from time to time, found his first right and followed that to Esplanade. Left on that was supposed to lead up to the I-10 onramp—and it did, into fast traffic going east.

Pierce wove into the stream of speeding cars and trucks, checking his rearview mirrors. He drove, watching out behind him, until the last of Lake Pontchartrain passed to the left, the flat gray water flashing like miles of mirror in the sunshine.

He drove, and no one followed him. No single vehicle, no team of cars and trucks and vans playing catch-up, changeover, and fallback to keep him covered. He was all alone in a thousand machines rushing east.

It seemed the Baileys were honest.

"Ted—you hear about this?" Agent Hildebrandt, walking in on Gottfried's late lunch. Out of his wife's sight, Gottfried tended to order in rich lunches, and this one was a roast pork sandwich, a pint of whole milk, and a narrow slice of apple pie from Bowsers.

"Hear about what?"

"Girl the Sweetwater killed? Latest victim?"

"Yes, but not our area, not our case. Thank God."

"A Lisa Pierce. Twenty-two years old."

"That's a shame. . . ."

"Pierce," said Hildebrandt. "*Pierce*. Guess whose daughter."

"Are you kidding me? —Our guy, our Pierce?"

"Sheriff Lotts says he's already on his way down to Florida for the funeral."

"Well, that *is* a damn shame. That's grim. Poor guy. . . ." Gottfried took another bite of his sandwich. Was there a better cold meat than roast pork?

Hildebrandt, leaving the office, said, "Could be interesting times ahead in the Sunshine State."

Full dark, Pierce stopped at a Motel 6 outside Mobile, Alabama. He'd driven the afternoon into evening with the expanse of the Gulf on his right, and enjoyed that as he'd enjoyed driving the wheatfields north of home. Same kind of spacious feeling, that there was no end to things. That you could keep going as long as you chose, and then if you chose there was even more room to go farther.

The Gulf was like that. A cloudy horizon that said, Come on—sail all the way to Venezuela, or out to the Caribbean islands, or down to Brazil if you care to. The whole world is waiting. . . .

Pierce had enjoyed driving that stretch, and stopped only once—for gas, and to go to a McDonald's to piss and pick up a strawberry shake and two Big Macs. Then he'd driven on, listening to Dorrie King sing country-western on the radio. Wonderful, wonderful voice; she sounded like an ordinary woman, a sad hard-working woman who'd been given an angel's throat to sing through.

When they put on some four-part gospel group next, Pierce had turned off the radio and recited Alfred Lord Tennyson to himself out loud, his favorite poet from the Kansas pen's library.

Though much is taken, much abides; and though
We are not now that strength which in old days

Moved earth and heaven; that which we are, we
    are. . . .

—It was his favorite poem of his favorite poet,
Longfellow coming second. . . .

Pierce paid cash at the Motel 6, signed R. Edwards,
and gave the clerk a slightly incorrect license number
for the truck. The Baileys remained a little on his mind,
and might after all have decided to send some people
after him. . . .

Still, when he drove around back to his room and
parked, he was surprised how relieved he felt not to be
carrying the gold anymore. All he had left of that was
five thousand in hundreds and fifties, Emma's garden
shovel lying in the pickup's bed, and a long account
number with a D at the end.

He didn't turn on the room's TV. Watching that was
a habit he'd lost in prison, hadn't sat staring at the set
the way so many did, to forget where they were. He'd
done better without it—seemed to him it made people
dumber.

He took a long hot shower, came out to towel where
it wasn't so steamy, then opened his box of pralines,
ate four of them and went to bed.

Pierce had thought he'd left the Café du Monde, but
he hadn't after all. He and Lisa were sitting there
together—and she was in her ranger uniform, even
though they were in New Orleans.

He'd been telling her how sorry he was for being
such a poor father, for leaving her alone and without
him all the years he was inside. But she was smiling at
him, didn't seem angry or resentful. Just . . . just
appeared happy to be with him, be seeing him at
last after only letters, and then the phone calls when he
was out.

She didn't like the chicory coffee, however; they
agreed on that.

"Ten years," Pierce said to her, that being how long it had been since he'd seen her, but Lisa didn't seem to mind that. She smiled at him, sipped her coffee—made a little face at the taste. The uniform looked good on her; she looked cute in it, wore the big hat and all to shade her from the sun. . . . The Florida sun must be something fierce; her arms were burned dark brown. Same warm brown as her eyes—and they reminded Pierce so strongly of her look when she was a baby. Those big eyes . . . soft, and questioning.

"I'm so sorry I disappointed you, sugar."

"Daddy," she said, and her voice sounded strange; it sounded rough. "Daddy," she said, "you were just a natural armed robber. It was just what you were good at. . . ." And Pierce saw why her voice sounded strange. There was a drop of blood at the right side of her smooth brown throat, and he decided not to say anything about it—but it grew and blood slid down onto her shirt, and as he sat across the little table, a red slit opened and opened slowly across her throat and blood came dripping, then running down, and her uniform shirt was ruined—and Pierce was too much of a coward to say anything to her about it.

He woke calling out. Then, when he was awake, couldn't remember what he'd shouted. He turned his face into the pillow and was startled to begin to cry. It was something he hadn't done since he was a little boy and his daddy'd beaten him, and it surprised him how much crying hurt his eyes.

Chapter 4

Carl was mowing. It was something that had to be done whether you wanted to or not. The grass didn't care what had happened, just kept growing. . . . If it was a choice between mowing and listening to some undertaker make his pitch about caskets and so forth, mowing won by a mile. —And of course it was good exercise, too. A man could be bald and carry a little extra weight and nobody thought anything about it. But let that man get really fat, and he was a figure of fun. . . .

Carl saw the red-and-white pickup coming down the street—and just like fate, it slowed at his house, then turned in to park along the sidewalk. Blocked his driveway—then pulled back to clear it.

Man got out in chino pants, boots, and a short-sleeve blue work shirt—and that was it, Tyler Pierce for sure, and Carl had never seen the man, except in some of Margaret's old pictures. Tall drink of water, didn't really look like a bank robber coming up the white-coral walk. And no spring chicken, either.

"Carl Hubbard?"

"That's right."

"Well—guess we were bound to meet sometime." Very strong handshake grip.

"Tyler."

"That's right. How's Margaret doing?"

"Well . . . well, Tyler, she's still pretty shaky. Doctor left some pills, actually had to make a call here.

And now she's in there with the funeral director's man. I just came out and started mowing."

"Don't blame you," and this Pierce was walking right on up to the house with Carl having to follow along as if 327 Jacaranda was Pierce's address and this was his house. Up to the front door, walked right in— and held the door for Carl as if he was a guest.

Margaret was sitting on the sofa with the funeral man, and she looked up and Carl saw an expression on her face he'd never seen from her when he walked into a room. She looked scared and pleased at the same time. It made her look younger, for a minute.

"Hello, Tyler. . . ."

"Margaret . . ." Went over there and kissed her cheek like a cousin.

"I'm just . . . I'm just doing some funeral stuff, and it's killing me."

This Pierce looked down at the funeral man and said, "You're not taking an advantage here, are you?"

"No, sir." Young man looked startled. "No, sir, I'm not. We're doing—it's going to be a modest service. Very nice, but not extravagant."

"We just can't afford to spend a lot," Margaret said. "My husband is a salesman, and he has emphysema." —As if it was any of this Pierce's business to hear all that. And she'd talked the same way to those reporters, too, told them this and that when they came sniffing around like a bunch of vultures. —They didn't know Lisa, and they didn't care a damn about her. It was just getting some news, to them. . . .

"You going to be staying with us, Tyler? You know you're welcome." Man had to be asked.

"Thanks, Carl. But I already took a room at the Roadside Rest out on—is that Pine Avenue, coming in?"

"That's right. Pine." Well . . . man was asked.

In driving down the center of the state, Pierce hadn't noticed much difference from any Southern pine barrens and sloughs. Stretches almost like that in southern Arkansas, and over in Texas. Nothing much different, except the heat. It was even hotter than New Orleans had been. A wet heat, and heavy.

Now though, down in Lake Palmetto—maybe just that much farther south—now he saw the difference. Semitropics under a blue-white sky and the sun up there just blazing—supposed to be closer down here, and by God it seemed so. . . . And plants appeared to be made of green rubber in this country, or were hard, thin-leafed, and spiked—and those looked to be saying, "Fall on me and you'll be sorry." Sandy country, and snake country where it wasn't settled and paved.

It had been a relief to drive into the town—strange trees or not, as long as they gave shade. A relief to get into a cool house, too . . .

Margaret had cooked a dinner that was Pierce's favorite a dozen years ago. Had gone out and shopped for that—broiled pork chops and yams (not sweet potatoes), and the small green peas and hot Parker House dinner rolls. Peach ice cream . . . She'd sat at the end of the table and watched him eat it.

It had surprised Pierce when he'd first seen her sitting in the living room talking with that young undertaker. He had . . . for some reason he'd expected her to be older—to look older, like an old woman. It seemed to be that long a time, that many years since he'd seen her. —But of course she wasn't old, was a few years younger than he was, matter of fact. Thirty-eight . . . thirty-nine now. Good-looking—elegant woman, thin, with that long Indian hair still black as night. Night with some silver in it now, but not much . . .

Wiry woman, too. Strong physically—she used to wrestle with him hard when they were screwing . . . making love. Hard time holding her down. He'd joked about it . . . saying it was like breaking a horse. Very active woman; must bounce poor Carl around something fierce. She'd been considerable in that way, in other ways not so much. But still it was strange to be sitting eating her cooked dinner, and talking to her.

Lisa, living, had been a reason to force them apart, Pierce being a convicted man. Now, dead, she had brought them together again . . . for a day or two.

"You still have your sweet tooth," Margaret had said—and after dinner, left Carl watching a cop show on TV and took Pierce out to sit on the patio. They had a fair-sized yard back there, and a pretty hedge around it grown up maybe eight or nine feet, so it made a wall of soft green—each leaf dark green in the center, light green along its edges.

Now, out on the patio—the heat being part of it, even with night coming on—Pierce felt again how different Florida was, felt the darkness and odors and heat come at him all together. It was pleasant in a way; seemed to be a lot to learn about it. More than there'd been in the evenings in Missouri.

It was pleasant to be sitting in an old canvas chair, with the strange person who'd been your wife sitting off to the side there, and you both were just fading . . . fading into night.

"Tyler, I don't know what to say to you. I know you're blaming me for not taking care of her, but I couldn't do it. You can't tell a young woman what to do. . . ."

Margaret's voice had changed very little. Maybe not changed at all—perhaps he'd forgotten in prison. He remembered that when they were screwing her voice would go up an octave to a farm girl's screech and all that office receptionist nearly-a-lady tone would disappear. . . . And she hadn't been a bad wife. She'd been a good wife. Had a very nice sense of humor—found a lot of things funny which many women wouldn't have. And she'd put up with a lot of his horseshit and taking risks and criminal acts and so forth. And could cook. Her voice had changed very little. . . .

"—Lisa had those two years of college and that was that; she came back from Gainesville and I just lost all control over her." It was a slowly vanishing woman talking now, though just over them the clouds still reflected a soft tangerine color from the setting sun. "I couldn't tell her what to do—Carl can't tell *anybody* what to do—and she wouldn't listen to Jason either. She was a sweet girl, but she was very headstrong. I said that was a dangerous job—and it turned out it was. A girl alone out there in that huge swamp—it just goes on forever. And now look what's happened. . . ."

"It wasn't your fault, Margaret."

"Oh yes it was," Margaret said, and began to cry. "It was my fault; there must have been something I could have done. . . ." She took deep breaths, trying to stop crying. "Tyler, you know I called her apartment yesterday? I called her apartment as if she was alive, just to see if maybe she'd answer. —Oh, I'm just going *crazy* . . . !"

"Shhh. It's all right."

"You're thinking, 'This stupid *stupid* bitch left me back then when I was in trouble—and she was no goddam use to our girl either and let her get killed by some fucking *maniac*. . . .' "

"No, that's not what I think, Margaret."

"Yes, it is."

"No. I went off robbing banks, and I got caught. You were right to leave me; I was a bad husband to you. And as for not taking care of Lisa—you did very well. I'm the one stepped away from my responsibility."

Pierce felt better for having said that much, and he settled back into his chair as if deeper into the night, where no one could see him or bring him any other bad news. He breathed in dampness and heat, and odors like a perfume counter's in a store. Jasmine, it smelled like . . . and gardenia too, or some flower like a gardenia. A slow breeze was drifting through the darkness—too far from the sea to be that. Perhaps from the lake they had here . . . or the swamps in the big park where Lisa had died.

"How far is it to that damn park?"

"Oh, it's . . . almost forty miles. It's a huge place— just miles and miles of wilderness is what it is. Supposed to be the biggest swamp except for the Everglades in this state. Full of all sorts of . . . things. It never was a place where a girl should be."

Listening, turning his head to watch her, Pierce saw through darkness her white summer dress faintly glowing in starlight, and a soft silhouette of a Margaret who might have been young.

"—You see that godawful swamp and everything, you can't *imagine* what a girl would be doing wandering around in there alone. Driving that jeep around . . . Young women think they're just like men now, and they're not. It's all just a stupid lie and they don't find that out until it's too late. . . ."

"Where's the police station in this town, Margaret?"

"Oh . . . that's . . . the sheriff's department is in the county courthouse, I think. But some detectives have already been out here. Some of them have been out here several times, and they stayed for hours. Yesterday and today are the first days they've left us alone. And I don't think they know anything; I just don't think they have any idea about this . . . goddam monster."

"I don't suppose they know much, or they'd have had him before now." There was a bird calling . . . seemed to be sailing back and forth through the air high above the yard. Some darkness bird, hunting moths.

"Listen, Tyler . . . the funeral is going to be day after tomorrow, instead of waiting till Friday. I don't want those reporters there, and the newspapers think it's Friday."

"All right. —I'll be paying for the funeral, Margaret."

"No, you don't have to do that. She was my baby . . . my daughter."

"Yes, she was—more your daughter than mine. But I'll be paying for the funeral, just the same. You tell me the amount, I'll give you cash." The moon was rising now, barely clear of the tall hedge fencing the yard—a moon just off the full, and frosted silver with streaks of red in it. It looked as if Florida's heat had risen to heat the moon. . . .

". . . Tyler, do you think about us sometimes, the way we were together?"

"No, honey, I don't."

Tim Macksie was one of those slender handsome young law officers who looked like clerks in expensive stores, until you saw their eyes.

Sheriff Macksie's eyes seemed to belong to an older man. They were dull gray-green as a snapping turtle's, and asked every cop's question: What have *you* done?

Pierce had been treated politely by the deputy in the outer office—a large man working on a late breakfast of two cinnamon rolls and coffee—and was left to wait only a little while. The sheriff's waiting room had *Reader's Digest*s and *Florida Today*s to look at. There'd been no mention of the Sweetwater killer in *Florida Today*. . . .

"I'm going to talk to you two different ways, Mr. Pierce." The sheriff had a very Southern voice, very country, it seemed to Pierce—likely out of one of the old Florida cracker families.

"First, I'm going to talk to you as that poor girl's father. And then, I'm going to talk to you as a convicted felon, subject of a fax we received yesterday from an FBI agent named Hildebrandt, up in Missouri." Macksie seemed very young to be a sheriff— must have won it by election. He wore his dark-brown hair cut neatly short, and was dressed in a tan summer suit. Where his suit jacket opened as he sat, a fat-butted SIG showed in a shoulder holster.

"So, first, I am very very sorry about what happened to your girl. It was the act of a mighty sick individual, and everyone in this department and in this county is upset about it. . . ." The sheriff had pictures of his family on his desk—but turned to face outward, to be seen by whoever sat across from him, as if to prove he was a man like any other man despite his badge and gun, his armed men, the cells downstairs. —A picture of his wife—very young, dark, looking Hispanic—and a baby, fat and smiling, held upright for the camera by a slim bare brown arm.

"—Mr. Pierce, we do not, I am real sorry to say, have leads and information strong enough for an arrest at this time. We have had five of these crimes, absolutely committed by the same individual, and all central or south-central in the state. And this one makes three in this county. Now, since the first victim was a serving Coast Guard officer, the federals are involved, and the state law enforcement people are involved, and my department is involved. And we are not any of us going to rest on this case until we have the perpetrator in custody and he is on his way to death row."

Sheriff Macksie hadn't blinked once while he was saying that. He'd watched Pierce all the time . . . muddy turtle eyes.

"—Okay. Now, second, we've been informed of your record, Tyler, and that you've come down here for the funeral and so forth. The federal people may be interested in interviewing you further concerning that big robbery up North—although you are not wanted, and apparently not considered a suspect in that." He paused, perhaps to see if Pierce had some declaration of innocence to make. "However, I can tell you that you are not a welcome addition down here. I don't like felons, probably responsible for numerous major armed robberies, running around my county. My people will be keeping an eye on you, and if you make a wrong move in a bank down here, you will be a real sorry ex-con."

All delivered as an item of information. The sheriff didn't seem a passionate type of cop. "—Now, I have some advice for you, and it's real good advice, too. My advice is, go to the funeral and then leave this area and get back up where you come from. Any information we get on the case, we will forward to Mrs. Hubbard. This is not Miami; we don't coexist with major criminals up here. You understand me, Tyler?"

"I understand you, Tim."

The young sheriff might have minded being addressed by his first name—and might not.

Lake Palmetto's library, set on a big corner lot with two banyan trees half-shading it, was a Spanish-style white stucco rambler with a very good orange barrel-tile roof—roof wouldn't do for hard-freezing weather, but perfect down here. . . .

"What are those trees?" Pierce had asked Carl about them after breakfast, when he was leaving and Carl went out with him to get the mail. "What are they?" Dark, dark-leaved trees spaced down the street with root edges raised out of the ground and snaking all around.

"Banyans," Carl had said—speaking as an old Florida hand, though originally from Delaware. "Roots grow down from the branches to the ground and dig in right there. . . ."

The banyans shading the library were huge, each a dark smooth-trunked forest in itself.

". . . Do you want to see the local paper?" The librarian was a man, young, with a blond beard and mustache. He didn't wear glasses.

"Yes—and the papers from the nearest big city."

"Biggest city would be Miami; we have those. — And only references to the Sweetwater murders?"

"That's right," Pierce said. "Everything you've got."

"Very well. It'll take a while to get the article dates and bring up those newspapers." The bearded man seemed to think it was an unpleasant request, but he went down his long desk and sat at a computer to begin.

This library was a step up from Carolyn's, in Dowland. Bigger, and with counters of viewing machines and computers. A step up from Dowland—a whole flight of steps up from the prison library. Still used grimy old card files in that prison. . . .

Pierce had bought a thick blue-covered notebook in a drugstore before he came over. A notebook and two ballpoint pens with black ink; he'd found black ink easier on the eyes than blue. He went over to a table under one of the windows, took out his reading glasses—how did anybody ever get used to wearing the damn things?—and sat waiting for the librarian to bring him the papers. . . .

. . . Marie Tessler—Lieutenant Tessler—had been the first woman killed. There was a picture, a photograph of her—tall, more handsome than beautiful—in uniform on the deck of a big white cutter.

On leave and in summer uniform, she'd been killed in her mother's apartment in the Sweetwater Residential Complex a few miles south of Fort Pierce.

Her mother had driven to the drugstore for antihistamines for a summer cold, and had been gone less than forty-five minutes. She found the apartment door open an inch or two, called, and went in carrying the little white paper sack of antihistamines and a romance paperback, *Eastwind*, by Susan Ashton.

She called, then found Marie on the kitchen floor, half naked, her uniform blouse torn off, and her throat cut so deeply her trachea had been sliced in two. Her breasts had also been severed and left beside her on the floor.

The kitchen was spattered and running with blood. Mrs. Tessler apparently had slipped a little in it, then knelt screaming . . . and had been found hugging her daughter, touching her wounds, trying to make her better. . . .

When Pierce read that, he saw Lisa in his dream of the Café du Monde . . . and had to stop reading, stop writing in his notebook. He sat for a few minutes with his head in his hands, worried he was going to be sick . . . and he didn't know where the bathroom was in this library.

He sat like that for a while, then noticed the librarian looking at him from behind his computer desk, took deep breaths, and straightened up to keep reading.

. . . The second was a police officer. A young Cuban woman named Mercedes Calderón, married, with a little daughter. Officer Calderón had been somehow persuaded out of her patrol car in Copper Beach, taken or led behind a closed Snookies sandwich shop, and murdered there in daylight by the Dumpster. Highway traffic going past all the time. Officer Calderón had not had time to get her pistol out. No time to struggle.

Her throat had been cut from behind; she'd staggered in bright sunshine, gargling, spouting blood, slowly collapsing in shock. She'd then been followed to the ground, her uniform blouse and her bra torn open, and her breasts sliced away.

There'd been tire tracks of another vehicle at the scene, printed into the crushed-shell fill and sand in front of the drive-in. The investigators knew there'd been such tracks, because the Sweetwater had taken the time to carefully brush them away.

The question of the amount of blood and blood-staining having come up, it was the general opinion of the coroners and police departments involved that the Sweetwater stepped behind his victims, reached over and deeply cut their throats—left to right, right to left, he seemed ambidextrous—then, avoiding the hemorrhage, stood back to let them stumble, strangling in their own blood, before stepping in to complete his work.

The Sweetwater's instrument was believed to be a straight razor. . . .

Rue Long had been a senior and cheerleader at Peace River College—very bright, very nice. The Sweetwater—the papers had already named him for Mrs. Tessler's apartment building—had caught her on campus in the evening in her drill-team uniform, apparently forced or persuaded her into an empty basement classroom, and slaughtered her. Same as the others— her throat, her breasts.

There were several photographs of Rue Long in the papers in her drill-team outfit. A very pretty girl, blond, and smiling. An article said she'd been a gymnast before she'd hurt her knee.

The librarian came to ask for the papers Pierce was finished with, and took those away. Two more dead young women were left . . . and then Lisa. Pierce read slower and slower. Made notes about everything mentioned, whether it seemed worthwhile or not, so as to delay coming to Lisa.

. . . Jo-Ann Dailey, just arrived home from her work as a Palmetto Lake meter maid, had died while her husband and young son were playing softball catch outside in the backyard. Her boy found her when they came inside. Mrs. Dailey had been killed in her laundry room. She'd either let the Sweetwater in, or been surprised while she was putting fresh-washed clothes into the dryer. The front door hadn't been locked.

. . . . Marcie Tredenberg had been a delivery person for The Emperor's Pizza, and had been wearing the restaurant's uniform, a Roman soldier's helmet, lace-up sandals, kilt, and armor (plastic). There was a photograph of her with two friends—delivery persons on different nights—all in those uniforms. One of her friends was pretty; Marcie wasn't. She was smiling, though—seemed to Pierce, just from the photograph, to have been a happy girl. Cheerful . . .

She'd been killed making a delivery.

The Sweetwater—his voice couldn't be recalled from dozens of others that evening—had ordered a small extra-cheese, waited beneath a flight of stairs going up to student housing at St. Catherine's in Katachee, and dragged Marcie down.

. . . Then, this year, just last week . . . the Sweetwater had murdered Lisa Pierce, a ranger twenty-two years old. Killed her in her Jeep parked a few yards off the Tucker Trail—a birdwatching trail—in the northwest section of Manchineel State Park.

She'd been found two days later.

The Sweetwater had taken her from behind, as he always seemed to do, and left her butchered behind the steering wheel. No one knew why she had driven her killer there, to the midst of wilderness.

. . . The police were puzzled about that, and apparently about everything. None of the young women murdered over the years had known each other, or had any friends in common. Their only likeness, the only connection at all, was their wearing uniforms of some kind, even inconsequential or silly ones. . . . There were no substantial clues, no convenient fingerprints. No witnesses.

Pierce made his last note, closed his notebook, and got up and left. He stood outside on the steps, squinting in the sunshine, its heat stinging his forehead. Then he went back inside to the desk and thanked the librarian for his trouble.

That evening, Margaret cooked Pierce's second most favorite meal—or it had been, years ago. Ham with cloves in it, corn on the cob, sliced tomatoes, and peach pie. She'd always been a good cook.

Pierce had gotten a haircut and a barbershop shave before he drove in from the motel to their house in the afternoon. Good haircut, bad shave; Florida barbers seemed to have forgotten the skill.

At first, he didn't know why he'd done that, gone to have a shop shave that way. Then he did. He knew why he'd done it when he felt the straight razor reached from behind him, to rest its edge at his throat. . . .

Jason Schroeder came to dinner—a stocky blond strong-looking boy wearing a heavy diver's wrist-watch. He was partners in a scuba shop north of Fort Talavera. Margaret had said he did well at it, but he seemed young to Pierce, to be a businessman. . . . He was short—maybe five-eight or -nine—but had heavy shoulders on him, and was tanned by years at the beaches. A handsome young man, with a round soft face that went oddly with the rest of him.

"Mr. Pierce," he said in the living room—Carl out in the kitchen with Margaret, making drinks. "—Mr. Pierce, I want you to know I tried to make Lisa happy. I loved her; I still do love her." The boy seemed afraid Pierce would blame him somehow, maybe do something to him, being an ex-con and bank robber and so forth.

"I understand," Pierce said. "Nobody 's blaming you." Though it occurred to him just then, how convenient the Sweetwater's killings would be for someone who wanted another person dead. Simply do it—or have it done—as the madman would have. . . .

"I just can't get it out of my mind. . . ."

"Give it time," Pierce said, found he didn't like the boy, and supposed he was jealous of what he'd been to her . . . that she'd loved him enough to marry him. What would he have said to Lisa about this Jason Schroeder?—if he'd come down here before, instead of wasting all that time working on the Michigan job. What would he have said to her about this boy when she introduced them, then later talked about marrying him?

"Your decision, sweetheart—although it looks to me like his face and his body don't match. Sort of thing might get on your nerves after a few years. . . ."

She would have laughed at that. She'd been a laughing sort of girl, apparently.

The ham was delicious; corn on the cob was very good. Pierce hadn't had lunch, was hungry and ate. And he noticed the boy putting away a big dinner, despite his sorrow. Of course, might have missed his lunch too. . . . Margaret sat at the end of their dining-room table looking better than she had since Pierce had come down. She looked better, and seemed satisfied watching Pierce eat her peach pie.

Over coffee—real coffee, not instant—Pierce told them he'd be leaving right after the funeral.

"Oh, no—not so soon."

"Margaret, I can't stay longer. Have some things to do."

"What in the world is so important to do up there, Tyler? You can fix roofs down here. Lisa . . . she told me you said you were doing roofing."

"That's right."

"Well, you could do that down here. You don't have any family up in Missouri except those Youngers. I don't count Nelsons—those people are just barely cousins to you."

"Can't stay," Pierce said, and finished his cup of coffee. "Good coffee. I had some of that New Orleans chicory coffee driving down. I guess that has to be an acquired taste."

"You are just so stubborn. . . ."

"Honey," Carl said, "leave the man alone. Maybe Tyler likes Missouri. Maybe there's someone up there special to him."

"Carl, you don't know anything about it. Is that true, Tyler? You have someone up there? —I hope it is, I hope there's someone to take care of you."

"There's someone," Pierce said, and thought how

much Carolyn would enjoy listening to this. Too bad she couldn't have come down; she and Margaret would have gotten along about as poorly as possible.

"A wonderful dinner, Mrs. Hubbard . . ." Jason, young dive-shop partner, had finished eating.

Chapter 5

The funeral was at ten o'clock in the morning at Mission Presbyterian Church, a pretty building right on the street, dark-cream stucco with a gray tile roof. Seemed to Pierce that every other building was stucco down here. . . . Margaret had been a Baptist when he'd married her; they'd been married at Jordan Baptist in Old Falls, Missouri. Apparently she'd decided to step up socially to Presbyterian.

"No reporters," Margaret said, getting out of Carl's Oldsmobile. "Those bloodsuckers can come here tomorrow and just waste their time!" She was wearing a new black dress, black shoes, and a black purse.

"Expensive outfit, but I don't care," Carl said to Pierce as she came up the church steps—and he took a look at Pierce's blue suit.

"Gentleman's Warehouse," Pierce said. "I got it yesterday."

"What are you, a forty-four?"

"Forty-four long," Pierce said.

"I'd like to go in," Margaret said, "if you two are finished talking about clothes."

They walked inside, Jason already there to meet them, and Pierce was surprised to see more than a hundred people sitting quietly in cool shade. It was as pretty a church inside as out, cream plaster walls with some dark wood trim . . . a tall, heavy wooden cross up above the altar. It was a bigger space than it had looked from outside.

His eyes adjusting to less light, Pierce saw most of the people sitting there wore uniforms. Park ranger uniforms—green uniforms. Two men, middle-aged men with weather-worn faces, got up from the pews and came back.

An older man with a turned-around collar came back with them. All three of them had something to whisper to Margaret and Carl, and then the minister shook hands with Pierce.

"You were her natural father, Mr. Pierce?"

"Yes, I am. I was."

"Oh, I think you're still her father. . . ." The minister wore glasses; Pierce could see himself in them—a curved shadowy church-light Tyler Pierce. "We have an open coffin, Mr. Pierce, and Lisa's looking very beautiful. Would you like to see her, say goodbye?"

"No," Pierce said. "I can't do that."

The minister looked a little puzzled, as if Pierce might be afraid of the dead.

"I don't deserve to see her," Pierce said, and the old man nodded and said, "I see." Then he reached out and stroked Pierce's arm as if that was where the pain was.

When the minister stepped out of his way, Pierce could see down the church aisle, and he saw—as if it hadn't been there before—the coffin shining dull bronze and banked on both sides with flowers. They weren't the flowers he was used to; they were tropical flowers, some white as white skin, others red as any blood he'd seen.

The minister and Carl and Margaret, with Jason and the two rangers behind them, were all walking down the aisle to look at Lisa. They were walking through organ music Pierce hadn't heard begin. Margaret looked back and beckoned to him, but Pierce shook his head and stayed where he was.

It was cool in the church; it was almost cold. Pierce stood and watched when Margaret got to the coffin.

Half of it was open, and Pierce could see white silk and an edge of bronze, and the flowers behind that.

Margaret looked in and bent down . . . bent all the way down to kiss. Pierce saw that, and he saw her straighten up again. She looked surprised. Pierce heard her say, "There's something wrong. . . . She's terribly cold. She's too cold!" Then she said—shouted—"Oh, my God! Oh my *God*!" and the minister and Carl wheeled her away between them and took her off to the side, and the organ music became louder.

The organ was playing a hymn Pierce knew. "There's a Wideness in God's Mercy, Like the Wideness of the Sea."

The organ was playing, but no one had stood up to sing; Margaret's calling out had upset things. Then one of the older men, one of the park rangers who'd come back to talk with her and Carl, stood up with a hymn book and started to sing. He didn't have much of a voice, so Pierce joined in—singing standing in the back, and he remembered a lot of the words. . . . But in the most surprising way, he suddenly missed Freddy Simmons, missed his voice—that deep dark voice all big black men were supposed to have, but Freddy had it. Could sing like an opera singer on the radio. . . .

"I do believe," Freddy'd said, the very first time they met, in the back of the River Lounge in Kansas City, "—I do believe you are the ofay kicked the shit out of my baby brother in the joint two, three years ago. Khalif? Khalif Simmons?"

"Yes," Pierce had said. "That's right." He had damn near killed that boy. Khalif had come up to him with some bullshit outside the weight room . . . made some slighting remark.

"Put my baby brother in the hospital."

"Yes," Pierce had said, "that's so."

And Freddy had smiled and said, "I owe you a *big* drink. That little motherfucker been lookin' for a beatin' since forever." And he and Pierce had been friends from then on, as if they'd known each other all their lives. And Pierce had asked Freddy in for the Michigan thing; and Freddy had come in. . . .

Everyone was up and singing by the end of that hymn, and it seemed to Pierce there wasn't much music better than hymn music, when people meant it and sang out. . . . The old minister and Margaret and Carl were back from wherever they'd been. Margaret, Carl, and Jason were sitting up front.

The minister went up to his pulpit, waited until everybody settled down from singing, then started to say his say. It was about what seems cruel and aimless in the world . . . and we were children who didn't understand, didn't know the half of it. But there was a plan like a painting—and every brushstroke that seemed tragic or mysterious was only a tiny contribution to that work of art that God was fashioning.

It seemed to Pierce that with so many nasty brushstrokes, God might be fashioning a mighty unpleasant painting, and nobody would know it until too late. . . .

. . . Some of the men from the park rangers carried the coffin, four to a side. The coffin was closed now; two men in dark suits had gone up to the altar and done it when the minister was finished.

Pierce watched the coffin come down the center aisle to him—such a shining heavy thing to hold a dead girl in—and as if someone had pushed him from behind he went up to the man in front on the near side, walked along with him, then said, "I'll do this," and moved in, moved the man away and took the weight of the coffin on his shoulder.

He took the weight and leaned into it, rested his cheek against the cool and shining bronze. He whispered, "Here I am. I'm here, sweetheart," as he and the others carried it out into the sunshine and heat, and carefully down the steps. Carefully down the steps and out to the undertaker's long dark-blue hearse. They had a metal rack and wheels waiting, to load it with.

* * *

Back from the cemetery and impatient to be going, Pierce stood on the house's front walk and said goodbye to Carl and Jason.

"Take care now, Tyler. You know you're welcome down here anytime. . . ."

"Thanks, Carl." Pierce shook hands with them both, and they went on inside.

But Margaret stayed standing on the walk, squinting in the sunshine. "Don't you want to come in, have some iced tea?"

"No, I need to be going."

"You going up home?"

"Not just yet."

"Why, what are you going to do down here, Tyler?" Pierce just stood there, and didn't answer her.

"Oh," Margaret said. "Oh, yes. God bless you." She stretched up to kiss him on the mouth. "My bad man . . ." she said, and watched him walk out to his truck.

It seemed to Naomi the old man was going downhill. Of course had been going downhill for some time— that was natural—but now going down faster. Sitting in his deck chair on the flowered terrace, looking out over the bay, Phil resembled an aging little dog dressed by children in a green nylon bathing suit.

—An old dog, one of the medium-sized gray poodles with its fur falling out. Same fat little elderly belly. Same eyes—little dusty gray monkey eyes.

"What the fuck are you starin' at? You're givin' me a once-over like a dead man."

"You don't look well, Phil."

"Oh, I have a whore come over here an' tell me I don't look well. I'm eighty-three years old. What the fuck am I supposed to look like? Fifty years ago? A handsome young guy?"

"I saw your pictures, Phil. You showed me the

Chicago pictures, and you were never a handsome young guy. You looked like a muskrat. Only thing missing was the tail."

Naomi was pleased to get a laugh out of him with that one. "Hee-hee-hee," like an old pirate in a movie.

"Hee-hee-hee. All right, I'm sorry I said 'whore.' "

"It's an ugly word."

"I said I was sorry. Want to play pinochle?"

"Can't we just sit here and enjoy the breeze, the water? You've got this gorgeous mansion, Phil, and you can't wait to go running in the house to play cards."

"I see this view all the time. It's a big deal for you, you come over here. It's not a big deal for me. Listen, you be good an' maybe couple days I'll take you out to Giacosa, get some veal."

"We'll go out to dinner? That'll be the day. . . . Look out there, Phil. You see that chop? Hurricane weather."

"You and hurricanes. —I don't believe any of the crap on the radio. That storm's a couple hundred miles out."

"Wait and see."

"Oh, sure. You an' the weather. . . ."

Two years before, recommended by Terry, bartender at the Miami Beach and Swimming Club, Naomi had been sent out to the bay islands to Phil Lombardi's. Five hundred for all night.

"He's interested in a grown-up," Terry had said. "A lady who's classy, knows the score."

"You mean an older woman he can get cheap. —Are we talking about an elderly man?"

"You got it."

"Is this a gangster or what?"

"He was a gangster; now he's long time retired and a decent guy."

"So you say," Naomi'd said, but she'd been broke— thanks to everlasting work on the fourplex—and had to go. A prostitute gets to be thirty-seven years old and can't undress in daylight with a client watching, it's time to be less picky. Past time.

And it had turned out very well. Ordinary old-man sex—a little huffing, a little puffing, and it didn't work. Then a little cuddling, a little loving, a gentle hand job, and it worked.

Better than worked, because a friendship had begun. Naomi was out of old Miami; her father had sold restaurant supplies, then managed a little hotel on the Beach—and Phil was out of old Chicago. "—But listen," he'd said to her once, when she'd come over and they'd had a loud argument about two-handed pinochle. "—Listen, I could see you were a little scared I started yellin'. Listen, Naomi, I'm not a bad guy, not a violent guy. I never was one of those 'You cocksucker, I'm goin' to cut your head off' kind of animals in Chicago. Okay? So don't be scared of me. I'm a rich retired bookie an' that's all I am. I never killed anybody; I never hurt anybody worse than a busted arm or something. —And you know those guys, those maniacs went around killin' people? *Boop boop*, puttin' 'em in garbage cans? Well, they're gone, an' I'm still here retired and doin' fine."

" 'Boop boop'?"

"Naomi," he'd said, "that's the sound a gun makes, when it's discussed by friends. . . ."

Naomi, who had her real estate license and sold small properties when she got lucky, grew to like Phil Lombardi very much and soon refused his money, though she needed it. —And she seriously needed some now, but it was the double curse of being a prostitute and a Jew that she had to be careful asking even a friend for money—especially a friend. It would be hard to take if Phil were to give her the Look, the "So for this Jew/whore, it was the money all the time" look.

She didn't want that look from this old man, didn't want to take a chance on it, so there was no asking him for money. She supposed she cared because Phil reminded her of the sort of old man her father would have been—and she did think of that sometimes, when they had what gentle sex he could. A perverse thought, but there it was. —And she loved his house, a small mansion, one of the finest causeway properties in Dade County. Almost an acre, with fifteen rooms of airy well-built fake English country, and a fifty-foot terrace right on the bay. Palms, croton, jacaranda, hibiscus, the works.

It calmed Naomi to come from her place—the four-apartment unit that had seemed such a good investment—to visit here every week or so, spend the day, play cards and have dinner. Always a good dinner, which she ate and Phil pretended to eat.

"I give him milk shakes," his old friend and houseman, Rudy, once told her when she said she was worried. "I give him milk shakes with an egg in 'em. That's my business, takin' care of Phil."

Naomi liked Rudy, but Rudy didn't like her. He was jealous. . . .

"Phil . . . !" Rudy, trotting out onto the patio, was as small as Phil Lombardi, but a few years younger. Naomi wondered what their mothers had fed these gangsters to have them grow up so small. Depression-era food . . .

"What is it? You see I got Naomi here; what is it?"

"Phil, a guy came lookin' for you. I got him waitin' in the music room."

"Who? What guy?"

"A guy—a . . . you know."

"You sayin' one of our guys?"

"No."

"Then fuck him."

"My job," Naomi said.

"Hey, come on sweetheart, don't talk like that. I said I was sorry what I said before."

"Phil, I got the guy waitin'. What do you want me to do?"

"Rudy, I don't know; you run my house. Who is he?"

"A Midwest guy . . . country guy. I'd say he's done time. I'd say maybe a stickup artist. You know, Jesse James."

" 'Jesse James.' That's good."

"Says Cipriano's people told him look you up."

"Paulie Cipriano? A Kansas City maniac; when he was a kid he was a maniac. You ever hear anybody talkin' back to Chris? Well, that Paulie did it. Told him shove it up his ass."

"Phil, do you want to see this person?"

"Rudy, what does he want with me? Lookin' for a handout or what?"

"No. He's got money on him."

"How do you know that, Rudy?" Naomi said.

"I always know a guy's got money. . . ."

"All right, Rudy, I give up. Make a couple calls, check him out. —He's okay, then he can come an' bother me."

"Thank you. I just needed a decision."

Naomi watched Rudy duck back into the house through the French doors. Rudy went through all doorways as if they were too low. "Rudy's upset. He doesn't like surprises."

"Naomi, for God's sake don't worry about that pansy. He's got moods like a woman."

"Phil, if you had someone come in at least to vacuum, he might get in a better mood. You have a lot of rooms, here."

"Okay. Number one, I don't want strangers roamin' all over my house. Number two, what the hell else does Rudy have to do? He doesn't have a goddam other thing to do than vacuum the floors, straighten up a little, make a breakfast, make a lunch, make a dinner."

"Phil, there's not a woman in the world hasn't heard that bullshit. And usually from some man sitting on his ass."

"Oh, come on—what is all this bad temper? Come

on, honey, be nice to Uncle Phil. Don't be cruel; I'm so old."

"You're so old. . . ."

"Well, I am."

"—And calling Rudy names. He's the only friend you've got."

"I don't mean he's a faggot. He's just queer— nothin' the matter with Rudy. You know he whacked a couple guys in his day. *Boop boop*."

"Again with the boop boop. . . ."

"Oh, he's a tough guy. I wasn't, an' he was. Sleeps downstairs an' he's got an Army .45. Anybody comes in here at night, they're goin' to get a surprise."

"Phil, I'll keep it in mind."

"Rudy took good care of me. . . ."

"That's right," Rudy said, ducking out the French doors. "—An' I still try. An' look at him; he doesn't eat. He's a bag of bones."

"Oh, get off it. I eat every goddam thing you put in front of me."

"Oh, sure. Well, I'm getting tired of it. I'm getting tired of trying to make you eat right."

"Then stop trying; do me a favor. —Who's the visitor we got in there?"

"I spoke to Kansas City. Looks like this is a legitimate guy—" Rudy glanced at Naomi.

"Oh, come on, Rudy," Naomi said.

"Well, he's a stickup person. Banks, and maybe somethin' else. Was a big guy in his line—an' word is, maybe not just 'was.' "

"So, what the hell does he want with me?"

"Phil, I don't know."

". . . All right. Let him come out."

Rudy ducked into the house, and soon ducked out again with a man following him—tall, and in his forties, Naomi thought. Early forties. He looked like an upstate farmer in chinos, zipper jacket, and boots. A good-looking man, if you liked them very country and weathered.

The farmer walked across the terrace to Phil and reached down to shake his hand. "Sorry to trouble you, Mr. Lombardi."

Phil shook his hand, looking up at him from the deck chair. "Jesse James," he said.

"What?"

"Nothin'. —You met Rudy. I want you to meet another friend of mine; this is Miss Naomi Cohen." A graceful gesture over to Naomi.

Jesse James smiled at Naomi, and said, "How do you do, Miss Cohen."

"So far, so good."

Kept smiling at her. Must have liked the answer—or had a thing for too thin and almost forty, with green eyes and red hair touched up in a major way.

"Have a seat there—get the guy a chair, Rudy—sit down, Mr. . . ."

"Pierce."

"Mr. Pierce. So, can I be blunt?"

"You bet."

"Mr. Pierce, I'm a retired guy; I'm out of the business for years. And I don't know you except for a phone call. Okay?"

"Right."

"Good call—don't get me wrong. But that's it. So, what do you want from me?"

Silence.

"Mr. Pierce, Rudy is my friend since we were kids. Miss Cohen is also a trusted friend of mine."

"Well . . . I need some names."

" 'Names.' Rudy, get Mr. Pierce something to drink. What do you want to drink?"

"A Coke."

"Rudy, please . . . a Coke. What names? What are you talking about, names?"

"Mr. Lombardi, some people I know in Kansas City

know you from way back. They said you were solid,
and you retired down here a long time ago. They said
you knew people down here, even though you were out
of it."

"So, that's what they said. I'm still waitin' to hear
what *you* got to say about 'names.' "

"I need a lawyer—somebody who has contacts both
sides, and knows the law down here and will keep his
mouth shut."

"Who doesn't," Naomi said. And got a look from the
farmer, but not a smile. The farmer had brown eyes,
but not warm brown eyes. She imagined him holding
up a bank somewhere in the Midwest. The First Corn
Exchange Bank . . .

"—I need that lawyer's name. And I need a psychiatrist—somebody really sharp that knows about criminal insanity. I need the name of a doctor like that."

Naomi glanced at Phil and had to concentrate so as
not to laugh. Phil looked like a stuffed old dog now.
His eyes were like little glass marbles, faced with this
apparent nutbag from the Great Plains. Needing a psychiatrist specializing in the criminally insane. . . .

"I need those two—and I need someone who knows
this state. Knows who's who down here. Knows what
the hell is going on—especially north a little. Palmetto
and around there."

"You just need these three people?" Phil said. "I'm
supposed to dig up these people for you?"

"If you can. If you'll do it. I'll pay you for your
trouble, Mr. Lombardi. It'll be worth it to me, save a
lot of time."

"Time for what, for Christ's sake? If you're planning
some fuckin' weird heist down here, I won't have a
goddam thing to do with it!"

"No. I'm looking for someone."

"Who?" Naomi said. "—If you don't mind my
asking."

A troubled farmer, now. "The person I'm looking

for . . . I'm looking for the man who's been killing young women down here."

"Lots of men kill their young ladies down here, Mr. Pierce," Phil said. "It's a sad fact of life."

"The Sweetwater is the one I'm after."

Naomi started to say something, but she didn't. Neither did anyone else. They were all quiet, and listened to the sound of a speedboat out on the bay. It was crossing north to south, thumping over the waves.

It got to be a long silence, and Naomi asked, "Why?"

"That man killed my daughter."

Another long silence, almost restful but not quite—and Naomi recalled, from last week's TV news, a snapshot of a pretty young brunette smiling under the shading brim of a park ranger's hat. . . . Pierce.

Phil Lombardi cleared his throat. "I'm very sorry for your tragedy, Mr. Pierce. But looks to me like you're headin' for trouble—either with the cops for interferin', or with this wacko cuttin' ladies' throats. And I have no interest at all in trouble."

"I can pay," Pierce said.

"Not enough to make me interested in trouble."

"Mr. Lombardi, the cops have not done jack shit in five years. If they had something—they would have done something."

"Doesn' mean they want you stickin' your nose in."

"What they don't know, they won't mind. I think I can go—with the right people to help me down here—I think I can go different ways than the cops can."

The old man had nothing more to say. Just sat there, brown and withered in the sun in his bathing suit, looking at Pierce.

Naomi thought she should probably keep her mouth shut, but she didn't. "Just some referrals, Phil. What can that hurt?"

"Naomi," the old man said, "this is not your business, dear."

Rudy ducked out of the house with a tray. A Coke

for Jesse James, and rum sours. Phil loved them, and
Naomi had learned to like them. Rudy always made
one for himself and drank it first, in the kitchen.

"Mr. Pierce," Phil said, "you don't want something
to eat? Please, have something—Rudy makes a fresh
tuna sandwich that's fabulous. On a bun."

"Another time." Pierce drank some of his Coke.
"You have a very beautiful place here, Mr. Lombardi."

"Better be, what it cost."

"I was thinking of a place in warm weather, like this.
Nowhere near so fancy, but someplace out of the
winter. You work on a roof in February in the Midwest, you start thinking of places like this."

"You work on roofs?"

"Yes, ma'am. I'm a contractor. Small-time." Pierce
took another swallow of his Coke, and Naomi was
interested to see he had an Adam's apple. Most of the
men she knew were too plump for that to show. . . . He
had his drink, put down the glass, then got up and went
over and shook Phil's hand. A bank robber with good
manners . . .

"I want to thank you for seeing me, Mr. Lombardi,
coming out of the blue like this. I appreciate it."

"That's okay. You don't have to run off; stay awhile,
finish your Coke."

"No reason to waste more of your time."

"Phil . . ."

"Honey, be quiet. —That's all right, Mr. Pierce. You
got a good attitude; you're a gentleman."

Pierce came over to shake Naomi's hand; he had a
hard grip, though she could tell he was trying to be
gentle with her.

"So long," he said. "Nice meeting you."

"Same here," Naomi said, and watched Rudy shep-
herd him down the terrace and into the house.

"Jesus, Phil—"

"Naomi, don't start. Don't start with me."

* * *

It was goodbye and gone, Pierce marching back through the house, the little butler or whatever showing the way. The house was like something in a movie. Even rich people, in Missouri, didn't live like this. . . .

Pierce went down the front steps, then walked around the big circular drive to the pickup. He'd parked on the far side so as not to block anyone.

He got into the truck, and sat for a few minutes checking the gas-station map—finding where he was again . . . then looking to see which way he had to turn once he was back over the causeway. It was a right turn. End of the causeway, take the first right . . . go two blocks. Then turn left on Sea Grape, and stay on that for the boulevard.

That would get him out to the motel. . . . As for the rest, without the old man's help it would just take more time, cost more money to learn what he needed to know.

He checked the map again, folded it and put it on the seat, then started the truck. He was coming around the drive when the butler, Rudy, came out the front door and waved to him to stop.

Pierce pulled up and the little man trotted over to the driver-side window.

"Figured you was gone. Phil says come back in. . . ."

So, back through the Hollywood house and outside, with that odd pair sitting watching him walk onto the patio, terrace, whatever they called it. The blue water was flashing with sunlight behind them. Sails out there . . . white against the blue.

"Please sit down, Mr. Pierce." The old man looked a little sour. "I'll tell you the truth. Go ahead, sit down. . . . I'll tell you the truth: I had a minute to think it over an' I changed my mind. An' I may be sorry, but what the fuck. Anyway, absolutely against my better judgment—"

"No, Phil, it's the right thing." The skinny redhead.

"You, you shut up; you said enough to me already.

—Pierce, I'm goin' to give you three names. People I know, an' they owe me."

"I want to thank you—"

"Just listen. Now, you call Walter Chetwin in Lauderdale. C-h-e-t-w-i-n. He's a lawyer had some problems, mingled his account and clients' accounts and so forth, but he's still practicin'. Represents some dealers up north there, around Palmetto. Very smart guy, maybe a little too smart for his own good, if you understand what I'm sayin'."

"Yes."

"—Then you give Hector Salcedo a call, S-a-l-c-e-d-o, in Miami. He's a shrink—was a shrink—had a problem doin' too many prescriptions for people had a monkey, you know? Used to be consultant with the Dade County coroner an' all that shit, an' he should fill your bill. Treated the daughter of a friend of mine—Ross Climenti's daughter, Carla, for boozin'."

"Spic didn' do her any good," Rudy said.

"Who asked you, Rudy? You talkin' here, or what? —Okay. Third guy is Mindy Kanin, also in Miami. That's Mindy K-a-n-i-n. He used to be a newspaper reporter, knows the state, knows what's goin' on. — Now, with Mindy an' with all of these people, you can use my name."

"Thank you very much, Mr. Lombardi. Chetwin in Fort Lauderdale. Salcedo and Kanin in Miami. I appreciate this, and I'd like to pay you for it."

"You'd like to pay me for it. Pierce, you are a novelty in south Florida. Let me tell you, my payment from you is goin' to be two things. —First, you already gave me an' interesting visit, which is unusual for me these days. —An' second, you will not come here again, get me involved in this shit any more than I am already."

"Okay." Pierce got up to go.

"Where are you stayin'?"

"Conch Shell Motel. It's out on Biscayne Boulevard."

"Where else. . . . Pierce, you definitely need Mindy or somebody steerin' you around. Cops are always checkin' those motels out there—because guys like you, just comin' into town, stay on that strip."

"I'll move."

"I would, I was you. An' Pierce, last word is, wise up fast down here—or that weirdo you're lookin' for is goin' to find you first."

Chapter 6

Out on the strip, heading north to the motel, Pierce pulled over at a branch bank, and went in to change a twenty-dollar bill into quarters.

It was interesting to see the layout of a strip branch down here. Heavy on security cameras—two were dummies—and light on personnel. It was a "Take-it" branch, all open counters in pretty colors, and low-guard glass wouldn't do the tellers any good. . . . People built this weren't interested in stopping the robber, definitely not interested in getting him trapped in the building. They wanted him in—and out.

And what he'd take wouldn't be much. —Two thousand . . . ten thousand, tops. Just cashier change. Silent alarms would go, and the cops would station a half mile up and down the highway; take him as he passed either way.

Robber here, would have to be a fool or a kid. And soon enough, the bank robber anywhere would have to be a fool or a kid. The currency, the real money, would be electronic entries—and that would be the end of big-time bank robbing. Would be no-gun white-collar stealing, then. Already was, most places.

. . . Of course, if a man *was* willing to go for short money, this branch could be taken. Absolutely could be taken—and the way to do it would be to hit their armored pickup. The truck would be the target, not the bank. It could definitely be done, and with the truck in there, done for better than short money.

And the cops waiting up and down the highway could be handled. —Pay two kids ten thousand each to speed both directions after the alarm went. Cops would take that bait, move out of position and chase them down . . . and find they'd only caught two speeders. No weapons, no bank money. Not even DUIs.

Absolutely could be done. The two car kids, and also two tough cracker boys from upstate. High school graduates—and brothers, cousins at least for the family bond. Then planning, and execution . . .

Pierce got his twenty dollars in quarters from a Hispanic girl teller. Nice-looking little thing, wore glasses and had skin like milk chocolate. —There were screamers, and then there were sensible girls who saw they weren't going to be hurt by reasonable men doing a job. This one was a sensible girl. . . .

His trouser pockets heavy with change, Pierce left the bank's air-conditioning for sun glare and a smothering weight of heat. He noticed he was tending to go from air-conditioning to air-conditioning down here, grateful for those islands of coolness.

This Florida summer heat seemed never to leave a man alone. It was there like a bully, leaning on you all the time you were outdoors. Worse than Midwest heat, or seemed so . . . Of course, it was also possible he was getting old.

Pierce drove a block farther down, and turned in at a Taco Bell with a phone booth beside it. He pulled around to the back lot to park, then walked to the phone.

It took two American operators and a handful of quarters to get to the Caribbean overseas operator and Lesser Cayman Island.

Then another operator—an island woman, by her accent—to get the Surety Island Savings Bank and a woman called Miss Warburten. She had the same singsong accent the last operator had had.

"And you're requesting a balance on a numbered account?"

"That's right."

"There will be a charge of twenty-five dollars for that information, sir."

". . . Okay."

"Very well. I am going to ask you specific questions, sir, which you will need to answer very accurately."

"Okay. Go ahead."

"What was the month and year of deposit to this account?"

"This month; this year."

". . . Is there a letter E or a letter S at the end of your account number?"

"No."

"What is the second digit in your account number?"

"Two."

"What is the fifth digit in your account number?"

"Three."

"Do you have eight digits in your account number?"

". . . No."

"Are your account-number digits grouped in three, then two, then three again?"

". . . No."

"How many zeros appear in your account number?"

"Two."

"Your current balance—minus our twenty-five-dollar balance-reporting fee—is eight hundred and two thousand, four hundred and sixty-five American dollars. Shall I repeat the amount?"

"No. No, I've got it."

"Do you have any other questions? There would be an additional fifteen-dollar fee."

"Wait a minute. . . . All right, I understand the interest being paid on the account is three and a half percent."

Silence.

"Is that right?"

"Yes, that's correct. It's the permanent annual rate."

"And there's a fee for another question?"

"Yes, there is."

". . . All right. Is it true I can transfer funds without coming out to the bank?"

"Yes. Simply write a letter to us, Surety Island Savings Bank, Fourteen Bay Road, Lesser Cayman—including your account number—requesting us to wire transfer any specific amount from the numbered account to any personal or business account in any bank in North or South America, Europe, or Asia. There will be a fifty-dollar fee for each transaction."

"Thank you very much."

"Happy to be of service," said Miss Warburten, and hung up.

Pierce stood there at the phone booth, feeling a tremendous relief. It surprised him; he hadn't realized he'd been so worried. —But now it was done for sure. Now that money was his, and no one knew it but the Baileys and that bank.

"Damned if I haven't done it," Pierce said aloud. "—Damned if I haven't." That money was his, and a weapon in his hand for hunting.

He went into the Taco Bell, ordered two chicken burritos, a side of guacamole, and a medium Dr Pepper, and ate sitting in an orange plastic booth by a window, watching the traffic go by.

When he was finished, Pierce went outside and around to the back parking lot. There was an old dark-gray Chevy station wagon parked beside his pickup, its engine running. . . . And when he walked to the truck to get in, a man opened the driver's-side door of the station wagon, got out and came around.

"Hey, asshole! Been waitin' for you."

A large young man in a black bathing suit and sleeveless black T-shirt, he wore dark glasses and was barefoot in sandals, his skin tanned deep. His brown hair was braided into a long pigtail.

"You talking to me?" Pierce said.

"Fuckin' right I'm talkin' to you!" The young man seemed pretty strong, and would have looked like a college athlete, but he had blue tattoos snaking down his arms, shoulders to wrists. "—You fuckin' dinged my car, man! You opened that truck's door into the side of my car when you parked, dickhead. And you just walked *away*?" He stepped in close.

There was a second young man sitting in the station wagon's front passenger seat. This one was smiling through the window glass; had the window closed for the air-conditioning.

"I didn't hurt your car," Pierce said. "Wasn't anybody parked in that space when I drove in."

"Well, dad, you're a goddam liar—and I want to know what the fuck you're going to do about this. I got a hundred dollars damage here, and you better come up with it, asshole. And I mean right now."

Pierce glanced around the lot. No one there, no one watching.

Young man noticed him doing that, must have thought he was looking for help. "—I said, you get that hundred up, and you get it up right now, cocksucker!"

"That much money?" Pierce said, and he took a half step back.

"Get it *up*—or I'm goin' to break your fuckin' jaw."

"I'm amazed," Pierce said.

"What?"

"I said, I'm amazed." And Pierce stepped in and kicked the young man in the crotch. Caught him solid, with a heavy thumping sound; boy's bathing suit wasn't much help there.

The young man bent and brought his hands down—couldn't help that, it was a reflex—and Pierce drew back as if he was going to throw a baseball, and hit him in the face. Almost always a bad thing to do, risk your hand against a man's head . . . hitting so hard.

Bathing Suit went back against the station wagon in a little spray of blood. Broken nose. And Pierce stepped away from him, opened the pickup's door and reached down under the seat for the tire iron.

The other man was still sitting in the car when Pierce came up with the iron—he wasn't getting out to help his friend.

Bathing Suit had some stuff. He was bent over and his nose was broken, but he came off the car at Pierce just the same, and Pierce brought the tire iron around and hit him hard across the side of the head and knocked him down. The iron stung Pierce's hand and hummed.

The young man was down with his face on the blacktop and his butt stuck up in the air. One of his sandals had fallen off when he was hit. Pierce swung the iron up to bring it down into this boy's backbone— and he would have, but he saw the other one, the one still sitting in the station wagon, staring at him with eyes big as a baby's.

. . . Neither of them was worth the damn trouble, and that was a fact. Pierce went over to the passenger-side window and struck the glass with the iron so it starred and frosted in the young man's face—then he reached across the hood and smashed the windshield, too.

By then, Bathing Suit was up on all fours, his head hanging down. Looked like a sick pup.

"I were you," Pierce said to him, "and not even good enough for door-ding scams, I'd find another line of work."

He put the tire iron back under the truck seat, climbed in, started the engine and drove on out to the highway. . . . Probably not a good idea to be parking in back lots down here. Area did seem to have a crime problem—one of those rare cases where the TV didn't lie. . . .

* * *

Pierce, glad to be back in his motel room's coolness—noisy air conditioner or not—sat on the bed and dialed the library's number in Dowland, but all he got was the motel office, and they had to give him an outside line.

The library phone rang a long time. It always did, because they kept the ringer bell turned way down so as not to bother a reader, so it took a while for either Carolyn or Mrs. Pelham to hear there was a call coming in.

Carolyn answered, though, and Pierce was touched to hear her "librarian" voice. Sounded like four years of college.

"Dowland City Library . . ."

"Hello. I'm looking for a Henry Miller book. One of the dirty ones."

". . . Tyler Pierce—you are a *mess*! Where are you and why the hell haven't you called me before?"

"I'm in Florida. And I sent you postcards."

"Well, I got the New Orleans card, and I did like it— I loved those little balconies. And I got one Florida card, where you wrote you were going to be looking for a particular person. . . . Which is what I *knew* you were going to try to do when you took off out of here. And I know why you wrote that instead of calling me and telling me, because you knew we'd fight over it. And I think it's very foolish, Tyler. I'll just tell you that right up front and then we can forget it. . . . But I missed hearing your voice, and postcards don't help that."

"I've been missing you, too."

"And you're not looking at those tan Florida women on the beach?"

"Haven't noticed a one."

"I'll bet. —Pauline's giving me the eye. Personal phone call on library time. Wait a minute. . . ."

Pierce sat on the bed, listening to the air conditioner.

Getting old, no doubt about it, to be so pleased to be talking to an assistant librarian in Dowland, Missouri.

"All right. All right; I told her it was a high school boy. Told her it was Dwight Kerner, asking about the New Deal and Franklin Roosevelt. —Now, where were we?"

"We were saying I sent you postcards, and I miss you."

"—And where are you in Florida?"

"Miami. And it's hot as fire down here. You take Dowland's summer, and double it."

"Well, look out for that heat, Tyler. You wear a hat. I know you like to think you're twenty, but you're not."

"Oh, I know I'm not. . . ."

". . . You went to Lisa's service?"

"Yes."

"And it was nice?"

"Yes, it was nice. People from that state park came. They'd liked her."

"Oh, Tyler . . . Can I say something to you?"

"You bet."

"I just want to say I don't know what there is after dying. And I've gone to church just about every Sunday—a habit, I suppose. . . . But if there is anything, then I know Lisa loved having you there. I know it kept her from being so lonely. —Is that . . . I hope that wasn't a stupid thing for me to say."

"No, it wasn't. You don't have to be scared saying anything to me, Carolyn."

"Oh yeah, sure. Things I've got to say to you would scare us both to death, Tyler. But listen, now . . . I'm glad you called me. I miss you, and not just the bed stuff—oh, you should see Pauline; she just gave me the Look. . . . It seems like you're getting to be important to me, Tyler. So, could I ask how long you think all this is going to take? How long you're going to be down there?"

"Honey, I'm going to be down here awhile."

". . . I see. Well, I'm not going to say anything more about it. About what you're doing down there."

"Carolyn, it just seems to be something I *should* do . . . at least I should try to do."

"Isn't that for the police? Isn't that their work?"

"They haven't got it done in five years of trying."

"Well, I know when to shut up. You don't think I do, but I do. . . . Just be careful. Tyler, you hear me?"

"I will be."

"All right. Is Margaret okay?"

"Yes, Margaret's okay."

"I'm scared the police are going to put you back in jail for doing this—and that's . . . that's all I'm going to say. I won't say anything more about it."

"Honey, don't be worrying."

"Oh, ha ha. That's a good one. . . . Well, listen, you better hurry on back up here, because you have another job. Mrs. Betts wants you to do her house. Mickey finished the garage, and she likes it."

"That doesn't make any sense at all. They have a good ten years left with the shingling they have on right now."

"Wants new."

"Doesn't make a lick of sense. Frank Betts go along with this?"

"What Martha wants, Frank'll do. Been that way forever."

"A real waste of money."

"You come on back up, Tyler. I mean, do what you can down there and then come back up. . . . Do you really think you have any chance at all to do this? Is it even *possible*?"

"If I'm lucky, I think it may be possible. I'll be going different ways than the police."

"That's what worries me."

"Carolyn, I'll be careful."

"Well . . . keep writing me those damn postcards. —Uh-oh. Pauline heard that, and here she comes."

"Good-bye, sweetheart."

"Bye-bye." And hung up . . .

. . . Pierce had gone to the office to pay cash for a tomorrow-morning checkout, adding the price of a Miami Beach postcard to be sent up to Carolyn—palm trees by moonlight, with the city skyline all lit up behind them—and was back packing his duffel when the phone rang.

"Mr. Pierce?"

"Yes . . ."

"We met earlier today, Mr. Pierce, at my friend's home."

"Right. I remember you." It was Miss Cohen, from Lombardi's house. Pierce recognized that sharp voice. Voice like a tough schoolteacher's.

"I'm sorry to trouble you, Mr. Pierce, but I thought you might need a little more information concerning Phil's recommendations to you."

"That so?"

"Yes. The other two are fine, but Mindy Kanin . . . Phil hasn't seen Mindy in two or three years, and doesn't know he isn't well anymore. I didn't want to depress Phil by mentioning it this afternoon. Kanin is elderly and retired, and he has early Alzheimer's. —I'm afraid he wouldn't be much use to you as a guide around the state, and I thought I'd call and let you know."

". . . I see. I appreciate this, Miss Cohen. Then I won't bother Mr. Kanin."

"No. And also I called because without Mindy you don't really have any notion what goes on around here. And I was wondering if you might want me to help for a couple of days. —I do know this state; I was born and lived all my life here, and I know who's who and pretty much what's going on from Pensacola to the Keys."

"You do?"

"Yes, I do."

"All right then, who's the sheriff up in Palmetto County?"

"The sheriff in Palmetto . . ."

"Right."

"The sheriff . . . sheriff in Palmetto . . . He's a new guy, young guy. Friend of Mark Spooner in Tallahassee, intends to go in the legislature . . . maybe try for Congress down the line. Ummm . . . what the hell's his name? His name is . . . Mooksie. —*Macksie*. His name is Macksie, and he's not in the business."

"What business?"

"Drug business. That's the big deal in Palmetto— transporting from the west coast over to Jacksonville, Palm Beaches and Lauderdale. Macksie's not in it, but some of his deputies probably are."

"Okay, that's good. That's useful."

"So, am I a consultant? Am I going to get paid?"

". . . Well, I suppose I could use you for a day or two, anyway. After that, Miss Cohen, it wouldn't be a good idea. Could be getting into problems after that."

"I understand, and I don't need problems. I do need some money, if you can afford it."

"A hundred dollars a day?"

"Can you afford to pay me more, Mr. Pierce?"

". . . Yes, I suppose I can."

"Could you pay me two hundred and fifty dollars a day?"

"Well . . . I guess I could."

"Then you've hired a guide, Mr. Pierce."

". . . Okay. It's a deal."

"Start tomorrow morning?"

"Six o'clock, over here."

"My God . . ."

"Seven o'clock?"

"Thank you. That I can do."

"See you then," Pierce said, and put down the phone. He'd never had a woman along in anything like this.

Any situation. And it was probably not the best idea. . . .

It was the first McDonald's breakfast Naomi'd ever had. Jesse James had turned down two decent possibilities, then steered into McDonald's as if it were home.

"Oh, no—we're eating here?"

"You bet."

They'd met in his room at that ungodly hour—both very formal, and his worldly goods waiting packed in a duffel bag—then had gone out into the parking lot. And there had been her beautiful (and temperamental) old Targa in German racing silver—and there also had been Mr. Pierce's big red-and-white pickup truck. And no question which they were going to take. "We'll come back for your car later." —So, there they were, Ma and Pa Kettle on the town, and heading for the nearest McDonald's.

Tyler Pierce, finding this was a first for her, had been amused—displayed a provincial smile, looking like a handsome middle-aged horse—and had ordered "The Big Breakfast" for each of them, with an extra biscuit.

She'd found it edible. . . .

And now—barely on the road again—had come his first question to Naomi, Girl Guide.

"Where can I get a gun?"

First serious question by this Wayfaring Stranger, first thing in the morning—and Miss Smart-ass with no answer. "You don't have one?"

"Miss Cohen, I'm a convicted felon. I can't be driving down from Missouri with a gun."

"But you can drive around here with a gun?"

"I think I better."

"Wait a minute. . . . Ummm, I need a phone. Find a phone booth."

". . . Rudy?"

"Yeah, what do you want?"

"Rudy, I need to know where people get guns."

Silence.

"Come on, Rudy. I'm escorting our bank robber, because Mindy Kanin is out of it."

"I knew he was out of it. But you're lookin' for trouble with Jesse James, there."

"It's a job, not love, Rudy. He's paying me a few bucks to show him around. So, please, where does he go to get a gun? I'm asking you as a personal favor. I don't want to bother Phil with this."

"You be sure you keep him out of it. I don't want Phil upset. . . . Okay. Go see Allen Mardanian. Got a big newsstand down the beach on Collins. World News." Then Rudy hung up.

. . . Driving over to the Beach, Naomi was occupied directing Pierce which way to go and how to get there—practically block by block.

"You need to stay in the right lane, Mr. Pierce."

"Okay. —Was that the ocean yesterday, in front of Lombardi's house?"

"No, that was the bay. The Atlantic's farther out, past the islands. Why?"

"I haven't seen the ocean. I came down the middle of the state on the turnpike, and then I was driving at night, and all I saw was motels. —I saw the Gulf up near New Orleans, but I haven't seen the ocean. Haven't seen the Pacific or the Atlantic."

"Well, you'll see the Atlantic in a minute. Just keep going; it'll be on the left." . . . What in God's name, what in *God's* name is Naomi Cohen—with her sun-ruined skin (and I was told; I can't say I wasn't told. Dr. Senise told me many years ago, "Wear a hat. Wear long sleeves")—what is this fading prostitute with her wrinkles, her dye-damaged hair *and* sun-damaged skin, doing playing sidekick to a bank robber from Missouri? Another bad choice in a lifetime of bad choices? As Mr. Pierce would say, "You bet. . . ."

"See, Mr. Pierce? Look—the Atlantic—there it is!"

"Um-*hmmm*."

So here we are. Naomi Cohen's bank robber and
bereft father sees his first ocean. Loves it.

Pierce parked in a small lot behind the newsstand—
looked more like a bookstore than a newsstand—then
came around to open Miss Cohen's door. Climbing
down in her flowered skirt, she showed tanned legs—
legs that seemed younger than she was. Sandals, bare
toes with red toenail polish.

They went into the bookstore—the space air-
conditioned very cold—with rows of newspaper
stands, some of the papers written in Japanese or Chinese . . . and shelves of books down both sides of a
long room.

"I'd like to speak to Mr. Mardanian."

"Well," the clerk was a black girl wearing what
Freddy would have called a major Rasta do. "Well,
perhaps I can help you."

"Next time, yes—if you carry all the Travis McGee
books. From reading those, that's all I know about
Florida. But right now, I need to speak to Mr.
Mardanian."

The girl said, "Okay," and led them to the back of
the store, and a heavy door with a two-way mirror
beside it on the right.

When the girl had buzzed and left to go back to the
register, Miss Cohen said, "This kind of thing frightens
me. Is it all right if I wait out here?"

"You bet. I'll be out in a minute."

And no sooner had Pierce told her that, and the door
opened, than she said, "No, I'll come with you," and
went on in.

Mr. Mardanian shut the door behind them, then
walked back into a big white-painted office packed with
books—in cardboard boxes, on steel shelves, and piled
on the floor against the walls. There were no windows.

Mardanian sat behind a desk scattered with books.

He didn't look Armenian to Pierce. He was short and barrel-chested, with a tough square face, light-blue eyes, and graying blond hair almost crew-cut. He was wearing a wrinkled blue summer suit, and looked like a cop—but wasn't, didn't have a cop's eyes. Also wasn't armed; didn't carry himself like a man with a pistol on him.

"I'm Allen Mardanian. And you are . . . ?"

"My name's Pierce. This is Miss Cohen."

"Please, sit down. Just take those books off the chairs. . . . And now tell me what I can do for you, aside from reserving a full set of John D. MacDonald's McGee series."

"Rudy Notunno, Phil Lombardi's man, sent us over," Naomi said.

"Did he? I see. . . . May I ask your full name, Mr. Pierce?"

"Tyler Eason Pierce."

"And you're new in this area?"

"Yes, I am."

"A Midwesterner. —Would I offend you if I asked where you've done time, Mr. Pierce?"

"Kansas."

"Kansas . . ."

"That's right."

"And Phil Lombardi would vouch for you?"

"I don't know."

"Yes, he would," Miss Cohen said.

"And . . . any other references?"

"Not down here," Pierce said.

"Paulie Cipriano, in Kansas City," Naomi said.

Mardanian smiled over the low stacks of books on his desktop. "You have a charming companion, Mr. Pierce. —I believe we have friends in common, Ms. Cohen."

"I'm sure we do."

"Well, to business. . . . Mr. Pierce, I don't believe in playing Let's Pretend. I knew who you were the minute you said 'Kansas.' A very messy job many years ago in Wichita, as I recall. Not at all the Iceman's usual neat in-and-out. As you'll gather, I'm something of a buff. . . . Now, tell me what you want."

"Would you have a Smith 625?"

"No, I wouldn't, though I could get one—but I'm not *going* to get one. In a world of idiots wanting nine-millimeter semiautomatics that hold fifteen rounds and frequently jam, a request by me to my various suppliers for a grown-up's gun, an unusual Smith & Wesson .45 caliber revolver, would be remarked on and remembered when they were busted and squeal-time-deal-time came around. —I don't want to be remembered."

"What can I have?"

"The magic phrase. —What I would *advise* you to have is also a Smith revolver, the Model 65 Ladysmith .357 Magnum, stainless, with three-inch barrel. Ammunition: Federal 125-grain Magnum, or the Cor Bon 115-grain .38 plus P's. This is a first-class and reliable firearm that several sensible local people have found very useful—so it's not *too* unusual. I should add the weapon will be new out of the box, and have a history of initial legitimate purchase and one dubious transfer. No record of theft."

"I'll take it."

"No pricing inquiry?"

"You'll charge me what you'll charge me."

"It's a pleasure dealing with you, Mr. Pierce—you're a breath of fresh air from the Heartland. I'll charge you eight hundred and fifty dollars—delivery late this afternoon—and throw in an Uncle Mike nylon under-the-waistband holster, a speed loader, and two boxes of ammunition."

"The Federal rounds."

"The Federal rounds, of course . . ."

"The 'Iceman'?" Settled in her seat, Naomi swung the truck's door closed. "The *'Iceman'* ?"

"That's old newspaper crap. Pardon my French."

"—How did he know about those books, the McGee books?"

"Microphone by the cashier. Just a way of keeping track." Pierce started the engine, backed out to turn into the street.

"Do you trust him, Mr. Pierce? —Just keep going the way you're going."

"Tyler. —No, I don't trust him very far."

"Well, Mr. Pierce—Tyler—do you trust anybody? I only ask because I long since learned the risks in doing that."

"I do trust people . . . except, you know, professionally. But there are a couple of people I'd trust all the way, even hitting places. —If I was still hitting places."

"You just fix roofs?"

"That's what I do." Pierce thought it was possibly a mistake, taking this lady along.

"Well, you're on a one-way street, and you're going to take a left up at the next corner. Better . . . better get over in that lane. —I thought bank robbers and those kind of Great Plains guys were all natural ace drivers. But I guess not."

"Being inside affected my driving. I know I'm not a good driver anymore. I just . . . I don't keep my mind on it."

"Okay. That's fair. . . . Can I ask how many years you were in there?"

"Seven."

"You don't mind my asking? —This corner's your left."

"No, I don't mind your asking, Miss Cohen."

"Naomi."

"Naomi."

"Okay . . . I looked him up, Tyler, and Dr. Salcedo is still at his old office address, even though his license was pulled. He is now a 'counselor—personal and family.' "

"But he was a doctor? A psychiatrist?"

"Yes—and very good, supposedly. University of Texas medical school, did his residency in psychiatry in Philadelphia. Then moved down here, was a big-time consultant."

"What happened?"

"I understand he wrote generous prescriptions. Too generous. Couple of hundred thousand dollars a year too generous—and the last ones were written for some cops."

"I see."

"Know what he said at the hearing?"

"No."

"It was in the paper last year. He said both cops had been seriously stressed and depressed—each having gender-choice and sexual-performance problems—and had been in desperate need of the medication prescribed."

"Cute."

"—And unavailing. Here's another left . . . and at the end of the block we'll be on Collins again and you take a right. Stay on Collins—we'll take the MacArthur over to Miami."

"The ocean . . ."

"That's right; there it is again. See those rollers? Weather coming in."

Chapter 7

Salcedo's office had still looked like a doctor's to Pierce, but the sign beside the corridor door had read: "Hector Salcedo Ph.D. Personal Counseling—Family Counseling." There'd been no receptionist, no nurse.

Salcedo had beckoned them into an inner office, shaken Pierce's hand briefly, and taken his hand back as soon as he could.

"And you're the woman who called?" Past middle age, Salcedo was very large and very fat in a light-gray summer suit. He was a rare fat man—restless and a pacer—and was moving as he talked, almost gliding back and forth along the window wall behind his desk.

"Yes, Doctor—Naomi Cohen. Mr. Lombardi suggested that Mr. Pierce consult with you."

Salcedo's hair, dyed dull black, was cut military-short, clipped close above his ears. It didn't make him look younger.

"Consult with me. . . . Philip Lombardi suggested this?"

"Yes. I understand you treated the daughter of a friend. Carla Climenti. An alcohol problem . . ."

"That was *not* an alcohol problem. All right. . . ." Salcedo came drifting back down the window wall, moving very smoothly. Pierce thought that being Cuban, the doctor was probably a good dancer.

"I expect to pay your usual fee, Doctor," Pierce said.

"My usual fee, Mr. . . . Pierce. My usual fee is ninety dollars per office visit of one hour."

"Fine." Thank God for the money.

"All right . . . all right." And it seemed to Pierce that settling his fee had soothed Salcedo; he stopped pacing and sat down behind his desk. His eyes were tucked into little pockets of fat, the pupils a sad dark brown. "—All right. What's the problem, Mr. Pierce?"

"I need to know . . . I need to know about killers. Serial killers."

"Do you? And why do you need to know that, Mr. Pierce?"

"Personal reasons."

"Well, I'm a personal counselor; it says so on my office door—a little inscription celebrating official hypocrisy. So, what are your 'personal' reasons?"

Pierce sat thinking about it, looking this odd fat man over. Salcedo stared back at him, waiting.

"My daughter was killed by one."

"Pierce . . . *Pierce*. Oh, yes, the girl last week. I am terribly terribly sorry, Mr. Pierce—what's your first name?"

"Tyler."

"I am terribly sorry, Tyler. Your only child?"

"Yes, Hector, she was." Pierce was interested to see that doctors, like FBI agents, didn't like their first names used by patients . . . suspects. Was interested also to see that Salcedo was first annoyed, then amused.

"—And you have some special regret? Something you did to her, or didn't do for her when she was alive?"

"I was in prison. I couldn't be with her when she was growing up—and then I didn't see her when I got out. I was . . . busy with something. I didn't want her anywhere near it."

"Well, Mr. Pierce, it sounds to me as though you fucked up royally."

"Yes, Doctor, I guess I did."

Salcedo settled into his big chair, getting comfortable. "When a man makes that kind of fool of himself, and neglects and hurts his little daughter for some criminal nonsense—then years later neglects and hurts her again, probably for the same reason, when she's a young woman—a man who does that has a lot to answer for."

". . . I know it."

"And what do you expect me to do, Mr. Pierce? Make you feel better? You *shouldn't* feel better. You should feel like shit for a very long time."

Naomi Cohen shifted in her chair, cleared her throat.

"I don't want you to make me feel better."

"—And what's all this about serial killers? You're curious about what happened to your daughter? You want to know how and why? Well . . . this interest is all too *late*, Mr. Pierce. It's interest the living girl should have received."

"I know that. But there's something I can do, to . . . to balance things up."

"There's a phrase. 'To balance things up.' —I suppose that means to try to catch this person, do away with him, whatever." The fat man looked tired. Pierce thought it must have been unpleasant for the doctor to be arrested, taken to jail. Then the court appearances . . . the story in the newspapers and on TV. His license taken away.

"—And I suppose there's nothing wrong with this improbable ambition of catching the person, so long as you're not kidding yourself. —Not kidding yourself that it will bring your daughter back in any way, or that it will lessen your failures toward her when she was alive."

"I know all that."

"No, you don't. You don't know the half of it, Mr. Pierce. —So, we have 'set a thief to catch a thief' and so forth. Well, I suppose you couldn't do worse than the police—and probably no better."

"Serial killers, Doctor—why do they do that?"

"Ah, there are two answers to that question." Salcedo straightened up in his big chair, looked more alert, interested. "—The first, and by far the most common reason is that they are paltry and third-rate human beings, so badly damaged—sexually or otherwise—that they can only feel complete when killing men or women or children happier, more beautiful, more coherent than themselves." Salcedo was looking over Pierce's head as he talked, recalling . . . addressing his office. "—They are a dreary crew, usually nastily childish, stupid, and uninteresting. A highly overrated set of losers . . . There *are* intelligent and fairly interesting exceptions—interesting because they have been so severely damaged, genetically or otherwise, that their intelligence is of no use to them."

"I see. . . ."

Salcedo smiled at him. "Not a helpful answer, was it, Mr. Pierce? Not what you needed to hear." He lifted a finger. "—But that was only the first answer, and applied to the usual run of that fairly rare group. There *is* a second answer, and it includes those individuals who are truly mad. And I use the term both medically and in its other sense, that of ungovernable fury. A rage caused by whatever conditions the killer finds insupportable, unbearable . . . Now, this is an unusual motivator. A fixed idea that grows within an individual like some monstrous plant." Salcedo made a graceful plant-growing gesture with both hands. "And a sign of this—very indicative—is the lack of what is so routinely present in the ordinary killings of ordinary serial murderers. Sex."

The fat man looked over Pierce's head, addressed his office again, lecturing. "—In this second, and thankfully very rare, category, sexual sadism plays no part at all. None. And that, of course—*despite* the quacks now advising the police—happens to apply precisely to the Sweetwater's murders. To your daughter's killing."

"But he does something. . . ."

"Ah, the severed breasts. You think that's about sex? —It isn't. The Sweetwater is not a sexual psychopath, no matter what anyone says. No sexual torture; no penetration; no bites; no ejaculate; no injury to the genitalia, not even the disturbance of clothing covering the genitalia. . . . The Sweetwater cuts their throats to kill them, then severs their breasts—but for a reason of his own, a lesson being taught to someone, or everyone. You might say . . . a message to the world."

"I see. . . ."

"And if the police—or very improbably, you, Mr. Pierce—ever discover what that message is, then the Sweetwater will be seen as clearly as if standing in sunlight."

"That sounds like it might be so," Pierce said. "Sort of thing that English doctor said, about craziness being just an individual point of view."

"Oh, very good! Spent some time reading, haven't you? Yes, R. D. Laing. And quite right, up to a point."

"Up to what point, Doctor?"

"The point of nausea, irreversible sadness, and murder, Mr. Pierce."

". . . Okay."

"Ah, the ex-convict is convinced. —Listen, I am a very good doctor, and I'm absolutely right on this, however wrong . . . however poor my judgment may have been about patients I considered my friends. . . ."

Dr. Salcedo sat suddenly silent as a run-down clock, seemed to have nothing more to say.

"Well . . . thank you very much, Doctor. I didn't mean to be a smart-ass." Pierce stood, took his wallet from his back pocket, and put two fifties on the desk. "You've been a real help."

"I owe you ten dollars' change," Salcedo said.

"Forget it."

"No, I will not forget it." Salcedo pushed back his chair and began rummaging in his desk's top right-side drawer. "I'm a professional, a physician—licensed or not—and I do not accept tips." He found a large yellow envelope, opened it and began taking out one-dollar bills. He put eight singles on the desk, then put the envelope away, opened the top left-side drawer, and made up the last two dollars in change. Quarters, dimes, and nickels. Five pennies.

Salcedo counted those out, sighed, and said, "One more thing. The police must have noticed this, but it hasn't been on the news. —In none of the Sweet-water cases has there been any evidence of struggle. It's as if, in an odd way, they were willing sacrifices. No sign of struggle; no scratches; no defense cuts on the victims' hands or arms. No trace of tissue under their fingernails . . .

"All six of those young women—one an armed police officer, one in the military—must have either trusted their killer, and allowed the Sweetwater to stand close behind them—or been taken by surprise in some sudden rush of assault. Which means either a very subtle killer, or a very sudden one."

"Or both," Pierce said.

"Yes—or both. If you're serious about even trying to locate this person yourself, you might keep that in mind. —And keep in mind as well that to persons such as this . . . executioner, the police are a faceless threat, like bad weather. An *individual* who tracks them is a different matter altogether, and is likely to be sensed as an animal would sense him. Then the hunted will turn, and become the hunter."

"Right. I understand that. I want to thank you, Doctor. . . ."

Out in the hall, Naomi said, "Poor son of a bitch has a worse dye job than mine. —Ready for lunch?"

Naomi Cohen was like several Jews Pierce had known. They stressed their Jewishness . . . waited for you to say something unpleasant. Like some Irish, and like blacks that way. It came, he supposed, from too much bad history.

Naomi had seemed to direct him all over Miami to get to this delicatessen for lunch. Maybe revenge for the McDonald's breakfast.

When they were seated in a big upholstered booth in the back, Naomi said, "You don't wear a hat."

"No, I don't."

"Down here, you ought to, Tyler. A hat *and* sunblock."

"You don't wear a hat."

"I wear sunblock, and in my case the damage is already done. I can't call back almost forty— I can't call back years and years baking at the beach. But if you're going to be wandering around south Florida all summer, you need a hat. A straw hat with a good brim, and sunblock."

"I just don't wear a hat."

"Okay, Tyler. Be unwise. . . . Want some soup? Matzo-ball soup? You might like it."

"Tell you what I'd like, Naomi."

"What?"

"I'd like it if you'd relax. . . . I know you're a hooker—or were a hooker, anyway. And you're Jewish, and I don't care. I know the Cohens were priestly families in the old days from the Bible, and you should be proud of that. The Pierces, in Scotland, just stole other people's cows. As far as I know, that's all they did."

"And you continued the tradition."

"Yes, I have. And I'll tell you something else: I tried matzo-ball soup many years ago, and I didn't like it. What I'd like in here are some potato pancakes with apple sauce, and a brisket sandwich on rye."

"So—I'm put in my place?"

"I need help down here, Naomi. But I spent enough time with people in Chicago that I don't need assistance ordering in a deli. Okay?"

"I'm put in my place. Except—referring to what you said before—I prefer the term 'prostitute.' "

"Fine."

"—And I'm curious how you knew that. How *did* you know that?"

"You angry?"

"Well, I could be."

"I just . . . knew it. I knew it from the way you talked, way you acted. Free and easy. Square women are more careful when they talk. . . . And you didn't have a wedding ring on; you never did have one. Wear a wedding ring long enough, it makes that knuckle swell a little. —And the way you and the old man dealt with each other, I figured you had him as a trick, and the sex thing worked out to become a friendship thing."

"Oh, that's really clever. . . . I didn't know you were such a noticer."

"You know, Naomi, we have working girls in Missouri too; I never thought they were bad people—and it's for sure I'm not any better. I was a bank robber, and I shot a couple of guys, and I took other people's money . . . just as much as I could carry to the car."

"And you're through with all that—and this money you're spending is from savings?"

Pierce took a pickle from the bowl of pickles on the table, and ate it.

". . . I'm sorry, Tyler. That last remark was rude. Out of line."

"That's all right. Don't be . . . don't be so nervous. Don't worry about it."

"Okay. —So, I've been playing Mommy?"

"You've been playing Mommy. Switch to Big Sister; it'll be just about right. . . ."

"Ready to order?" The waiter was Hispanic, and had brought ice water with him.

"My brother would like the brisket sandwich on rye, and an order of potato pancakes with apple sauce—*and* sour cream. He still has something to learn."

"All right . . . And for you, miss?"

"My sister," Pierce said, "will have the matzo-ball soup."

"You're leaving town today, Tyler?" Naomi looked odd sitting in the pickup, didn't seem at home in it. She was sitting up straight, as if she was getting out in a minute.

"Yes, after I pick up the piece. Don't see any reason not to get going to Fort Lauderdale, and see that lawyer—maybe make it late today."

"Well, I heard about Chetwin, Tyler, I mean before Phil suggested him. He was the lawyer for some drug people up there, but I don't think it was their money he took."

"I'd say probably not."

"Took his ordinary clients' money. —And he had a hearing, but nothing much happened. I think he just said it was an accounting error, and he returned the money with interest."

"Okay."

"What I'm saying is, another attorney would have been disbarred for that. And I think Chetwin wasn't, because he knows where too many bodies are buried."

"Sounds like just the man I want."

"Be sure you don't trust him, Tyler—you know, on so-called confidentiality. I wouldn't trust him on that or on anything."

"I don't intend to."

"And there's something else." Naomi opened her purse on her lap, and began to search in it. "—In this state, local law-enforcement people are supposed to cooperate with the state investigators. And the state investigators are supposed to cooperate with federal. But here, that doesn't always happen."

"In every state."

"But here, especially—" She took a nail file out of her purse, and began working on her nails—long nails,

the red polish chipped from being bitten. "—Here
especially, and the reason is the drug money. In Miami
and on up the state, it just swamps everybody. So what
I'm saying is, you could run into a cop who's straight
on everything but drugs. It's just too much money."

"I can see that."

"Federal prosecutors down here—when their terms
are up? Some of them start right in practicing as
defense lawyers for the drug dealers. It's just so much
money. . . ." She held the little file aside, and nibbled
on a hangnail. "I used to bite my nails," she said. "But I
stopped."

"I'm not going to be getting around the trade,
Naomi. It's none of my business."

"Tyler, if you fool around with Chetwin and those
people in Palmetto County, you're going to be fooling
with their commerce one way or another, because
that's the action up there."

"I'll stay clear of it."

Naomi looked over at him, then down at her nails,
went back to filing. "Listen, can you afford to keep
paying me, just a few days more?"

". . . I guess so."

"I know it's a lot of money for you."

"I can afford it."

"Oh? Do I sense some satisfaction there? Have you
been bad, Tyler? —Oh, my God! A smile!"

"Okay . . . okay. I can afford to pay you, Naomi.
That doesn't mean I'm going to let you get in deep."

"So don't. I stick with you a few days, make enough
money for the plumbing bill, and give you the benefit
of wisdom earned by a lifetime down here—earned
occasionally by blow jobs and other undignified stunts
with undignified people from Tampa to St. Pete . . .
you name it, including Palm Beach. But I was never
with a Kennedy."

"I'm relieved to hear it."

"So, keep going and we'll pick up my car—my

beautiful Porsche—at the motel, and then you follow me down to Coral Gables and the Vampire of Southwest Forty-sixth Street."

"Doesn't this look great, Tyler? Bought it six years ago."

Pierce had trailed Naomi's German sports car several miles to this residential block, and a narrow parking lot beside a two-story quadriplex. Cream stucco and a brown cheapo-shingle roof.

"—What do you think? Doesn't this look like a retirement dream? And on a nice lot? Four one-bedroom units with kitchenettes and big living rooms where you can have sleeper sofas. Stacked washer-dryer in each unit. The owner—that's me—lives in one, rents out the other three." Naomi stood beside her little silver car, surveying the property.

"—This was supposed to be my retirement, and it has become a nightmare, a running sore. I still owe a fortune on the mortgage. I have a tenant in One-B, a woman, who is too messy, too dirty to be human—and I have a couple in Two-A, and the man is some sort of car-repo hoodlum and they haven't paid rent in two months. And I have one decent tenant, a nice young guy who's an airline mechanic. And that's it." Naomi got her keys out of her purse and led Pierce across the parking lot toward the front ground-floor unit. "—I call this place the Vampire; it's been sucking my blood for years. The goddam original builder used galvanized iron pipes throughout, and they're failing—or so I'm told."

"You should have had a tile roof."

"Oh, great. Do you know what barrel tile costs?"

"Well . . . this climate, you're going to have trouble with the fiberglass shingling up there. That's low-end, not even architectural."

"Do me a favor, Tyler, don't look at my roof anymore.

Just come inside and you can watch TV while I pack for this adventure."

. . . The apartment was bigger than Pierce had expected. Nicer, too—very clean and classy-looking. A white carpet. There were photographs on the walls instead of paintings—but they were very good photographs, nature things. Birds and so forth. And the sea.

"Really nice."

"I'm glad you like it. Do you want a beer? . . . Wine? Your traditional Coke?"

"Nope. I'm fine." Pierce took out his wallet, counted out five fifties, and handed them to Naomi. "First day's pay."

"Oh, God bless you. From you—through me—to the plumber, that rich thief."

"Do you need some in advance, Naomi?"

"No, I don't. This is not a prostitution situation; this is pay as you go. —So, watch TV, watch a game, make guy noises when some overpaid brute fumbles whatever. I'll pack, and I'll be right out—well, not out immediately, but fast as I can."

Naomi went down the hall, and Pierce walked back out the front door. —They were really nice units. If she owned them all paid for, then the plumbing and maintenance wouldn't matter so much. Mortgage was what was eating her up. Bank would be expecting these units back in a few years—sell them off to somebody else hadn't done their arithmetic. . . .

Pierce walked over to the staircase; nice wrought-iron railing—cast-iron actually, needed that black paint right now. He went up to the breezeway and knocked on the door to 2-A.

A woman with long blond hair down her back opened the door to TV talk-show sound. The woman was in her thirties, a little heavy, but pretty.

"Ace Management and Collection," Pierce said, and stepped in so she had to back out of the way.

"Kenny!"

Pierce stood in the living room beside her, and waited for Kenny. They—or the lady—kept the unit clean and neat, and the TV wasn't on too loud, either. Good tenants, Pierce thought, if they'd pay their rent. . . .

The toilet flushed down the hall, and a man in slacks and a white sports shirt came out and into the living room. He was a medium-sized wiry man with a big nose and glasses. Looked like a country-type person, and tough.

"What in the fuck are you doin' in my house?" Came right up to Pierce, looking mean.

"Where are you from?" Pierce said.

Kenny seemed surprised to be asked. "I'm from North Carolina, and what the fuck is it to you?"

"Thought you looked country," Pierce said. "Seems to me you'd know better than cheat a lady on her rent."

"What did you say? *What* did you say?" Real angry face, a pinched face. Kenny looked ready to start punching, didn't appear to be worried about his glasses.

"We're Ace Management and Collection, and I can't stand a welsher—somebody that owes and won't pay. That's really unfair and out of line. You owe two months' rent, but I'm collecting three. Get it up and don't give me any checks. I know you keep cash, because *I* keep cash."

"Kenny, let's pay him."

"Good advice, Kenny. —And you can forget that bad-ass look. I come from people just like yours, and if you make me put my hands on you, I'm going to throw you off that balcony out there—you have my word of honor on that. And then I'll throw all this furniture out on top of you."

"Kenny—Kenny, get the money."

"Listen to her," Pierce said. "She's a real smart lady. You're lucky to have her. A lucky guy." And could see

Kenny wasn't going to start punching after all. That time had passed.

"Then what about my goddam plumbing? What about *that*?"

"Kenny," Pierce said, "it costs management money for a plumber. Now you get up your share right now— and a third month's in advance for being so damn late. And don't you make me come up here again. . . ."

". . . What's this?" Naomi had changed into a sort of light-blue suit with pants. She had a big black purse slung over her shoulder, and had brought out a green Samsonite suitcase. She looked like a woman ready to travel.

"That's from Two-A, three months' rent. He should be on time from now on."

"My God, Tyler . . ."

"Just something to do."

"But it wasn't your *business* to do it. Wasn't there . . . was there any trouble?"

"No trouble. He just needed to be talked to. I told him I was Ace Management and Collection—told him we'd be taking care of it from now on."

"Just like that . . ."

"You bet. Reasonable guy; he just hadn't understood the necessity of getting that money in on time."

"Well, please, please don't do anything like this again. I mean, I appreciate it, but please don't. You didn't . . . you sure there was no trouble?"

"Naomi, there was no trouble."

". . . Well, thank you. Thanks. —And you can give me a hand with my shutters. There's a storm coming; I can feel it."

Pierce helped swing the heavy window shutters closed, fastened their latches, then carried Naomi's suitcase out to the truck. It was a big suitcase, and heavy-loaded. "What have you got in here?"

"I don't have anything in there I don't need."

"Mmm."

"Don't 'Mmm' me, Tyler. We may want to go to a nice restaurant. —And do we have to take this damn truck? Why not my wonderful car? —Which is always breaking down, but at least is beautiful."

"No." Pierce opened the pickup's door and put Naomi's suitcase in the back, behind the seats.

"Well, it'll be a change," Naomi said, sighed, and climbed in.

"Got to stop on our way out of town. Pick up that revolver."

"Oh, of course. Have to do that. . . ."

Chapter 8

The baby, late-term, came salted out at half a pound, wrapped in bloody tissue and convulsing.

The Angel received it, took it away to the freezer room, and blessed and baptized it in privacy there at the sink. A blessing, and another blessing, and a kiss.

The baby trembled in the cup of the Angel's hands, opened slate-blue eyes, and died—but not unsaved. And the Angel, who had once been only human and free of duty, filled out an abortion tissue-disposal form for the state, and one each for the county and city departments of health, then wrapped the baby gently in a paper towel and laid it in an insulated Disney's Dumbo lunch box, where a small block of dry ice smoked slightly.

The Angel put the lunch box in its locker, and went back to the OR and work.

It had been a difficult day, in which the need to go outside for a moment to glance at His glory, only in passing, had been constant as hunger.

But those glances, those swift looks—sometimes steady looks—had slowly blinded the Angel's right eye, its master eye, shaded and clouded it so even Dr. Torguson had noticed and said, "What's wrong?" when handed an Acheson clip #3, instead of the #2. They were the same size, only the teeth were different, so it was an easy error to make.

Torguson had said, "What's wrong?" but Dr. Rosales, an ophthalmologist, knew. "What in hell have you been doing? You've got a damaged retina here!"

"Looking," the Angel had said, before Karen could say anything.

"At what, for Christ's sake? The sun?"

"I had an accident with my binoculars, out bird-watching. I picked up a flash of the sun."

"Well, I have to tell you this is permanent damage. You've lost some sight in this right eye, and you're not going to recover that. —For God's sake, you can't pick up *any* direct sunlight in an optical instrument down here. Where do you think you are? You have permanent damage. . . ."

So, to maintain its ability to serve, the Angel could no longer look into the sun.

First thing before a morning of D&Cs, D&Es, and the saline-injection baby—the only one whole enough, living long enough to be saved—there'd been a wonderful seven-o'clock breakfast with Marion out at Charlie's on the lake. Soft-scrambled eggs, iced coffee, and a hot cinnamon roll with sweet butter—such a body's thing that the Angel part, the important part, withdrew and drained like cool liquid deep inside along the spine, and left the rest to Karen.

Marion had said to go after the job at County Central, come back and work with her. "Susan McNernan's leaving, and they're going to need an OR service nurse. They miss you—you were their ace."

"Marion, I'm not interested in medicine anymore. I don't see the point to it."

"Karen—excuse me? Don't see the point? The point is to make people well."

"But why? Why make such a fuss about doing something temporary? It's just interfering."

"Listen, sweetie, what do you think you're doing in Torguson's little death factory? I'd call that interfering. —And why in God's name you went over there, I'll never know. Is he still doing those real late-term ones?"

"Someone has to be there," Karen said. "And he applies for waivers—he gets medical waivers for the late terms."

"I'll bet he does. What a cutie." Marion had signaled to the waitress for more coffee. "—Making his bundle before the metho-and-miso prescriptions put him out of business."

Karen hadn't answered her, hadn't said anything more about it. She'd finished her cinnamon roll. She didn't have a cinnamon roll every morning; then they'd be less and less enjoyable. She had one once a week.

Only the pleasure of light grew no less. It was a pleasure increasing as she rose slowly from this place toward the Sun. She was rising and was still here at the same time; it felt very odd, and she supposed that was her wings . . . that feeling of rising.

"Your modest sun is all you can see of me," the light had said to her on the afternoon of August 16, more than four years ago. —And when it said that, in a casual man's voice, as if it knew her and intended to know her better, a band of striped light-and-dark came over her eyes and made her sick. It covered, then uncovered them in the summer's bright baking heat on the bus-stop bench, and Karen saw clearly how incomplete things were, how much in need.

There'd been voices before, when she was seventeen, but they'd murmured like a TV next door, a classic indication of developing adolescent schizophrenia which had turned out to be just . . . upset from what she'd done. —This voice was very different. It wasn't only a voice; it was a person speaking to her— God, or a god, speaking to her as a person through the Sun's brightness. If the voice had been foolish, Karen would have thought she was going mad.

Sitting on the bench, she'd said, "Can I talk to my

baby?" and a woman sitting beside her had glanced at her, then looked away.

"*No,*" the sunlight had answered her, shining red through her closed eyelids. "*—Never.*" And it was the comfort she had waited for.

By moonlight, when no voice could be expected, the Angel and Karen mixed like shook paint and took her gardening trowel and small shovel and drove the Toyota out to Lakeside and into the cemetery by the access road along the water. There were odd warm night breezes blowing this way and that, as if to introduce a greater wind coming.

Nearly all Karen in the dark, she took her lunch box from the car's backseat and carried it out to the bank. There she lifted sod and dug a small square hole between bronze markers set down into the grass so as to leave it clear to mow. Finished, she opened the lunch box, took the chilly baby gently out . . . murmured the secret in its tiny ear, and set it into the ground wrapped in its paper towel.

Then she scooped in the soil, reset the sod, tamped it down and went home, very tired. Duties upon duties pressed on her, and weighed her to sleep with Grumble in her arms. . . .

. . . Karen woke feeling better and anxious for the Sun, not to look at, but to feel across her shoulders. Grumble was awake already, the cat poking her with his nose, impatient to go out.

Karen had wanted a little dog a few years ago—they were more active company, and she'd been so lonely. But she couldn't have one; dogs didn't like her anymore. Now, it was just her and Grumble.

She'd had a relationship with Stan Parmenter back then, just to have someone near her. He'd been company, and she'd done whatever he wanted so he'd stay over—and Marion had thought she expected Stan to marry her.

"Doctors stopped marrying nurses a long time ago, honey. Now they can get bank loans to pay back medical school. . . . And has our energetic orthopedic surgeon been fucking you?"

"We've made love."

"I'll bet. But honey—what he's had, he doesn't need to pay for. And I can tell you, what Dr. Charm wants to marry is some young society pussy from Cypress Road."

"I don't want to marry him."

"Then for what? Fucking? Companionship?"

"Companionship," Karen had said.

"Oh, great . . ."

But just a little after that, the light had come down at the bus stop, and there was no time for people like Stan Parmenter—who'd gone to St. Petersburg, anyway— no time for anyone, any of her friends, from then on, except to pretend to them that she was still alone.

Grumble poked at her again. If she didn't get up, he'd start kneading with his claws extended just a little.

"All right . . ." She got up in her pajamas, and Grumble thumped off the bed, trotted after her to the back door, and was released into the little yard of small date palms and hibiscus hedge.

"—Too small," Marion had said, and Bud and Lorrie had said the same thing. A four-room stucco cottage on a side street with fishermen and God knew who. But Karen had bought it, taken a mortgage out. It was old and canary-yellow, and tucked into its small lot as if, injured on the street, it had backed away.

It was the first house she'd owned. Before, had been apartments. And it was from this small yellow house that she'd walked the first year she owned it . . . walked to the bus stop around the corner to go to work four-to-midnight shift on the children's ward at County Central. She'd walked that afternoon—hot, a terribly hot day—to sit and wait for the bus. Then the Sun had spoken to her.

"My Danite," it said, among other things. *"My avenging angel."*

She'd listened to it for days and nights and hadn't slept. It told her stories so interesting she couldn't do anything but listen—and once a boy, Barry Hoyt, had come to do the yard, and came to the kitchen door afterward to ask her something or get his money for the work. But Karen had been sitting at the kitchen table, listening, and could hardly hear him.

After a while, he'd come in and asked if she was all right. Then he shook her shoulder. He went away, and came back in a while, and spoke to her and took her by the shoulder again, but she was still listening. So the boy had kissed her neck, then kissed her mouth.

Then, as she sat still, listening to the Sun's story about another Sun—much older—the boy, Barry, had said something and opened her pajama top and felt her breasts, then knelt down by her chair and sucked her breasts as if she had milk in them. Karen had looked down, listening, and seen his narrow, handsome head nestled there . . . felt his teeth on her. It was stranger than the story of the older Sun; she thought she was imagining it.

She'd listened that day and then another day, until she felt weak and sick and had to lie down. The afternoon of the second day, the boy came back and he had a friend with him. The boy called into the house, called and then came inside and into the bedroom and asked if she was all right.

Karen could almost say "I am," but not quite, there was a story, not yet ended, she didn't understand.

The boy came and stroked her hair and asked her another question, but she could pay no attention. He unbuttoned her pajama top and said something, and the other boy came to the bed to see.

They talked to her, but she was sick, and busy listening, so they took off her pajama pants and looked at her. They felt her, and then took off their clothes and got onto the bed, and one looked at her and pushed her legs apart and then began to have intercourse with her, which her body enjoyed though nothing else did. And the other, the friend, masturbated and then put his penis in her mouth. They were there all afternoon, and did things to her which her body enjoyed. Grumble lay on the windowsill—the sun, through the blinds, bright stripes on his soft black stripes—and watched.

They were gone before the story ended.

When the story was over, Karen got up and went to the mirror, and saw that she could do what was necessary. She was taller than most women, and strong, and good-looking at thirty-one. —She saw also how badly she needed a shower. She smelled of days without washing, and of her sweat and the boys' sweat, and their semen was dried in the dark hair at her vulva, and between her buttocks, and on her face. She was sore.

—But that happened early in the messages, before she'd changed her job, and when the boys came again a few days later, calling . . . calling, and came into the house to see if she was all right, they met the Angel and left. The Angel had grown inside Karen as she'd listened to the Sun, and now it wore her like a robe.

It frightened her at first, so she wept and wanted to go up to strangers on the street and ask for help against it, but the Sun calmed her, and the Angel was always polite.

In the afternoon—a busy afternoon, with Drs. Torguson and Bessler finishing another saline and doing D&Es—the Angel was able to baptize only one. Four others were tiny, dead, and lost before they were expelled. The fifth—who kicked, and though salted wouldn't come—was scissored in the uterus and taken out in little pieces.

There were shouts outside, and several people carrying signs and doll babies. Fran, at the front desk, came back frightened to tell Torguson she'd called the police again; Fran was the eighth clerk The Clinic had had in seven years. But before the police came, the people outside had left. It was too hot for them to be standing on the sidewalk, out under the summer sun. So it seemed to Karen that even His casual glory had been too much for people who only shouted, who taught no lessons.

But that afternoon, the rarest thing, only the seventh since the Light—a Must-be Mother came in to talk.

She came in wearing dark glasses, canvas Keds, a blouse and jeans—but filled in the form, *Stewardess*, along with her ID and present address, so was bound to wear a uniform at work. And if she wore a uniform—and especially since she flew nearer the Sun—must be aware of the architecture of order, and know she proposed to violate it. A deliberate violation.

It was upsetting to have another Must-be Mother, intelligent, handsome, and uniformed at her work, come in so soon after the last lesson—and since it was late and the only saved baby safe in its lunch box, the Angel flowed down inside to fill Karen's legs like water and took her into the office to listen to Fran run through the descriptions and questions and choices state law insisted on.

"I am *really* not interested in hearing this. . . ." Moira Durchauer was small, tanned, and neat, in her thirties, with soft gray eyes and a tomboy face. She sat back relaxed in one of the office folding chairs, a small brown leather wallet-purse on her lap. Her hair, sun-streaked light brown, was cut like a teenager's—short, and close to her neck in back.

She was smiling while Fran read the pamphlet to her.

"Listen," she said. "I don't want the baby—I want the baby gone. Why, is my business—but one reason is that I'm being transferred to the New York–Europe route, and I can't be transferred pregnant. . . . And I have another reason, a better reason than that, okay?"

Fran finished reading choices out loud, and Moira

Durchauer only sat and smiled, but her small hand
gripped her purse as if it were a friend. Then she said,
"Can we get on with it? An appointment?"

Karen stood in the office at the file cabinets, listening . . . listening for doubt, but didn't hear it. She
heard only cowardice.

It was serious news. There would be no way to travel
to New York and Europe later, for Moira's lesson. No
time to wait months for safety's sake. Moira's lesson
would have to be taught much sooner. . . .

Fran put the required pamphlet away, gave Moira a
confidential code number, and started a chart with only
that number on it, which was done so no one would
ever know the names of women who'd been to The
Clinic.

"Appointment?"

Fran looked in her book, and said, "Next week.
Wednesday, two o'clock. —And payment is by cash or
check, unless you're on a program."

"Oh, I'll pay cash," the stewardess said.

And so a Must-be Mother, perfect for her part,
had come to disappoint the Light, and wouldn't be
persuaded. . . .

After she'd changed her white uniform for a skirt,
blouse, and sandals—though the demonstrators knew
her, knew she was a Clinic nurse—Karen left the
building with the Angel asleep in her throat. One
person had come back and was standing across the
street with a sign.

Karen drove to the Ace Hardware out on Hibiscus.
She hadn't gone to that store for anything in three
years.

She bought two seventy-five-watt light-bulbs, a
toilet plunger, and a heavy-duty utility knife whose
blade, four inches of scored razor-edge, slid in and out
when a button was pushed along its gray-plastic
handle. She paid and took those things home, and the
Angel woke as she fed Grumble.

* * *

Moira Durchauer woke crying, said "You bastard," to the empty place in the bed beside her—and got up, still weeping, to blow her nose with toilet tissue in the bathroom.

She showered and felt better—looked in the long door-mirror as she dried herself. The baby didn't show, wouldn't show much for another month, even if she was going to keep it. Which she wasn't.

One of the few . . . really the only pleasure would be to walk into the cockpit on some Rome–New York flight, have Wayne say, "Hey, it's the Midget! How's it goin', Moira?" and answer, "Well, Captain, it's going fine now. Sorry I had to abort your kid a few weeks ago, but I really didn't want him . . . or her."

That would be worth it, just to have the chance to say that to him with the crew sitting there. See how Captain W. Henrici handled that fastball. . . .

When Moira walked out of her apartment building, a woman standing beside a white Toyota smiled at her across the parking lot. Smiled, gave a little wave, and walked over. Blue blouse, white slacks, blue purse, white sandals. A tall woman with big bones—but nice-looking, tanned, with short black hair . . . natural curls . . . .

"I know you don't remember me. I'm a nurse at The Clinic. I saw you yesterday." And this big blue-eyed woman—five-nine? five-ten?—still smiling, apparently expected that to be a really good memory for Moira, seeing her in that place, under those circumstances.

"Yes, I think I remember you in the office." Moira gave no smile. Lady, what in the world do you want with me . . . ?

"You see, I was staying overnight in a friend's apartment here—they're painting my place—and I saw you, and I thought, Oh, I'll take a chance on being told to fuck off."

"I won't say that, but—"

"But why am I bugging you? I don't know; an angel said, 'Walk across this parking lot, and see if she's had breakfast.' "

"I've had breakfast." Moira saw a white mark in the woman's right eye. A little slice of white into the blue.

" '—Then see if she wants to go shopping, have a cup of coffee . . . whatever the hell.' My name's Karen Yeager. —I saw how frightened you were in the office. You know, terminating a pregnancy doesn't bother some people. Other people, it bothers a lot."

"I wasn't frightened. I'm pretty tough."

The tall woman leaned down a little, smiling, as if she were going to tell Moira a secret. "Listen, I've been a nurse for nine years, and I've seen a lot of people act tough—you know, the way you were acting—but I haven't seen a single one that *was* tough. . . . Except maybe once or twice, on a children's cancer ward. I suppose I saw one or two tough kids there."

"Are you—is this something about getting me to change my mind?"

"No. I'm not allowed to try to change your mind. The mothers have to decide for themselves."

"Well, I've decided."

"Have you?"

"Yes, I have."

"Okay." The woman—tall, so tan, and almost beautiful—stood smiling down at Moira. The sun was in her eyes, but it didn't seem to bother her.

"—And I'm not really worried about it," Moira said. "I'm sure it's pretty safe."

"It is. It's very safe, very unusual to have serious complications. —So, if you don't think I'm just some wacko who needs to mind her own business, what about a cup of coffee?"

". . . I was going shopping."

"What are you looking for?"

"Oh, some summer things. But for Italy—nothing with palm trees on it."

"Did you try Peninsula?"

"They're just too expensive. It's ridiculous."

"I know, but they're having a sale—which, believe me, is the only reason I mention them."

"They're having a sale?"

"Today and through the weekend. I think that's right; it was in the paper. Peninsula . . . and Carstairs, too, but I think that's just beach stuff."

"Well, I can look. . . ."

"—And stand some company? Because if you'd really rather be alone, no problem. You don't have to put up with me at all. —In fact, *please* don't tell any-body I even said hi. Clinic personnel aren't supposed to have any contact at all with patients or possible patients."

"Oh, I won't. . . . It's Karen?"

"Karen." The tall woman had a rich smile, like a pleased child's.

"I'm Moira—as I suppose you know already. And I guess . . . I guess I could stand some company."

"Well," the woman said, and took her arm, held it lightly with cool strong fingers. "—Then awaaay we go!"

Chapter 9

"Do you like honey, Tyler?"

"Yes, I like honey."

"Then pull over—pull over there. I'm going to get you a treat."

Naomi had directed Pierce off the turnpike just north of Miami. "We've got time to show you some Florida," she'd said. And it had been all secondary roads since then—going west and inland for miles, turning this way and that way on narrow county blacktop with heat dancing off it. Passing busted-out little gas stations on white sand and crushed shell with stretches of groves, palms, scrub and Spanish bayonet. . . . Then swampland. Forever swampland, it seemed to be. "You're looking at the Everglades, Tyler. . . ." And all of it— flat as a flapjack—seemed to shiver in the heat, the glare of the sun.

When Pierce had mentioned the heat, Naomi'd said, "Always worse before a storm, and there's one out in the Atlantic, getting strong—early in the season, too. Heard about frying eggs on the sidewalk? Well, I've seen it done. Nineteen seventy-three, in August. Eggs *and* ham, and they fried fast. . . .

"Pull over!" . . . Naomi swung her door open and hopped out of the pickup while it rolled to a stop in front of a tired-looking fruit stand, with a tired-looking lady staring out over heaps of grapefruit.

Naomi seemed to Pierce to be pretty energetic for a whore—a prostitute. Most whores he'd known were bone-lazy, but Naomi was very lively. Talked fast, moved quick as a girl. —Pierce could see how Jewish women ran their families the way they were said to do. It was an energy thing. Their husbands and kids just couldn't keep up. . . .

And Naomi was right back in the truck, quick as a terrier. "—Here." She twisted the top off a little jar and handed it to him. Pierce stuck his fingertip down in the honey, then licked it.

"What do you think about that?"

"Well . . . that's real good. It's particularly good honey." And it was, it tasted of oranges—like marmalade, but richer.

"That, Mr. Missouri, is real Florida orange grove honey—and besides some stuff from Greece, and raspberry honey from Washington State, that is the best honey in the world." She took the jar back and stuck her finger down in the honey . . . licked it off her finger.

"That is good honey." Tyler could taste it lingering on his tongue.

"And the lesson there, Tyler, is no matter how fucked-up and tacky this State of Florida gets, there is a sweetness and richness about it that's valuable."

"I believe that," Pierce said. He started the truck and pulled back onto the road.

"I've always loved honey," Naomi said. "Sometimes, I'd come back from being with a client—maybe something very unpleasant—and I'd go in my kitchen and have spoonfuls of honey. It's such a good, sweet, strange thing. Bee spit, bee pee—I don't know how those little darlings do it, but God bless them and I don't care."

"I understand that very well," Pierce said, and surprised himself by telling a secret. "In Kansas, when I was inside, they'd have chocolate pudding a couple times a month. Day that happened—we had that—that made it a good day for me. You know . . . just a treat."

"What a sad couple of aging birds we are, Tyler," Naomi said. "—You with your guns and banks, and me with my old clients, my loveless twat." And then sat quiet, looking out over the backcountry.

It was country that now, with roads run through it, looked only rough and overgrown where there were no groves or tacky houses—sandy, flat, and hot. But Pierce had listened to Naomi lecture on the state's history, leaving Miami, and could imagine the trials those little Spaniards must have suffered, marching in their half-armor through miles and miles of this tropic scrub, its biting bugs and snakes. Sticking themselves on thorns and poison vines. Hard little men, marching through this furnace, with their homes so far away . . .

"We'll head over into Lauderdale pretty soon, Tyler—plenty of time to catch the thief Chetwin in his office."

"Good."

"Can I ask you something?"

"You bet."

"Just between us two . . . I presume, if you ever catch this nut, that you intend to kill him. —Now, don't give me the Look. It's a reasonable question. I mean, you could turn him over to the cops."

"No."

"Just 'no'?"

"That's right."

"Well, with the Look, I can imagine you robbing banks. —What's that? Not another *smile*?"

They drove into Fort Lauderdale late in the afternoon. The traffic was worse than Miami's.

"My God, Tyler—didn't you see that man signal? The man was changing lanes!"

"Then let him wait."

"You're tired."

"I'm not tired, Naomi."

"You don't realize how tired you are."

"Naomi . . ."

"All right. You pay me to point things out, and I was just pointing something out. —Take a left up here on Sixth Avenue. We'll go up to Las Olas, and take another left. . . ."

Chetwin's office was on the top floor of a round building in bronze and black glass—and was lively, with a client couple waiting and two receptionists, one busy at her keyboard, the other—very beautiful—there to greet and advise. There were small trees growing in the corners of the room. Between them, a long glass wall looked out over a canal with three huge white motor yachts parked along it. —It seemed to Pierce that whatever trouble Walter Chetwin had got into, borrowing his clients' money, he'd got out of it.

"It's a shame," Naomi said, when they'd been noted as having no appointment—previous call or not—and been asked to sit and wait.

"What's a shame?"

Naomi nodded at the beautiful receptionist. "Wasted gorgeousness. If I had that face, that body—if I'd ever had that face, that body—I'd be Queen of the Universe."

"You're nice looking."

"Oh, please . . . I'm almost forty and I have skin like an old wallet. And Gary Senise warned me about the sun; he *told* me."

They waited an hour—waited until the other couple had gone in and then come out, then waited some more. After an hour and a quarter, Pierce got up and spoke to the beautiful receptionist.

"Buzz him, tell him we're coming in."

"Oh, I'm sorry, but Mr. Chetwin is consulting with clients on the phone—a conference call—and I think you'll just have to wait."

"Do what I told you." Pierce had lowered his voice. "Do it right now."

". . . I can't."

"Sure you can, honey." Speaking so softly now, the girl had trouble hearing him. "—Do it."

". . . All right. All right." She leaned away from Pierce as if he'd threatened her, and pushed two buttons on her phone set. "Mr. . . . Mr. Chetwin, there's a man here who has to see you. —No. No, he has to see you right *away*. Right now!"

"Thank you," Pierce said. "Don't be scared, miss. Isn't going to be any trouble. . . ."

". . . What in the world did you say to Gloria? Sounded like she was losing her lunch." Walter Chetwin was younger than Pierce expected—a good-looking young man in a blue summer business suit, light-blue shirt, and lighter-blue tie—and was as pale as if he lived in Canada. His hair was a blow-dried reddish blond.

"I wasn't nasty to her."

"Um-hmm. And you are?"

"Pierce. Tyler Pierce. —This is Miss Naomi Cohen."

"Oh, yes. . . . You called the office yesterday, Ms. Cohen? Is that right?"

"That's right. And I was *told* I had an appointment."

"And you mentioned a mutual elderly friend—not, I'm afraid, a very important friend anymore."

"Then make a new one, Counselor," Pierce said.

"Any relationship between us, Mr. . . . Pierce, would depend on what your problem is."

"His problem," Naomi said, "is that the Sweetwater has murdered his daughter."

". . . Oh, *Pierce*. Yes, I see. And I'm very sorry."

"—And, and he intends to do something about it. Find the killer. And to do that, he needs the scumbag contacts that only a legal weasel such as yourself can provide for points north and west, particularly Palmetto County."

"Have we met before, Ms. Cohen?"

"I suppose it's possible."

"And, Mr. — what do you *do*, Mr. Pierce?"

"I'm a roofer."

"He used to rob banks," Naomi said.

"Ah . . . well. The thing is this, Mr. Pierce— not rob banks in this state?"

"No, the Midwest."

"Oh, all right. . . . The thing is, I am not about to abet any interference with even an unproductive police investigation of several murders. The notion of offending the police—and possibly a homicidal maniac as well—does not appeal to me." Chetwin shook his head to show how little that appealed. "So, I will not be representing you, or lending you aid in any way. Clear?"

"Counselor, I'll deposit fifty thousand dollars into any account you say. Wire deposit within three days."

". . . Into any account I say? "

"That's right."

"Three days? Full amount?"

"That's right."

"Well . . . Well, I've reconsidered. I feel, in the cir- cumstances, with a client so tragically impacted by these crimes, that I *should* offer any help or informa- tion I can—particularly in order that there be no inter- ference with the current official investigations." A decisive nod. "—You have a lawyer, Mr. Pierce. My secretary will give you the corporate name and account number—it's a Delaware bank—where that deposit may be made."

"Which secretary?"

"Not the beautiful one. The other one."

"All right," Pierce said. He stood up and leaned across Chetwin's desk to shake hands with him. Chetwin seemed surprised to have his hand shaken.

"Now," Pierce said, and sat down, "seems to me, and seems to a doctor we talked to, that the women this Sweetwater kills are the key to *why* he kills them. In other words, they provide him a reason for what he does."

"Uniforms . . . ?"

"Maybe. But if that was all, why wait a year or more between murders? I don't think those uniforms are enough reason."

"Not to a reasonable man, Mr. Pierce. But we're not talking about a reasonable man, are we?"

"Then why doesn't he kill men?"

"Sex. The odd pleasures of sex, I'd say."

"No. The doctor said there was no sex in these killings, even with cutting their breasts. He doesn't . . . molest the women's private parts."

" 'Private parts . . .' Sounds like a play. Who is this doctor?"

"Hector Salcedo, in Miami," Naomi said.

". . . Salcedo? Had some prescription problems?"

"Yes."

"Right . . . right, I got him. Familiar with that one. That was a good one."

"You think that doctor's wrong?" Pierce said.

"No, Mr. Pierce, I'm not saying that. I'm saying that you're trying to make sense out of a madman's murders—and I don't think you can do it."

"I'm not trying to make my kind of sense. I'm trying to make his kind of sense."

"Find the reason—however unreasonable—and you find the man. All right, what do you want from me?"

"First, I want to know what the police know about this—and especially about each one of those women that were killed."

"Oh, shit—you've got to be kidding."

"There are deputies in Palmetto taking from dealers transporting across the state up there—people you represented in court. I want the name of one of those sour cops."

"No *way*. Even if I had a clue—"

"Tell you what, now," Pierce said. "You can collect that fifty thousand and do the job you agreed—or you can have personal trouble with me. This is not a money matter, or some robbery or dope deal. This is a personal matter."

"Okay . . . okay. I didn't mean to be flippant, Mr. Pierce. I know this is a very serious situation for you—and there's no need for threats. I'll do what I can. And what I can't do, I'll explain to you." Chetwin paused, seemed to be giving the matter serious consideration. ". . . You see, the problem with naming any police officer who might be . . . dishonest, is that to do so I'd have to violate client privilege. A client of mine who might have an arrangement of that sort—"

"What's the officer's name?"

"I told you, I can't tell you that."

". . . If you don't," Pierce felt everything slowing down around him. "—I'm going to have to do something to you."

"Well." Chetwin tried to smile. "Mr. Pierce, you have a very bad temper there. It's . . . as an attorney, I can tell you that losing your temper is always . . . *always* a bad idea. Ms. Cohen, would you talk to your friend?"

"Tyler, please," Naomi said, and got up, "please don't do anything until I get the hell out of here!"

She went to the door as Pierce stood up and Chetwin said, "No—don't go. The officer's name is Burney. George Burney."

". . . Thank you," Pierce said, and meant it. "You just saved both of us a whole lot of trouble." He stood looking at Chetwin. "I'll be in touch when I need some more help from you, Counselor. —No hard feelings?"

"No hard feelings," Chetwin said, and managed a smile when Pierce reached over his desk and shook his hand good-bye.

. . . In the outer office, Naomi said, "Just a minute," turned and went back inside.

"What now?" Chetwin said. "—And where the hell do I know you from?"

"Bar association conference about three years ago. You were at the Fontainebleau."

"No . . . I still don't— oh, *Christ*."

"And what a sad creep you were."

"Thank you. So I wept—big deal. And you, as I recall, were . . . actually pretty memorable."

"Once reminded."

"Three years. Give me a break."

"And what do you think of my friend? What do you think of his chances?"

"I think your friend is an obsessed man, and a dangerous man, Ms. Cohen. He scares me—and I've been scared by the best. . . . And as far as catching that lunatic, I suppose he has as good a chance as the police do, which isn't saying much."

"And were you going to make a call to your client, to warn that dirty cop?"

"You'd advise against that. . . ."

"I don't want Tyler Pierce coming back down here and killing you."

"I see. And you have a point."

"Good-bye."

"Good-bye, Ms. Cohen."

When they walked out to the parking lot, throwing long dancing sunset shadows in front of them, Pierce said, "I need to make a phone-booth call, transfer some money—then I want to get up to Palmetto and get going on this."

"Do we have time for dinner?"

"You're hungry. . . ."

"Damn right. —And I know just the place. We'll do the Renaissance out on Racquet Club—try without reservations. It's got tropical plants; it's got a waterfall; it's got a pond with fish. You'll love it, Tyler. — I'll have the crab cakes, you have a steak."

"All right, but I want to get north," Pierce said, unlocked the truck, climbed in his side, and reached over to unlock her door. Even so late, the truck's cab was an oven.

"What about me driving?" Naomi said. "I can drive this truck."

"No. Get in." Pierce would have liked to smoke one of his cigars—no chance with this lady in the truck. Wasn't even worth a try.

"All right. Let's see. . . . We have to get out of here, then over to One, and up to Sunrise. Take a left when we get to Sunrise."

"Which way do I go out of the lot?"

"Right . . . Wouldn't you like me to drive? It's part of the service."

"Naomi, just tell me which way to go."

"Go right out of the lot over to Seminole. Then right on Seminole up to Sunrise Boulevard. Left on Sunrise . . . You never drove the getaway car, did you, Tyler? —Ah, another of those rare smiles."

"I know my way around Missouri . . . Oklahoma. I know my way around that part of the country."

"Oh, sure. Seminole's coming up—just get on and go north."

"That was a rich neighborhood back there." Stopped at a light, Pierce noticed an odd pair—didn't seem to intend to cross the street—watching him from the curb. A tall man, big and very tan, with close-cut sun-bleached hair and pale eyes . . . looked a little tough. The other man was older. Short, squat, arms hairy as an ape's . . .

"Neighborhood? Oh, the Isles—all the yachts and canals and so forth out the shyster's window? Oh yes, very rich. That's money above and beyond money. . . . And speaking of your new attorney, Tyler, may I ask what was that 'I'm going to have to do something to you'? What was that? —A bluff, I hope. In which case, remind me not to play poker with you."

The light went to green and Pierce pulled away, that

mismatched pair still standing at the curb, watching him go.

"I wouldn't have killed him, Naomi."

"I see. Good news . . . good news."

The moon was up as Pierce drove north through Palm Beach County. Driving through a haze of insects that swam in the air in front of the truck, flicked up into the headlights . . . then into the windshield with small *ticks* and yellow splashes.

Naomi, tired after that big dinner—or maybe just relaxing, getting used to him—had stopped talking, eased off and ridden in silence through the dark for a long while. She'd said only which highway to take— another narrow two-lane blacktop swinging back through the boonies—and that she had a surprise for him. Then she'd fallen asleep leaning against the passenger-side door—overtaken, he supposed, by the early hour he'd made her start. Once she was breathing deep, Pierce had reached across the seat to lock her door.

He would have preferred driving along the ocean, but Naomi'd said, "If you want the feel of this country, drive inland—the coast is for the tourists." So here he was, driving a roofing truck through moonlit country strange enough there should be dinosaurs in it. Spiky little scrub plants, and palms, and some sort of cypress. There was an irrigation ditch running alongside the road. . . . Heavy odors of night flowers were ruffling through the windows on warm air. He'd gotten tired of air-conditioning. That fancy restaurant had been air-conditioned, but you hardly noticed it because of the plants, and the pond and waterfall. Naomi had been right . . . been worth going out there for dinner. Cost a fortune.

Carolyn would have loved the waterfall, would have liked the little fish in the pond. Carolyn liked anything little—puppies, whatever it was; if it was little, she liked it. Liked bugs, and would go put them outside rather than kill them. Probably missed having some kids, and that's what that liking little things was all about. . . . He'd bought her a postcard in a place near the restaurant. Bunch of kids on the beach in Fort Lauderdale. Little kids, with red pails and shovels and so forth. Signed this one "Love," too. —Once he'd started doing that, it was hard to see how he could stop. . . .

Very little traffic was coming this way, and not a house to be seen except one farmhouse fronting orange groves miles back, with no lights on. . . . Driving through strange country with a strange woman asleep beside him. A woman like some men he'd known— maybe himself, in a way. Seen too much, and done too much. Left worn out and disappointed with herself, and nobody else to blame.

As if his thinking about her had woken her up, Naomi straightened beside him in the dash light's dull yellow glow, took a deep breath, and said, "Welcome to Palmetto County, Tyler—we're coming north on their secondary county road." Naomi's voice was hoarse with sleep. "—You want to get out of Palmetto County fast, going south, this is the way. Atlantic Coast is forty-five miles east, Gulf Coast is ninety-five miles west. A lot of the county is swamp—biggest in the state, after the Everglades and maybe the Myakka. . . . Manchineel is their big city—at about forty, fifty thousand. Smaller town over on the coast is Fort Talavera, with Palmetto Lake, county seat, in between. Also not very big."

"I was in Palmetto Lake a couple days ago. Ex-wife lives in that town. Buried my daughter there."

"Oh, that's right. I'm so sorry, Tyler. It's just such a loss, and in that dreadful way. . . . I never had any kids, but you know what I do? I've done it for years. Sometimes at night, I lie in bed and imagine I did have them—Joshua and Rebecca." Naomi was sitting up as if she was looking out into the night, but her eyes were closed. "Is that ridiculous? Is that sad? I dream years of having those two children. Their being my babies—twins, born the same time—and I just imagine them growing up, day by day, month by month, year by year. Sometimes I lie there for hours, doing that—and not all good times, either. Josh started with pot when he was fifteen, and I almost killed the little shit! Well, I say 'little'—he was already taller than I was. . . . Is that ridiculous?"

"No."

"I still pretend I have them, and they're in college. They don't write, of course."

"You'd have been a good mother."

"I would have driven those kids crazy. They'd hate me."

"No," Pierce said. "They wouldn't."

Naomi, looking tired, looking older in faint instrument light, took an Almond Joy from her purse, unwrapped it and ate one section, then handed the other to Pierce. "Here, eat. And keep your eyes open. . . . Too bad we bypassed West Palm—it's an interesting town. My father was in restaurant supply, and when my mother died, he took me with him all over the state. — Your parents still alive, Tyler?"

"No."

"My father said West Palm used to have two bests: the best doctor in the state—doctor named Michael Smith, who saved my dad's life, once—and the best hot dogs. A place called the Hut, little curb-service drive-in on Lake Worth, served those. Split hot dogs on toasted buns, and a mug of ice-cold Hires root beer. They brought them out to the car on a tray, and my father said they were the best in the world. All gone, now. . . . Keep your eyes open, Tyler."

After another mile, they went through an amber slow-blinking crossroad light—houses and stores there all dark under the moon—and across the intersection.

A very high, heavy-duty hurricane fence with a deep concrete ditch visible behind it began along the right side of the road. The truck's headlights shone bright orange across the steel mesh as they went by. The fence ran straight along for a distance—and Pierce saw something come suddenly into the headlight beams. A group of bright yellow coins over there, reflecting back the light.

"What's that . . . ?"

He slowed, and saw through the fence a pride of lions gathered behind their concrete moat, staring. "Jumping Jesus!"

"You like that?" Naomi said.

"You bet . . . !"

"Rift Valley Preserve—besides the swamp, Palmetto's major tourist attraction, and big rivals of Lion Country down in Palm Beach County. They have everything in there."

Pierce slowed the truck, stopped, then backed down the road to where the lions stood watching. "Will you look at that? Look at the size of those cats. . . ." He turned off the headlights, opened the truck door and got out, and walked around to the highway's shoulder. He stood there in moonlight, looking through the fence at the lions, as they looked at him.

"Tyler Pierce and the lions," Naomi said, sitting in the truck, watching. "And what in God's name am I doing here?"

Chapter 10

After midnight, Pierce pulled into a Motel 6 across the first Manchineel turnpike interchange, went in, paid cash for two rooms, and came out to the truck to wake Naomi.

She grumbled like a sleepy child, following along as he carried her suitcase down to number 17, ground floor. He unlocked the door, carried the suitcase in, and put it on the bed. Everything in the room was colored orange.

"Good night," Pierce said. "I'll come get you pretty early."

"I don't doubt it. . . ."

Pierce went to his room—number 23, ground floor, everything in there light blue—locked the door and put down his duffel bag. He turned on the air-conditioning, went into the bathroom to get a hand towel, then came back to the bed and drew the Smith & Wesson from its holster at the small of his back, under his windbreaker. A handsome piece, though he liked the longer barrel on the 625.

Pierce sat on the bed, released the revolver's cylinder latch to dump the loads on the bedspread, and checked the weapon's bore by the light of the bedside lamp. There was no wear on the forcing cone, no wear in the rifling, and only the usual Smith & Wesson gap to the cylinder. He thumbed the cylinder closed, held the piece up and shook it. No rattle, no movement.

Pierce stood up, relaxed, and slowly turned this way

and that, dry-firing . . . squeezing the trigger to that neat click as the hammer came down. The revolver's muzzle traced the room, passing over some things . . . the pistol snapping at others like a quick-tempered little dog as it noticed them.

About a ten-pound pull, and just about right. Ten pounds, double-action. Almost five, single-action. A friendly gun—just heavy enough to handle the full-house Federal .357s and still steady down for a fast second shot. A class revolver . . . Enjoyable, the weight of a fine weapon in his hand.

Could use a fancier holster, a little slicker on the pull. But the nylon would do, do better than leather in this climate. —And also in this climate, even stainless, the piece would need a light rub with Hoppe's oil, and sooner rather than later.

Pierce dry-fired a few more times—worked left-handed for several passes after that—then picked up the six loose rounds, wiped his prints off them in case he had to dump the empties fast and leave them, and loaded the revolver.

He thought he'd have to get a couple of those big loose beach shirts tomorrow; zipper jacket was way too hot for this weather.

Pierce went into the bathroom, took a shower, and came out wishing he hadn't eaten all the New Orleans pralines. . . . Wishing for Carolyn too, to have her here in the room with him—just being in the room, and maybe talking about the library and doing ladies' hair at Snip N' Style. Small-town talk, and pleasant to listen to . . .

He turned off the air conditioner and the bedside light, then opened the room's window, pulled back the bed covers and lay down in the dark. He heard the highway traffic . . . and under that, from some vacant lot, the sounds of nighttime insects. Tropical insects, waiting for time and heat and wet to rot the highways, he supposed. Rot all this and all the people away, and leave the country to them again.

He got up after a while, closed the window, turned the air conditioner on and went back to bed. He was tired as if he'd worked all day on a steep roof. . . .

Pierce had mentioned getting some hot-weather shirts, out-shirts, to Naomi first thing after breakfast at the motel restaurant—pretty good pancakes, syrup not so hot. It was a foolish mention, because Naomi had gotten excited and insisted on going shopping for the shirts right away, and it cost them a half hour driving down Manchineel's strip looking for a clothing store. Then a lot of time in the store looking at tropical shirts. Rayon, cotton, everything.

"Guayaberas," Naomi said. "—Two nice cream guayaberas."

"What's that?"

"Really pretty tropical shirts—you can use them semiformal. Usually cream or white, with a little lace pocket, a little lace down the front."

"No."

". . . Oh, of course not. What was I thinking of? . . . Well, they have to be cotton, anyway. Or cotton-polyester; rayon just doesn't hold up." And Naomi kept talking about shirts and bringing them back for Pierce to try on—and each one, he looked over his shoulder in the dressing-room mirror to make sure the revolver didn't show in his waistband back there. So the shirts had to be pretty big—the clerk thought they were too big—and any one of them would have made him the talk of the town in Dowland. They had pineapples on them, or palm trees, or beach scenes—and one of them, bright red, had vines and monkeys.

Pierce was taking off one of the shirts—green, with big red flowers on it—when Naomi came back to the dressing room with another one.

"Oh, my God," she said. "Your *side* . . ."

Pierce said, "Buckshot," and handed her the green shirt.

They finally settled on three really expensive cotton-polyester shirts in extra-large long. Silk-screened. A dark blue with pineapples; a black one with palm trees; and a cream-colored shirt with small blue flowers on it.

Naomi tried to get Pierce to buy a straw hat, but he wouldn't.

When they were finished shopping, Pierce stopped at a 7-Eleven, filled the truck's tank, and bought three Almond Joys and two packages of Backwoods cigars. Then he used the pay phone to call Chetwin in Fort Lauderdale—told the girl he was their newest client—and was put right through and charges reversed.

"Counselor?"

"Yes?" Chetwin didn't use his name, didn't sound pleased to hear from him.

"Yesterday, I transferred an additional sum into your account, along with your fee. The additional is one hundred thousand dollars. Should be in there today or tomorrow. You'll be my banker as regards that amount."

"Oh, for God's sake. . . !"

"—For which service, add ten to your fee."

"Oh. . . . Well, that's all right. That can be done."

"Now, here's what I want you to do. I want you to contact a good document man—do you understand? And send him up to Palmetto tomorrow. Motel 6, at the Manchineel interchange, room twenty-three."

"There's no way I could do that. I would have no idea—"

"I think one of your other clients can probably help you with that."

"Absolutely not."

"A good document man, tomorrow, Motel 6. And have him bring the additional amount transferred, minus your money."

"Are you serious? This person brings the money?"

"Yes, I am. Pay the man a mule fee."

"Jumping Jesus Christ."

"Good morning, Counselor. . . ."

. . . Officer George Burney wasn't in the phone book.

"Didn't expect he would be." Pierce got into the truck. "—Didn't expect it; cops are usually unlisted."

"I know." Naomi, in the passenger seat, had made entries in Pierce's blue notebook. "I already looked that up while you were in there buying those ridiculous cigars. There were two other Burneys in the county. A Mrs. Maude Burney, and Arthur D. Burney."

"Yeah, I saw 'em. Maybe mother and brother," Pierce said, and started the truck. "I'm going to try the lady first."

"I'll try the lady."

"Naomi—you're here for information, not to be doing anything like that. And you need to be going home, anyway. I don't need much more advice."

"You've got to be kidding, Tyler."

"I mean it."

"So do I—unless you can't afford me."

"I can afford you—"

"Excuse me for interrupting, but you're heading for Tallahassee. Cane Lane is the other way on this county map—and that's for Mrs. Maude."

"Okay." Pierce pulled into a laundromat lot, turned, and drove out going east.

"There you go. You were saying . . . ?"

"I was saying, I can afford you—and you can earn your money looking stuff up back at the motel. You don't need to be driving around with me."

"Right. And then you could call me from Tallahassee."

"I can read a road map."

"Tyler, you have other things on your mind—you'd better have—and that's why I'm here. Little chores, little reminders, useful information from a woman's point of view—such as that no police officer's mother or grandmother or aunt is going to tell a big tough-looking man, who is obviously *not* a cop, anything about their Georgie."

". . . All right. You can talk to the woman."

"Thank you. And I'll need to rent a car. I can't arrive at Mrs. Maude's in a roofer's truck. —You're not going to smoke that thing in here, are you?"

"I'm not going to light it. Just chewing on it . . ."

"Fabulous . . . Shirt looks great, Tyler. Those little blue flowers are nice. Very . . . festive. And you can't see the gun back there at all."

"Naomi, give me a break."

Just about every one of Maude's friends was absolutely locked to their TVs all morning, staring pop-eyed at some silly soap opera. Hairy young men and starlets or whatever—those girls still not too old for a good spanking—doing everything but having sex right in front of you.

Watching that stuff was some people's idea of how to spend half their day. . . .

"Well, what do you do with yourself, Maude?" Doreen would ask her that, and Sonya. "—Mom, what in the world do you do all day?"

"I work in my yard. I bake Key lime pies for the church. I wash Little Boy—and he digs out back so he needs a bath just about every day. I go shopping. I follow the stock market report on the radio, and I read a book every now and then, which is more than I can say for most of my acquaintances *and* my daughter."

"George doesn't read."

"My nephew is a police detective—and that means he's too busy to read."

"Any excuse for George," Sonya would say.

"George comes by, Sonya. —You don't."

. . . This morning was pie morning, and Maude had four of them finishing—secret being *real* Key lime juice from real Key limes—four of them made and almost done. There wasn't one time she'd had a pie left unsold at St. Ambrose's. Not one.

Maude had spread clean dishtowels on her kitchen counter, ready to set the pies out to cool—and every time she had to do that, she regretted changing her old tile countertops for this laminate stuff. You just looked at that laminate—put anything hot down, whatever—and you could kiss it goodbye. . . . Just had got ready to set the pies out, and there went the doorbell.

. . . It was a woman, standing on her front steps with a notebook in her hand. Maude had never seen this lady before in her life—thin woman wearing dark glasses, and trying to look younger than her years. Hair dyed brick-red, and she was forty if a day.

"Mrs. Burney?"

"That's right."

"Mrs. Burney, I'm Charlotte Gregg, from the *Miami Post*? I'm a reporter for the paper."

"I don't read that paper."

"No . . . I'm not—we're not going to put you in the paper."

"I particularly don't read the Miami papers or the Tallahassee papers. I don't read the Jacksonville papers either, and I do a lot of reading."

"Well . . . I am really terribly sorry to bother you, but your name was in the phone book—Burney. I know this seems . . ."

"No, go ahead, say what you came to say. I didn't mean to be rude, Miss Gregg."

" 'Miss.' You noticed the no ring?"

"I noticed the no ring."

"The reason . . . the reason I came out is that we're doing a series on law enforcement around the state—the officers in the front lines, people who really do the work. . . . And the person, the detective, your sheriff's department said I should interview is Sergeant Burney. But those people wouldn't give me the man's address! —Apparently, detectives' addresses are big secrets.

They only gave me his phone number and he's not at home; I've called several times. And I saw your name in the phone book and just decided to come over to see you, since your name is Burney. . . ."

"It's George's golf day. He always plays golf, off shift."

"Oh, thank God. I hoped you were a relative of some kind."

"Aunt."

"And he's playing golf?"

"George always plays golf, off shift."

"And where is he playing golf? I only have today. . . ."

"He plays at Bonny Dune. —And you better come on inside off those steps, or you're going to melt. Do you like Key lime pie?"

"I love it, when it's the real thing."

"The real thing is all I make, dear. . . ."

"I'm not charging you enough, Tyler." Naomi busy buffing her nails as they rode back down the Manchineel strip after returning her rental car. She'd taken the red polish off.

"What was that stuff?"

"What stuff?"

"You took the . . . the nail polish stuff."

"Nail-polish remover, Tyler. Acetone, to you. I'm sorry if I've offended with a very slight odor of acetone in your truck. —And as I was saying, I'm not charging you enough."

"Why's that?" It had seemed to Pierce that even the early morning had been hot. And the day at noon was much hotter, and fiercely bright.

"Because I feel like a shit, that's why. I lied to that nice old lady—who looked at me, at my nails, as if I'd come down from Mars—and you're going to do God knows what to her nephew."

"I'm going to make him take a lot of money." The

air conditioner was doing pretty well for the truck cab but there was a haze in the air past the windshield, and what seemed like a dust of gold—as if the air itself was reflecting heat.

"Even so, I feel like . . . It's an unpleasant feeling."

"Naomi, you wanted to do it and now you're sorry. . . . Tell you what: you need to back off from this. You need to stay in the motel, or get back down to Miami. You've been a big help—"

"Bullshit. I've been essential."

"—very big help, but you don't need to get in any deeper."

"Sit in the motel or go home."

"That's right." . . . How in the world men worked on roofs down here, in heat like a furnace fired up high.

"And I will go home, Tyler, just as soon as I can do it without leaving a babe in the woods. Do you happen to know the name of the major dealer up here?"

"No, I don't."

"Well, last night—and when you check your motel bill, which you should always do, you'll see the call—I talked to a really vile professional acquaintance of mine in Coral Gables. . . . The important dealer up here is a Jim Clarence. And do you know what that means?"

"No."

"Clarence is an old name in south-central Florida. And it means he might be Seminole, or Creek, or Miccosukee—or part Indian, anyway."

"Okay. That's . . . that might be handy to know."

"Here's something even handier. The tribes will dislike Mr. Clarence in a major way. They'll consider him a disgrace—consider any Indian drug criminal a disgrace—so the people he uses will be whites and Hispanics."

". . . Well, you need to stay back at the motel, anyway."

"Sure . . . Are we doing lunch?"

"You bet."

"Not—don't tell me. Not fast food."

"I don't have time for a fancy lunch, Naomi. "

"Tyler, how can you go from dinner last evening at the Renaissance—and you ate half a cow, blood-rare— how can you want lunch today at McDonald's? You don't notice a little taste difference?"

"That was a good restaurant. Good steak, real nice salad."

"And the wine, you had wine—and the pond. You liked the pond and the waterfall. . . . You've got a right turn coming up in about half a mile."

"Okay. —I liked all that, Naomi; it was a nice water-fall. But I like eating at McDonald's, too."

Naomi stopped doing her nails and looked over at him. "Tyler, you're too good to be true."

"Well, I *do*. I've eaten in fancy restaurants in Chicago. I mean French restaurants, the whole nine yards. Years ago, I ate at the Bakery there—and that was a very good restaurant, one of the best in the country. And I've had really great steaks in Kansas City. And barbecue. —But I do like McDonald's. I think their french fries are very good. And the Quarter Pounder is good."

Naomi went back to her nails. "Mr. America," she said. "You're very cute. It's getting tough for me to imagine you robbing banks, Tyler."

"Well, I did."

"So you say. . . ."

They found a McDonald's on Second Avenue, just off the exit from the fourth interchange, the last at Manchineel.

Naomi had the Quarter Pounder, a Sprite, and a small fries. "My taste buds must be going. Can I ask you something, Tyler?"

"Yes, you can."

"You expect this supposedly crooked cop to give you information on Lisa's case?"

"That's right."

"And you're going to bribe him for that?"

"If I can. —Naomi, don't worry."

"Oh, please . . . Has it occurred to you that Chetwin might have given you an *honest* cop's name, just to get rid of you?"

"Oh, yeah. That occurred to me."

"And? —You going to use that ketchup?"

"No, take it. —First, I don't think Chetwin knows many honest cops. I think he and his dealer client up here—probably your Mr. Clarence—I think they stay away from those officers. And second, if Chetwin screws this situation up, he would have a serious problem with me."

Naomi tore the ketchup tab, squeezed some on her french fries. "Tyler, can I ask you another question?"

"You bet."

"A personal question."

"Sure."

"Have you ever killed anybody?"

"Nope."

" 'Nope'? —And you're threatening people like Chetwin? Who's a coral snake in a hundred-dollar necktie? And I suppose you intend to lean on this crooked cop if you have to."

"Naomi, do I have a choice? Now, do I have a choice but to deal with these people? Do I have a choice except just go on home and forget my Lisa? —Forget any other girl this crazy man decides to murder, year after year?"

"Your daughter wouldn't want you to get killed down here, Tyler. —I can't finish these fries. If this is the small, then what the hell is the big order like?"

"I don't intend to get killed down here, Naomi. And if it comes to it—you asked me about it, so I'll tell you—if it comes to putting somebody down, I can do it. I always knew I could do it, because to tell you the truth I come from bad blood. I could do it, but I just never had to." He drank some of his Coke. "And I'm not proud of that, but there it is. You asked me, Naomi."

"I know I asked you. It's just . . . Tyler, you have to touch so many dangerous bases around here—and God knows what monster is waiting at home plate."

"Well, you finish your french fries—"

"I can't. They're not bad, I'm just full."

"All right then—if you're finished, come on. I'll drop you back at the motel, because I'm going to try for that first base this afternoon."

"I'll go with you."

"No, you will not."

There was nothing much out on Appochokee Road— a county road, but still hard to find on the Palmetto County map. A few small houses—board-and-batten, and looking tacky-built—were scattered along on little sandy lots, with long stretches of scrub and what Pierce thought might be date palms between them. Plastic toys in the front yards . . . Little houses looked to be cooking in the heat, the plastic toys ready to melt.

The fanciest thing out on Appochokee was the sign, when he came up to it. Two tall square red-brick pillars stood each side of a turnoff, and held the sign arched over the black asphalt between them. *The Bonny Dune Golf and Country Club.*

The sign was white. Lettering, dark blue.

There was a smaller sign, also white-and-blue, stuck on a post at the side of the drive. *Private—Members Only.*

Pierce drove on in, the truck dipping and rocking along on blacktop sagging from having been laid out on sand—seemed to have been no roadbed prepared at all. Some contractor doing his friends a hasty favor . . .

The drive rose off the level and began to swing in slow curves along the sides of what appeared to be sand dunes, rises just barely covered with coarse weeds and some sort of green tangle. Sea grapes, maybe.

Something . . . No trees—not even palms. No grass. It didn't look like golfing country.

And where the sand lay uncovered, it seemed to burn white as ash in the heat. Looked to Pierce like powdered glass; there were little blue and diamond sparkles off it in the light.

The drive took a jump and bump over a bad section, leveled down, and swung left into a small parking lot.

Past that lay bright-green grass. The grass spread only a hundred yards wide, and ran on out between scrub-covered slopes, never becoming wider . . . then turned out of sight past a distant hill like a hotel hallway carpet gone around a corner. There were marker flags out on the greens, and people walking pulling their golf bags with them on little wheels.

Sprinklers going. A whole line of them along one side of the grass—spray twinkling in hot sunshine. Seemed a waste of water not to wait till night.

There were only a few cars parked in the lot. Pierce pulled into an empty space, opened the truck door, and stepped down onto black asphalt gluey with heat. The air trembled above the pavement.

The only building was a long white double-wide mobile across the parking lot, and Pierce walked that way . . . thinking it might have been smart to take Naomi's advice about getting a hat. Dark glasses wouldn't have hurt, either. His boot soles were sticking a little to the pavement, and he threw the darkest shadow he'd seen as he went along.

. . . The mobile's big rectangular room was paneled in paper-print fake oak, air-conditioned to a chill, and almost empty. What looked like a small pro shop—a few shelves of shirts, display cabinets, and a rack of golf clubs and bags for sale—was tucked down at the far end of the room. . . . A long pine-board bar was set on its back wall, and a very thin boy with a blond crewcut was sitting behind the bar reading a magazine.

Four women—golf widows, Pierce supposed, and

each with a beer mug in front of her—were playing cards at a table to the right of the door. All four were middle-aged—two of them probably sisters—and all four wore glasses. There was a green plastic bowl of pretzels in the center of the table, and used paper plates. The women all looked up at Pierce as he came in, then went right back to their cards. No talking. It appeared to be a serious game.

There was no one else in the place, and no decoration except golf clubs—old putters and drivers arranged in patterns on the walls like ancient weapons—and a few little plastic boxes of individual golf balls dotted around on wood brackets. Pierce supposed they were hole-in-one mementos; each bracket had a white card tacked beneath it. . . . There were big square posters of fancy golf resorts or golf tournaments running down both sides of the room. It was a dedicated clubhouse.

The boy barkeep stood up and smiled as Pierce came over; seemed pleased to have company. He was wearing a white Bonny Dune T-shirt—the club name, in slanting letters, over a sand-yellow patch with a strip of fairway green running across it.

"Somethin' cold?"

"Not a member."

"Oh, that's okay. Bar's open to guests."

"Not a guest, either. I'm just looking for somebody."

"Well . . . hell, have a drink anyway." A nice boy.

"Okay. I'll take a Miller Draft, if you have it."

"We got it, but you can have hard liquor if you want. Private club . . ."

"Brew's fine."

"Okay. Have to charge you two dollars and fifty cents. That's what they run." He seemed worried Pierce would change his mind over the price.

"That's all right."

The boy stooped to a counter refrigerator, took out the bottle of beer, and made a little production out of wiping away the condensation with his bar towel, turning off the cap, choosing a glass from the rack, and snapping the coaster down on the bartop. A nice boy, and bored.

Pierce paid him, and left fifty cents on the bar. "Reason I came by . . . friend of mine, state trooper out of Tallahassee—"

"You from up there?"

"Yes, I am. —Well, my friend said, 'Look up old George Burney, you get down around Manchineel . . . Palmetto.' And I understood Sergeant Burney played golf out here."

"You an officer?"

"Nope. Not in law enforcement at all."

"Well, you just missed him maybe forty minutes. Everybody had lunch—we got a microwave and can do pizza, anything you want—they ate and just took off out there for their second round."

"I see. Well, it's no big deal. I'll be in town and I'll get with him later. —You know I have no idea what the man looks like?"

"Well hell, I'll show you. You can still see him. . . . How about I run out there and bring him in for you?"

"No, no. I never interfere in a man's pleasure on his day off."

The boy came out from behind the bar—he was tall, but very skinny. Never played any football in high school, for sure. He beckoned Pierce over to a window. "He's out there, but he's way out."

"Which bunch is he in?"

"Not the two close in. See the three of them out by the first rough?"

"All looks like a rough to me."

"Man in the khaki pants . . ."

"I see him," Pierce said, and could barely make out the man's features. He was a couple of hundred yards away, standing leaning on his club, watching another man swing. Burney was a tall man. Sizable. And had a mustache. "Man with the mustache?"

"That's him. I could go get him."

"No, don't do that. I'll be around for a few days . . . catch up to him at the sheriff's office."

It was a major pleasure just to stand in cool air, drinking a cold beer. Would be a pleasure to stay for an hour of cool air and cold beers. . . . Golf. Pierce had never had the time for it, though he'd had friends who swore by the game. Men he knew, a couple of them, would go robbing—and one of them killing a time or two, as well—and come back and get right out on that golf course, said the game got in your blood. . . .

Never had seemed to Pierce to be time enough for playing games. Then, inside in Kansas, nothing but time—and nothing but trouble or handball to play.

No, there'd never been time for games, or real grown-up work, either. No time for Margaret or Lisa. Iceman was just too busy for all that. . . .

"Another beer?"

"No thanks. Think I'll be getting along. I appreciate the hospitality; you got a nice place here."

"Best course between Palmetto Lake and Ocheeka—and built against the odds on all this sand scrub. My dad was contractor for the road and for the sprinkler system, too. First sprinkler system he ever put in. We do paving, mainly."

"Did a real nice job," Pierce said.

Pierce parked on the shoulder on Appochokee Road, a few yards down from the club's sign, and set himself to wait for a few hours. He turned off the engine, rolled the truck's windows down, and settled in. He made the mistake, getting comfortable, of resting his arm out the window on the doorframe. —Got a little burn from that, told him not to be touching metal that had been out in this sun.

He found it hard to get the heat out of his mind.

There seemed something personal about it, as if it was against a man, trying to smother him, make him sick. Naomi had said this was unusual, even for south Florida in midsummer, and he hoped she was right. Hard to believe people could prosper in this sort of weather, air-conditioning or no air-conditioning. . . . Here he was, sitting still in a truck with the windows open, and he was already running sweat. Missouri got hot, very hot in the summer, but not like this.

When he'd dropped Naomi off at the motel, she'd said, "One hundred and three degrees, and ninety-four percent humidity, Tyler. Drink water—and get a hat!"

Well, he'd had a beer, and wished to God he had another. . . .

. . . At twenty minutes after five—and not a bit cooler at all—the seventh car came out through the gate. And this one, a white Camaro, was driven by George Burney. The sergeant—appeared to be a handsome man in the door mirror—pulled out of the drive and took off down the road toward Manchineel as if he was late for a date.

Pierce started the truck, U-turned, and drove after him.

Burney was a fast driver, with a local police officer's unconcern about speeding, and the Camaro made such time that Pierce had to nearly floor the accelerator to keep after him . . . then slowly catch up to run close behind. He saw the sergeant glance into his rearview mirror—and right after that saw a mild curve and crossroad two or three hundred yards ahead.

The truck's weight told as they went into the curve; it sat stable on the road—and Pierce swung out to pass . . . but didn't, only ran alongside the Camaro deeper into the curve and stayed there in the other lane, hoping to God no traffic was coming his way.

Then, just before the crossroad, he blew his horn— signaled to Burney to take that right—and as the sergeant stared over at him, looking startled, swung the truck to the right, struck the car lightly, and crowded it over into the turn.

They both swung over, both braking hard—the Camaro took it well; the truck's back tires broke free to skid . . . and they went turning right together in a plume of sand and dust, turned and turned and ended half on a rutted country road, half off it onto sand and shell.

The Camaro stopped sooner than Pierce could, both braking in showers of gravel. Then it was very quiet.

Burney got out first. The sergeant jumped out of his car and was coming up to Pierce, black loafers kicking up loose pebbles, as Pierce climbed out of the truck. Burney was wearing a light-blue sports coat, and khaki slacks. His face was flushed dark under his tan.

"You stupid son of a bitch." He wasn't shouting. He was angrier than that. A tall man, with clear gray eyes in a square, handsome face. Almost handsome enough to be a movie star's . . . Pierce thought the sergeant must be catnip to the ladies.

"Sorry to pull you over so sharp," Pierce said. "Be happy to pay for that damage to your car."

"Oh, you're going to be sorry," Burney said, and was reaching out, apparently intending to get his hands on Pierce and proceed however from there.

"Wouldn't do that," Pierce said—and was interested to see Burney hesitate, standing there in front of him. The dust was settling back at the crossroads, where they'd skidded.

"What the fuck—? What the *fuck* do you think you're doing? You could have killed us both—and you are God damned right you're going to pay for my car. Every fucking penny!"

"Oh, I'm going to give you a lot more money than that, George."

"What—"

"Shhhh. You stop talking for a minute, George, and just listen to me. My name is Tyler Pierce. My daughter was killed over in that swamp you have here. . . ."

Burney stood staring at him, seemed confused to be off the subject of his car. There was sweat on his forehead from the heat. It was hard heat to breathe in.

"—Now I intend to do something about my daughter's death, Sergeant, because—no insult intended—law enforcement down here is not getting the job done."

"You are out of— Who the fuck are you?"

"I just told you. My name's Tyler Pierce."

"I mean who the fuck do you think you *are*? I am a goddam police officer! —And you run my car off the *road*?"

"I needed to talk to you in private, George."

"Well, pal, you just got yourself into some serious trouble!" Burney looking like a real tough cop, now.

"Sergeant, what I want from you is the sheriff's office case summary on the Sweetwater. I want to know the current major leads and suspects—if any. And I want to know the *conclusions* your people have come to. I don't need a file cabinet full. I just want some pages; I want your people's conclusions on those crimes."

"Oh, you kiss my ass!"

"And I'll pay you very well for that report or whatever, George. I'll pay you as well as this drug dealer you dirty for up here."

". . . Pierce, you're crazy and you'll pay me shit! . . . And if I tell you I don't know what the fuck you're talking about, and I'm a police officer and you're looking for trouble and you're about to get it—what then?"

"Well . . . then I'd have to see to it you change your mind right quick."

"I'd say the court would call that a threat, Pierce," Burney said, and he reached up and across to a shoulder holster under his blue jacket. He was fairly quick, and had an automatic almost out—something bright and stainless—before he stopped and stared into the Smith & Wesson's muzzle.

"Jesus," he said.

"Last thing I want to do," Pierce said, "—is kill you."

". . . Well, we have a . . . we're in agreement about that."

"You put that pistol up, and we're going to talk."

"I guess we are. . . ." In slow motion, Burney tucked the shiny pistol away. "Easy on that trigger, now."

"You bet. —Now, as I was saying, I have a business proposition for you, Sergeant." Pierce reached back to holster the Smith & Wesson under his shirttail. "I'm going to pay you ten—nope, twenty thousand dollars for a summary of the case information the sheriff's department has on the Sweetwater."

"I couldn't do that. —I wouldn't do it, either."

"Sure you would. You're talking to at least one drug dealer up here all the time. Maybe Jim Clarence?"

"Bullshit."

"—What do you say to that man, George? What do you tell him? You tell him where the sheriff's going to be looking next? You tell him who's a narc and who's okay?"

"That's a fucking lie." Burney looked into Pierce's eyes, a straight steady look from a man with nothing to hide.

"—So I figure you're not a real cop at all. You're just a criminal with a badge, and I can deal with you."

"You kiss my ass."

"Now don't you try and be tough. Too late for that, George. We're just going to do us a deal, here." Pierce reached into his back pocket—which made Burney start—took out a roll of hundred-dollar bills, counted out twenty, and dropped them on the ground between them. "There's two thousand there—another eighteen thousand when I get that paperwork. You have my word of honor."

"Get serious, you asshole. I wouldn't touch that shit!"

"Oh, yes, you will. You will touch it, Sergeant. Because this is very important for me, to have that information. . . . So now, you pick that money up and put it in your pocket."

"No way. And you are getting yourself into major trouble. You already are in major—"

"Pick it up, Sergeant, or I'll have to kill you right here."

"You're out of your . . . you're fucking *crazy*! I am a police officer!"

"I already said you're no police officer. You're dirty as dog shit and you belong in the pen with better men than you are. . . . Now, I can't leave you to walk away clean and go talk to the sheriff, get me harassed out of here. I can't have that happen. —So, you are about to get shot dead right here, you don't bend down and pick . . . up . . . that money."

"You just—you better just take it easy. . . ."

"I can smell the yellow on you, George—coconut custard right down your back. And I'm going to count you to ten. One, two, three—"

"Come on. . . ."

"Four, five, six—"

"Come on, now. . . ."

"Seven, eight—" Pierce, in no hurry, reached back under his shirt. "Nine—"

"All right, all *right*. Jesus Christ!" Burney stooped, then hunkered down to collect hundred-dollar bills out of sand and sand burrs.

He stood and stuffed the money into his left trouser pocket; it took him two tries to find the pocket. He looked tired, not so good-looking, as if getting down like that for just a minute had worn him out, made him older. "You wouldn't have shot me."

"Yes, I would," Pierce said. "I would have shot you in the head and left you right here with your brains out on the dirt. —And you can bet the next crooked cop I came up to in this county, after that, would have done what I told him real quick."

Burney's attention was wandering, drifting away. It was a look Pierce had seen during robberies and in prison, the look a person had when he was dreaming whatever it was wasn't really happening, and everything was the way it had been.

"Hey," Pierce said. "*Hey*. Don't go away on me, George. You hear me?"

Burney stopped looking out across the dunes, the scrub pines.

"You pay attention, now—you all right?" Pierce gripped Burney's shoulder, gave him a little shake. "I'm going to give you an extra five thousand to fix that pretty car up just perfect. You all right?"

"Yes. . . ."

"Okay. You just do what I say, and nobody will ever know about you, about your being crooked and all, except me and that dealer you work for. —And about your being a coward? That'll be just between you and me. Nobody else will ever hear of it."

Burney stood and listened.

"Nobody's perfect, George. Everybody shades a little. And nobody wants to die—you shouldn't blame yourself for being human." Pierce put his arm around Burney's shoulders, patted him gently.

The sergeant stood in slowly failing heat and light, quiet under Pierce's arm.

Chapter 11

There was a white van, a new Club Wagon, parked at the motel lot when Pierce drove in under a furnace-red sunset. *Flash & Photo* was painted in rainbow colors along the van's side.

Pierce parked the truck, got out, unlocked his room and went in. He had time to take a piss and wash his hands before there was a knock on the door.

"Oh, yes, you're the person. Pierce." Almost a child's voice out of a very small man in gray slacks and a white dress shirt with no tie—a Chinese or Vietnamese, Pierce thought. He was carrying a heavy brown-leather briefcase. One of the old-fashioned ones, with straps and buckles.

"Vietnamese," the little man said, as if Pierce had thought out loud. "We have big heads. Chinese have small heads. Japanese also have big heads. And that is how you can tell the difference."

Pierce shook hands with him—felt a wiry little grip. "Come on in."

The small man walked in, sat in Pierce's only chair, opened his big briefcase, and took two small thick brown-paper packages out. "I'm the identity man. My name is On Nguyen, Mr. Pierce." He handed the two packages over. "—By the way, Mr. Chetwin has already given me a certain amount of money to bring these to you."

"All right." Pierce put them on the dresser. "—Now,

Mr. Nguyen, let me tell you what I need. I need basic travel ID. I don't need the stuff going back to birth certificates, school transcripts, military discharge and all that. I just want a picture driver's license, vehicle registration, Social Security card, credit card—"

"These are names I have on credit cards I have." Mr. Nguyen bent over his briefcase again, fingered through it, and came up with a small yellow ringbinder notebook. ". . . I have Wybranch, Nearing, Teller, Donaldson, Jerome, Boyce, Arguella, and Byers."

". . . Boyce."

"So . . . Gilbert Cullin Boyce."

"Okay."

"On that credit card, charges all right up to eight thousand, but only for two more weeks—week and a half, better. Then Mr. Boyce will get his bill. And everything else will be Mr. Boyce's—Social Security, driver's license . . . everything in his name."

"That'll be fine—and will I have his true address?"

"Yes, you will. . . . You going to pay this man back afterward, what you spend? He's only liable for a small amount."

"Just the same, I take something from a man, I feel better taking it direct, not be running around sneaking his money off him with a bank card."

Mr. Nguyen nodded, seemed very amused—stared down at the carpet as if he'd start laughing if he looked at Pierce.

"—And I'd like any stray stuff you can give me. Library card, bank checks, deposit slips . . ."

Mr. Nguyen liked that. "Library card is a smart thing. I have library cards."

"—And all this just has to be good enough so a motel clerk or a traffic cop won't question it. Just good enough to hold for a day or two, after an arrest—until I can make bail. A confusion thing, that's all."

"Florida, Georgia, Alabama, Kentucky, New Jersey.

I have those blanks with me, Mr. Pierce. And I have
license plates for those states, if you don't want from
Boyce—want it a rental."

"What's Boyce's state?"

"Kentucky."

"No, make it Kentucky."

"No library card for Kentucky."

"Then skip that."

The little man shook his head. "No. I'll make. I can
make a card. —And everything Gilbert Cullin Boyce."

"And what's this all going to cost?"

"Ummm. Cost you three thousand dollars."

"Make it three thousand, five hundred. —Good
will."

"All *right*. That's very nice. Mr. Chetwin told my
friend you were a bad man, Mr. Pierce—but I see he
was mistaken."

Pierce didn't know what to say to that, and Mr.
Nguyen sat examining him, then nodded toward the
dresser. "You should look and see what I brought.
Make sure."

"Not necessary," Pierce said, and the small man
seemed to think that was funny too, and stood up smiling. Pierce seemed to have amused him considerably.

"Mr. Pierce, I'm going to take your picture—bring
some equipment in, take your picture in here. And then
it will be about three, four hours work in my van to
finish."

"No problem." Pierce took him to the door, and
when he opened it, there was Naomi in a fancy-looking
black dress, black high-heel shoes.

"Secrets?"

"Just some business," Pierce said, and Mr. Nguyen
smiled at Naomi and walked past her.

" 'Business.' Tyler, I know it's not a requirement—"

"Come in."

Naomi walked into his room, looked around as if

another Vietnamese might be inside. "I know it's not a requirement in this fiduciary relationship, but I would have liked to have been told that you were back . . . that, for example, your crooked cop hadn't killed you."

"I should have let you know. I had company."

"Right. Ho Chi Minh. Just passed me by."

"Doing some documents for me. Different IDs. I want to be able to change motels, things like that, without leaving 'Pierce' everywhere."

"Ah, the photography van in the lot . . ." Naomi went to the dresser mirror, stood looking at herself.

"Right. Must have a whole setup in there. . . . Name'll be Gilbert Cullin Boyce. Gil Boyce."

"Not terribly imaginative. And what about my ID, Tyler?" Naomi reached up and touched her hair.

"You won't need it, Naomi. Nobody up here knows who you are, knows your name. And you're not going to be here long, anyway—another day or two—so you just stay right here. Stay put."

"Stay put."

"That's right. I'll be leaving tomorrow morning, getting into a different motel down the strip. Different motel—I'll use the Roadside Rest—and the Boyce name. You can still help without running around with me for everybody to see we're together."

Naomi made a face and looked up and to the right, as if there were someone up there listening to this. "And if I should need a car for the next couple of days—just for basic transportation, for research?"

"Rent it in your name, and I'll reimburse you."

"And you will let me know what you're doing. Every morning—breakfast, or at least a little phone call? Just so I can keep you from making any really fatal blunders in this snakepit of a county?"

"I'll keep in touch."

Naomi sighed and turned from the mirror; didn't

seem pleased. "I hate to say it, Tyler, but you're making sense. You do what you do, and I'll do what I do."

"*You* don't do anything, Naomi."

"Um-hmm." She gave Pierce a look. "And you are going to get rid of your truck."

"No, I'm not. There's some body work, and I'll have it repainted."

"I see. . . . What color?"

"Blue."

"Please, do me a favor, Tyler. Do green, not blue."

"All right. Green."

"Thank you—and did I hear 'body work'?"

"Little dings on the passenger's side . . ."

"Ah . . . And how did things go with the crooked cop?" She turned back to the mirror as if something might have changed in the last couple of minutes. Reached up and touched her hair again, seemed disappointed.

"He was at the golf club. We had a meeting."

" 'Body work.' And you had your meeting, and he's *going* for it?"

"I think so, if things move fast enough. Burney's not . . . he's not real quick."

"We hope. . . . Well, this I have to hear blow-by-blow. Let's discuss it over dinner, Tyler—and I don't mean fast food. I checked with the office clerk, and he says there's a really good—and expensive—seafood place out on Hammock, so—as you can see—I'm dressed and ready to go."

"I've got to get my picture taken first."

"I'll want a color print, eight by ten."

"Karen . . . ?"

"Yes."

"It's Moira. Moira Durchauer?"

"Hi! What are you up to?"

"Well, yesterday I had a flight, and I caught a commuter back up late and I didn't get much sleep—but it's a great morning, and I thought I'd see if you wanted to do something."

"Sure. —Still like the pants?"

"Well, I do. I tried them on when I got home with them, and I thought, Oh, no, they're just too floppy! But then I tried them on again this morning, and they really look all right. And *really* all right with the linen blouse."

"Oh, they looked great on you."

"You don't think they're too floppy? I'm pretty short to be wearing that much material, Karen—and ice-cream white, too."

"They looked wonderful. Very sophisticated. I'd keep them—I would definitely keep them."

"I am. I'm probably going to keep them. And I'm keeping the suit for sure—I know that looks really good."

"It does. Moira, I think you made great choices right down the line."

"Well, if I see women in Rome and Frankfurt looking at me as if I've gone crazy, I'll know I goofed. . . . I could have just shopped over there."

"Uh-uh. I had a girlfriend who went over on vacation, and she said they just don't have the selection. Their good stuff is very good, but the selection is much more limited."

"That's true. I was over there for a few weeks a couple of years ago—air charter. I mean it was the airline, but they were doing lease charters. And it's true, they don't have as much choice."

"No, you absolutely shopped smart. So . . . you're definitely going to work out of New York, and over to Europe."

"I think so. . . . Oh, Karen, I just—"

"It's your decision. Your business."

"Well, there's stuff I haven't told you. . . . Listen, the reason I called? You said this was one of your days off, so I thought I'd see if you wanted to drive over to

the coast. We could go to Fort Talavera, get some sun-
blocked rays on the beach."

"I'd like that."

"Now, are you sure? Because, you know, if you're
with some guy . . ."

"No. I'm free and lonely."

"Great, I'll come get you."

"No, don't bother. Why don't I meet you at Googy's
on the beach over there—you know, in front of the
deck."

"An hour?"

"Hour and a half."

"Okay. Surf's up . . . !"

. . . It seemed to Moira that the people at Fort
Talavera had done a great job on their beach. For a
small town, they'd spent a lot of money on it. Even in
the two years she'd been flying out of Miami, then
commuting into Palmetto, they'd cleaned up the beachfront and had bike cops patrolling it. And two other
restaurants—more upscale than Googy's—had opened
on the esplanade. The walkway there was new, and
curved away under the palms almost all the way out to
the lighthouse point, with awnings and flags fluttering
in the breeze from the Atlantic. . . . The big rollers
were coming in all along the beachfront, heavy gray-
green waves that were almost transparent as they
curled, then broke and fell, and shook the ground a
little. Supposed to be a big wind coming in. . . .

Now, this was probably the most beautiful beach in
southeast Florida—a little too upscale for a really old
rust-colored bathing suit that sort of hung off her hips.
Moira'd put her new suit, her good suit, on first, and it
still fit, but she had this idea it was pressing on her too
tight across the stomach, even so early. . . . A stupid
thing to worry about, considering.

She'd looked in the mirror after she'd changed, and
there was this little woman in a bad bathing suit—not a
girl, and not a young woman either anymore. A

woman, small and thin, with a too-short haircut, no tan to talk about, and a face getting older by the minute. . . .

Moira had rented a big furled blue-and-green-striped beach umbrella from weird Terry at the stand up on the esplanade. She stood leaning on its wood handle in front of Googy's beach deck, her straw tote on the sand beside her. People were sitting at the restaurant tables, eating their cheeseburgers and fries, looking out over her head as if she weren't there. . . . It was odd, because she loved the beach and the sea and swimming—and she used to look great in a suit, even with small boobs. It was odd, but she'd gradually felt less and less comfortable lying out on the beach with hundreds of strangers. And not only about men doing those shifty little glances when they went by—but just all those people she didn't know, women and kids too . . . all of them running around half naked, and she was just another body lying out there in the sun.

It was silly, but it began to bother her a little, so she'd started to rent beach umbrellas and just leaned them on the sand so at least in the shade there, she had that little bit of privacy.

It was tremendously hot, the sun really blazing, and it wasn't even noon yet. The sand was almost too hot to stand on. A lot of people were going in the ocean, even with such heavy surf, and it wasn't surprising. It would be a pleasure to get in the water . . . get cool.

Moira saw Karen Yeager coming down the beach from the esplanade—could see her over the crowd, she was so tall. Karen was wearing a barely-there black two-piece suit and that was it. And carrying a gray canvas book bag.

She looked almost like an Indian walking on the beach she was tanned so dark, as if she'd never heard of skin cancer at all—and Moira saw some people look at her as she walked past them. So big and strong-looking, great legs, and burned bronze by the sun. She wasn't really beautiful, but people looked at her just the same. Major bod, if you were a guy and liked big ladies . . . which apparently some did. . . .

"Hi—I made it!"

"Damn, Karen, you look disgustingly great."

"I don't, but thanks."

"I feel like a pale worm."

"You're very cute, and I'm too big. Big bones—I can't help it."

"Let's go on down. —How do you *dare*? That's what I want to know—how do you dare tan like that?"

"The sun would never hurt me."

"Doesn't your doctor tell you not to do it?"

"Oh, I don't have a doctor. Don't need one. —How about here?"

"Can we go down that way? It's just too crowded— it's like, you know—maybe it's from flying, all those people jammed in—but crowds bother me."

"Come on. . . ."

They found a good spot near the water, but thirty or forty yards down from most of the crowd. The surf was heavier here; there were fewer swimmers in it.

Moira opened the big umbrella . . . then set it down on its side, the striped canopy turned to shield them a little from the crowd. It threw a curved blue-green shadow on the sand.

They tugged the beach towels from their bags, shook them out and laid them down—Moira's a stolen Palmer House bath towel from a Chicago stopover.

"Ready for this?" Karen took a thermos out of her book bag and shook it gently—ice rattled softly inside. "Margaritas."

"Oh, God. Oh, you angel!" And when she said that, Moira saw Karen do something odd—hold her head a funny way as if she was listening to someone calling down the beach. Then she looked at Moira, and there was no expression on her face at all.

". . . To bring the margaritas. . . ." Moira thought

Karen had been upset by what she'd said, though it was nothing bad. Thought maybe she was real religious and didn't like anybody to say, "Oh, God."

But then Karen smiled. "Drinks now, or wait?"

"Karen, I do not want to wait."

"I made them very light—you know—in case you decide to keep the baby."

"Oh, right. . . ."

They sat on their towels drinking margaritas out of little clear plastic cups—they each had two drinks—and talked about clothes, and that turned to talking about men, and why women kept building their lives around men as if that were the most important thing, the only thing—and then when you got them, what was the big deal? And Karen told about the doctor she'd been with, who'd come to her place for more than a year but only stayed over on weekends. How clever he'd been . . . and cold, except for screwing.

"You are describing two pilots of mine, and one high school halfback."

"Well," Karen said, and finished her drink, "they're different animals from us." She took Moira's cup, got up, and walked away down to the water to rinse both cups in the sea. She had long strong legs, almost too heavy with muscle and bone . . . and delicate muscle moved across her dark tanned back as she walked. Fine white sand was stuck to the sweat on her right forearm, where she'd leaned up, drinking.

When she came back, she said, "Let's swim." Reached down for Moira's hand and pulled her up to her feet.

Moira had always been a very good swimmer, and didn't mind surf as many women did. Didn't have to worry about her hair, cut so short. She waded out . . . felt the Atlantic cooler than usual, then slid into a collapsing roller and stroked through it. Surfaced . . . and swam on out in a steady crawl . . . out to where the waves heaved up in great slow swells as the beach began to shelve. She turned there, looked back for Karen, and couldn't see her.

Treading water, waiting for a wave to pass by, still watching, Moira felt a sudden smooth brushing past her leg. She jolted in the water, stared frightened down, and saw Karen beneath her through foaming green, sliding under and past.

Karen surfaced a ways away, called, "Sorry—didn't mean to scare you," and went back under.

They swam for some time there just behind the breaking waves, keeping out on the swell. Farther down the beach, a shifting school of surfers were paddling out, then riding the big rollers in. . . . Moira swam the surface, Karen beneath the sea—both swimming also against a slight southern riptide running down the coast. The swells came in under and past them like green dunes, regular, rising high and very heavy, and the sea where they swam trembled slightly as the waves crested, curled, and broke to strike the beach.

After a while, Karen surfaced, shook water from her black hair, smiled and gestured them in.

"I wasn't tired." Moira had to step faster through the shallows to keep up with Karen's longer stride.

"No, you're a smooth swimmer. I was tired. . . ."

They lay down on their towels side by side, Moira half in the umbrella's shadow, Karen out in the sun, the sand almost too hot beneath them.

Then Karen sat up and said, "You'll burn. Where's your sunblock?"

"Oh, in my bag, but I don't need it."

. . . Before this—Karen rubbing the sunblock cream on her back—Moira had wondered a little if she was a dyke, she'd been so nice to her. But Karen was just getting the sunblock on and it was definitely nothing personal, not that kind of touching. A girl—well, a woman, another stew—had come on to Moira once, and it had been a really uncomfortable situation. The idea of lying around in bed with a woman playing kissy kissy . . . it was absolutely not comfortable. Of course, Karen looked so strong—almost big as a man—it would probably be a definite fuck, whatever it was. But still creepy. . . .

"Karen, I really don't think you were tired."

"Tired of what?"

"Tired out there swimming. I think you're just wanting me to be careful. Not drink too much, not get tired out and so on—am I right?"

"So?" Karen finished Moira's legs.

"Well, so . . . it's really nice of you. And I know you're concerned, but it's probably wasted effort because the truth is I just don't plan to have this kid."

"Your decision."

"That's right. . . ."

"You're done," Karen said. "You can get the front."

"I just don't like that stuff—it's so greasy."

"Better than developing a melanoma."

"You don't worry about it."

"No, I don't."

After that they lay quiet, side by side, and Moira almost drifted off to sleep. This was the nicest time at a beach—tired and hot from swimming and the sun, and just lying so warm, hearing the sea, hearing people far enough away so they sounded nice, and weren't going to bother you. ". . . This is my last day of freedom. I'm scheduled out again tomorrow. And I'll be flying the day after, too."

"You like flying?"

"I used to." Moira turned her head, and saw in Karen's right eye, as she lay listening, that little slice of white into the blue. "—You know what happened? I lost two friends, two good friends, in that accident over Toledo three years ago—well, almost three years ago. Girls I'd known for years. They had a midair and just fell out of the sky." Moira turned over on her back; remembering made her feel restless. She lay on her

back with her arm across her eyes. The sun was . . . it
was really a very hot day, even for almost August.

"—And it sounds strange, but I knew exactly how
it was. I knew exactly how it was because I dreamed it
right afterward. Is that weird, or what?"

"No, I believe that."

"—Food and trays up in the air, just sailing around
the cabin—a mess—and everybody screaming. Screaming in their seats and sort of flopping back and forth as
if a wind was blowing. I could see their heads going
back and forth. And in my dream, I saw Nancy up in
the air—you know, sort of swimming over the aisle
and all those screaming people strapped in their seats,
and she was trying to hold on to a seatback. And she
looked so terrified . . . she just looked awful, and they
all were falling and falling. . . . They fell ten thousand
feet out of the sky. I still dream about it. . . ."

"That's terrible, Moira. And terrible for you."

"Well, it scared me. And it cured me of the romance
of flying, I'll tell you that. After the Toledo thing I
used to vomit in the airport bathroom before my
flights, I was so scared. —But being a stewardess is
what I do. I can't *do* anything else, not and make
money. I had one year of college, and that was a joke.
I'm thirty-five years old, and I want to get married." It
seemed to Moira it was easier to talk with her arm covering her eyes—as if what she couldn't see couldn't
see her very well either.

"—I'm not ashamed of saying I want to get married.
I'm not ashamed of saying I want a man to take care of
me. Flying scares me now, and life scares me, and
that's just the truth." Boys, some noisy people, were
shouting farther up the beach. It always seemed
strange, how boys couldn't just be quiet.

"Life scares a lot of people."

"Not you, I'll bet."

"Oh, it used to."

". . . About the baby, Karen. You've been so nice, and I don't want you to think . . . Well, the nitty-gritty—and I wasn't about to spill my guts in that clinic office—the nitty-gritty is I had amnio two weeks ago in Chicago. They didn't want to do it so early, they wanted to wait, but I just said they had to." Moira took a deep breath, breathed in sea air, salty air that didn't care about anything. "—And the news, the big news was that my baby is going to be a girl, and she's got an extra twenty-one chromosome. And what that means—"

"I know."

Moira was surprised to begin to cry. She'd thought that, the crying, was all over with. "—It means she'd be retarded, a little Mongol girl. Down syndrome, and she'd be retarded and she'd look funny—and I know they're supposed to be like everybody else, but they're *not*. It's a goddam lie! And I'd love her, I know I would, but what man would ever love *us*? What man would marry me and take us both?"

"Her father?"

"Ha ha." Angry tears, now. Moira supposed tears got hotter when people were angry. "—That'll be the day, that Wayne Henrici divorces his wife and lets her take his two boys—that he's crazy about—and marries me with a little girl like that. He'd give me some money to help support her—maybe, if I took him to court. And what other man would want me and a little retarded girl? I'm nothing special, Karen. I'm just an ordinary person and I'm not that young anymore."

"But it could happen. A man might love you both."

"Oh, sure . . . It could happen, but what are the fucking odds? You tell me that!"

"Not good."

"You are goddam right 'not good.' And Karen, my parents are dead and I don't have anybody. . . . I've never been a lucky person."

"You'd have a daughter."

"Oh, right. I've read all about that; I spent the last two *weeks* reading about it. Down's people die young. She'd live just long enough so no man would have me—then she'd die. They die *young*."

"Not always . . ."

Moira took her arm down and let the sun shine red through her eyelids. She opened her eyes the slightest bit and the sunlight flashed and sparkled through her tears. "Karen, I'm not brave enough. I'm not strong enough. —I don't want to kill my baby, but I don't want to be some sad old woman all alone except for a retarded daughter, and still flying when I'm fifty and vomiting in airport bathrooms!" She got up on her elbow on the towel and looked for a tissue or something. All this was pushing waterproof makeup pretty hard. And she had to blow her nose, too. "It doesn't mean I'm bad."

"I know. Want a Kleenex?"

"Yes. —And I'm telling you this because I didn't want you to think I'm just another selfish lazy bitch, some asshole who'd kill her baby because she doesn't want to be bothered."

"I don't think that. I don't have a tissue."

"Oh, shit. And Karen, I just have to ask you. Forgive me, I know we don't even really know each other but I have to ask you. Please tell me . . . just tell me what you would do."

"Honey, I can't tell you."

"But you know what you'd do."

". . . Yes, I know."

"You'd have this little girl, wouldn't you? You'd have her and take care of her no matter what."

Karen leaned over through the umbrella's blue-green shade, and kissed Moira on the forehead.

"—Isn't that true? Isn't that what you'd do?"

"I can't tell you."

"Oh, but it's my whole *life*. . . ." Moira sat up on the Palmer House towel, searched in her purse for a tissue.

"Yes, it is. —Now come on, honey, blow your nose and we'll go up to Googy's for a little comfort food. Cheeseburgers and shakes, on me."

Chapter 12

"Sideswipe with a white General Motors car."

"That's very good," Pierce said. They were standing out in furnace-hot morning air, in the yard at Ronald's Repair and Body, seven blocks west off the strip.

"Paint's the clue. Crappy. An' it was a low car. . . . Camaro?"

"*Very* good—and how much is this going to cost me?"

Ronald Fiala was a slight man in his fifties, bearded, and wearing washed-out blue-denim coveralls. Looked like an old hippie. "Mr. Boyce, it'll cost you . . . six hundred to body the truck. Fifty on top of that to match the paint—you got Ford red *and* white there."

"To like new?"

" 'To like new' will cost you a hundred more. Less filler, more hammerin'."

"And I want all new paint. Green."

"Green? A green truck?"

"I've seen lots of green trucks."

"Well . . . depends on the green," Fiala said. "You go British racing green, you got something."

"And I'll bet that's expensive paint."

"Wouldn't have mentioned it if it wasn't." A smiling old hippie.

"How much for like new, and painted?"

"Whole thing'll go for a flat one thousand, an' that's fair. That's not outrageous."

"*You* say."

"You won't find anybody else short of Jax do the job we do."

"I'll bet. —And by tomorrow, day after?"

"Absolutely not. Maybe a week."

"Day after tomorrow."

"For two-fifty more, day after tomorrow."

"You run pretty costly, Ronald."

"Well, that's true. I'm pricey, but I'm pricey so I don't have to cheat the work."

". . . All right. Do it like new and paint it that special green," Pierce said. "—And by day after tomorrow." He shook hands with Ronald on that, and walked out to his rental, a gray Nissan four-door with a bad radio. Mid-State Rental had accepted Gil Boyce's card.

It was the tall trees and shade, the neatness on both sides of the road—even without the big carved wooden sign—that showed where the state park started. But it was a neatness that went back only a couple of yards off the two-lane blacktop's shoulder. Beyond that, on either side and as far as Pierce could see, it looked like the rough beginning of the world.

Palmetto scrub, and little fat palm trees, and thorny tangle in long clumps here and there . . . then cypress standing in forests out to the horizon, their trunks throwing late-morning shadows over lagoons of still black water. That water looked to contain anything— and one of those things, a mile farther down the road, Pierce saw lying by the side of the pavement. An alligator up on its forelegs—the reptile five or six feet long, looking rough-carved out of wet black wood and resting there in the heat off the highway. Pierce saw its eye as he drove past. And there was nothing in that pale-yellow eye but observation.

It gave him a jolt, a memory of seeing Marty Lubeck staring out of his solitary cell on Deep Four. Lubeck had been in there, except for weekly exercise, for four-teen years, and he'd looked out the little door window just like that as Pierce went by. Observation. Waiting for something to come close enough. . . .

This swamp, the state parkland, had been a sudden shady change from the endless flatlands turned to crops all the way from Manchineel. That cultivated country had been flat as a tabletop, and with distant fountains here and there, irrigation water being pumped as if by great fire hoses through the air.

Pierce supposed the cropland had been swamp a few dozen years ago. Wild country. And gone now to filled soil and tropic sun and pumped water that must grow crops the year round. Cropland would get bigger, wild land smaller. . . .

Wild land still big enough in here, though. The state park was a major piece of country. He'd driven miles into it now, and seen nothing but wilderness and signs for this area or that area. —Wilderness in the real sense of the word, meaning it could kill a man in a night and a day and a night, just being out in it with nothing for protection—having no mosquito repellent or netting. Having no boat, no knife, no matches, no gun. And worst of all, having no notion of the way to go to get out.

. . . Margaret had said this was no place for a young woman alone, and she was right. In this piece of country, life meant nothing at all. Death would be the standard here.

People talked about going back in time. Seemed to Pierce there was nothing easier. Just park your car and start walking . . . start wading into the out-there. After a mile, two miles—and all turned around, lost, splashing through sun-hot black water . . . swimming, crawling and struggling out of mud onto some hammock for a rest where a cottonmouth slid past you— you'd have gone back to the time before there was any time at all.

. . . Pierce had called Burney at work first thing in the morning, and assumed calls to the squad were taped. "Detective Sergeant Burney, please . . . George? This is your old fender-bender buddy. How is that pretty white car?"

" . . . It's . . . it's a mess."

"Hell, told you I'd pay for it, and I will. All my fault, brush-blocking you that way. And listen—why don't we have some lunch?"

"I don't have anything . . . I don't have anything for you."

"Estimate on that pretty car? Sure you do. You bring all that paperwork along—every bit of it—and I'll see you at the main picnic grounds out at Manchineel State Park. Say one o'clock. I'm playing tourist out there."

". . . Can't make that."

"Sure you can, you want your money."

"No, not today."

"Today or never, old buddy. See you out there." And Pierce had hung up. . . .

There was almost no traffic this morning, as if the heat had slowed it, thinned it out. Heat, and a cloud-striped sky—looked like animal stripes up there, blowing away thousands of feet high in streamers of dirty white and smoke gray. Blowing away from the coast. The Nissan's radio, between hissing and spitting, had mentioned the storm out to sea. A hesitating storm, it seemed to be. Threatening to come this way . . . threatening to be a hurricane, and already named Olivia.

"Hold on to your hat, Missouri." Naomi at breakfast this morning, discussing the weather. —She'd already had something to say about sausage biscuits. "Absolutely could not be worse for you." Then went ahead and ate two of them.

"I've seen tornadoes, Naomi."

"Not three hundred miles across, you haven't. . . ."

And if there was no wind out here along the ground, it was true there was wind somewhere higher. Pierce had smelled the sea when he'd rolled the car's window down.

. . . The swamp and jungle opened up to the right, out of increasing traffic. Opened into a big parking lot—looked like two paved acres—with rows of cars and five big tour buses lined up in blazing sunshine and heat. A crowd of tourists bright as bugs were walking along a sort of causeway beyond the buses—a bridge on tall concrete pillars curving away out over the swamp. A viewing walk, it looked like, and a place for the people and their kids to stroll above those ancient reptile times. Safe, with their video recorders and funny clothes.

There were buildings each side of the lot—flat-roofed, and one-story—rest rooms, snack bar, ranger station. But a big sign carved into knotty wood read *Park Headquarters* and showed a carved arrow aiming on down the road . . . so Pierce speeded up again, passed the second lot entrance, and kept going. More traffic on the road with him now.

At the headquarters turnoff, to the left, Pierce drove a curved paved drive through foliage too thick for full sunlight . . . then out of that to a clearing with a long handsome rambler—built board-and-batten out of knotty pine—set in the middle. There was a graveled parking area beside the rambler, with twenty or thirty cars in it, and a second, smaller structure behind that. . . . Both buildings with the solid, quality look of paid-for-by-your-taxes. All old-time local-style construction. —No pine shakes on those roofs, though. Heavy-duty composition; shingles looked like brown Alaskans.

Pierce pulled in between two park department Jeeps—Wranglers, painted dark green—and walked into the building past a group of women with field glasses walking out. . . . Inside was about the coldest air-conditioning he'd found down here. Almost uncomfortable, it was that cold. State people weren't worried about those electric bills.

They'd left most of the interior open—like a very big cabin. A long room with a peeled-pine beam ceiling, and paneled with the same knotty wood used on the outside walls. Glass display cases and framed maps and photographs—wild animals, birds. The pictures reminded Pierce of the ones Naomi had in her apartment; nature photographs instead of paintings. Seemed to be a Florida thing. . . . Pierce found a nice postcard for Carolyn—big white bird just taking off from a branch covered with shiny dark-green leaves. Really pretty white feathers on the bird.

There was a line of tourists at a counter to the side of the room—a few of their kids were ducking around, complaining—all waiting to see an almost elderly ranger with a short gray-white beard. He was wearing the green state park uniform the men had worn at Lisa's funeral . . . but this man hadn't been there. Must have had the duty, that day.

Pierce waited in line, listening to the mothers trying to keep their kids behaved and still. The fathers said nothing, just stood there and let the women try to handle it. . . . Strange how that had become the way now to treat kids when they acted up—just talk and talk at them as if they were grown-ups, and then do nothing so the mom got a look of contempt and the child was off and away again. . . . Seemed to Pierce it made a lot more sense to just whack their butts one good one, and set 'em in place to behave under their daddies' hands. Sure made more sense for the parents. Probably the kids would prefer it too, rather than think their folks were fools, and weak—too weak to protect them, take care of them.

Pierce stood waiting as the line slowly moved, listening to the children running around, making more noise each time after their mothers had called them in and had long conversations with them about what they'd agreed to that morning. There was an unhappiness there, disappointment both sides. You could hear it in their voices. . . .

"How can I help you, sir?"

"Well, I could use a good map of the park. . . ."

"Here you are. —And these pamphlets on the Manchineel's plants and animals."

"Thanks. Now, let's see. . . ." It was a sizable map, and Pierce, unfolding it on the counter, found it not much help. "The bird areas . . . the more wilderness areas . . ."

"Any place you go off paved road, sir, you'll find pretty much wilderness—except for the causeway in A, over here. . . ." The ranger's age showed in a brown-spotted hand, a pointing finger that trembled slightly.

"Area A . . ." The Miami paper had said D was where Lisa had been found. "—And D is here?" It was a peninsula of darker green at the park's upper west corner.

The old ranger was a patient man. "Yes. That's several miles west. It's a wilderness viewing area for tree-dwelling birds, rather than waders. You'd see waders over at B. But you'll see occasional reptiles in D— timber rattlers rather than moccasins, and one of the very few habitats where you'll find timber rattlers this far south. It's slightly higher ground—maybe that makes the difference. Coral snakes also, under dead-falls and so forth. It's a good area to stay on the path. Stay in the cleared viewing sites. Not a good place to put your hands under brush, or stones or fallen branches."

"I'll bet."

"Some idiot apparently was keeping funnel-web spiders in this part of the state; I don't know how he got them out of Australia. They're extremely poisonous— about three times more so than black widows—and very aggressive. Several apparently got away from him, and now—along with a lot of other unpleasant foreign fauna—we have them to deal with. Two of those spiders have been confirmed in the park, and killed."

"D."

"That's it. You might also—if you have time—take a look along our swamp trails in Area E. They really give you an experience of the swamp, as well as a small section of saw-grass wet prairie. It's spring-fed, but very similar to virgin Everglades farther south."

"Well, okay. Thanks."

"Enjoy yourself, sir. . . ."

It was a long drive through the park to that area. But on the map, not even all the way across the park. And with miles of that wild country still to the north and south.

Pierce saw the sign for Area D, turned right up a short stretch of paved access and into a narrow graveled parking lot. There were only two cars there, and a small shed-roofed pine lean-to with a big map against its back wall, and glass display cases . . . printed information on a bulletin board.

Pierce parked, locked the Nissan, and walked over to look at this map, a more detailed map of the area. He was at the base of a peninsula maybe two miles long, more than half a mile wide. Crisscrossed by five separate trails that intersected here and there. . . . There were two access roads dotted in black, *Park Department Vehicles Only*.

There was a plastic shelf on the shed's side wall labeled *Area Maps*, but they were all taken. He'd have to go back to the car, get his notebook, and sketch out the big map in enough detail to use.

"Are we out?"

Pierce turned and saw a short, sturdy woman—a ranger—sitting in one of the park's green Jeeps. She was a dark-skinned lady with a round pleasant face, looked part Indian.

"—We out of maps?"

"Looks like."

"Well, no problem." She had a young voice, clear as a girl's. "—I've got one you can have." And leaned over in the driver's seat to reach the Jeep's glove compartment. She was wearing a pistol. Stainless, a big Beretta; it looked too thick in the grip for her.

"Appreciate it," Pierce said, and walked over.

She handed him a folded map—and seemed surprised by something, gave him a black-eyed look. There was a lot of Indian in those eyes. "Aren't you Mr. Pierce?"

Nothing to say to that but yes or no. "Yes, I am."

"I saw you at Mission Presbyterian. Lisa's funeral. And Andy Pullings said you were Lisa's dad."

"Yes, that's right. I saw a lot of park people there— and I appreciated that, thought it was good of you folks to come out."

"She was a nice girl. She was . . . well, you know what she was like."

"No . . . I hadn't seen her in a lot of years."

"That's too bad." The lady ranger leaned out of the Jeep to shake Pierce's hand. "Fern Ketlow."

"Tyler Pierce."

"And you came out here to see where she died, Mr. Pierce?"

"Yes, I did."

Ms. Ketlow started her Jeep. "Well, I'll go against regulations and give you a lift out there. You wouldn't find it if I didn't—and you aren't supposed to drive park access roads anyway. Hop in. . . ."

"Thank you, but I wouldn't want to get you in trouble."

"It wouldn't be all that bad trouble. Hop in."

. . . Women in uniform. Softness and hardness all together, and maybe the cause of confusion in the Sweetwater's mind, though Dr. Salcedo hadn't seemed impressed by the uniform thing as a reason.

Pierce closed his eyes for a minute, riding along

through heat like a hot shower's. Uniforms . . . It had
been a hot day in Wichita, too. Hot, but not not as this.
And there'd been nothing wrong with that job, until
getting out. Getting out was where it fell apart. One of
those little teller girls had tripped the silent alarm; no
other explanation. . . . And even so, even so, they
almost got clear. He and Ed Sonnenberg were out and
in the first car and gone down the alley to Second
Street. Some gunfire, just a few shots, but they were on
their way.

"Where's Pete?" Ed had said. "He ain't comin'
behind us."

"Stop and back up."

"Tyler—you fuckin' *crazy*?"

"Do it."

"Holy shit. . . ." But old Ed had done it. Stopped
dead at Second, with whoop sirens coming in from all
over town. Stopped, then raced the Buick, backed it up
that alley again and out into the bank lot.

Looked like a cop convention in that lot. Police officers crouching behind three cars taking shots at Pete
Mulhune, and he was down.

"Where you goin'? Where you *goin'*?" —And
Pierce, quick, quick before he had time to think about
it, was out of the Buick and running across that hot
pavement, pulling the .45 and taking a passing shot at
one of the cop cars to keep their heads down. Took that
shot and another to worry them—and there was Pete,
sitting on the blacktop with blood spattered around him
like spilled red paint, and he was laughing.

"You dumb fucker," he said, like Pierce was the funniest thing he'd seen. And Pierce bent and had him up
and slung over a shoulder as if Pete weighed nothing at
all. —And then it was a run. A few yards that took forever through the heat and the crack-*bang* of the rounds
coming in. Pierce threw back another cover shot to try
to keep those cops' heads down, keep them from
drawing a fine bead—and he was almost to the Buick,

saw Ed staring at him from behind the wheel, face
white as a lady's. And the Buick's rear window went
right then, just blew away, and little bullet holes
popped into the fender, the rear door. Things snapped
and hummed in the air.

Even so, Pierce was almost to the car with Pete's
blood running down his shirt. Just a few steps to it,
when they hit him.

. . . Inside, later, a con had asked Pierce what it felt
like to take a load of Magnum double-ought buck. And
Pierce had told him. It was like being kicked there at
his side by a big draft mule. A big mule with steel
needles set into his shoe.

It struck him so hard, Pierce thought his neck was
broken by the impact. And it knocked him flat, Pete
and all.

Pavement was hot against Pierce's face, and he was
just able to get his hand up . . . wave Ed away, see the
Buick head out, chunks getting blown off it as it went.
Head out and away into more sirens down the alley.

Lying there on his belly—Pete stretched out dead a
ways away—Pierce couldn't feel his left side at all.
Figured that was pretty much gone. He heard no more
shots, only footsteps running toward him . . . and he
felt a tremendous anger at the police and at himself,
too. A rage about something . . . He kicked and heaved
and rolled over in blood, and the Smith & Wesson was
in his right hand, the only friend still with him. And
there was a woman police officer coming running—
anxious, he supposed, to be the first to reach him, put
handcuffs on him.

He rolled onto his back—it felt like his left side had
been torn off him—and the .45 came up and leveled
right on her. The policewoman stopped just a few feet
away as if she'd hit a glass wall. Stood staring into the
muzzle of that big revolver.

A stocky brunette with wide hips and a considerable
bosom in her uniform shirt. She had a heavy black

automatic pistol down in her left hand. Had all that equipment on her belt, had that pistol. . . . And she was dead and she knew it.

Pierce saw her mouth in a soft O of fear, brown eyes wide with it. It was just an instant there, in the heat and after all that shooting, other footsteps running to them. It was just her and Pierce, and nobody else in the world.

She looked too scared, too soft to kill.

Pierce said, "Oh, the hell with it. . . ." And put the revolver down gently on the pavement beside him. Hated to scratch and mar the finish on a fine weapon. . . .

"—Mr. Pierce?"

"Yes?"

"It's up around there, past these cabbage palms. I'll leave you there, if you want—then swing around the area . . . be back for you in less than an hour."

"I'd appreciate that. Want to thank you for going to this trouble."

"No need to thank me, Mr. Pierce." She turned right onto the access road—barely wide enough to earn the name. More a track, it looked like, between tall clumps of spiky green growth with needle tips, and another plant with fleshy fat light-green leaves that looked like they would bleed. They were crowding the road narrower from both sides, and scraped and thumped along the Jeep's metal as it rolled past.

"We have to bush-hog these every month or two, cut the vegetation back. . . ."

Then she turned a sharp left, and they were clear and onto a small rough pad of graveled asphalt, with not much more than room for the Jeep. There were walls of every different shade of green rising around this little clearing—vines roping up into scrub and trees. Cords and cables and curtains of vine . . .

"This is where . . . ?"

"Yes, Mr. Pierce. They found her right here, in her vehicle."

Straight ahead was the only break, a few yards where the bank had fallen away to mud, and taken trees with it. Through there, Pierce could see a great distance of water flashing bright as broken glass in the sunlight. Here and there, huge cypresses stood up out of it, shaggy with moss.

"That," Ms. Ketlow said, "is where the Scamander flows in, real shallow . . . and two, three miles wide some places. The Scamander River—I don't know where they got that name—and it's drug-running heaven. They caught a probationary ranger one night, doing some signaling with a flashlight right here. Warning somebody the state people were out with airboats, waiting for them."

"Airboats?"

"They're a shallow kind of flat metal boat, with an airplane engine in the back."

"Oh, I've seen those. Saw them in a movie."

"Well, that's what that fool was doing. But nobody could prove anything, so they just fired him and that was that."

"Lot of drugs get run?"

"Just pouring right across this state. —And they like the park because it's so wild with the swamps and shallows and hammocks and gator holes. They love it out there. Come in all the way from the mangroves and Gulf bays in airboats, canoes, dugouts, swamp buggies. You name it. . . ."

"Long as it pays the way it does, folks are going to run it. —I understand your people won't work the trade."

"My people? . . . Mr. Pierce, I'm from Oklahoma— my people are Cherokee. I'm not a Florida Indian."

"Oh, I'm sorry."

"No need to be sorry. Tribes down here are nice people, and you're right, they don't like drugs. Our people have enough trouble with alcohol—we sure don't need any more trouble like that." She put the Jeep in gear, and Pierce climbed out.

"Thanks again, Ms. Ketlow."

"Mrs. —Married Dave Ketlow the day he got his electrical contractor's license, and two years later we came down here from Oklahoma to do hurricane damage repair. See you in less than an hour." She backed the Jeep neatly out, turned on the narrow access, and drove away.

There was no silence when she was gone, only a different sound. Like someone frying bacon, but softer. Pierce thought it might be one of those airboats running past in the distance, but then a sort of veil came drifting out of the green and wrapped itself around him, and it was tiny insects . . . gnats of some kind. They didn't bite, just stayed with him as he walked and looked around this small space of asphalt, so he saw everything through that little cloud of creatures.

Those insects were making some of the sound. Others, back in the green, were adding to it. Insects, or frogs.

Where he stood, looking out through the cleared fall, out to the wide swamp river, was where Lisa must have sat at the wheel of her Jeep. Looking out into early evening and talking with the person she'd given a ride to, as Mrs. Ketlow had sat talking to Pierce.

And that person had climbed over the passenger seat—maybe supposed to be getting a hiking pack out of the back, or some camera equipment. Had climbed into the back . . . turned, still talking, taking a razor or whatever out. —Then gripped a handful of Lisa's hair, yanked her head back hard, reached around and cut her throat.

Then leaned back, back and away to avoid being spattered while Lisa struggled with her death behind the wheel.

"What I'm seeing right now," Pierce said, aloud.

"What I'm seeing now. . . ." What he was seeing now, the space where the mudslide had carried plants down to the river, was what Lisa had seen in sunset light. Listening to the insects singing in the jungle all around. . . . Listening to the person moving to get his gear together in the back.

Then a hand in her hair, and that strong sudden hauling back. And something quick and bright before her eyes.

Pierce went to his knees, then all fours . . . and crawled on the rough pavement, its surface cracked and worn by heat and rain. He crawled in a slow circle looking for any odd and tiny thing that might have been missed . . . looking for traces of dried blood, for any dark stain. He thought for a moment he'd found something, wet a fingertip, and tasted only oil from some parked Jeep. Lisa's or someone else's . . .

He felt if he could only find a trace of her, it would bring them closer. As if then she might be able to murmur some clue to him. Say something, if not right now, then later in a dream.

Pierce crawled through the heat, and saw a thousand tiny plants, so very small, commencing to grow up through fractures in the asphalt. Another few years, there wouldn't be any paving here. Only green.

He got to his feet, and it was difficult, as if he'd suddenly grown old.

He stood still for a long time, then began to walk slowly around the perimeter of the clearing, staring at the ground . . . trailed by the cloud of gnats. He and these little flying bugs went around and around to the singing of other insects, and frogs—and Pierce looked out to the clearing's center several times, as if he might catch sight of that Jeep there, and Lisa sitting at the wheel looking out over the Scamander River. . . . As if he might catch a sight, out of the corner of his eye, of the Sweetwater just behind her.

". . . You okay?" Mrs. Ketlow driving in off the access road.

"Fine."

"Well, hop in. I'm late on rounds."

Pierce climbed into the Jeep, and as she backed and swung around to the access, took a last look behind him at the clearing.

"Well, I guess you needed to see the place. I didn't find her, thank God." Mrs. Ketlow slowed as a clump of the sharp-pointed leaves from whatever bush scraped and sprung along the Jeep's side. She had to lean away from them. "—Chester Budyear found her, just doing regular rounds. And I don't think he's over it yet."

"Lisa must have given somebody a lift, too."

". . . Yes, I guess she must have. She had Wednesday evening, and that's a slow shift. We do that sometimes, if it's slow—take people out to special areas for bird-watching, take hikers back to their cars—things like that. Not supposed to, officially."

"She did a favor. . . ."

"I guess."

"Mrs. Ketlow, I'm supposed to meet somebody. Could you tell me where the main picnic area is?"

"You leave headquarters. Take a right—the way we went—and stay on the main park road for about half a mile. You'll see a sign on the left—'Second Campground. Picnic and Recreation.' "

"Okay. . . . And thank you for taking me out there."

"Better world, Mr. Pierce, you wouldn't have anything to thank me for."

Chapter 13

The Palms apparently was the jewel in the crown of Palmetto Lake retirement homes. Naomi had rented a maroon Mercury convertible—what the hell, why not?—and was glad she had when she pulled up the drive to what looked like a two-story coconut cake with light-blue icing and a columned entrance.

They even had a doorman—elderly and black, in a gray coat with epaulets. He let her leave the car in the drive—a maroon convertible was all right for the drive.

"I'm up from Miami to see my aunt."

"Are you? *Are* you?" Big smile. The ladies must love this old guy. "And who is the darling?"

"Mrs. Keith. Jackie Keith."

"Oh, that sweetheart. She's goin' to be so *pleased*!"

Naomi began to pity the man, having to butt-kiss rich elderly white ladies. —And one that wasn't even a lady. . . .

The doorman passed her through into a long lobby with a small fountain at the back, a woman behind a desk up front. More businesslike at the desk. No "darlings" or "sweethearts."

"Mrs. Keith is having her massage. She's scheduled for that and she should be having it now. But if you'll wait, Ms. . . . ?"

"Naomi Cohen. I'm one of her nieces, from Miami."

"If you'll wait—if you'd like to sit over in our lounge, at the fountain? I'll call upstairs."

"Thank you. . . ."

. . . Jackie came across the lobby twenty-five minutes later, large, tall, and palely wrinkled. She wore pink plastic-rimmed glasses and a light-green slacks suit. "Oh, for God's *sake*. What a surprise!"

"It's been a while, Jackie." Naomi rose out of a too-soft sofa in pale powder blue, gave Jackie the slightest hug, and kissed her cheek. Jackie looked eroded, old for only five years gone by.

"Pretty grim, hmm?"

"No, Jackie, you look great. Very distinguished. Some handsome, icy old duchess."

"Bullshit. I'm a wreck. Don't let anybody tell you estrogen keeps you young. Only for that—and for absolutely no other reason—I occasionally miss my balls, because do you know the latest? You've heard the latest. The latest is it's fucking testosterone that keeps you young. . . . Who *knew*?"

"Well, this place looks wonderful. . . . And you have a doorman."

"We have a doorman for three hours in the afternoon—usual visiting time—then William goes back to changing lightbulbs."

"And Jackie, I meant it when I said you look good. Very elegant, *soignée*."

Jackie sat down, with elderly care, in the sofa's companion chair. "Well, I dress carefully. That, at least, I have some control over. The face and the body are the problems—as I see you are beginning to discover. No longer the Princess of the Desert, are we?"

Jack Keith had had his operations too late. He'd changed, but been frozen with his change not quite complete. Naomi remembered very clearly being held down on a bed by Tom Oppert, and then being beaten by Jack, who was using a wire hanger that had been heated on his apartment stove.

She looked into this old lady's face, a little shriveled beneath a neat silver-blue hairdo, and found only an outline of the man she'd known—then already well past middle age, but still a prime pimp and owner of two outcall services.

A very intelligent man. Violent, handsome in an old-fashioned lean good-profile way, and very hot for cock. Liked a girl with them too, to keep the other man interested.

He'd beaten Naomi for making separate arrangements—separate arrangements with two clients, and no payments made to Lila-Lee Companions, or to Close Encounters either. They'd discussed the situation first, and Jack had said he quite understood an intelligent girl was bound to branch out. He'd added that intelligence was always reinforced by the experience of logical consequence, and had Tom hold her down while he went to heat the coat hanger.

"—And what, what in the world brings you up out of Miami? Surely not an urge to visit an old friend?"

"Oh, I'm on a job."

"Naomi, I hope it won't hurt you if I say that you're getting a little too old for the Life. Unless . . . migrant camps?"

"I know I'm getting too old—and this is a legitimate job, or nearly."

"Oh, sure. Some nice guy . . . ?"

"Money, Jackie—the rest of us haven't pimped a fortune."

"You watch your mouth. I'm old enough to be your goddam mother."

"And the old ladies—the *other* old ladies here—they don't know?"

"They know me as a sharp-tongued and amusing woman, healthily elderly, who has deliberately estranged her talented and successful children and so is never bothered by them. The women here envy me for not having to do the Sweet Granny bit."

"God, Jack—Jackie."

"And let me tell you something else: after all . . . after all I went through, the grief which one or two very selfish and cruel young men caused me—and I'm not even talking about the surgery, *surgeries*—let me tell you something that may surprise you, and has pleasantly surprised me. I absolutely love it here." A pause, while she smiled, nodded agreement with herself. "—I love it. It's beautiful, it's quiet, it's calm. It's expensive, but beautiful, quiet, and calm. And here I can be the woman I've always wanted to be—but without the boyfriends and the arguments and the fucking and the abuse and the heartbreak. None of that. Just a woman among women, affection, and respect."

"Wonderful."

"Believe it. I've found the secrets of happiness—and they are, in order, money, no balls, a healthy old age, and a fabulous hair-person. Mrs. Rickart—fabulous. In fact, you ought to let her do you. That hair belongs on the stroll on Eighth Street."

"Thank you."

"You were never able to make the most of yourself, Naomi. And now it's too late."

"Thank you. I'm so glad I came over."

"You came over because you want something. You're such a softie—you always were a tough-talking softie. You can't hustle me, honey. Tell me what you're after."

"You were damn glad to have this softie holding your hand at Mount Sinai."

"That was my surgeries, and long ago. I was sick and in pain and that wasn't the real Jackie. This is the real Jackie, so what do you want from me?"

"How many women live at The Palms?"

"Including me, in the whole complex, one hundred and twenty-seven. Moneyed crones and hags and a few great gals. —Almost all being wished to death by middle-aged sons and daughters that are sick of them. . . . There is such a thing as staying too long at the party."

"They talk? They gossip?"

"Only constantly, of course. Why?"

"And they know this area . . . know the people in the county?"

"They *are* this area, Naomi. The people in Palmetto County are their people—or work for their people: sons, daughters, sons-in-law, daughters-in-law, grand-children, nieces, nephews, old friends, old enemies. Why do you ask?"

Naomi searched in her purse, found the list she'd written on Tyler's notebook paper, and handed it over. "Those names, they're all girls . . . young women. . . ."

Jackie took the note, lifted her bifocals slightly to center the reading prescription. "Um-hmmm. Yes, they are . . . and I remember these names. These girls are all dead."

"The Sweetwater killed them."

"Busy bee."

"I'd like to know what the women here have to say about these dead girls—whether they knew any of them or have heard anything about them. Heard any-thing at all."

"Ooooh . . . smart! Smarter than the local cops have been. The Palms is Information Central—for sure members of our little community have known, or known about, some of these goners. Really, very smart to check in with them." Jackie, finished reading, adjusted her glasses. "—But what the hell is it to you?"

"It's part of my job."

"Your job?"

"I'm working for a man who's looking for the Sweetwater. The Sweetwater killed his daughter."

"Ah, a great light dawns. A man. What a sap you are, Naomi."

"I'm being well paid."

"Well paid? To stick your nose in a maniac's business?"

"I'm not going to be that involved."

"Sure. . . . All right, then tell me this: what's in it for

me? Talk to me about money, Naomi. Do you know how expensive this place is? I'm in my seventies; do you know how expensive it will be to stay here another ten or fifteen years? Hmm?"

"If you come up with something, I'll . . . he'll pay you for it."

"Oh? Do we have a rich man, here? Of a certain age? And does he know what you've been doing in Miami the last couple of decades?"

"He's not interested."

"Sensible man. —Now, how do I know I'll get paid?"

"You have my word you'll get paid."

"That means bupkis. It's not your money."

"Jackie, he's not a square john. He's . . . he's a retired bank robber."

Laughing, Jackie looked suddenly younger.

"—So if he owes," Naomi said, "he'll pay."

Jackie laughed a little longer. ". . . Oh, that's wonderful." Subsided to chuckles. "I'm glad you came up. That's wonderful." A sigh. "And who does he know that I know?"

"He knows me, Jackie."

"Honey, you're just pussy and you don't count."

"He knows Phil Lombardi, and Rudy."

"God. Old Phil's still alive?"

"Yes. And Rudy Notunno."

"And Notunno said he was okay?"

"Yes."

". . . Well, I will want—is he good for twenty?"

"He'll give you ten, Jackie."

"Fifteen."

"Ten."

". . . All right. I will want ten long for anything—*anything* germane I come up with, Naomi."

"All right."

"We have a deal—your responsibility?"

"We have a deal."

"Done. If there's anything here, I should start collecting it pretty fast, in a day or two. —And your having held my hand in Mount Sinai or not, if you fuck me over, Naomi, I'll rise out of my satin-upholstered coffin and come looking for my money."

Sergeant Burney, in brown slacks and light-brown sports jacket, was sitting, restless, at a long cypress-wood table at the edge of the picnic ground. Must have been waiting for a while. A newspaper was folded on the table in front of him. When he glanced up and saw Pierce walking across the grass, he looked impatient, a detective with other, more important things to do.

He seemed to have recovered his cophood.

It could almost have been a setup, but Pierce had driven the circuit of roads in and out of the recreation and camping area. There'd been a lot of people— tourists, and a couple of rangers. But no cops trying to look like tourists. Nobody too busy doing nothing.

"You're late."

"Yes, and I apologize," Pierce said. "Do you forgive me?"

Burney's tan darkened a little. "And this is an insecure place to meet."

"You want your money, Burney, you better show me something for it."

Burney reached for the newspaper, and Pierce saw it was folded too flat to cover a pistol. Burney pushed it across the table. "And that's it. That's all I could get and that's all I'll be able to get. And I could be in deep shit just doing that."

Pierce pulled the newspaper over, the *Palmetto County Advance*, and unfolded it. Inside, was a softbound report, looked like a professional printing job. The cover was dark blue, and had a seal . . . some official seal embossed on it, and CONFIDENTIAL printed across the top. Whole thing was only about an inch thick.

Burney cleared his throat. "That's the summary—"

"Are you trying to fuck with me?" Pierce forced himself to sit still, not reach across the table for this man.

"No. No, that's *it*. That's the last report out of the task force. That's what went right to the governor. That report right there."

"Where are the goddam *working* papers?"

"Now, come on. Come *on*. They're all over the place—every squad, every . . . the state people and the federals. The sheriff has the department's stuff in his secretary's office. You expect me to go in there? Come *on*. . . ."

Pierce left the report where it was, and stood up.

"Hey, *hey*. Listen, Pierce, that's everything we got right there! You think we had something, we wouldn't tell the governor? That's it. . . . 'Working papers,' that's a laugh. There's no leads, there's nothing solid on any of those homicides. We've got crime-scene reports, license-plate write-ups, family interviews—a million bullshit phone-in leads from nuts all over the country . . . and interrogations on every bum that came down the coast and got busted for anything the last four, five years. —Come on . . . come on, now. This is all we've *got*. If we had some more, we'd at least have a possible perp indicted."

Pierce sat down.

"—And if we had heavy leads, if we had serious information, we'd have the fucker who did it!"

"Why should I pay you for nothing, Burney?"

"You agreed. That was the agreement—you pay for what we have."

"Pay for nothing?"

". . . Well, maybe this'll tell you who he *isn't*. Maybe our people've been working on it too long."

"Pay you to find out who he isn't. . . ."

"I did what I could, and you said you'd pay me. That's what you said; that was our deal."

Pierce sat and looked at him.

"—And . . . and if I find out anything new has come up, you let me know where I can reach you and you have that information for free. That's a guarantee; I'll check around again. We want to see this guy caught, just like you do."

"Not like I do," Pierce said, and sat watching Burney a little while longer. Burney looked down at the table's dark-gray wood, pursed his lips and made a faint ticking sound with his tongue, waiting. He'd shaved very neatly around his mustache.

Pierce picked up the report and took a thick brown envelope out of his back pants pocket. He slid it across the cypress table. "I'll call you, Burney. *Tomorrow.* And when I do, you better have asked around, you better have more than this official horseshit to tell me. You don't, I'll take it as a personal thing." He stood up.

"You got it. Whatever I can dig up; you've got it. Don't worry about that. . . ."

Pierce walked away . . . and could tell Burney was still watching him. Walked away feeling bad about this . . . the meeting, the talking they'd done. He had the report, and there might be something in it—and he'd paid and the cop had taken. But talking with the man had gone wrong, there'd been a wrong tone to it, like listening to a bad song.

Burney hadn't been afraid of him.

"The old ladies weren't a bad idea."

"I hope so, Tyler. We'll see. —And you can go over to Palmetto Lake sometime, and meet Jackie. She'd like you."

"What's funny?"

"Nothing."

"Naomi, pass me the ketchup."

"Ketchup on spaghetti?"

"Ketchup on this spaghetti."

They were having dinner at the Gondola, in downtown Manchineel. Very classy and going to cost a fortune, with paintings of Italy across the walls. Bridges. Not bridges—aqueducts . . . This Jackie Keith had recommended it to Naomi, and here they were. There were no tomatoes in the spaghetti sauce at all. Just oil and pieces of garlic. Garlic on the bread, too.

"It's good for you, Tyler." Naomi, after his first bite.

"If it doesn't taste good, it isn't good."

"Well, an acquired taste . . ."

"I'm not going to acquire this taste."

". . . I know you're disappointed with the report, and your crooked cop."

"I suppose I am."

There was an olive-and-salami dish that wasn't bad, and an okay salad. Pierce had asked for French dressing, and the waiter had given him a look.

"Jackie's asking for a lot of money, Tyler."

"You told me—and she can have it if she gets something for us. But give me a day; I put the heavy cash into a safe deposit box, under Gil Boyce. Barnett Bank, on the strip. And they charge plenty for those boxes."

"So tell me—what bothered you about the sergeant?"

"What bothered me was, he wasn't bothered."

"Maybe it was a setup?"

"No setup, no stakeout people. And if he had told his department, he wouldn't be able to keep the money."

Naomi was eating her spaghetti in a strange way. She was winding it around and around her fork, holding it against a soup spoon so it wouldn't fall off . . . then sticking that whole thing in her mouth.

"What's the matter?"

"Nothing."

"Tyler, the whole world does not use a knife to cut up their spaghetti in little pieces before they eat it."

"I didn't say they did."

"You know, it's possible Burney just decided you weren't a killer—that you wouldn't have shot him after all."

"Then he's a fool."

Naomi was winding up another forkful. "Could be. . . . And there's nothing useful at all in that report?"

"Oh, I read that damn thing one end to the other—and what's in there is a lot of excuses, mainly. How come this boyfriend and that boyfriend couldn't have done any of them. How there were no connected motives. No opportunities. Pages of transcripts of talking to those boyfriends."

"Lisa's boyfriend?"

"Oh, Jason's in there." Pierce drank some wine. The wine was pretty good. "—And he was over at the beach in his store the evening it happened. A calm boy, no crying from him on those tapes. . . . You know what they say on the transcripts where some of those men cried? They say, 'Subject wept.'—And they don't have detailed autopsy reports in there, either."

Pierce had some more wine.

"That's all right, Tyler. Don't worry about the autopsies. You don't have to see everything."

"Yes, I do. . . . They have a lot of maps in there, have some graphs. They have a psychiatric profile of the Sweetwater from the FBI, sounded just like any member of Congress."

"Pictures?"

". . . Yes."

"I'm sorry, Tyler."

"You don't have to be sorry."

"Well, I am. You let *me* look at that fucking report. Give it to me tonight, and I'll go over it for you page by page. With so much, there's got to be something we can use."

"Well, Burney did say it would eliminate a lot of possibilities, and I guess it does. I guess that was worth the money. And he's still supposed to be asking around. I'll give him a call, tomorrow. . . ."

"Don't be discouraged." Naomi did another one of those wound-up spaghetti bites.

"I'm not. I'm not discouraged at all. I've got years for this, and I'll never let it go."

"It would make a sad life for you, Tyler."

"You're wrong. This is the best thing I've ever done. —I can't understand why they couldn't put tomatoes in that sauce."

"Italians eat it this way lots of times."

"They were raised to it. I wasn't."

Pierce had read in bed before he slept. Read carefully through the picture pamphlets from Manchineel State Park. One had photographs of all the plants and trees—orchids, black mangrove and red mangrove, cypress, gumbo-limbo, black cypress, oak, sweet gum, and pages of others, cabbage palms, pines, and lots of little shrubs and flowers. The animal pamphlet was mainly birds, egrets, herons, mostly wading birds . . . and then the alligators, snakes—rattlers and moccasins and corals and so forth. Only thing they didn't have was crocodiles. Crocodiles were down south in the Keys. Insects, though. Place apparently was insect heaven. Mosquitoes.

Pierce had read through the pamphlets carefully, then put them aside and slept. He was worried he'd have a bad dream about Lisa, but he didn't.

He dreamed he was walking through walls of green leaves, and never coming clear enough to see the country. The leaves were vined together like hanging curtains, with still more curtains behind those. All green, the color certain even in his dream. . . . He walked though, and felt the leaves as he put his hands into them, drew them aside to another curtain of green. It didn't disturb him. He felt he had time to walk through them all, and was troubled to be waking to the ringing of the phone.

"Mr. Boyce—we don't usually put calls through after midnight. Just . . . would you please let your party know—"

"Okay," Pierce said. "—Okay." And heard the connection.

"—Tyler? *Tyler*?" Naomi, her voice pitched high. "It's Naomi, and somebody's been in my room and went through everything!"

"The report?"

"I've got it. I've still got it. I couldn't sleep, so I went out and walked down the strip for coffee. I took it with me to read it, and when I got back my door was open."

"Whoever it was, was watching—saw you go, and took the opportunity. Where are you phoning from?"

"Outside the motel office. I'm in a pay phone on the street."

"You stay right there where people can see you. Don't go back to your room! You understand me? Stay where you are, and I'll be right over."

Pants, shoes, shirt, gun, and wallet, and Pierce was out the room door and into the gray Nissan rental. The Motel 6 was almost a mile up the highway. . . .

". . . I was scared to death. I always thought I was tough, but just a messed-up motel room scared the shit out of me!"

"You're okay, Naomi. Come out of the phone booth. Come on—go and sit in the car."

Naomi came out of the booth. "I'm all right. And I apologize for the panic call."

"I know you're all right, honey. Get in the car and wait. I'll be back in a minute."

Pierce went trotting up the dark motel drive and then along the line to room 17, the room numbers hard to make out between shadow and dim lighting. Most of the rooms were dark, people asleep despite the highway noise. . . . But he could see the door to 17 was open. Naomi had lit out and left it that way. Or someone, once she'd run, had left it that way.

Somebody'd seen her go . . . then broke in. Or somebody had gone in and not cared if she was there, maybe had wanted her to be there. —Or had done it only to bring Pierce trotting along, bring him out where he could be got to. . . .

Pierce drew the Smith & Wesson from under his shirt, then slowed . . . walked toward that open door. But paid more attention to the cars parked angled up and down the row. Paid more attention to those cars, and to shadows. Watched them, and saw nothing there.

There was a soft thump thump thump of thunder. East, from the sea.

Room 17 was dark past the open door. There was no use staying out in the light. Pierce slid inside, pistol first, and kept moving through dimness to the dresser. Before he reached it, he knew the room was empty; the pressure of another person was missing. Maybe in the bathroom; not here.

And there might have been a slight smell remaining . . . a man's odor. Very slight thing, but could be there over the sweet smell of woman and perfume Naomi had left. Pierce stood in the dark awhile, he and the Smith & Wesson patient together. Then he checked the bathroom.

". . . I think I better go back to Miami." Naomi was wandering around her motel room, picking things up then putting them down. She was supposed to be packing. —The room had been turned all the way. The dresser drawers were out and stacked upside down, bed linens stripped. Bedside table and its drawer both upside down. Curtains taken from the track above the window and spread out on the floor. The carpeting had been pulled loose and turned up a few inches away from the wall all around the room. The wall mirror was down. The black plastic casing had been taken off the phone.

The bathroom, a smaller space, had been done the same. But nothing broken in either room. Nothing

dirtied or torn. And nothing missing. It troubled Pierce
the man had been so careful. Courteous, in a way.

"I guess your crooked cop wanted that report back,
Tyler."

"Maybe." Pierce was sitting on the bed, watching
Naomi wander. The small room was bright, all lights
on and blinds down.

"The motel people must have told him we came in
together."

"Could be. And they wouldn't find a Tyler Pierce
registered on the strip at all, now. So they went back a
night here, and that gave them you. Motel people pretty
much have to tell cops anything they want to know."
Pierce saw Naomi put the first thing away in her suitcase. Looked like a pair of blue pants . . . slacks. She'd
folded them very neatly. "Careless to be doing that, us
coming to register together that way. I blame myself."

"Before, you said 'Maybe.' 'Maybe' it was your
crooked cop."

"I'm just surprised, that's all. I wouldn't think Burney'd be so neat; I'd've thought he'd make a mess. He
didn't like me—and no reason for him to like you."

"Neat or messy, I suppose it's back to Miami for
Naomi."

"No, I wouldn't do that. I wouldn't go back down to
your place right away."

"Why not? Seems like a really great idea to me,
Tyler." Into packing, now. Suitcase filling up. Seemed
to Pierce she'd brought stuff she'd never need in a million years.

"Why not? Well, Naomi, he knows you. —Or who-
ever it was knows you. The cop, or someone from
Chetwin, or that little forger. Or maybe your friend
Jackie. No big deal to get your home address."

"How? *How?* I had my purse with me."

"Have any prescription drugs in the bathroom
cabinet?"

"Only my . . . Primarin."

"Doctor's name? Your name? Prescription number?"

"Shit . . ." Slowed her up on the packing.

"Your friend Jackie—you said she'd been bad. You go see her, you ask her to ask some questions, and the next thing you know somebody's turning your room—maybe would have turned you, you hadn't gone out for late coffee."

"Jackie wouldn't do that, tell somebody about us."

"No?"

". . . I suppose she might, for money."

"Um-hmm. . . . Well, it was probably Burney, looking to get the report back. Then he'd still have my money, but I wouldn't have that report and he'd be home free. —Except maybe for dealing with me." Saying so, Pierce recalled the sergeant hadn't seemed worried about that, out at the park. "—Probably was Burney, but you don't want to be going home just yet, Naomi. You don't want a visitor to come see you down there when you're alone."

"Then stay *here*? I'm not going to stay here!" Putting little jars and bottles in a small zipper bag with flowers on it.

"No. We'll find you someplace else. Someplace a little more private, a little safer than this."

"A lot safer, if you don't mind." Small zipper bag went into the suitcase.

"Well . . . would you be interested in bunking with my ex-wife?"

"Your ex-wife?"

"Margaret and her husband, over in Palmetto Lake."

"Tyler, I'll tell you . . . I haven't met Margaret, but I have a feeling we wouldn't get along."

"Right about that. . . . You two sure wouldn't get along."

"Then if you don't mind, let's skip Margaret."

"Okay. We'll find a place for you; don't be worried about it, Naomi."

"What about my rental car, my convertible?"

"Leave it here. I'll return it."

"I'm not going to have a car?"

"Naomi, you can use the Nissan. My truck's supposed to be ready tomorrow."

Naomi put a pair of shoes in a cloth bag, tucked them into a corner of her suitcase. "And all this—this break-in, this room-searching—it doesn't scare you, Tyler? Oh, pardon me, I know it doesn't *scare* you. I mean, does it concern you?"

"It concerns me. . . ."

They were out and cruising through almost no traffic down nighttime blocks, when the rain came.

Pierce had never seen anything like it. It came with a sudden shoving wind against the right side of the car, and then a pouring flood, so the Nissan staggered and its tires skidded and spun a moment in the wash.

Pierce couldn't see through water running down the windshield in sheet on sheet and he braked and skidded again. "Holy cow!"

"Did you really just say 'Holy cow'?" Naomi said, apparently feeling better—and was answered by a crack and white blaze of lightning that lit them like flashbulbs . . . and then thunder that hurt Pierce's ears. The car seemed to jump to that sound, and Naomi was saying something more but he couldn't hear her.

He looked at her in another lightning stroke and saw her lips saying *Pull over*. He drove blind to the right, saw the highway curb in another sizzling flash of white, steered over and along it, and stopped with a narrow swift stream of water already foaming along the gutter past the Nissan's wheels.

"Told you so," Naomi said. Thunder came again, and her lips said *Weather*.

Chapter 14

Pierce lay in cool darkness, listening to the rain. The rain came blowing in, hissing against the room's window, along its walls. Came in like waves on the shore, a series of rainstorms ... and then silence except for the building's gutters gurgling, drumming with water. No traffic sounds.

"This is nothing," Naomi'd said, going into the bathroom. "What's something is what's pushing it. A big wind is what's pushing it."

"That rain was big enough for me." Pierce was already in bed in his boxer shorts, under the covers. He'd thought that Naomi—a professional, after all—wouldn't be concerned about sharing his room, but she'd been nervous as a cat.

"I don't want the bed near the window" had been the first thing she'd said when they came in.

"No problem. I'll take that bed."

"But the other bed was yours. We should change the linen."

Pierce had looked at her. "Naomi, it is almost three o'clock in the morning. We're not changing any goddam linen. Go in the bathroom, and then get out here and get to bed."

"Yes, sir!" she'd said, but seemed satisfied. She'd taken things out of her suitcase, made that remark about the storm, then gone into the bathroom and stayed a long time.... She'd come out in yellow pajamas and a green robe, and had done something to her hair. "I trust," she'd said, "there'll be no attempt at romance."

"No hanky and no panky. Go to bed, Naomi. . . ."

And now he lay listening to rain, and a tired woman's soft purring snores. Surprised him, how much he'd missed that sound. How much he missed Carolyn. Even tonight, with this little jolt, this little reminder it was no Florida vacation, it would have been nice to have Carolyn here—if she was in a sort of shark cage or something, if she was safe.

He'd written Carolyn about Naomi on a postcard— about hiring a lady for a guide—and thought Carolyn would like her. She'd think Naomi was funny. . . .

. . . Now take this Jackie Keith. Naomi goes to see her—tells her what's up, promises her money—and just a few hours later Naomi's room gets turned. Turned very neatly, with nothing broken. People had an odd idea about old folks, that they were different inside because they were old. —Anybody had done hard time, met some of those old boys been inside thirty, forty years . . . anybody'd met those old boys knew you had to watch your back with some of them just like you would with any kid, any hard-rock. You watch your back or old dad'd shove a spoon-shank in your kidneys, teach you some manners. So, it could be that Jackie figured where there were a few thousand, there might be the chance at a lot more. And it could be that Jackie had other old friends out of Miami, a lot tougher friends than Naomi.

. . . He'd intended some snappy maneuvers back and forth along the strip to shake anybody following them from Naomi's. But the rainstorm had taken care of that; no one could have seen through it to follow anybody.

Jackie . . . and Mr. Nguyen. And Chetwin. Chetwin and Mr. Nguyen—they knew where Naomi was staying, where Pierce had been staying. And they knew the new name—Boyce. But Chetwin was a lawyer, and a coward. And the little Vietnamese had struck Pierce as a professional, not likely to step out of his MO. A cautious little man—a grown-up, that gun dealer Mardanian would say.

Mardanian . . . Older man, and seemed settled in his business. Most gun suppliers didn't mix in.

Even so, plenty of people to consider. All of them, except Naomi and Rudy and old Lombardi. Naomi a sweetie, whore or not. And Lombardi and his man were out of it.

Still, plenty of people to consider—and not even touching the Sweetwater yet. But no matter what a man is looking for, the deeper he digs the more dirt he turns.

The rain, the rain was coming in again. Brought a salt smell with it from the sea. . . .

Naomi'd given up fighting for fancy breakfasts. She was having an Egg McMuffin and a buttered biscuit on the side, hash browns, and coffee. She was dressed plainer than usual, it seemed to Pierce. Blue jeans and a white puffy-sleeve blouse. Naomi looked better, dressed that way, like a handsome skinny country-woman—except for her hands, and her hair, and that bright-red nail polish that she'd put right back on after taking it off.

"Thing we need to do," Pierce said, "is rent you a room in somebody's house. Somebody doesn't keep daily check-in records for everybody to see."

"I guess that's a good idea."

"Too bad you and Margaret wouldn't get along."

"Tyler, I thought we settled that. Spare me."

"Probably be sparing both of you." Pierce was having one sausage-and-egg biscuit. Had used to have two or three of them for a breakfast and not think a thing about it. "—So we'll rent you a room for a week or two. And when this all settles out, you can go on home."

" 'Settles out'?"

"Any matter like this, I don't think it'll last

long—considering somebody's already sticking his nose in what's none of his business."

"And the Sweetwater?"

"Oh, that part could last a good long time. I meant . . . all this interfering. This Burney, or whoever."

"Tyler, if your Lisa were sitting here, eating this . . . this God-help-me breakfast, I know what she'd say. I *know* what she'd say. She'd say get your middle-aged butt back up to Missouri."

"I don't doubt that's what she'd say."

"And you wouldn't pay attention. You'd just go on with this."

"You bet."

"Oh, for Christ's sake. . . . Tyler, just finish your breakfast and we'll go look for a room for me."

"We'll stop and check on my truck, first. —Try some of that apple jelly on your biscuit. Except for Kentucky Colonel's, this is the best not-homemade biscuit you can get."

"Oh, please. . . ."

"It was supposed to be ready today." Warm rain, almost hot, had spattered their rental, coming to the garage . . . then had spattered Pierce as he got out to hear this car guy's crap.

Ronald Fiala nodded, very agreeable, comfortable in the noise and odors of his garage, his shop. "It *is* ready. You could take it out right now. It's ready, but the paint's still tender. Take it out in the sun now—or this rain—and it could cloud. Really needs another twenty-four hours, slow drying. This is special paint."

"Special paint."

"That's right."

". . . And I didn't ask for a racing stripe."

"That's not extra, Mr. Boyce. Stripe's not going to cost you a thing."

"Yellow."

"That's right. Complements that British racing green."

"Big yellow racing stripe on a Ford 250 truck?"

"Why not?" Fiala appeared surprised at the question.

It seemed to Pierce that his truck didn't look like his truck anymore. Looked like some rich boy's quail truck, but bigger.

"—And have you seen better bodywork than that, Mr. Boyce? Touch of filler and *only* a touch of filler."

"No. That's fine." And the bodywork was good; no sign of that sideswipe left. "Twenty-four hours?"

"If you want this fine paint to last. We got two undercoats buffed and sanded, and two finish coats sanded and buffed. You tell me if you want to ruin this paint. —And we got weather coming in. Coming in right now."

"All right. Twenty-four hours . . ."

It had seemed better to Pierce to look for a place miles away from Manchineel or Palmetto Lake. And they'd found notice of a Fort Talavera room for rent—at 407 Buttonwood Lane—tacked up on a supermarket's business-card and for-rent board, past the checkout. They'd gone in so Pierce could get another pack of Backwoods cigars.

"What are you doing with those things—eating them? You just bought some."

"Like to have 'em on hand."

"They're your lungs, Tyler. I'm not going to say anything more about it."

"Um-hmm."

They'd left the market, gone several miles, and turned onto the highway east to the coast when Tyler found something troubling him. Couldn't think what it might be. . . .

They drove down the road and out from under the rain into strange late-morning light. It was a spotted light—sunshine, then cloud shadow—first one, then the other, so it wasn't restful. The day was coming as hot as the day before, a heavy still heat. It was no cooler when the cloud shadows passed over; the Nissan's air conditioner had its work cut out.

But it wasn't the wearisome weather troubling Pierce. He'd glanced into the rearview mirror when he changed lanes to pass a stakebed truck carrying watermelons. And a gray sedan—Ford, maybe—two cars back, had pulled out to pass just after he did. . . . He'd seen a gray car like that twice before. Once as he came out of the market, and thought nothing of it. And once again, turning onto the highway behind him.

Now was the third time.

"What's the matter?"

"Nothing, Naomi. Bad driver back there, driving all over the road."

"Sounds like somebody I know. . . ."

There was no gray sedan following as they took the Fort Talavera turnoff to Fourth Avenue . . . none in sight when they pulled up to the curb so Naomi could check the map for Buttonwood Lane.

". . . It's on this side of town. Tyler, what was the number?"

"Four-oh-seven."

"Shit, it's south of us. We've been going the wrong way. You really need to start learning these maps—"

"Naomi, that's what I pay you for. But I am going to learn them."

Naomi sighed. "All right. Just . . . just make a U-turn and go back under the overpass and keep going, keep going straight. It's all the way to hell an' gone back there. . . ."

Fourth Avenue cut through a neighborhood of residential blocks—little stucco bungalows with small lawns and low hedges of some green-and-purple plant. Driving past, Pierce saw several people putting heavy shutters up on their houses. Believed in that hurricane coming in. . . .

Buttonwood Lane intersected almost a mile south. "Low-rent district," Naomi said after they made the turn. And as they drove across a second intersection and into the next block on Buttonwood, a gray sedan, a Ford, turned out of that cross street and after them. Not coming fast. Coming slow . . . slower, and dropping back.

It seemed to Tyler that whoever it was had been running parallel to them, one avenue over, then got anxious.

"What is it?"

"Nothing."

"Bullshit . . . Bullshit!" Naomi turned in her seat to look back. "Who is it? Is he following us?"

"Nobody's following us, Naomi." And as Pierce said it, they reached the next intersection and the gray car turned away and was gone. For a moment, Pierce thought of going after it, pulling it over—but he had Naomi with him . . . and there were a lot of gray cars. Too damn many. Too many gray Ford cars for him to be forcing some people over—people maybe not following at all—and putting a pistol on them in the middle of town.

"They were following us."

"No, I don't think they were. They're gone."

"Tyler, please don't shit me. You saw them before. You saw that car before."

"Maybe—but probably not."

"Christ . . . " Naomi's hands were trembling. She clasped them together, held them in her lap.

"Don't be scared. Chances are those people weren't following us . . . had nothing to do with us. Lots of people have to be going the same way we're going."

"I know that. But neither am I stupid, Tyler."

"Whoever, they're gone now. And they have no way of knowing whether we're staying on this street and for how long—or turning off to someplace else."

"We hope."

"I apologize to you for this, Naomi. My fault for letting you get in it at all."

"It is *not* your fault. I wanted to do it, and I needed the money. Besides, it's an adventure. —And if it was anybody, I think it was just that crooked cop, and he's pissed off and following us and the hell with him." She took a deep breath. "—And Tyler, speaking of your cop, let me keep that report he gave you. I saw some things in there. I think there are things in there you missed."

"If you can find anything in that worth a damn, you'll be doing something. It's just excuses every page; that's all it is. What we pay our taxes for is just crap like that and nothing getting done. Government has got too damn big for its britches."

"Well, let me keep it. . . ."

Pierce turned left off Buttonwood onto a street called Surf. He drove almost a mile, watching behind them . . . checking to each side as he passed an intersection. There was no gray sedan.

He took a right onto an avenue—Third Avenue—and the next right after that to go back the direction they'd come.

"Nothing?"

"Nothing," Pierce said, took another right onto Surf, drove two blocks, and pulled over to the curb and parked in front of a small house with a plastic red fox on its lawn. Red fox and three fox kits, life-size in plastic. Pierce sat for a few minutes, watching the street up and down, watching the traffic going through the next intersection.

". . . Either there wasn't anybody, or he's lost us."

"From your lips," Naomi said, "to God's ear."

Pierce started the car, drove up to the intersection, and turned left onto Buttonwood Lane.

"I'll leave this car with you; it's rented under the name of Boyce. Gil Boyce is on the contract.

—I'll pick up another rental here to drive back to Manchineel."

Number 407 Buttonwood was in a block with only a few fat little palm trees on it. Older houses—wood clapboard, not stucco—with more yard alongside them than in front. People on this street showed no plastic birds or animals on their lawns; seemed to favor low chain-link fences to protect their few square feet of green-yellow grass, drifted sand, and sandburs.

The house was a narrow two stories—storm shutters already up—and had a side drive. Pierce pulled into it and drove on through to a one-car garage and paved backyard. He turned in behind the house, out of sight from the street.

"Just being extra-careful," he said, and Naomi gave him a look.

They got out, walked back down the drive, and around to the front door.

Pierce rang . . . and after he'd rung again, they heard someone coming to the door. When it swung open, Naomi took a quick step back and bumped into him.

A man in outsized black trousers and a triple-X white short-sleeved shirt stood in the doorway. He was old, and a giant—inches taller than Pierce, much bigger, and deformed. His jaw shelved out thick as a two-by-four plank . . . all the bones of his face were swollen out of shape, grown heavy, ridged, and wrong. His arms were pale, very long, and lumpy with growths of bone and muscle down to hands twice the size a man's hands should be, the huge fingers splayed and bent like roots. . . . He stooped in his doorway, staring down at them as if they were children in a fairy tale, come to some monster's house.

"Was that you around back?" He had an ordinary voice, not as deep as Pierce had expected.

"We parked back there," Pierce said.

The old man looked at Pierce, then at Naomi. "Never

saw anything like me, did you?" He had narrow blue eyes that seemed to belong in a different face.

"We're here about the room," Naomi said.

"Didn't answer my question."

"Don't think I have seen a fellow like you," Pierce said.

"Rare condition, now." The old man turned and seemed to duck under his hall ceiling. "Come on in back. I'm cooking. . . ."

They followed him down the hall to his kitchen—a long room decorated country-style, with baskets and pictures of yellow chickens on the walls. The old man went to his stove and began stirring in a wok with a long-handled wooden spoon. "Fish and stir-fry vegetables. People eating soft stuff are making a big mistake."

"You hear that, Gil?" Naomi said. "He means fast food."

"Terrible." The giant added some sauce to his pan. "Only reason I'm still here with this condition is I eat right. —Now, you see one of my ads?"

"Yes, we did."

"Front room with kitchenette, ground floor. Suitable for only one person."

"It's for me," Naomi said. "And you're Mr. . . . ?"

"Name's Charlie Montfort. Of course, way back when, the family name was *de* Montfort, for sure. You wouldn't know, probably, but the de Montforts were a very old Norman family." He shook more sauce into the stir-fry. "—Norman barons way back, and that same blood flows in my veins. Charles or Carl or Carolus—of the strong, or fortified, hilltop." He turned from the stove and gave Pierce a careful look. "How tall are you?"

"I guess about six two and a half."

"Well, you're not. You are six-three—and you've been cutting that extra half inch off when you talk to people because you're sensitive about your height. Am I right, or not?"

"Right," Pierce said.

"You're a long drink of water, and I'll bet you're strong. But let me tell you something, son: you're not as strong as I am. I have acromegaly—you know what that means?"

"I know," Naomi said.

"It means I have areas of uncontrolled bone growth, as you can see. Arms, legs, jaw, brow ridges. And where that bone has grown, so the great connections of cartilage and tendon have attached to it. The leverage is terrific." He stirred his fish and vegetables again. "—I'm convinced it's the de Montfort blood. I believe the name was given to the de Montforts because of this hereditary illness, which turned their men huge as hills, and terribly *fort*, which is French for strong."

"I believe it," Pierce said.

"Don't make fun."

"I'm not. I believe it—seems reasonable."

"More than reasonable. If I'd had the sense to get out of plumbing and get an education, I'd write a book proving it." He bent over the wok to smell his cooking, and said, "Oh, boy."

"My name's Naomi Cohen. This is Mr. Boyce."

"Is that *Cohen*—or *Cohan*?"

"Cohen. I'm Jewish."

"Thought so, looking at you. Reason I asked, I'd really prefer not to have Irish in the house. I've known many Irish people, and they're charming but they can't hold their liquor worth a damn. And I should know, since I was married to an Irish lady—Irish-American— for thirty-three years. . . . Now, as I say, it's the front room out there, ground floor, big studio room and a little kitchenette and your own bathroom. I'm gone fishing most of the time, and I'm a widower, anyway—so no woman is going to be minding your business, poking her nose into your room when you go out—which, believe me, Catherine would have done in a minute. Cost you one hundred and twenty-five dollars a week in season."

"And now?"

Mr. Montfort turned down the heat on his stir-fry. "Cost you ninety dollars a week with a ninety-dollar security deposit. Your own key, you come and go as you please, park in the back if you want. You have the first space there by the back door; that's your space. I use the garage."

"Who else do you have renting here?" Pierce said. "My sister's a worrier."

"Your sister? Cohen and Boyce?"

"Half sister," Pierce said. "Mom married again after my dad died. Change for the better, frankly."

"Well, she doesn't have to worry." Mr. Montfort spooned some pieces of vegetable and fish out of the wok onto a white china platter. "—Doesn't have to worry. Life's too short to have trash living in my house. Two other people rent here, upstairs. A couple, and the man's a bank teller. And I don't allow pets or children; I don't give a damn what the government says. Government can kiss my you-know-what, which I'd say if there wasn't a lady present."

"That smells wonderful," Naomi said.

"Seafood stir-fry. I use mackerel, and no other fish whatsoever. —I'd offer you some, but I have a friend coming."

"Oh, we've eaten, anyway. . . . Could I see the room?" Naomi said, and the giant put down his wooden spoon and led them back up the hall to a door on the left, unlocked it, and gestured them in.

Pierce liked it; a big sunny room with a blue convertible couch and little palm plants in pots. It reminded him of his apartment in Dowland, made him miss Richard . . . wonder how the old dog was getting out to the sunflowers to pee.

"It's charming, Mr. Montfort," Naomi said. "I'll take it."

. . . Pierce, having paid out the one-eighty and listened to more sales talk about eating fish, came back to
the room, sat on the blue convertible couch, and
watched Naomi unpack and put things away. Had done
a lot of watching Naomi pack and unpack. Getting to
know just how she did it, every item.

"Naomi, there're not so many ways over here to Fort
Talavera. Not so many streets *in* Fort Talavera.
Chances are that car wasn't following anybody."

"Bullshit, Tyler." Ground that out real rough, putting
her underwear in a dresser drawer.

Pierce saw what he should have seen before. More
scared Naomi was, the tougher she talked. Like a child,
that way. "—Listen, you ever fired a revolver?"

"Yes, I have. I shot at beer cans from Gary
Gustafson's boat many years ago. I did not hit a beer
can."

Pierce reached back under his shirttail—shirt was
the dark-blue one with pineapples—drew the Smith &
Wesson, and put it on the lamp table beside the couch.

"Oh, no. No thanks, Jesse James. I don't like them
and I don't want it." Naomi hung her green bathrobe on
a hook on the inside of the bathroom door.

"Tell you what now, Naomi: you just keep this for
tonight . . . keep it till I come see you. I'll be by
tomorrow or the next day—and if you're out, I'll just
wait."

"I don't want it, Tyler. You keep it."

"I know you don't want it now. But you tell me
this—if that car *was* following us, got a good idea
where we are, where you're going to be. . . . You tell
me this: with that old man gone fishing, if somebody
comes through your window—just curious, got some
questions to ask you and maybe have a little fun—*then*
are you going to want this revolver? You answer me
that."

Naomi had nothing to say. Her suitcase was all
unpacked.

"Okay? . . . Now, I'll come by and get it in a day or two. Meantime, you keep it near, keep it with you when you go out. —All you do, if something bad happens, someone comes against you . . . all you do is grip it hard with both hands, point it at that person's belly button, and pull the trigger back smooth, all the way. You do that—and never mind the noise and all—you keep doing that as long as anybody's standing there scaring you. And pretty soon, they won't be."

Naomi closed the dresser drawer. "Wonderful. — And right now I could be in a cheap hotel room on Miami Beach, giving some nearsighted tourist a blow job. . . . We just don't know when we're well off."

The Angel, full of chili after lunch, lay sleeping in Karen's belly—in it, or around it; she wasn't sure. An easy morning of one saline, one evacuation, had ended with lunch at the Boca Chica on Orange Avenue. A bowl of chili, medium-hot, with chopped onion and shredded cheese sprinkled over it. Chili, two corn tortillas, and a can of Tecate with salt and a slice of lime.

Now, back at work, and laying instruments out on trays in Number Two—their fine steel still hot from the old-fashioned autoclave—it was the Angel who stirred and woke and ran up into Karen's throat like syrup at a voice she only recognized then.

A voice with Fran's, in the office.

Karen walked down the corridor and saw Moira sitting there in loafers, khaki slacks, and a yellow blouse, talking with Fran. And the Angel had known before.

Moira saw Karen in the office doorway, and said, "Hi."

"Hi."

Fran was leafing through her book. "If you have to have today, we could schedule you for two-thirty. . . ."

"Just so I get it over with." Moira looked across the office at Karen. "I'm sorry," she said.

Karen didn't say anything. She felt the Angel

turning slowly inside her, pushing against her in there. . . .

Two patients later, Moira lay surprisingly small on the table in Number One. In the dressing room, Karen had seen her pregnancy only in the slightest softness and shining china-white of her belly, the darkness and size of the areolas. Her body otherwise was almost adolescent for a woman five years from forty. Her arms and legs slender, muscular as a twelve-year-old tomboy's. She'd had a rapid pulse, somewhat elevated blood pressure, but all within parameters.

Moira had said, "I guess now you know what kind of person I am."

"Your decision, sweetheart." Karen had taken the plastic wrap off a blue paper gown, shaken it out, and held it for her.

"Right. That's right," Moira'd said. "But I know what you think."

Now she lay prepped and scrubbed, knees up and spread wide, feet—in white cotton clinic socks—tucked into steel stirrups. Karen held her hand.

"How're we doing?" Torguson, in from an afternoon meeting at the bank—Dr. Bessler taking some patients for him—had been a little late scrubbing. He glanced at the chart. "How're we doing, Moira?" Torguson was a big man, bulky, with a broad tanned face and milky blue eyes.

"Okay."

"Okay!" He looked over the chart more carefully. "You seem to be in very good health, Moira, a healthy woman. I don't see any reason for any concern whatsoever."

"Good . . ."

"Now first, we're going to give you a little sedative—"

"Administered, Doctor."

"We've already *given* you a little sedative. —Thank you, nurse. And pretty soon, this will all be over and done with." He leaned down so that Moira could see his face, see he was smiling. Torguson never presented himself first to a patient wearing his mask. He was a good surgeon—or was supposed to have been, in his previous practice—and was gentle, considerate of the patients as if they'd held carefully to term, and had come to the clinic to have their babies.

"We're going to go in and give you some dilation, first—open the entrance to your cervix just a little. That'll take some time, hour or two, but don't worry, we won't forget you. And a couple of times you'll feel stings when we deaden that area as we go on with the procedure. —Okay?"

". . . Okay."

"Then, when you're ready, we'll finish the procedure and you'll rest for a little while in our recovery room. Then you'll be on your way, and that'll be it!"

"Thank you, Doctor."

"Don't thank me. I thank you, for being such a good patient. . . ."

The Angel poured down into Karen's hand, and Moira murmured at that change in grip before Karen let go to assist. . . . Then, when the cervix mouth was injected and packed, the doctor gone to the clinic office, the Angel stayed to watch over Moira and wait with her for a while. . . . Moira dozed and woke, and dozed again, riding the sedative. If her eyes had not been closed . . . if she had opened them for only a moment, she would have seen the radiance the Sun allowed its daughter.

Almost an hour and a half later, Torguson came back and sat on his small stool. He opened Moira's vagina and looked into her for dilation, pulled out the packing and dilator, and found enough. He held his right hand out as if for a gift, and Karen laid the long curette—a number-seven Ostholm with a small slightly hooked blade—in it. When that went up into her, Moira made a sound. And when the doctor began to scrape down the uterine wall, Moira groaned and said oh, oh,

SACRIFICE 241

oh, as if he were having sex with her, as if that were
what he was doing with the steel.

She made those sounds, and several drops of blood
ran down from the blade. They spiraled along the
narrow instrument out of her vagina, and spattered
between her legs, just a little. Moira said God and tried
to lift herself away from the blade, but Karen put her
hand on Moira gently, and held her still.

"Shhh," Karen said. "Almost done."

Torguson scraped . . . and scraped a little more.
Then slid the Ostholm out and blood and tissue came
with it.

"Ringner."

And Karen put it in his hand as he said it. The Ringner
was tipped with a small half-round scoop, like an ice-
cream scoop but much smaller. When this went into her,
Moira made her sounds again, but louder. And with this
instrument, the Ringner, Torguson was slower, more
deliberate. He took his time . . . and turned and turned
his strong wrist this way, then that way.

"Okay," he said, and sounded pleased. He gently
withdrew the instrument, and Moira's twelve-week
daughter came out in a little knot of blood. More blood
and tissue came out after her. Moira's little girl came
out the size of the Angel's thumb, and was put in a pan.

Chapter 15

In Fort Talavera, Pierce had taken a cab to Sunstate Rental and driven out a black Dodge Dart. No problem with the Boyce ID. The car was all right, but its air conditioner just wasn't up to the weather. Wet heat. Heat that made it hard to breathe—and the air conditioner not making much difference.

Naomi, still nervous, hadn't wanted him to leave, kept trying to start some argument so he'd stay a little longer. Then Montfort had come up the hall like Frankenstein's monster, asked her to feed his outdoor cat while he was gone fishing, and Pierce had left while they were talking cat chow. The cat was old and had weak kidneys—couldn't eat much protein. . . .

Down along the sea after an Arby's lunch—Pierce had taken a wrong turn, a left to downtown instead of a right to head west—he saw a bank of phones along the esplanade, and pulled in to park.

He called the sheriff's office and asked for the detectives. The police operator, a man, switched the call, and there was a trace pause . . . maybe ten seconds. Pierce had heard more and more law enforcement was doing that—setting up automatic trace systems they could follow up or not.

He waited the ten seconds listening to Hawaiian music, and then a detective came on—Lieutenant Pittle, Pickle, something like that. Burney was out of the office; due back in maybe half an hour. Pierce thanked the detective and said he'd call back, that it was just a personal call anyway.

He got back in the Dodge Dart and drove a way up the beach walk to a different set of phones. It was too soon to call again, so he put fifty cents in the parking meter, locked the car, and walked down red brick steps to the beach. It was very pretty, a very pretty situation with the low clouds all blown over, and the sun out now—a strange sun, hot, swollen, and red as infection. Only a few high clouds, long clouds streaming . . . and the beach a bright, bright reddish gold, curving away as far as he could see.

The ocean's complicated roaring noise . . . Pretty loud, too. Seemed to Pierce those were big waves coming in, and he didn't see many people going swimming. There were a lot of people on the beach, but not going into the ocean.

He took his shoes and socks off at the steps, then walked down the beach through hot sand—hurt your feet, it was so hot. He supposed he looked all right for the beach in his pineapple shirt and slacks. Clothes seemed pretty Florida to him. . . .

There was an odd light along the beach—maybe reflected up off the sand. A yellowish light and really fierce. The heat and the light were just . . . like one thing, and you went wading in it. Pierce thought maybe Naomi had been right, and he should have bought a straw hat . . . baseball cap or something, heat was that bad. But no saying this wasn't beautiful. Carolyn would love it down here.

The ocean. The ocean; name for it sounded like what it did, rolling in, hissing in. The *ocean*. . . . Wind coming off it, good hard breeze coming off it out of a blue-white sky. Could be the storm coming in, that pushed that rain in front of it. . . .

Pierce walked down to the sea and stood where the surf just ran up, so the water raced and foamed around his ankles . . . wet his trouser cuffs. Being there at the

sea, with the wind coming in and it being so hot, the
sun stinging his skin . . . being there was what convicts
dreamed about. Dreamed about more than fucking,
more than money. More than their kids.

This was the kind of dream that came back and back.
Being out and alone in some big place with just fields,
or a lake. Being out where there was only land or
water, and wind. And nobody else knew where. . . .

After a while, Pierce walked up off the beach, out of
the hot sand—sand so hot he started to hurry—and up
onto the walkway. The breeze was coming stronger,
blowing in warm gusts, rippling the flags they had on
tall poles along the esplanade. Blowing the flags out
popping and snapping in the wind . . . blowing the
leaves—fronds—the fronds on the palms there, whispering and rattling. Coconut palms. There was no
saying it wasn't pretty, heat and all . . . so different
from Missouri. . . .

Burney was in, and sounded better than at the state
park. Not so snotty.

"Hey pal, glad you got me. I have some really good
additional information for you. Could be about a certain lady—she's been askin' about you. So let's get
together, and I'll fill you in. Change your mind about
some golf, Thursday?"

"No, George, golf's your game. You're not taking
me for another twenty. But I do have time for some
lunch. . . ."

"You're on, buddy. Tell you what . . . meet me out at
Shell Road and Second. —Where are you calling
from?"

"Talavera."

"Well, come over to Palmetto Lake, meet me out at
Shell Road and Second, one o'clock. I'll introduce you
to the best fuckin' Mexican food you ever put in your
mouth."

"You got it, George. See you there and then."

Seemed to Pierce that Sergeant Burney was used to

handling that kind of phone call, good as an actor on TV. . . .

. . . There was a gas station at the Second Avenue intersection in Palmetto Lake, and Pierce drove in and parked away from the pumps to clean the Dodge's windshield. There were bugs pasted all over it just from the drive from Talavera, and he'd made the mistake of trying the windshield wipers on them. Sunstate Rental hadn't filled the wiper-fluid bottle.

He'd about gotten the mess off with cleaner and paper towels when somebody blew his horn, two short ones out on the avenue, and Pierce looked over and saw Burney at the curb in a light-brown Chevy four-door—an unmarked cop car, and looking like an unmarked cop car. No white Camaro; must still be in the shop.

Burney was wearing dark glasses and a straw hat, a Panama hat just like the one Naomi had wanted Pierce to buy. He made a follow-me gesture and started up, drove slowly down the avenue.

Pierce pulled the Dodge out into traffic a few cars back, but Burney wasn't hurrying. He drifted along until Pierce came up behind him, then still held to pretty slow.

Burney made two careful turns, then led south out of town on a straight two-lane with a canal running beside it. Apparently a cautious crooked cop. Must be getting worried Sheriff Macksie had some doubts about him, to be scooting all the way out to the boonies for a meet. . . .

Following just behind, and tired of the air conditioner's trying, Pierce shut it down and lowered the Dart's driver's-side window. Steam-hot air came blowing in, driven on gusts of wind that shoved the car slightly. The sky, which had been nearly clear on the coast barely an hour back, was ribbing up now with those high long clouds. High clouds and darker.

Weather so changeable and sudden might be that storm
of theirs, that Olivia. . . .

Out here was flat saw-grass country, with long
stands of those cypress trees, the Spanish moss on them
fluttering in the wind. Looked like Florida for sure. . . .
There were wading birds in the canal along the
highway. Big white birds—maybe the egrets from the
park's pamphlets. The great egret. Several of them, and
a blue heron. Pierce had seen blue herons before,
hunting the Missouri Breaks when he was a kid.

There was a big stand of cypress up ahead, the trees
stretching out to the right for a couple of miles . . . then
other stands beyond that. The cypress trees were dark
gray and green, their leaves moving in the wind. Pierce
could see slow traffic up ahead . . . the two-lane
opening into a three-lane. They'd dredged and routed
the canal away from the highway here, but the birds
were still in the water, fishing for whatever. Frogs,
salamanders. Little trash stickle fish, likely.

Up ahead, Burney had stayed in the right lane behind
a line of very slow traffic.

Pierce saw cars there turning off to the right . . .
under a sign of some sort. And when he got closer, following along, he saw the sign was in the shape of a
huge alligator, arched across the turnoff. Lettering on
there said GATOR COVE.

He'd seen billboards for it, leaving town. Another
animal attraction, like that African animal preserve a
few miles farther south, but a lot smaller operation and
just reptiles. After Pierce turned off, the advertise-
ments along the access road showed only alligators and
snakes. . . . Then a bigger sign of a water moccasin
with its mouth open, arched over the entrance to the
parking lot.

Pierce followed Burney's car across the lot, and
pulled in to park five cars down from him. A nervous
detective sergeant for sure, to come hiding among the
tourists. . . . The cop got out of his car—didn't look at

Pierce—and walked away toward an admissions gate through a pretty fair crowd of people. Better than fair, considering the weather was so hot and windy, and looked to be getting worse.

People milling around, getting their kids out of the cars, herding them together. People just like cattle in a feedlot. Cattle with sunglasses on even with no sun shining now. Sunglasses and short pants and video cameras. Seemed to Pierce he could damn near hear them moo. —Probably exactly the way the locals thought about them. A herd that came down into the state every year, got milked, then went on back where they came from.

There they were, filing in, paying to see some snakes—and, from the signs, see somebody wrestle an alligator. Pierce wondered if Burney was having a little fun with him, bringing him all the way out here like some secret agent. To look at reptiles . . .

At the admissions gate, they had a big sign showing the alligator wrestling. A strong-looking Indian grappling with an alligator that looked the size of a trailer truck. Water splashing all around . . . Seemed to Pierce, the Indian on that sign was in trouble.

And Gator Cove wasn't cheap. It was a ten-dollar single admission to get through the gate. Burney was two people ahead, still playing "I don't know you," and Pierce spoke up loud enough for him to hear. *"Sergeant, you owe me this ten bucks."* —Could tell Burney didn't like that a little bit.

"Let's get to it," Pierce said, coming into the place.

Burney looked away from him and said, "Back of the building, for Christ's sake!" And went strolling off that way, toward a high board fence, painted green. There was a heavy wooden door in the fence where it joined the south end of a long metal shed. . . . Looked like storage, a fenced lot back there.

Pierce followed Burney over while the crowd was going off to the right, down two graveled paths to a big round of wooden bleachers. Pierce could see through an entranceway between the bleacher stands, and there was a pool down there. Looked like a little round swimming pool.

There was something in it—something black, looked like an alligator for sure. Black—two, maybe three yards long, and wider in the middle than you'd expect. He supposed that was the alligator was going to be wrestled. —And since he'd paid the ten dollars, he didn't see any reason not to go watch the wrestling after the cop had told him what he had to tell, even if the wrestling *was* some sort of cheat. Might be interesting to see how a man handled a thing like that. . . . Likely the reptile would be fed or doped up, so it wouldn't do anything too sudden, turn the theatrics into a late lunch.

Burney was at the wooden door set in the board fencing. He opened it, looked back at Pierce and made a little beckoning motion with his head. Pierce went on over, stepped through the door, and closed it behind him. Burney was standing waiting for him by another long shed across a small muddy yard . . . and shook a cigarette out of a pack, offered one to Pierce as he came over.

"No thanks," Pierce said. "Let's get to it."

"Sure thing, asshole," Burney said, reached behind him, opened the shed door, and stood aside.

A handsome man—looked Hispanic—stepped out of the doorway, smiling. He was wearing a neat summer suit, white shirt and tie.

Pierce turned to run back to the fence, the wooden door—and stopped, since two men were standing there already, must have come out of the long building at the fenceline. They were Mexicans; young men, looked like farm workers. Another Mexican, older, walked out of the building and stood by them.

Then a very short plump young man, looked like an Indian, came out of the same building. He was wearing gold-rim glasses and overalls, and carrying a cane-bottom chair in one hand, a dead chicken in the other. Chicken looked to be a barred Rock hen.

Pierce heard something behind him. The handsome man had stayed back by the shed door, and another man had come out to stand beside him—a white man, older man going bald. He was holding a sawed-off shotgun.

Burney was standing nearer. Looking pleased.

Seemed to Pierce these damn buildings were like clown cars in a circus, everybody popping out of them. These people appeared to favor a theatrical style. Six of them, and the shotgun.

" 'Welcome to my parlor,' said the spider to the fly, and so forth. . . ." The Indian put the chair down in the mud in the middle of the yard, took the chicken in his lap, and began to pluck it, the feathers falling, swirled this way and that by the wind. "—My name's Jim Clarence. This hen was called Cootie; now she's dead." The young man smiled at Pierce in a friendly way. His glasses lenses were round as his face and body; he looked made out of circles. His eyes were brown, shading to black. "Always a mistake," he said, "to make a pet out of dinner. And this one's for us— my famous chicken and dumplings. The gators eat them spoiled, and with the feathers on."

"He could be carrying." The handsome man in the suit, still back at the shed door.

"No, he isn't," the young Indian said. There was a sudden thump and boom of recorded drums coming out of loudspeakers all around. Very noisy drumming and Indian music, Indian chanting. Show must be starting. . . .

One of the three Mexican men at the gate came over to Pierce, said, "Excuse me," and patted, stroked him down for a pistol.

"Nothing."

"Told you. It's a posture thing. . . ." The young Indian

leaned back in his cane-bottom chair. "I understand, Mr. Pierce, that you're some sort of old out-of-state badman—and you're down here on a personal thing." Still plucking that chicken. Doing a neat job, too. Seemed to Pierce the boy'd plucked chickens before. "—Sad to say, you have interfered with my business. We thought we had you located a couple of days ago, but you disappeared on us. There was a Pierce on the strip—then there wasn't a Pierce on the strip. So this is really good, that our Georgie brought you out here." He tugged a clump of feathers out of the chicken—and Pierce took a quick false step, then turned and ran at Sergeant Burney as fast as he could go.

He saw the man back there with the shotgun step aside to get clear—and angled as he ran, to keep Burney between them.

"Going for the cop's *gun!*" Jim Clarence. Smart young Indian.

Pierce felt a hand grab at him from behind as he came up on Burney while the sergeant was backpedaling, getting his hands up.

Pierce kicked Burney in the knee to slow him, got a grip on the detective's jacket with his left hand to hold him still, then hit the man in the face as hard as he could.

Almost always a mistake to hit at a man's head—good way to break your hand—but Pierce had no time not to. He hit Burney in the face, felt teeth crack under his knuckles, and the cop went down flat on his back with Pierce on top of him and two men come to grapple him from behind.

"Get on him!" Clarence calling that out—and a man, one of the Mexicans, got an arm around Pierce's throat from behind and was choking, hauling at him. Somebody else was hitting him, hitting him in the head.

But Pierce let them do it, didn't care about that. He had Burney's jacket torn open and the butt of that stainless automatic showed holstered there and he reached and had it.

"Stand fucking clear!" Man with the shotgun, no doubt. But nobody stood clear.

And Pierce had the pistol in his right hand, only Burney's face down there beneath him, bright with blood, and Pierce was coming up with the pistol from under all those people like furniture piled on him—and there came a pair of brown hands that fastened on his right wrist and wouldn't let it go.

Pierce tried and tried to turn the gun to use, and it was his right arm against that brown man's both, and it was all that mattered. The rest of them and their choking and yanking and punching didn't count at all, and it was so hot, like in a sweat bath.—The brown man, one of the Mexicans, was a strong person, work- hardened, stocky, and young—so it was only slowly, slowly, that Pierce was able to move against him, one arm against two, but turning, turning so the pistol's muzzle was coming up and around out of this bunch of men.

"Mother*fucker*!"

Then the handsome man, who'd been standing watching, came over in his neat suit and kicked his way into the scramble to get a second hold on Pierce's right arm. And that was that for the pistol.

Pierce let them keep that grip—and being choked and hit hard, up on one knee, he set himself and got to his feet. He came up biting, clubbing with his free fist and kicking, and men spilled off and came back slugging and trying to hold him.

He saw the young Indian for an instant as he fought, saw him through a run of blood come down his forehead. Clarence was still sitting, plucking the chicken. He didn't seem troubled.

Pierce got just room and time enough for one more good lick. Hit one of the people a good one, and was satisfied a bone had busted somewhere, man's jaw or his own left hand. A bone had busted somewhere. And right after that, like sudden night, a shadow came and he was hammered down into it. Hammered on his skull so light flashed and flashed, but didn't light the dark.

"I have seen shit, and I have seen shat," someone said. "But I never saw no shit like that."

Pierce tried to open his eyes, thinking a screw was at his house's bars, running his mouth. He tried to open his eyes, but only one of them opened; the left eye was stuck shut.

It wasn't a screw talking, because there was no uniform. And there were no bars, either. A short heavy young man who looked like an Indian was standing in T-shirt and blue-jean overalls, looking down at him. Young man wore glasses and seemed familiar, so Pierce took a deep breath that hurt his chest to breathe—and as if it had been a magic breath, pictures came fluttering into his mind like thumbed-through pages that showed him the Michigan job and roofing and Carolyn and coming down here, and why.

"Ah, old dad is with us again," the young Indian—Jim Clarence—said. Pierce was lying on a shed floor, hands and feet tied tight. Pole-barn shed . . . He felt sick as a horse.

"Crazy fucker." Someone else said that, and Pierce saw out of his unstuck eye that three other men were standing around, looking at him.

"No such thing," Jim Clarence said. "Just an old-fashioned badass." He bent over Pierce. "You were hot shit in your day, I'll bet."

Pierce didn't say anything. He didn't think he could try to talk without having to vomit. Seemed like they'd fractured his skull, it hurt so bad.

"But," Jim Clarence said, "your day's done, dad. Sure as hell's done around here. —Horacio, will you get me a chair?" Having asked, Jim Clarence stood waiting, looking down at Pierce as Pierce stared back up at him out of that one eye. "You are a mess, man. Look like forty miles of bad road. . . ."

Pierce tried to say something after all. Had to clear his throat, and finally said, "Kiss my ass." But his jaw wouldn't open very wide, and his voice sounded squeaky as Mickey Mouse's. Jim Clarence smiled.

"He needs to be put in." The handsome man in the suit said that, standing looking down at Pierce. It was this man had waded into the fight and caught hold of Pierce's gun arm.

"Here you go." One of the Mexicans brought in a chair—looked like the chair Clarence had been sitting in out in the yard, plucking that chicken.

"Thanks, Horacio." Clarence sat down, seemed more comfortable. Appeared to be a sitting sort of young man. "Dad, you hear that, what Tomás just said about 'putting you in'? You hear that?"

Pierce had nothing to say.

"Well, let me tell you what that means. It means Tomás wants us to put you in the big tank out back here, our acre pond. Means I should feed you to Big Louis."

"Right on." The Mexican, Horacio.

"See? Now Big Louis, Mr. Pierce, is a sixteen-foot American alligator. Weighs—oh, I guess about a ton and a half. Big Louis eats twenty chickens once a week."

"And one Colombian asshole." Tomás, the handsome one, pushed back his suit jacket's sleeve, looked at his watch. He didn't appear to want to waste any more time with Pierce.

"That's right," Jim Clarence said. "An occasion when Big Louis got to eat from the top of the food chain. And I suppose we should have shot the Colombian first, because it was a truly unpleasant scene. . . . Man was weeping and he shit all over himself. White summer suit, too. Shit all over himself before he went in."

"Louis didn' mind." The white man, older man, stood against the shed wall. Still had his shotgun.

"No, certainly didn't seem to," Jim Clarence said. "It looked like sort of rough dancing, you know, the way old Louis just dragged him off the bank and then went into that big slow spin they do. . . . He'd get a grip and pop a leg bone, then he'd get another grip. Dude squealing for his mom. —Sounded like a four-year-old in there, didn't he, Tomás?"

"About that old."

"It was a mess." Jim Clarence sat for a moment, eyes half shut, apparently recalling it. Then he looked down at Pierce again. "—As for you, dad. . . . Well, what you have done is commit the cardinal sin: you have interfered in my business. You have threatened and bribed an officer of the law in my employ, and you have threatened and bribed my own attorney—an officer of the court, for Christ's sake! . . . And the reason I know these things, way I found out these things, was I was talking to old George-the-Cop a couple of days ago concerning some trade matters—and something I said must have worried him, because all of a sudden he started squealing like a pig at a barbecue about you being so threatening and cruel to him and he just couldn't help it and didn't want to take the money."

Clarence shook his head, smiling. "Just . . . 'couldn't help it.' And of course, Counselor Chetwin was the only out-of-organization person who knew about our detective sergeant—and you'd be amazed if I told you how fast that legal beagle folded when I got him on the phone. Weak reeds . . . bogus reeds to be leaning on."

"Got that right," the white man said.

"See," Jim Clarence said, "people like that, it's just a question of who scares them last."

Pierce had nothing to say.

"Nothing to say?" Jim Clarence had stopped smiling. "No more 'Kiss my ass'?"

"Put him in, J.C." The handsome one, Tomás.

"Well, I'm thinking about it.... And also, Mr. Pierce, there's the damage you did right here at Gator Cove, demonstrating what a hard-rock you are."

"Cop to the dentist." Horacio.

"That's right. You listening? Poor Georgie's going to have a difficult time explaining to Sheriff Macksie where all those teeth went."

"—An' Juano in the hospital."

"Hear that? You broke the man's jaw, showing off. So my problem is: what the hell to do with you? Now, it's true, if you go to Big Louis, you're gone and that's that."

"Right on." Horacio.

"On the other hand, you're down here on a personal matter, and I have some sympathy for you there—and, *and*, if I start murdering every person who inconveniences and annoys me, who interferes even slightly in my trade, I'd soon get a reputation as some sort of weirded-out psycho. —And that would discourage a sensible businesslike attitude on the part of associates and customers. We could get into some really nightmarish relationships. . . ."

"God forbid." Tomás looked amused.

"—As you apparently know, Mr. Pierce, ours is basically a transport operation. Across the state and back across the state through our fab wilderness areas and so forth. I'm in touch with a lot of people—and I can't have them wondering when I'll lose my temper and toss them to Big Louis."

"Understand the problem," Pierce said. Still the squeaky voice. His jaw wouldn't open much, and when it did there was a little grinding sound on the left side.

"Well!" Jim Clarence turned to look at his people. "Hear that? Dad is waking up, becoming an interested party. *Okay!* Okay, big guy!"

"I'd still kill the fucker." White man with the shotgun.

"Who asked *you*?" Jim Clarence said, and the white

man didn't say anything more. "I give you people leeway, and you take advantage, become impertinent. . . . So, Mr. Pierce, all that's on the one hand, and to your advantage. But on the other hand, you have abused and used an important informant of mine— someone under my protection. And you have also stepped between me and my attorney—you have damaged our relationship of trust." He tilted his chair back a little, rocked slightly, easily balanced. "You have gotten severely in my face, and I can't let that pass. To do that, to show clemency, weakness, might give ideas to people who ordinarily never have ideas. Do you understand me?"

Pierce said nothing.

"I think you do. And you understand an example has to be made. . . . What I'm going to do . . . what I'm going to do is put you in a position to learn more about our Sunshine State. A position, by the way, that my law-abiding tribal brothers would wish for this drug-dealing young Indian—well, half Creek anyway. Hell, they'd be happy to see me tied to a manchineel tree, let that sap eat my skin right off. . . ." Jim Clarence sighed and stood up.

"—But that's my cross to bear. A detribalized, deracinated young Gainesville graduate, just out here with his motley crew of necks and beaners, trying to get along, make a modest living." He smiled good-bye to Pierce, and walked away.

"Horacio," he said as he went, "—you can hit old dad again. Lay a good one upside his graying head."

Chapter 16

Jackie regretted her breasts no end.

The hormones had grown them to a modest size so many years ago—and of course she hadn't been satisfied. Not satisfied. Had Dr. Wigand tuck some cushions in there as well—and all to please two . . . three good-looking young men who'd been happy to lie suckling at those knockers like huge handsome puppies.

Had smelled a little like puppies too, the darlings . . . that young, *young* milky breath. The sweethearts had accepted her as an "attractive older woman," and that wonderful wonderful make-believe had worked like magic. . . . Later, not so well.

The fucking had always hurt a little—a surgical pussy is only a surgical pussy—but that had been so minor, so unimportant compared to the enormous relaxation of being herself at last, hugged and held by those delightful, clumsy, and so dear creatures.

But now, the implant tits were out of control. A fat old lady's ponderous boobs on a skinny old lady's body. Set free, they made clothes with even senile chic just impossible. —Of course, there was always the surgical reduction thing. But when one is operated *out*, has been put under, sliced, stapled, and put under again—and all that several times—well, the rolling gurney becomes a little death wagon to a room full of knives. And the body knows. It says, "Oh, no. Oh, no, please. . . ."

So strap those honkers flatter, Jackie love. You
wanted 'em; you got 'em; deal with 'em.

Then the peach dress—ankle-length, thank God, for
the ugly-veins problem. Extra femme today, for poor
Naomi, apparently come for *news*. Poor Naomi—didn't
that just say it all? What sadder weakness in an aging
whore than sentiment, loneliness, affection? Weakness
and available money—the combination for profitable
prey. Had it ever failed the strong . . . ?

. . . Naomi had been watching the wrong way down
The Palms' lobby. She heard high heels behind her and
turned to see Jackie coming around the little alabaster
fountain. The fountain was working, a soft fan of
floodlit water. Jackie smiled; she was wearing a really
pretty pleated dress in soft peach. A dress too pretty,
too young for her—so her face, above its soft collar,
looked ancient. And she'd done something to her top.

"Christ, Naomi, you've been rained on and you look
terrible. Bad night—or good night? And what are you
doing to your hair?"

"Good morning. —Nothing. I'm not doing anything."

"That's what I mean, dear. Has a nice, neat, short
'do' occurred to you?" Jackie sat in the chair across
from Naomi's love seat. She sat carefully, as if her
knees hurt.

"I don't want to cut my hair, Jackie."

"That long, it just makes you look older. And I'm
not even commenting on the color. What is that—
antique-brick red?"

Naomi thought of mentioning the peach dress, how it
made Jackie look old as Egypt. "I like my hair long,
Jackie. I like it this color."

"Well then, I won't say any more about it. A French
knot might help. And at least a few streaks of gray . . ."

"Jackie, I just stopped by to see if you had anything
for us."

"Us?"

"That's right."

"Still raining out there?"

"It was. It's sunny again, now."

"Jackieee . . ." A tiny and very elderly lady was trotting by, hanging on to a rolling aluminum walker.

Jackie waved and called, "Dorisss . . . !" as the little lady was past and down the lobby, moving fairly fast.

"Doris Griest," Jackie said. "Nice gal. Old as the hills and a tough cookie. —Have you had breakfast?"

"No."

"Then you're a lucky girl! Today is Brunch Day, and you can be my guest. We have it once a week."

"Thanks, Jackie, but I'm really not hungry."

"Oh, bullshit." Jackie struggled up out of her chair. "Come on into our fabulous Garden Café and have the best *huevos rancheros* you ever put in your mouth."

"I'm not that hungry—"

"Hungry for news though, aren't we? You want some news? Then get your buns in gear. . . . Give me a chance to show off my company to the girls. I'll tell them you're my oldest niece, a demi-Jew and a bitter disappointment to me."

Jackie led the way—still a man's height, three or four inches taller than Naomi. The nape of her neck also a man's, too thick though almost hidden in blue-white waves of hairdo. . . . Naomi followed out of the lobby, then to the right along a wide corridor with a series of fairly good prints of Florida history along the wall. Indians on a beach . . . then Spaniards in their armor and odd crescent-moon helmets. Then the Americans . . . and Flagler's railroad. Then Walt Disney World.

Naomi smelled food—cooking ham, peppers, and something else—and Jackie pushed polished double doors open onto a long sunny room, the left side all glass . . . rising two stories high, then curving in to meet the building's stuccoed side. A narrow garden of croton lay outside, the shrubs' thick foliage of poison

purple-and-green leaves twisting and spiraling together
into a rough rag quilt under hot sunlight.

Quarry-tile floor and festoons of hanging lobelia and
clematis. A pretty space, with at least a hundred elderly
women—and very few men—sitting eating in groups
of four at tables in two rows down the room. There had
been conversation and china-and-silver noises as the
double doors opened—much less now at nearby tables,
as Jackie and Naomi walked in.

A hundred pairs of eyes lifted from their plates. Eyes
dull, and eyes sharp as sandburs, eyes washed almost
clear of tint by time. And being watched by them for
that moment as she and Jackie walked in, being examined by those ladies—all shrunken gray and white
though wearing colors—Naomi realized what Jackie
apparently hadn't, even after years: that her secret was
no secret to many of these women, and hadn't been for
a long time. Only, taking such a grand and consistent
attempt as good enough, they had chosen to let it pass.

"We'll do a table for two." Jackie led the way to a
table against the wall, away from the bright expanse of
glass, the croton garden. "Usually I eat with Carrie
Potter and crew, but weekly brunch is a free-for-all."

The table was set with linen and good stainless, and
they'd just sat down when a very dark Mexican girl as
small as a child came to them. She wore sandals, and a
pale lavender apron over a brown broom skirt and
blouse.

"G'morning, Ms. Keith."

"Good morning—or good almost noon, Estrella.
Estrella, this is my oldest niece, Naomi, and she's been
a disappointment to the whole family."

"I don' believe that, Ms. Keith. You always sayin'
things."

"It's true," Naomi said. "They wanted me to at least
finish college."

"Lots of people don' finish, an' they go back later.
—You want *huevos*?"

"Yes, and plenty of 'em," Jackie said. "And coffee, *please*."

The girl smiled at Naomi, and left.

"In the bad old days," Jackie said, "I would have little-girled that cute beaner—taught her some shy-child glances . . . done the book bag, bare legs, white socks and Buster Browns bit. The Catholic schoolgirl thing. And she would have turned for thousand-buck tricks."

"Ah," Naomi said, "the good old days."

"Don't be snotty, sweety, just because you're aging out of the Life. I can recall you performing in some scenes easy to remember."

"—And difficult to forget. Jackie, what have you got for us?"

Jackie unfolded her napkin, tucked it across her lap. "I will not—I absolutely will not drop fucking eggs on this dress. . . . What have I got for you? Well first, let me congratulate you on the smarts to have come to see me at all . . . to realize just what a major information bin my fellow crones have become. And they have; it surprised *me*. Turns out that very little of what has happened in Palmetto County over the years has escaped their attention." Jackie picked up her fork, examined it. "Found a dirty one, once. —Turns out they hear all, see all, know all, particularly regarding any kind of nastiness. It's a little scary . . . and, if I were a different type of person, would also open up some blackmail opportunities with their friends and relatives you wouldn't believe."

"And information for us?"

"Again with the 'us.' And when do I get to meet the other half of the team? Attractive? —I mean, for an armed robber."

"He's a nice man."

"If you're not in the bank when he comes calling."

"He's nice."

"Okay . . . Sore spot? Affection not being returned?"

Jackie, looking perfectly like a woman now, sat watching Naomi, satisfied.

"Jackie, if you got some fucking information from these people, then give it to me if you want your goddam money."

"Oooh. *Sore* spot. —And, as a matter of fact, I do have two— no, really three very interesting items concerning the serial victims of your serial killer. And here's what I'm going to do. I'm—"

Estrella arrived balancing a heavy round tray too big for her, slid its rim onto the table edge for support . . . and unloaded two oval platters of *huevos rancheros*, a basket of hot corn muffins, a saucer of butter pats on cracked ice, a small silver bowl of salsa, and a coffee pitcher, cream, and sugar.

"We don't fool around here," Jackie said, "when it comes to eating. It's all we have left."

"Enjoy!" Estrella said, lifted her empty tray, and was gone.

"Thinking of what I said, weren't you? The schoolgirl act. Wasn't I right?"

"On that shit, Jackie, you were rarely wrong. Want some coffee?"

"Immediately. —Could have made a fortune with that, rented her out to groups for the weekend. She shows up with her Barbies, and worried her momma will find out. Almost in tears, frightened, alone with all those big men. . . . An absolute *fortune*."

"I don't doubt it for a minute. But spare me."

"Take a muffin—they're no good cold. . . . Have to shave her pubic."

"Jackie, you were saying what you had for me?"

"How're your eggs?"

"Wonderful."

"Well, as I was saying, I have three items about one victim. Then, two special things about another one. Now, for the first girl the agreed-upon payment is dandy. But for the second—stuff's so *specific*—I will require a little additional."

"You shit," Naomi said. "You better not try to fuck—"

"You keep—keep your voice *down*! You keep your voice down and get it through your head that this is business, Naomi. . . . Don't sit there glowering at me. Eat that muffin—wonderful hot, lousy cold. Now listen, I know you're on a crusade and making chump change and being a partner and a pal to your bank robber—but this place costs *money*. I have years and years to go, and where am I supposed to live? My friends are here and it's my home, and if I have to charge your buddy a little extra for a name he could never never find on his own, what business is it of yours? . . . Are you going to eat that muffin?"

"Yes, I am."

"Then eat the goddam thing and stop playing with it. You are just hopeless. *Hopeless.* I could have made you rich and you just fought me every step of the way. Annie Busano is rich. She's got a fucking boat in Lauderdale as big as the White House, and she didn't have your ass, your legs, your boobs or your smarts. And there she is with an ex-john who owns every other pink grapefruit in Florida—and here you are, playing seeing-eye for pennies with your hair dyed God knows what color that's supposed to be."

". . . What have you got for us, Jackie?"

"Eleanor Cernan is one of our originals here, a truly poisonous hag. But one of her old friends, now gone, was the mother of the first girl—Marie Tessler, the Coast Guard girl. Eleanor gave me the whole rundown while costing me my bridge-playing reputation for years. I will never partner the senile bitch again. —Three never-made-public items. One, our young victim had been requested to separate from the service for the *good* of the service."

"Why?"

"Eleanor didn't know, so I don't know. And, by the way, neither did the girl's mother. Eleanor thinks that Marie might have been screwing an enlisted man, or something equally no-no. Certainly had been screwing somebody, because she got pregnant the year before it all happened, and had to get rid of the kid."

"I read the police summary report, Jackie. She had a current boyfriend, and they interviewed him."

"Where'd you get the report?"

"Never mind. But they interviewed the boyfriend."

"Who got you the police stuff?"

"I *said*, never mind."

"Did your bank robber get it? I'll bet he did, and I wonder how. . . . Well anyway, Dan Taftner, the boyfriend—then a young electrical engineer, now an older electrical engineer working up in Jax. Our Dan—as you've probably already read—was way over in San Francisco when Marie was cut up in her kitchen. He'd wanted her to leave the Coast Guard, and apparently the Coast Guard also wanted her to leave the Coast Guard for being naughty or whatever." Jackie swiftly ate two forkfuls of eggs. "—Marie's mom liked young Dan, and young Dan liked her mom. But Eleanor met him several times, and says it would never have worked. The suctioned-out infant apparently hadn't been his, but he was this really unbearably squishy forgiver." Jackie reached in the basket for a muffin. "You finish 'em, or I will. —Anyway, Eleanor said Marie was a nice girl. Good-looking in a sort of military way, and a good sense of humor."

Naomi made notes in Pierce's blue notebook. "All right. But you said you had three things for us."

"Doesn't the boyfriend count? He could have been pissed off she'd made it with somebody else . . . waited a few months to be safely way out of town, then paid to have her chopped."

"No. He doesn't count."

"Okay. All right. The third thing about Marie was

that she may have been a little bi. Her mom told
Eleanor she was going around with some brawny beach
bunny for a while. But that was the year before she
died. —Even so, it occurred to me if it was true, that
might be the reason the Coast Guard was willing to say
bye-bye. May have suspected some pussy hunting in
those close quarters at sea."

". . . And that's it?"

"Naomi, did you know any of this before?"

"They had Taftner in the report—that he was out of
town. And that she'd been pregnant at some time; there
was scarring in the uterus."

"The famous police report. How'd you get that?"

"Jackie, why do you care how we got it?"

"Because it interests me, that's why. And you didn't
have any of the Coast Guard stuff, did you?"

"No."

"Naomi, when do I get my money?" Jackie finished
the last of her eggs. Mopped them up with half a
muffin.

"I can get some of it for you, Jackie. But you're not
going to get it all until we have more than this. I don't
think this does us much good."

"Now, you listen to me. —Want more coffee?"

"Yes, just half a cup."

Jackie was pouring when Estrella came back with
her empty tray.

"You both finish?"

"I think so—Naomi, are you going to finish your
eggs?"

"I just can't. They were very good."

"Okay. Estrella, we're finished."

"She didn' leave much. . . ." The girl loaded her tray
with platters and dishes. "You wan' dessert? We got
raspberry scones."

"Scones?"

"Naomi, try for a little class for Christ's sake. —No,

Estrella, we'll pass on dessert. Make sure Willa doesn't put dessert on my bill."

Estrella said, "Yes, I will," and carried the tray away.

Jackie turned to watch her go. "The only thing you have to watch out for at The Palms is special meals. Ordinary meals are paid for, part of the deal—so for the brunch, or birthdays, they try to get cute on the bills."

"It was really good."

"Then you should have finished your eggs. —Now, as I was saying . . . you listen to me, Naomi. I don't give a fuck how much good those first items do you. You offered money for what information I could get—and you *will* pay me. And if it's special information, you will pay me more. Do you understand?"

"Nobody's going to cheat you, Jackie."

"Oh, you got that right. Several bad boys tried moving in on Jack Keith in the old days. 'Just a pimp.' 'Just a faggot.' Well, the faggot pimp is still here—and those bad boys are out there trying to drink the Gulf Stream. So don't make a mistake with me, Naomi, just because I'm old."

"You don't have to threaten me, Jackie. We—he wouldn't cheat you. And if you have something that really helps, I think he would pay you more."

"And does this 'he' have a name?" Jackie drank coffee, looking at Naomi over the cup's rim.

"Yes, he does, and it's none of your business. And I'll give you some advice, Jackie. If you meet him, don't try talking to him the way you talk to me."

"That's a laugh—you're trying to tell me how to relate to a man? Who's had the long-term lovers here? Who's had the real many-year relationships with those interesting beasts? Hmmm? Did I come to you in the old days, crying? Or did you come to me?"

"You came to me once."

"Yes, all right. About Lonnie. That one time. . . . Do

you know I still dream about him? Do you believe that?"

"He was very sweet."

"He was a con-artist son of a bitch, and he never loved me."

"Yes, he did. He told me he did, but you were just impossible, Jackie."

"He said he loved me?"

"And you were impossible."

"I had my fucking *operations* for that man!"

"Jackie, keep your voice down."

"All right. . . . I am."

"Now, what else do you have?"

". . . The 'else' I have, is that another one of the oh so pitiful victims was dealing coke and Mexican brown at the time of—or shortly before—her demise. Interested?"

"That wasn't . . . there was nothing like that in the report."

"Oh, no! The cops *missed* something? Did they miss that this girl, with no straight income to speak of, garaged a new Mercedes convertible back of her uncle's house? They *missed* that? Uncle's dead, but Auntie isn't. She lives here."

"That's . . . I guess that could be important."

"Oh, think so?" Jackie poured more cream in her coffee. "I'd make a note of it if I were you, Naomi. And you could add that this same girl's longtime on-the-QT boyfriend since high school—I guess the cops missed him, too—did three years of hard time for knifing two—count 'em, two—grown men almost to death."

"What's his name? Which girl?"

"Gee . . . you know, I just forgot. Just slipped my mind, Naomi. Know when I'll remember? I'll remember when I have my original ten thousand and—*and* an additional five thousand dollars placed in my spotted, withered hand. . . . Now, you haven't finished your coffee. I'm paying, so drink up."

And as she said it, a shadow slid across Jackie's face, and on across the room. The shadow came in with the sound of rain . . . then sheets of rain beating, running down the room's glass wall.

"Olivia is what they're calling it," Jackie said. "—Due tonight."

At the tables through the dining room, gray heads lifted, veined hands paused above plates as wind came gusting after the rain, drumming, making the high glass hum.

Chapter 17

Pierce couldn't breathe, and it woke him.

There was soft stuff in his mouth and up his nose, and when he tried to breathe in he felt it tickling down his throat.

He smothered—and woke, and sat up into gray daylight and a drifting rain. He put his hand to his mouth and tried to spit and wiped away a thick soft handful that crawled against his palm—mosquitoes. He blew his nose in his fingers and there were more of them in gray clots and smears of his blood.

Now he felt them biting, looked down and saw he was naked and sitting in muddy coarse gray-green grass. His head hurt so it made him sick, and he lay back down on his side in the grass, shivering, covered with mosquitoes like a shifting sheet of dark felt. He lay still for a few minutes, then vomited a little, and felt better.

The mosquitoes were at his eyes, and he had to keep them squinted closed. Better anyway; it helped him remember.

After a while, Pierce recalled everything. His head hurt as if his skull was cracked from side to side, was so damaged it would kill him, and he tried to vomit again but nothing came out. When he moved his head, even a little, it hurt more. . . . It seemed cold for a summer day in Florida, but he supposed that was from lying out naked in this rainy weather. He thought about being cold, and then he slept. But not for long.

The mosquitoes woke him. They covered him even thicker in a moving gray-black mass, the countless little bites becoming slowly one big bite and making him feel sicker. It was frightening, as if they would kill him if they kept on. Would take all his blood. . . . Pierce sat up and wiped them away in gray-and-scarlet smears, but more came clouding. They didn't appear to mind the rain. He could hear nothing but their whining in his ears.

"Get up." Pierce said it to himself out loud. "Get your dead ass up!" And he rolled onto his belly, then got his knees under him in sharp-edged grass, and heaved up to all fours. Then he stood, and staggered a few steps, dizzy. The mosquitoes were stinging and stinging him with tiny whips. Their high thin whining threaded through everything.

There was water on one side of wherever he was. Black water dimpling in the rain. Holding his head with his left hand as if that would hold it together, Pierce stumbled to a shallow bank—stepped off and half fell, half slid naked down a slick of mud, and went on down into the water. Warm . . . warm as blood, and he felt the coating of mosquitoes come loose from him as he turned in the water. Come loose in soft sheets and drift. Then he went under all the way.

Oh, wonderful. Wonderful. That felt so wonderful to him. Comforting as warm bathwater after a harsh day. His head hurt; he felt it beat in rhythm with his heart.

Blinking in darkness, rolling a little side to side, Pierce stayed under as long as he could, and when he came up—just put his head out into the cooler rain— there were no mosquitoes. So he rested there, looking across a wide stretch of water to a stand of cypress . . . their drapes of Spanish moss dripping in the rain.

Some water plants beneath them over there, and a long rough log floating, shifting in the current.—Then the mosquitoes came back and Pierce ducked his head. When he lifted it again, something had changed, and he floated, looking around like a baby in its bath . . . and saw through a mist of rain that the log was gone from over there, only a slow swirl of black water left behind.

"Oh . . . *oh!*" He called that out as if to warn another Pierce, turned and thrashed and lunged up through warm water and soft cool mud onto saw-edged grass— and scrambled out out *out* onto the hammock. He went on all fours up to its highest place, a little rise and patch of scrub hardwood, and turned and stared behind him, wrapped in a mist of mosquitoes. His feet hurt, cut on the grass.

Below, the black water still moved where he had been. And as it grew quiet, Pierce saw nothing. He watched that place . . . then looked out a little farther. Twenty feet off the hammock's shallow bank, two green-gold eyes more than a foot apart—and seeming to float there on a small raft of rough bark—lay watching him. A dozen feet behind them, there was the slightest very slow side-to-side disturbance in dark water.

The rain drifted and drifted away on a wind that gusted and grew stronger, so Pierce's robe of mosquitoes was torn and fluttered and blew away. Horsetail clouds were streaming over in silver gray, sailing across a slate-gray sky as fast as sailing ships. He stood shivering, streaked with mud and smears of blood, and looked out over the country.

Five white birds—egrets, they looked like, big birds beautiful as angels—flew past. The black water snaked out on every side for a mile and more, what might be a shallow river dotted with island stands of tall cypress . . . and, far distant, a low hammock of hardwood along the horizon. There was no sun showing to give east or west or the time of day. Nothing but wilderness and water, and rain blowing across the country on a gusting wind. But the storm coming in, and coming in fast, brought direction with it. There was a slight taste of salt in Pierce's mouth—blown west on wind from the sea.

. . . They'd carried him deep into the Manchineel—by airboat, canoe, or skiff—and left him.

Pierce stood swaying on grass-cut feet, listening. Listening through the wind sounds and rain sounds, and a soft chorus of tree frogs. Listening for a distant noise of traffic on a faraway road . . . or the sound of a skiff's outboard, some swamp fisherman foolish enough to be out with a storm coming in.

There were no sounds like that. Only frogs, weather, the occasional whine of a mosquito coming back to him. He was standing at the beginning of the world.

And no way to blame the Indian boy for it. Jim Clarence could have saved himself even this trouble by putting a bullet through Pierce's head. —Only person to blame had been so prideful, so foolish, as to follow a spoiled cop behind those buildings like a sheep up a slaughterhouse ramp. And unarmed. . . . Pierce blamed himself more than the Indian boy and his people. He had come to them asking for a whipping, and he had got it. —And all of it time wasting while Lisa lay dead.

Pierce turned and turned and looked out all around him. There was nothing to tell him which way to go, except the wind. And the wind, which must be from the sea, was growing stronger and stronger, the sounds it made slowly going up in pitch like a lady singer at Sunday church. There'd be no traveling into that wind. It would blind him and chill him. Beat at him and weary him to death fighting it every step.

He'd have to go with the wind—and that would be to the west, the salt marshes reaching in from the Gulf, and many miles.

He'd have to go. If he stayed, and stayed naked in this country more than a day or two—storm or sun—it would kill him.

Pierce heard some noise beneath the wind, started and looked around, frightened the alligator had come crawling up after him. But there was nothing down the shallow bank . . . nothing lying out in the black water under the rain.

He wished for a rock, something to hold, a stone only a little bigger than a fist and with a sharp point to it. A rock like that would seem the best friend a man could have. That would make such a difference. . . . And not wishing for a gun, not wishing for a knife or ax. Let those go. Let those go, if he could find a good rock. . . .

And if not, a stick.

Pierce stood shivering in the wind and took the time to think, make up his mind about several things. He regretted he wasn't younger; a few years less would have made a difference, doing this—but he couldn't have those years back. He had no weapon or tool, but he would have made decisions . . . and having decided might make the difference.

First—discomfort mustn't count. Not his head hurting so much, not his feeling sick. Not the mosquitoes, chiggers, horseflies, yellow flies, mud and grasscuts and the wet and cold today and the heat sometime later. None of that could be allowed to count at all, or it would wear him out regretting his lost comfort.

Second—no more being afraid. Not of alligators or snakes or poison this or that. There was no use to it. If he was in the water and a gator seized him, all he could do was try to turn with it when it rolled, so it wouldn't take his leg off. Turn with it, and do his damnedest to reach for its eyes . . . distress it enough maybe to let him go, even torn up. —And if a snake bit him, it bit him, and likely wouldn't kill him. Would likely only make him very sick if he kept his spirits up.

Third—drink water while it was fresh, and eat whatever creature could be gotten.

So—if not discomfort, or a danger that crippled him or killed him . . . if not thirst or hunger, then what was there to stop him going where he wished to go? Only the time it took and the effort to do it. . . . Pierce stood in the rain and thought about those decisions, and it seemed to him they made good sense.

The wind was coming booming now, combing the saw grass and sedges, bending them west so there was a harsh dark-gray beauty to this country, and Pierce walked to the far edge of the hammock, saw grass cutting his feet up pretty good. He marked cypress standing away west, walked down into the black water there, and began to swim.

It was farther than he thought, and wind gusts were coming along so hard they shoved his head nearly under from time to time—but other than that, and having to forget about alligators, it was all right swimming. Pierce took his time, didn't try to hustle through the water, just stretched out and stroked out. It was odd swimming through water so warm and dark. Black water. It was like swimming through a summer night.

Fresh water though, and Pierce drank it as he swam; it tasted like tobacco. Drank himself full and almost sick to his stomach, swimming toward the stand of cypress. Big trees, coming closer very slowly . . .

Under them, in among the big gray knee roots rising from the swamp water, in among the vines and foliage that sheltered there, Pierce felt easier, as if trees were friends of man. The wind was buffeting, moaning through their branches, whipping the long beards of moss straight out . . . tearing one away. Pierce saw it go, tried to stand up there under the tree, and just barely could, touching cold mud on tiptoe.

Here he could climb out, up into the tree roots, and roost there like a hen, but the wind came whistling—carrying things now, small branches . . . pieces of stuff as it went by. He could climb out and crouch there in the cypress roots and wait, but the wind would whip the heat out of him, chill him and wear him down. And when the storm, this hurricane, was gone tomorrow or the next day, the sun would come out and beat down on him, and he still left in the middle of this country.

Pierce let himself back down into the water, and commenced half swimming, half wading through the cypress grove. The day was getting darker under a darker sky, but still leaving a silvery soft light, as if that was the color of the wind rushing through. In Missouri, such a sky would have been a tornado sky stretching for a few miles . . . but here it ran out as far as he could see. A sky bad enough so it was a pleasure to be in under the trees, and not see too much of it.

He was in deep mud now. Mud up to his ass in places, so he had to lunge and struggle out of it—grab hold of cypress roots and haul himself out of it. He thought he saw a snake slide away off a thick angle of root. . . . Slim little dark snake there, getting out of the weather.

He waded from behind a big tree, stood up in soft mud out of the water, and the wind came and slapped his back, the back of his head, like a rough joker. That jolt to his head made Pierce feel weak, nauseated, but he kept wading. The wind beating at his back gave him his direction. He would be worse off without it. "Worse off without it!" He said it aloud to hear his voice, any human voice, and kept wading to the last cluster of big trees.

So much did he want to get up out of the water, climb up on those thick tree roots and rest, lean against the trees' smooth bark. "Sorry," he said, talking to himself out loud again, and swam to those last trees . . . found mud there and waded in among them, in among wet tangles of plants and vines that shook and whipped and tore away in clumps under the wind. Another slender snake—he just saw it as it slid away under the green.

"Good luck," he said . . . then thought there was a rule he should have made with the others about discomfort, and being afraid, and drinking and eating where he could. He should have made a rule about not talking to himself. . . .

From here was only wind and water a good quarter mile west, over to what seemed in silver light a long low hardwood hammock. What had the park pamphlets said? Pond apple, bustic, live oak, royal palm and gumbo-limbo . . .

Pierce stood in warm black water and took deep breaths . . . steadying down. The sound of the wind was now many sounds: whistling, howling, and over all a tremendous roaring rushing noise, like a waterfall falling forever, never striking the rocks below. Pierce had to turn his back to it to catch his breath.

He leaned down into the water to begin to swim, and a *crack* as loud as a dynamite stick's sounded above the wind—and like a swift shadow the heavy topmost crown and branches of a big cypress, leaves fluttering, flew past a few yards over his head. Flew fast and sailed away on the wind. Pierce ducked, though it was already gone . . . ducked, leaned into the water and began to swim.

It was not like swimming he had done before, in swimming pools and rivers, and stock ponds as a boy. It was swimming as swimming must be in the sea. Across this open stretch, unshielded, the wind had only the water to deal with, and it dealt it up into waves, whipped the tops of those away and spraying like hard hail. The water boiled around Pierce, and the waves shoved him sidewards, and he had to glimpse the hardwood hammock so far away, then keep his eyes tight shut again against the wind-blown water.

It was wearing him out. It was wearing him out and not even half the way across. "Won't do," Pierce said to himself aloud, and opening his mouth had been a mistake because the wind caught him from the side and blew his mouth wider, ballooned his cheek and forced water in hard enough to hurt. Should have made the rule no talking. . . .

He swam and swam, but the wind came and pushed him sideways, ducked him, and struck him when he came up again so his head made him sick. Won't do, he thought, and went under and this time tried to stay awhile. He swam frog-style down there as he had when a boy. Cupping the water in both hands and drawing it back along his sides . . . kicking out, doing the frog kick. He supposed any alligator passing by would find that way of swimming pretty funny. But it was peaceful, better down here, even without air to breathe. A temptation in a way, to stay . . .

He surfaced and had trouble getting a breath; all the air was turned to blowing water coming hard enough to hurt. The noise was like a train going fast across a trestle just above him. A long two-locomotive freight running very fast.

He turned his head away and managed to sip a breath of air. Sipping little breaths until he felt better. He squinted to see if he was going right, going with the wind to that low hammock of tall trees, and thought he saw it. It looked too far away.

Pierce gasped a last breath in, sank, and began to frog-kick his way along through darkness. The quiet, only the softest drumming roar down here, was a great comfort. And the warmth, out of the wind. It seemed a very good way to travel, but slow.

Something passed him in the water. He felt the soft strong pulse of it going by. Pierce stopped swimming and let himself drift, ready for a sudden terrific pressure on one of his legs. Maybe an arm; he brought his arms in to his sides. Maybe his head. —Anything wanted this head, could have it.

He drifted and thought, I'm wasting time and wasting air, and whatever it was is likely gone.

He drifted a little longer . . . then kicked up and surfaced into an explosion of noise. It was like being shot at at close range, that roar and blast and impact. In this country, he'd seen the beginning of the world . . . and this the end of it.

He breathed. He managed his breaths, took water in with them, and sank coughing back into darkness. It had become his home. He took his direction down there with him as best he could, and went back to frog-kicking, blind as any little animal grown up in a cavern, and could see how much peace there was to that sort of life.

. . . He swam, and rose and sank time after time, disliking the surface more and more—the jarring waves, the dull silver light and the wind come pounding over him. The wind was making a noise like police sirens, whooping and yodeling, and he thought for a moment once, going under, that he was back in Kansas in the parking lot and hurt, and had found the asphalt soft enough to dive beneath and was swimming away as the cops roared back and forth above him.

Swimming away . . .

It was his hands that found the land. He hadn't been able to see the hammock the last two times he'd tried; the wind had blinded him when he rose up to it. His hands found a slippery small root . . . then mud, and Pierce continued his frog-kicking and it became a mud-stirring . . . and then a slow slow crawl up and out into terrific sound.

Things were hissing through the air, and he climbed up a steep wet bank on all fours, keeping low. A branch went whirling away with a snoring sound amid the rushing, rushing of the wind. Pierce felt rough grass under his hands and knees and lay down, shivering. The wind was screaming around a tree trunk just beside him. Pierce took the deepest breaths he could, turned his head and suddenly vomited, and the wind took that and whipped it away.

"Get up. Get up," he said to himself, but not out loud. He wanted to go back into the water. Under the water.

Pierce lay there on harsh grass, the wind rolling over him like heavy swift soft wheels, lay waiting to feel stronger, not so tired. He held his hands over his ears because of the noise. He lay waiting . . . but didn't feel stronger or more able, and knew waiting wouldn't do it. He got up to his hands and knees again—felt suddenly dangerously lighter, light as paper, and the wind was around him and under him and lifted him a little and almost turned him over, started him rolling—so he dropped onto his belly and began to crawl with his eyes squeezed almost shut as the wind and blown water beat at him.

He was looking, but didn't remember what he was looking for. He felt thorns hooking him as he slowly went, clawing down his nakedness. Thorns and sharp twigs. Everything sharp or hooked or pointed came to him as he crawled, eyes almost closed. Water ran over the hammock inches deep, was driven up and along, hissing into him and past him. There were places . . . there were places he came to behind big trees, where the wind was bent and broken and spun on itself with a rhythmic engine sound and things whirled up in mud and water. Even so, it was better there, behind big trees.

He crawled across the hammock and the air was full of things above him. He crawled across to the other bank and could hear less and less. The wind was deafening him.

Whatever it was, he hadn't found it.

He turned and went on his belly, slid his face along in water and mud, held to the mud and torn grass with his fingers. Now he was crawling into the wind. Now, if some heavy thing came flying so low, it would smash his skull, or break a shoulder and leave him to crawl in slow circles until he stopped.

He crept along until going in this way—crawling against the wind—began to seem the only way possible, and walking or riding in a machine only nonsense, fantastic as a dream.

Yards up the hammock, he found what he was looking for. Knew that as he reached to touch it. A big live-oak limb, ripped from a tree with an angle of the trunk torn with it. Twelve, fifteen feet long, and almost a foot thick, it lay dark, soaked, trembling in the mud as if waiting for more wind to come for it, lift it, whirl it away through the air.

Pierce crawled up onto it and over . . . reached back blind to fumble for a grip on a smaller stub forking off, and tried to drag the oak limb behind him. At first he couldn't move it . . . then he could. He crawled at right angles to the wind—right ear deafened, right eye blinded by it . . . and very little by very little dragged the limb after him through wet mud to the hammock's bank . . . and down it, hauling the heavy branch through blowing vines and brush that whipped him as he passed.

As his hands had found the land before, they found the water now. And in the slight shelter of the bank, Pierce turned to face the oak limb . . . and almost sitting up, yanked and hauled at it, his braced bare feet running blood the rain took to be blown away. Hauled at it as he backed down into the water. Hauled at it as if he was as strong as the wind.

The thick branch shook and resisted, and then it came. It slid and rolled and lumbered down into the water with him, and Pierce shoved and shoved out from shelving mud—and they were floating free, out from the hammock's edge, and Pierce climbed half onto the limb and hugged and gripped thick round rough bark, and the oak leaves whirred and seethed and rattled around him, and they were drifting out, drifting out . . . sailing west with the wind.

Silence woke Pierce. Silence and bright and perfect light.

He lay aching and sick half across the big limb, his
left side and left leg resting warm in the water. The
branch's bark had rubbed some skin from his belly; he
was stuck to the wood with blood.

The light hurt Pierce's eyes; it took a while to
become accustomed to it. The oak limb drifted on the
river's black water as it had sailed, wind-driven,
through the night. He had hugged it and gone with it
for furious miles as all its clustered leaves, its small
branches, were blown away. And after a while, he had
heard his mother calling him to supper on the wind.
Heard her, but paid her no attention. He'd assumed it
was the hurricane's trick to make him leave the oak
and go down in dark water to stay.

Now, in silence, he opened his eyes to a brightness
like sunlight seen through a held-up glass of water, that
gold-silver shining. He moved on the long branch and
tore loose where blood had dried beneath him. It hurt
to do it, but not as much as moving his arms and legs
hurt. They felt frozen, but they burned when he shifted,
tried to bend them. Hurt enough so he called out,
"Whoa . . . *whoa*," as if the pain was a horse, gone running loose.

It took a time to set that discomfort aside, and the
sickness.

He moved again, slid slowly off the thick round of
oak and into the water. The water hurt his belly,
then felt very good to the rest of him, so soft and warm.
He held an angle of branch with his right hand and
began to move in the water there, slowly kick to swim
alongside.

The sky was rounded out above him, a great cylinder
of clouds that rose right up to the sun, and the sun rode
above it as over the gate of paradise. Beneath this was
gleaming and gleaming air, and Pierce swam beside his
limb of oak in the center of the light.

There was no sound, and no wind. Only brightness.
It was prettier than any place Pierce had ever been.

He ducked his head to drink, and tasted salty water.
Salty water . . . The river had run west and become a
salt marsh. To his left, drifting by, a little island of low
trees and bushes was propped up on clusters of roots
rising out of the water. Mangrove. He remembered it
from the park pamphlet. . . . Red mangrove.

It was warm—hot here, really. And the breeze that
just began was warm . . . came warm and riffling
across the dark water, the stillness broken. A breeze,
and distant thunder.

Pierce swam beside his long oak branch, and a fat
black snake came and swam near, curving and curving
through black water. They swam together past that
small mangrove island, and then another, but by then
the snake had gone away. . . . Pierce heard behind him
nearer thunder and a rising whisper of wind, as if the
hurricane had followed and found him, and he turned
and looked back and the great cylinder of light was
folding in upon itself, miles high, the still, bright eye of
the storm slowly closing.

Darkness settled, and the wind caught its breath and
came booming.

Pierce lost his oak limb a little later. The wind came
and turned it and spun it in the water, and he couldn't
climb on, couldn't hold to it. It tore from his hands and
swung and swung away as the water was skinned by
the wind into sleet. He sank down and swam beneath,
tasting salt water, salt water burning his eyes.

He swam the way he'd swum before, but not as well.
He couldn't hold his breath; he came up too soon each
time and the wind struck at him. Then he went down,
went down again and swam, but not nearly as well,
swam like a man who couldn't swim, his arms and legs
not moving together. But he got up to the surface, got
up and caught a breath through the blowing spray
before he sank. The train had come again. Had turned
and turned and come roaring and rumbling over its low

trestle so it shook the water he swam in, made it tremble even under and deep.

Pierce went up again, tried to breathe and couldn't, so he sank and did without, swam without having breathed any air, but slower and slower. It was easier than going up into the storm. He heard Carolyn talking just as clearly as if she stood beside him. Talking about a movie she saw up in Jefferson City. . . .

He swam only a little way before things came and took hold of him.

He struck and kicked at them underwater in the dark, felt them slim and slippery. Tree things . . . roots. And then he struggled up so long a way to air—and came up among fencing mangrove roots into a foam of blown water, and was able to turn his head away and get a breath.

Pierce got that breath, and then another and twisted and forced his way deeper among the roots rising around him, felt cold soft mud slide away under his feet. And he hung on and clung amid the mangrove roots, where the wind could beat him, but not carry him away.

There was roughness in the mangrove roots that moved and touched his hands, but he couldn't see it. Touched him many places. After a time when he hung with his eyes closed against the wind, he opened them to a lightning strike some way away, and saw that small crabs crawled in thousands among the mangrove roots, and crawled on him.

"Great God in Zion," a man said, his voice very clear through the wind. "I'd call this a tight . . . but I seen worse on the border."

There were spurred muddy high-top boots swinging in the wind above Pierce's head, and he looked up and saw his great-great-grandfather sitting in the mangrove branches. Knew him from the tintype. Moses Pierce was smiling down, hatless, teeth missing from his lower jaw. He had a face like a hunting bird's, and unpleasant eyes. The wind seemed to be only a breeze to him, gently stirred his hair. He wore grimy black and a dirty flannel shirt with a black tape tie knotted in a bow. Two big long-barrel revolvers—cap-and-ball Remingtons, they looked like—were stuck down through a brass-buckle belt.

"It's a tight," he said. Nodded, looked out over the country. "But had you been with us when Pleasonton's troopers caught up at South Station, you'd think this a Sunday chicken dinner. Yessiree, you would—peas an' biscuits an' peach pie an' all. Had men's brains blowed out, shot out all over me. Come at us like we was rats in a grain store . . . like us Quantrills wasn't regular cavalry at all."

"Get out!" Pierce said. He was afraid he was dying, for a dead man to come talking to him. *"Get out!"* And Mose Pierce melted as if the wind was catching him, had caught a tuck of him, slowly unraveled him and blown him away. A spur still shone on the shadow of a boot, glinted silver, and was gone.

Pierce would listen to no more voices, so no more voices came. He closed his eyes and closed his mind, and held hard in his tangled cage through dark hours of the day, until the storm's greatest weight was done. Then, in that silence and soft rain, his skin torn in small spots here and there where the crabs had been at him— torn most on his legs, where he couldn't reach to knock them away—Pierce opened his mouth and drank what rain he could. Then took a crab crawling on a branch above him, broke it in his hands, broke it open, and ate.

Felicio Ruiz, an old man as far as these grove workers were concerned—more than half of them illegals—was still in charge and had taken care they should know it. To these young ignorants, mountain peasants who'd never seen an orange before Florida, to be driven in an evening out to groves of wind-broken trees was nothing but an opportunity, camping for a few days' work clearing and burning.

They were not intelligent enough to realize they were seeing the ruin of good people here. Not intelligent enough to think how long it took to grow new groves of prime grapefruit trees, prime oranges. These peasants were ignorant as owls, and that was the truth.

The levee road was littered with blown brush and branches. Snakes. There were snakes everywhere, come up on this raised road from the hurricane.

It was getting dark. Ruiz reached to the dash to turn the truck's headlights on—and when he looked up, there was a pale thing, a small cabbage-palm trunk in the road, so he slowed. Then saw it was not a piece of palm trunk, but a man, naked and left dead on the road by the storm. . . . It was absolutely the worst bad luck he had ever seen to start a job. A bad job of ruined trees, and now started with this bad luck. . . .

He stopped the truck, climbed out to the peasants' questions, crossed himself, and went to take a look.

Chapter 18

"Feeling better?"

"Yes. Took a day or two, but I'm feeling better." Moira's voice, or her phone, sounded odd. Storm damage.

"D&C's no fun."

"Karen, it sure as hell wasn't. What happened to that no-pain thing?"

"Well, we don't put people under. Just ameliorative locals."

"Well, it wasn't enough."

"But you're okay? You're feeling okay?"

"Yes. I mean, a few tears, but I guess that's normal, because it's not every day . . ."

"Honey, are you all right?"

"Karen, you've been such a good friend. . . . Oh, boy, the water works are starting up again. I just cry at the drop of a hat. Anything I see on TV, anything with little kids in it and I just start bawling. *Boo-hoo, boo-hoo.* It's ridiculous, because I'm actually tremendously relieved. What I want . . . I guess what I want is to have my little girl—and I don't give a fuck if she's not very smart! I just wish I had her, was going to have her—but I wouldn't have to *worry* about her." Karen heard Moira blow her nose. "Excuse me. —Well, I suppose that says it all, doesn't it?"

"Just about."

"But you still . . . you understand."

"Yes, I do."

"You understand, but you don't respect. Right?"

"That's right."

"Shit . . ."

"Did your transfer go through?"

"Oh, yes it did! Well, I was sure to get it—it really wasn't a maybe thing. And . . . and as of eleven days from now, yours truly is going to be based in New York, and flying out of Frankfurt and other Euro alternates, and back and forth. It's going to be just fantastic. Thank God for reciprocal agreements."

"It'll be wonderful for you, Moira."

"Well . . . it will be. They're doing a really new thing."

"Time for a good-bye lunch before you go?"

"Oh, sure! Yes. We could go out—not tomorrow, I'm doing end-of-lease things and getting rid of a ton of stuff—we could go out day after tomorrow. Do a big lunch at the Patio and get drunk out of our minds."

"Sounds good. But let's do a picnic instead."

"Okay! You want to come get me, or you want to meet?"

"No, I'll drive us out there. And I guess we'd better meet, because I have to do something first. . . . Why don't you park at the mall, in front of Sears, and I'll pick you up out there at twelve-thirty."

"You got it. —And Karen, thanks so much for being a buddy. And I really want to tell you I appreciate that you didn't just bullshit me. You know?"

"I know."

"Okay . . . So, see you out front at Sears day after tomorrow!"

"It's a date."

"How long?" Pierce said.

"Well, welcome back to the world!" The nurse looked too young for the job. She looked like a junior high school girl dressed as a nurse for a school play.

"How long?"

"How's your vision? Is your vision okay?"

". . . Fine. I can see all right. How long have I been in here?"

"This is the second day you've been a patient here. And this is late afternoon. —You're in Coast County Central, and you're doing just fine." She walked out of the room as if that was all there was to say.

"Goddammit," Pierce said. Seemed pretty rude. . . .

After a minute or two, the nurse walked back in, smiling. "The doctor will be by in a minute. . . . And you have no permanent injuries, just abrasions and insects and exposure. You were out in the boonies, and some grove people brought you in."

"This is the second day. . . ."

"That's right, and we need your name, because you had nothing on, no clothes, no ID."

". . . Name's Boyce. I was out there fishing, like a damn fool. Thought I had time to get in, but I got caught instead. Don't know how I lost my clothes and stuff. . . ."

"You're very lucky it wasn't a major hurricane, Mr. Boyce."

"Not a major hurricane . . ."

The doctor came in—Hispanic, and looking much too young for his job. Another kid. "How's our survivor?"

The nurse patted Pierce's hand. "Name is Mr. Boyce, Doctor. He was out fishing in the Manchineel when Olivia came through."

"Aha . . . Extremely unwise. And how are we feeling, Mr. Boyce?"

"Just fine . . . A little tired, but I'm feeling fine, and I want to thank you folks . . . but I'm going to have to get somebody to come over here and bring me some clothes and pay you people."

The young doctor had listened to him carefully, seemed to want to be sure Pierce had all his marbles. He listened, then he leaned down close and looked into Pierce's eyes. "Good. Good . . . Well, tell them to come out tomorrow morning, Mr. Boyce, and you'll be ready to go. You were suffering from some contusions, concussion, exposure—little core temperature problem— and countless assorted insect and other bites. Also, something took little pieces out of the skin on your legs."

". . . I believe it."

"You're lucky to be alive—and very lucky it wasn't much of a hurricane."

". . . Seemed like a considerable hurricane to me."

The doctor smiled at that, picked Pierce's right wrist up and took his pulse. "Running like a Rolex," he said.

. . . After supper—a not-bad supper of sliced ham with pineapple sauce, rice, yam, and a glass of milk—a different nurse, a grown-up black woman, connected Pierce's phone, warned him the hospital would charge him plenty each call, and left him alone.

Pierce sat up, hitched around so he was sitting on the side of the bed, and noticed for the first time that he was in a room for two; there was an empty bed with white curtains drawn against the wall. When he was sitting up, he was sorry for it because he felt sick to his stomach—must have sat up too quick—and he had to lean forward, put his head down, to keep from throwing up that ham and pineapple sauce.

He sat there for a minute with the phone in his lap and his head hanging down. A sick pup for a little while. He was looking down at his legs, and there were small white bandages stuck all over them. . . . Then he slowly felt better, and was able to straighten up. Took deep breaths.

He had to ask the hospital operator for the Palmetto County area code. Then ask their operator for Mont- fort's number. There were two numbers, and the hall- phone number had gone right out of his head. . . .

"Hello?"

"Naomi, it's me."

"God*dammit*, where the hell have you been?"

She sounded so much like a wife that Pierce had to laugh.

"It's not funny, Tyler. It's not funny at all!"

"No, I guess not. Has there been any trouble there?"

"No. Nobody's bothered me."

"Storm do any damage?"

"No. A few trees, a few windows some idiots didn't tape or shutter. Lines were down, but they're up now."

"Good. Now listen, and don't get all excited—"

"I won't get 'all excited,' Tyler."

"I need you to pick me up some clothes. Slacks, shirt, sneakers, and socks. Sneakers size eleven. And bring money—or your credit card—and I'll reimburse you when I get the cash out of the bank box."

"Are you in jail, Tyler?"

"No, I'm not in jail, Naomi. They have me in a hospital over here, and—"

"What is it? What's the matter?"

"Naomi, nothing's the matter. I got caught out in the storm, and I'm in the hospital over here for nothing serious and I'm ready to get out."

"What do you mean, 'for nothing serious'?"

"I mean nothing *serious*. I got rained on and mosquito-bit. It's nothing to worry about. So, would you please get me some clothes just to travel in, bring money or your card and drive over to—what the hell is it?—to Coast County Central Hospital. You come tomorrow morning, and we'll be out of here."

"You're in Coast County? How did you get over there?"

"Honey, I swam. Now, I'll see you tomorrow morning."

"Tyler—"

"Tomorrow morning."

Pierce hung up the phone, and sat for a minute, resting. Just talking on the phone made him tired. . . .

Then he got the operator back, and placed a call long-distance, up to Carolyn's house in Dowland. Hospital was going to charge him a fortune, making these calls. . . .

There was no answer, and Pierce thought of calling the library or Snip N' Style, but he couldn't remember which one Carolyn would likely be at in the evening, whatever day this was. And also didn't feel like talking to somebody else first, before they put her on. . . .

. . . It was strange that in his last dream that night, in a sleep that had been rich with dreams, Pierce found himself back in the Manchineel. Found himself swimming beside Lisa in black water under a haze of insects that had been the wind all along. That sound was theirs; the wind was the wind of their wings. There was nothing strange in that. The strangeness was in his ease at being there, as if the place was home to him. Lisa swam smiling. She was smiling twice; her mouth was smiling, and her cut throat was smiling. She was in her ranger uniform and swam the way the black snake had, curving and curving through dark water. . . .

Breakfast was scrambled eggs and something supposed to be country sausage—might as well have been a rubber fender flap. Naomi came in while he was working on it with a white plastic knife no way up to the job.

"Tyler. . . ?" She was in the doorway carrying a big brown cardboard box, and smiling not too good a smile. Pierce supposed he didn't look his best.

"Are you all right?" She came over to the bed and bent down as if she was going to kiss him, then straightened up instead and took his hand and shook it, held on to it. "Are you okay?"

"I'm just fine. Don't tell me I look that bad."

"No, no. You just . . . look tired."

"That bad?"

"No, no! You look fine."

Pierce got out of bed—took a little effort to do that—put a hospital robe on over that damn no-ass

dress they'd put on him, and went over to look in the
room mirror by the door.

"Jumping Jesus Christ . . ."

"Tyler, what happened to you?"

"Goddam mosquitoes and things, I guess. . . ." A
movie monster was looking out of the mirror at
him. Tall thing with a puffy bruised pumpkin face and
little swollen squinty eyes. Long legs with bandages up
and down.

"And they're just letting you *go*?"

"That's right. Guess looks don't count. . . ."

"It's not funny," Naomi said. She put the cardboard
box on the bed, opened it, and took out a plain white
shirt, gray trousers, and a pair of white canvas tennis
shoes.

"Thanks for bringing this stuff," Pierce said. ". . . I
need to call Carolyn. She should still be home."

"Well, call her, Tyler. —You want me to go stand in
the hall? Go in the bathroom?"

"You don't have to do that, Naomi."

Pierce sat on the bed, dialed the hospital operator,
and gave her the number.

"Hospital's going to charge you an arm and a leg for
these calls," Naomi said. She took a magazine about
sports fishing from his bedside table, and went to sit in
a chair across the room. "Oh, God," she said. "More
fish . . ."

Carolyn's phone rang up there a few times, and Pierce
had decided he'd missed her, when she answered.

"Hi, sweety."

"Tyler?"

"How are things going?"

"Going lonely for me."

"I know—me too."

"Have you had any trouble? Has there been trouble
down there? You sound strange."

"No trouble. Haven't really had any trouble worth
worrying about," Pierce said—and Naomi gave him a

look across the room. "It's just mainly hunting around
. . . you know, asking questions."

"Are you sure you're all right, Tyler?"

"You bet. I'm fine."

"I just . . . I just wish you weren't messing around in
those killings. I know I shouldn't say that, but it's what
I feel. I just think it's so unwise. But I understand, I
understand why you're doing it."

"I know. I know it's how you feel, sweetheart. And
I'm sorry it's a worry to you."

"Well . . . anyway, I do like the postcards."

"Well, I'll keep 'em coming."

"Tyler, are you really . . . are you getting anything
done down there?"

"Yes, we are."

" 'We'? Oh, that lady. You wrote me about her."

"Naomi's been a major help."

"Tyler," Naomi said, "let me talk to her." She got up
and came over. "—Let me talk to her for a minute."
She took the phone, covered the mouthpiece and said,
"—No *trouble*?" to Pierce. Then she took her hand
away and said, "Carolyn? Carolyn, this is Naomi."

"Hi."

"Hi. Listen. I am just the guide dog down here, and
we *are* getting somewhere, even though I know it's
hard to believe. It's hard for *me* to believe. —And I
just want to say that as far as your guy is concerned,
there has been no fooling around. Period. It's business,
with maybe friendship thrown in. *Period.* —Okay?"

". . . Okay."

"So, I will try to keep him presentable, try to keep
him from smoking cigars while I'm in the truck, and
try to keep him *out* of trouble. I have not been able to
keep him from eating fast food, and now he's got me
doing it."

"I believe that. He's very stubborn."

"Let's just say, honey, that I think you have your
long-term work cut out."

"I know it."

"So, you take care—and don't worry about me in any way at all, you understand?"

"Yes, I do."

"I'm not saying he isn't cute, for a bank robber."

"Give me a break," Pierce said. "Let me have the damn phone."

"I know. He is cute."

"I'm just saying I'm not even in the game, Carolyn. —Okay?"

"Okay."

"Will you let me have that phone? . . . Hi, sugar. That's Naomi—don't pay any attention to her."

"I like her. . . . Tyler, are you being careful? Are you both being careful?"

"Careful as we can be, sweetheart. I don't think this is going to take much longer."

"Well, for God's sake be careful."

"We will."

". . . You have jobs up here, you know. Mickey's always calling saying people are calling him about jobs. Bob McReady at the hardware?"

"Right."

"He's thinking about doing his roof, and that would be a big job. It's really two connected buildings."

"I know, and he needs a new roof. And he'll buy the cheapest shingling he can and not give a damn how long it lasts. I'll be surprised he uses me, and not some kids with a staple gun."

"Well . . . well, I miss you. And I'll be honest—I miss you in bed, Tyler."

"Not like I miss you."

"That. And more than that."

"That's right, more than that. . . ."

When Pierce hung up, Naomi said again, "No *trouble*?"

*   *   *

—Naomi said it a third time driving back across the state, driving through cool damp morning air over wet blown litter on the highway. Past occasional billboards knocked over, and several trashed fruit stands. "No trouble . . ." she said. Then later said, "Not funny," after Pierce laughed, describing his journeying buck naked, and concerned about alligators.

"Well it is, in a way. It is funny."

"That son of a bitch. Fucking redskin asshole—a goddam drug dealer! He was just . . . he wanted to *kill* you."

"Nope. Old Jim Clarence was trying to avoid it."

"Tyler, what are you going to do? Don't tell me you're not angry. Don't tell me you're not going to do something."

Pierce thought about it. Thought looking out at the country they were passing. Settled green-and-brown crop country, most of it. Had been like the Manchineel once, though—had been that pretty, that various and savage. Now it was just flat plowed-and-disked table-land as far as you could see. No sign except for shallow pools of water here and there that a hurricane had just passed over those fields. ". . . I'll tell you, first I saw I was in that country, I figured to come out and kill him."

"If you . . . I'd help if you want."

"Naomi—thank you, honey—but I'm not going to shoot that boy. Because it was me got into his business, not him that got into mine. . . . I mean, if he makes me do it, then I will. But what I really want is to get that wallet back. I got all the Boyce ID in there—and some money, and I want that back too."

"Next time, he'll kill you."

"No, he won't. You bring my revolver?"

"Yes, I did. It's in my purse. But Tyler, you're not well enough."

"I'm fine. Just a little creaky; feet are sore from

grass cuts. But I'll wait a day or two before I go see Jim Clarence. —Bites itch, I will say that."

"We'll get you some calamine."

"And I need to pick up my truck."

"We'll get the truck."

"Now go on about your buddy, Jackie. —Wants more money for a name?"

"He was one of the girls' boyfriends, a bad boy. Apparently both into drugs. Supposedly, she was dealing when she was killed."

"—And you're thinking what I'm thinking."

"Tyler, Jim Clarence runs the drugs in Palmetto County. He's run them for several years."

"Young for that . . ."

"The previous man—I think—was named Ned-lund. . . . Something Nedlund. I suppose Jim Clarence started working for him, but anyway nobody has seen Nedlund for some time."

"Big Louis."

"What?"

"Nothing. . . . It's true a Sweetwater gives folks opportunities to do killings of their own. Pass them off as his."

"Tyler, if a girl worked for Jim Clarence—"

"Muled for him maybe, brought stuff across the state. —And then, could be there was a disagreement. I suppose Jim Clarence or one of his people might take advantage, do that girl the way the Sweetwater does, so she'd be put in with his killings."

"My God. . . ."

"—And that first girl was a Coast Guard person. An officer. Mighty handy for drug people to have a Coast Guard person in their pocket. None of my business, though."

"Why *not*?"

"Because that's something that Lisa wouldn't have had to do with—that trade. Nobody would have had that reason to hurt her."

"Unless she was in their way somehow, Tyler, out at the park. Had seen something, or learned something out there."

Pierce said nothing for a while, rode looking out at the country. Then he said, "I want to meet this Jackie. I want to meet her first thing tomorrow—see if that drug shit makes any sense at all."

"You're going to pay her?"

"I'll pay her and she can have the extra five—but by God she better be worth it."

Naomi speeded up a little, passed a white Chevy pickup, then got back into her lane. She looked over at Pierce.

"Tyler, are you sure you're okay? Should we go see a doctor in Manchineel?"

"No. Naomi, I'm fine."

"Tyler . . ."

"Yes?"

"I think I'd better tell you about Jackie. . . ."

. . . They had driven into Palmetto County, and Pierce was still laughing, feeling much better than he had.

"It's not that funny, Tyler. Really, it's sad."

"Hell, I think it's pretty damn funny, living with all those old ladies."

"Don't think Jackie isn't tough."

"Oh, I'm sure he is—she is."

"Well, she *is*. She's had some people . . . you know."

"I'll bet. Oh, me. Oh, Lord . . ." And that started him off again.

"If you're going to deal with her—well Tyler, you can't be doing this . . . this gay prejudice shit."

"I'm not," Tyler said, and managed to stop laughing. "I'm not prejudiced." He took a breath and sat up straight. "It's just—it's just the situation."

"For God's sake, Tyler. You're such a hick. . . ."

* * *

Jackie came downstairs in a cream pantsuit, sky-blue silk scarf, black high heels. It seemed to Naomi she'd taken extra care with her hair and makeup this afternoon. Coming to meet a man . . .

"Where is he?"

"Parking the truck."

"The truck?"

"Truck."

"I see. . . ." Jackie led the way past the fountain to a love seat and armchair set behind a potted palm. They'd put colored dye in the fountain. Tangerine. Under the lobby lights, it looked like urine.

"Any Olivia damage?"

"Naomi, this place is built like a bunker. It's not-to-worry land—and that includes minor hurricanes. We lost a window. Two windows and the Dumpster, and that's it." Jackie sat in the armchair, arranged herself . . . carefully crossed her legs.

"Dye in the fountain . . ."

"Naomi, we always have dye in the fountain for birthdays."

"Looks like pee."

"I *know* it looks like pee. I told them, but they didn't have any more blue. It's a vegetable food coloring, is what it is—and this dye is what they put in the Key lime pie mix."

"Why do it at all?"

"Naomi, it's a tradition. Okay? This is Phyllis Moffat's birthday. I suggested pink. I suggested blue. But this is what they had, and it doesn't really make a hell of a lot of difference, because Phyllis has MD and is blind as a bat."

"MD?"

"Macular degeneration. —And where is our attractive middle-aged bank robber? He could have parked in the drive."

"He's not very attractive at the moment. Hurricane caught him out in the Manchineel."

"And what the hell was he doing out there? . . . Hello? No answer?"

"You don't have to know everything, Jackie."

"Oh, yes I do. I do have to— Oh, my God. The poor *man*!"

Pierce was coming across the lobby in fresh chinos, loafers, and his tropical shirt—the cream-colored one with small blue flowers. He was limping slightly, and had a folded newspaper in his hand. . . . Naomi thought he was looking a lot better than he had the day before. They'd driven to his motel room, and he'd taken a shower, come out to lie down for a few minutes . . . and slept through the night and into the morning while she sat reading the task force report on the Sweetwater, making notes. She hadn't slept at all, had left early and had breakfast and come back, and he'd still been asleep.

"Well," Jackie said. "We're wearing complementary creams and blues."

"He's lucky to be alive," Naomi said.

Pierce was close enough to hear her, and said, "We're all lucky to be alive." He went to Jackie and reached down to take her hand. "Gil Boyce. —And you're Jackie Keith, elegant as described."

"Right on," Jackie said, and seemed to Naomi to be pleased. "But what the hell happened to your poor face, and where did you get that godawful shirt?"

"I suppose I had what you could call a wilderness experience," Pierce said, smiled at her and sat on the love seat beside Naomi. "And I'm not responsible for this shirt. I was bullied into the thing, and that's the truth."

"Naomi, you dope, why didn't you get this poor man a couple of off-white guayaberas?"

"I tried. He didn't like the lace."

"Hmmm. A 'wilderness adventure.' Trouble?"

"That's right," Pierce said.

"Ah, *trouble*. It's the one thing I really do miss in the

square life. Trouble. I used to wake up in the morning eager for it—though I do think I gave more than I got. It was like a heavy habit. Wake up and have a trouble shot, then a dealing-with-trouble shot, then a having-dealt-with-trouble shot. . . . And who was it gave you this trouble, Mr. Boyce?"

"Gil."

"Oh, I doubt that. 'Gil Boyce . . .' It's not bad, but I don't believe it for a minute. I remember your poor daughter's last name. Who are you, really? Come on, fess up to old Jackie. . . ."

"No way," Pierce said. "You might take advantage."

"Heavens no. —And just who dropped you in the swamp, *Gil*?"

"Locals."

"Hmmm. Not for welshing, I hope. I do hate a welsher."

". . . You're not trying to be unpleasant, are you, Jackie?"

"Wha-oh! *Temper* . . . I apologize."

"It was a . . . territory thing. A defensive thing."

"And locals. So, not Eli Palacio down from Jax, and not the people from Miami. The local trade people?"

Pierce smiled. "How did you folks do through that storm?"

"Two windows," Jackie said. "And a Dumpster. And I do want to say, considering what you're doing down here, that I'm very sorry you lost your daughter. I remember her picture in the paper; she looked like a good girl, and pretty."

"I think she was."

"Okay . . . So, I understand you have some money for me. Naomi—dear girl—has guaranteed ten long up front, and another five for the extra."

"She told you right, Jackie. But the five depends on something very solid."

"Um-hmm. And did she tell *you* that old as I am, I'm not too old to deal with anyone who fucks me over?

Not too old to make a phone call and get piano wire stuck in somebody's brain, stuck right in through the ear."

"That really work?"

"Gil, it works like sixty. There's just one little drop of blood to clean up with a Q-Tip, and that's it. A stroke—and a real tragedy."

"Sounds like big-city shit to me," Pierce said, and he and Jackie laughed. ". . . Tell you what, you can have your ten." He unfolded the newspaper, and handed Jackie two thick manila envelopes.

"Oooh, it's Christmas," Jackie said, opened the envelopes in her lap, and thumbed through the money. She looked down the empty lobby, then took a few bills out and held each up to the light. "—And they're straight! You *are* a regular guy."

"That's ten," Pierce said. "And I can get your five extra right now—it's in my spare out there. You earn it, you'll have it. You don't, and you won't."

"All right," Jackie said. "For you, since Naomi likes you, I'll break a rule. I won't ask for the money first. . . . The girl was the third one killed. Rue Long. Rue, for Ruella—and why a parent would name a white girl Ruella, escapes me. A golden girl, a gymnast, one of those muscular blond princesses. . . . Her aunt lives here, Myra Pinot, almost senile but not quite. The girl was in college, Peace River, north in the county, and she was killed in a basement classroom. And, according to Auntie, a confidante—parents are always the last to know—according to Auntie Myra, our blond coed had led a secret life for some time."

Jackie rearranged herself in her armchair, recrossed her legs. "Her old boyfriend on the sly—boyfriend since high school, according to Auntie—was a young Mexican, Tomás Seguin. Very handsome, but hasty with his knife. He almost killed two sportfisher crewmen in an argument behind the Conch Club. It's a bar out on De Soto. . . . Now, all this was years *before* the girl was murdered, so according to Auntie the police either weren't interested in ancient history, or don't know it. It hadn't been an advertised relationship—the golden girl and her hoodlum beaner." Jackie pursed her lips, considering the relationship. "—Though actually, some of the boy's relatives appear to have been respectable. An older brother is a venture-capital person up in Jax, according to dotty Myra, who heard it from a friend. Doing *very* well."

". . . Tomás," Pierce said.

"Tomás Seguin. Ring a bell?"

"Go on. . . ."

"Auntie Myra thinks her princess's decline began all those many years ago, being banged by young Tomás—so handsome, brown, and nasty. The Sweetwater, apparently, only the *coup de grâce*." Jackie looked at her watch. "Are you two staying for dinner? Because I have to tell them if I'm going to have guests. They serve early here. It would be hamburger steak, mashed potatoes, string beans and dinner rolls tonight. A forties classic, and a big favorite with the ladies."

"No," Naomi said. "I don't think we'll stay."

"Why not?" Pierce said. "Hamburger steak sounds good. We'd like to, Jackie, as long as you let us pay for our dinners."

"I do love a gentleman."

"Now, go on with what you were saying."

"Well . . . I'm sorry to have to reveal it, but when our princess was murdered, Auntie Myra had reason to believe that she had a little coke habit—thanks to the old boyfriend—and was also *the* coke-seller on campus. Took orders, and filled them. . . . Auntie believes it because our all-American girl once—very high—confided in Auntie and then burst into tears. She also, for a while, garaged a new Mercedes 450 convertible behind their house. Said it was a loaner from a rich boyfriend, and not to mention to anyone that she was using it. The registration, though, according to nosy Myra, read Ruella Dorothy Long."

"Holy shit," Naomi said.

"You've got the five," Pierce said. He got up and limped down the lobby to The Palms' entranceway. William, on duty now and in uniform, opened the door for him.

"Jackie, that's amazing."

Jackie had been watching Pierce. "If you think that's the most amazing tale to come out of this nest of aging carrion birds, you have another think coming." She turned to Naomi. "—And you *told* him, you bitch."

"Jackie, I work for him."

"And that excuses treachery?"

"Jackie, it doesn't make any difference to the way he feels about you."

"You say!"

"I think he likes you."

"Oh, 'he likes me.' Great . . ."

"Well?"

"Well what?"

"What do you think?"

"That really is a dreadful shirt."

"Come on."

"All right . . . He's personable. Very tough, obviously an ex-con, and I would say was—probably still is—big in his field. Where in the world do you think all that money is coming from? And by the way, he's armed."

"I know."

"You know. And are you keeping in mind that what this is all about is your armed robber looking for a homicidal maniac? And that when and if he finds him, he is going to blow his head off? You *are* keeping that in mind?"

"Yes, I am."

" 'Yes, I am.' . . . Well, he's polite, and middle-aged attractive—despite the mosquito bites—in a lanky, well-hung rural way. Sure you haven't gotten a piece of that, you greedy girl?"

"We're friends."

" 'We're friends.' Naomi, you are the sap of the world."

"But you like him."

"Naomi, I'm not your mother."

"I know you're not my mother. But you like him."

"He's . . . he's an old-fashioned type. He's a man."

"I thought you'd like him, Jackie."

"Honest to Christ, Naomi, you're forty years old—"

"I'm not."

"Almost forty, and most of the time you act like a hard broad who's been around and fucked and been paid for it by twenty years of men. And then suddenly sometimes you start dreaming, as if you have not yet wakened to smell the roses."

"Jackie, be a friend."

"Sweetheart, I don't have it in me to be a friend. I'm just an old acquaintance. Does Jesse James— What's funny?"

"Nothing."

"Does Jesse James have a little woman back home?"

"He's not married, Jackie."

"I know he's not married—I can smell those. But there's someone rolling pie crust in Indiana or wherever?"

"He sends her postcards, and calls. I spoke to her. She's nice."

"Ah. 'She's nice.' —And has he sent her a carved-coconut pirate head?"

"He will, if he sees one."

"Men . . ." Jackie said. "Aren't they a trip?"

Chapter 19

Karen had brought the food, and they'd had a picnic on the quiet side of the lake. Away from the highway and houses.

On the northern edge of the city, Palmetto Lake was big enough that only an occasional jogger came along the paths so far around it. Live oaks grew at the edge of the water, grew so close their lower branches sometimes drooped their leaves to touch the lake, dipping in breezes.

The hurricane had torn some limbs away, scattered a trash of branches and dead leaves over the grass and down the bank to the lake. It had torn the clouds away too, and left the sky clear and cooler, a sweeter blue not burned blue-white by the sun.

They'd each had a bottle of Beck's beer, half a big delicatessen liverwurst sandwich, pickles, and potato chips.

"It feels so strange," Moira said. She was sitting with her back to the trunk of a small oak. "You can't imagine how strange it feels. You know—to have done it. Have it all over with, but it's still sort of with you."

"I know how it feels." Karen was lying beside her, on a beach towel. She'd taken her blouse off, was lying in the sun in her jeans and bra.

"No, you have to do it . . . have done it."

"Moira, I know how it feels." Karen sat half up, rested on her elbow, and drank the last of her beer from the bottle. "—When I was fourteen, I got pregnant. My brother was nineteen, and he had sex with me." She lay back down and closed her eyes. ". . . Well, I couldn't bear having my parents find out, so I tried all kinds of things. I tried everything I'd heard of. I fell down on my stomach as hard as I could on the back steps. And I drank kerosene."

"God," Moira said.

"—And I tried other things, but nothing happened, and after a while, after four months, I could see my stomach." Karen reached down and gently patted her stomach. "I was really starting to show more and more, and pretty soon even big sweaters weren't going to hide it. . . . So, I straightened a coat hanger and lay down naked in the bathtub late one night and put that up me. I pushed it up as hard as I could."

"*Jesus*. Karen . . ."

"—Well, I fainted; you can believe it. . . . And when I woke up, there was blood in the bathtub, and I pulled the piece of wire out and I fainted again. . . . When I woke up the next time I was hemorrhaging and lying in all that blood, and my baby had come out."

"Oh, that's so *terrible*. . . ."

"He was smaller than a kitten . . . and attached . . . and he moved a little at first, and then he didn't. I was so . . . I was very confused. I picked him up and hugged him, but we both got cold. We lay there all night long, and I tried to go to sleep, but I couldn't. And in the morning my mother came in."

"Oh, my God. . . ."

"Then, I really thought it was a great tragedy. I dreamed about it all the time and I heard my baby talking to somebody, and really made myself sick. . . . But now, I understand I was only ignorant—and I'd failed in responsibility through ignorance."

"That's . . . that's the worst thing. . . ." Moira had tears in her eyes. "And I've been talking so damn much about *my* problems . . . *my* baby."

Karen opened her eyes and lay looking up at the sun.

"I'm not supposed to do this," she said. "But it's hard not to, because He looks back."

"Do what?" Moira said.

"Look at the Sun," Karen said. "I'm not supposed to." She sighed and got up, folded her towel, and went over to her gray book bag. She unzipped it, put the towel in, and took something out. "Are you missing your baby?"

"I guess I always will, in a way," Moira said, and reached over to pick up her crumpled sandwich paper and a leftover pickle slice, and tucked them into the delicatessen's paper bag. "Finished with your beer?"

"Here." Karen brought the beer bottle and a napkin to her, and Moira put them in the paper bag. "—Well, you won't. Not much longer."

"Not much longer what?"

"Miss your baby," Karen said, and made a soft clicking sound with something. "Get up," she said.

"What?"

"*Up.* I've got something to show you, sweetheart, and it's real important." And she bent and took Moira's arm and lifted her up. Lifted her gently as the Angel had to do, or the arm would have been broken.

"What is it?"

"Come down here with me," the Angel said, and its voice buzzed like a bee's. It tugged Moira gently, guided her puzzled down the bank to the lake. "Now look," it said.

"What? Look at what?"

The Angel pointed to the Sun's path gleaming, sparkling, shimmering across the lake. "There's the very best way. That's the way you should go."

"Go where?" Moira said. "Karen. . . ? What's the matter?" And tried to pull her arm away.

"Listen to me," the Angel said, and held her. "And I promise you'll be safe."

"Please . . . let me *go*."

"—Moira, you take exactly that way to the Sun, and

don't be frightened by how far and dark it is—don't be frightened by the emptiness on either side. Sweetheart, you stay on the bright way, regardless." Then it made a clicking sound with what was in its other hand, and reached around and cut her throat.

Moira yanked free and leaped a little away, and turned gargling and spitting blood. She tried to say something but it flew spurting past her red tongue and spattered scarlet down her T-shirt, drenched it so her small breasts printed through. Taking little staggering steps this way and that, Moira tried to breathe, and breathed blood. She put her hands to her throat, fumbled in spraying wet . . . then, staring at the Angel and the Angel's blade, knelt awkwardly as if a better place were there, just along the grass.

The Angel saw she had begun to understand.

Moira knelt, then lay down on her side—staring past the Angel now—her small mouth stretched wide and draining bloody foam. Then slowly she commenced to convulse and kick in a drift of windblown leaves.

The Angel knelt to her to remove breasts unearned—smiled, tucked Moira's soaked T-shirt up, and said, "Don't be afraid. It's almost done. . . . Your little girl is waiting in the Sun."

The signs were down for Gator Cove.

They lay shredded in late moonlight along the side of the road. The hurricane had torn the arched sign away from the turnoff, sailed the painted alligator out over the swamp.

Pierce turned off the truck's lights, slowly drove the access road for twenty or thirty yards, then pulled over to the shoulder and parked. There'd be a little while waiting, waiting the moon down for darkness. . . .

He'd wakened late, at almost noon, and lain thinking for quite a while—considering that odd Jackie and her news the day before, and the conversation over the hamburger-steak dinner, with all those old ladies grazing around them in that fancy glassed-in dining room. . . . Pierce had known several pimps in Kansas City; knew one in Chicago. He hadn't cared for them. All had a nastiness to them—came, he supposed, from abusing women—and Jackie had that meanness, no saying she didn't. An untrustworthy person, but humorous . . . good company.

Now, why would people in the trade go and kill a girl so savagely—feel they had to do that, cover it with the Sweetwater's murders, rather than shoot and bury her and be done with it? Just have her disappear. . . .

Why? —So as to have all questions answered, leave nothing for the police to wonder about, nothing to make them go any direction but toward the Sweetwater. It was a good enough reason. And if good enough for one killing—why not for two? Or more?

Use a pretty young woman—a classy-looking young woman in a fancy car—as a transport mule across the state. Do that while the law was looking to wilderness, airboats and the like, for your way to go. And then, after a while, if the young woman began to use the stuff herself, or got quarrelsome . . . why, there was the Sweetwater's way to deal with her.

One done that way, for sure—and maybe more than one.

Rue Long . . . Pierce remembered her face from the newspaper at the Palmetto Lake library. A smiling, pretty, *pretty* girl. Looked like a college girl in a movie.

Pierce had spent some time lying in bed thinking about her, and what had happened to her. Then he'd gotten up and dressed—feet still a little sore, but his face looking better—and driven down the strip to a Taco Bell for a big lunch. Pleasure to have his truck again, even duded up.

After lunch, he'd gone back to his motel room and called Naomi over in Talavera to be sure she hadn't been disturbed. —Only person who'd bothered her had been old Montfort; he'd come in from fishing and spent the morning talking with her about trolling for mackerel. Seemed that was the only way to catch the only fish worth eating.

Pierce had listened to Naomi on the subject of fishermen, also listened to advice on soaking his grass-cut feet in warm water and Epsom salts. Then he'd said good-bye, hung up, undressed, and gone back to bed. He'd watched some fools on television, then slept again.

After dark, he'd wakened feeling just fine. . . .

. . . Pierce sat in the parked truck a good while, watching the moon, listening. No one turned down this way. Only a few cars passed on the highway behind him; it was late for traffic out in the country.

He waited awhile longer, until the moon's edge sank into treetops, then opened the truck door and stepped down into the coolest night he'd known in Florida. Down into the night's odors, and the tree frogs' high-pitched rattling singing.

Pierce walked down the road past two more ruined signs for Gator Cove. The wind had snapped one sign right off a four-by-four post. The broken wood shone pale in the last of moonlight.

Pierce went past that, and past the driveway entrance to the place. There was a pole light, a security light glowing back there in the parking lot. He went down the road past the wooden fence bordering the property; it was a six-foot fence, roofs of sheds and outbuildings showing over the top.

When the wooden fence changed to five-strand barbed wire, Pierce jumped the roadside ditch—his feet still tender—climbed the wire, and came out on the other side into sedge and swamp. He walked down into that and darkness . . . waded through mud and shallows, and worked his way around to the property's back. Another section of fence there—wood, old and rotten. He broke through that quietly as he could, twisted out two boards, and squeezed through.

There was rough grass and a dirt bank. Pierce's sneakers and trouser legs were wet and black with mud. The smell was almost the smell of the Manchineel.

Once up the bank, he stood and rested a minute, listening. There was a big pond off to the left, its surface shining soft silver in starlight. More than an acre of water, with cypresses around it. Place where Big Louis lived . . . Pierce walked slowly, carefully, through low scrub, setting the branches aside as they touched him in the dark. He saw a small ruined building just before he reached it, and went on as quietly as he could—sliding along the building's wall.

He heard a radio playing Hawaiian music, but paid no attention to it. It was the man left on guard that interested Pierce, and he left the ruined building, and crossed to another, looking for him.

He saw a cigarette coal glow . . . and dim, and glow again.

The Mexican, Horacio, was just visible sitting on a shed's doorsill, smoking pot. Pierce could smell the smoke. . . . There was a shoulder arm—looked like an automatic shotgun—lying across his lap. It was a sign of an organization slipping, for a night guard to be sitting out smoking pot. Organization slipping, or been too successful for too long—getting careless.

Pierce took his time and went slowly past another building—smelled like a stable; likely had been a stable at one time—went around that, came to the back of the shed . . . and slowly down its side to the front, smelling the pot smoke as he went.

Horacio looked up as Pierce stepped around the shed's corner.

He looked up, and grunted as if he'd been hit. Apparently thought for an instant that Pierce was dead, and come back anyway.

Horacio started to yell the same time he reached

down for the shotgun—but accomplished neither.
Pierce bent down and slid the Smith & Wesson's
muzzle gently into his mouth.

"Shhhh."

Horacio stared up at him, seemed to be relieved that
Pierce was real. Relieved it was just a matter of a gun
barrel stuck in his mouth.

"Up," Pierce whispered to him. *"Up and inside."*

Horacio said something around the gun muzzle, then
pulled his head back a little to speak more clearly.
"Don' kill me."

"Shhhh."

"Don' kill me, man."

Pierce took the revolver's muzzle out of Horacio's
mouth, lifted the shotgun away as the man backed into
the shed. . . . A shadow of a bulb was hanging from the
ceiling, and Pierce set the shotgun against the wall,
reached up, found the light, and switched it on.

"No hard feelin's, man," Horacio said.

It was such a funny thing to say that Pierce had to
smile. He holstered the Smith & Wesson, reached
down for the shotgun, drew it back over his shoulder
like a baseball bat, and swung the butt into Horacio's
head. The Mexican gave a sort of jump and dumped
over, his feet—in fancy high-top sneakers—flying up
in the air almost in a cartwheel.

The shotgun stock was one of the new black plastic
ones. It hadn't broken.

"No hard feelings now," Pierce said, and hunkered
down on the shed's splintery pine floor to wait for
Horacio to wake up.

. . . It took a while.

Such a while, Pierce was concerned he might have
killed the man, and got up to look. But Horacio was
breathing . . . appeared to be having a bad dream. He
dreamed and muttered for some time, then groaned,
and groaned himself awake. Said something in
Spanish.

"Last thing I want to do," Pierce said. "—You listening? Last thing I want to do is make a man a cripple. But I don't have time to fool with you."

Horacio was lying on his side, curled up for comfort. He looked at Pierce as if he'd never seen him before. The right side of his face was red, shiny and swelling. Pierce supposed he'd broken the man's cheekbone.

"You understand what I'm saying to you?"

Horacio seemed to think about that, then nodded. There were tears in his eyes . . . probably from being hit so hard.

"—I just don't have the time to waste."

Horacio nodded as if he certainly could understand that, a man being too busy to waste time.

"—So, first time you lie, or don't answer me, I'm going to thumb an eye right out of your head. Second time, second eye. . . . So don't you make a mistake, now. Don't you be forcing me to do something that cruel."

Tears ran down Horacio's cheek. Pain, Pierce supposed, from that busted cheekbone.

"You understand what I said?"

Horacio nodded. Sniffled like a child with a cold, drainage from the broken sinus on that side.

"Say it. Say you understand."

"I . . . understan'." Horacio sounded different, nose all plugged up. Sounded like a comedian pretending to have a bad cold. And sounded more sensible than scared . . . a pretty good man.

"Who else is on the place tonight?"

". . . Me and Jim Clarence."

"You sure?"

"That's all. Just me an' him."

"All right . . . And your handsome fellow, in the suit—Tomás. What's his last name?"

Horacio sighed. "Seguin. Tomás Seguin."

"Okay. —Now, did you people use a woman named

Rue Dorothy Long to run some stuff for you? Mule it over in a fancy car?"

". . . Before my time. Man, all that shit was before my time." Horacio's face was swelling fast. It looked like a spoiling vegetable in the bulb's yellow overhead light—a melon frozen in the field and spoiled.

"I asked you a question. Better answer it pretty quick."

"*Yes.* . . . I heard we run her for a while."

"Did you people have a problem with that girl?"

"I think so. . . . Before my *time*."

"Too bad," Pierce said, leaned forward suddenly and put his left thumb against Horacio's right eye. "Too bad."

"No *no*! No no no. They had trouble with her. She was skimmin'. She was peelin' a little every shipment and sellin' on her own. Bitch was a user, man. Feedin' that fuckin' habit!"

Pierce took his thumb away, and Horacio said, "Oh . . ." turned his head and tried to vomit on the shed floor. He tried to vomit, but nothing came up. He took a while to catch his breath; then he said, "Before my time . . ."

"You people do her?"

Horacio said nothing until Pierce shifted his weight, leaned down. Then Horacio said, "I heard that. That's what I heard, that she had to go." He was breathing deep, seemed to Pierce he was trying to keep from being sick. . . . There was only the sound of his breathing in the shed—and from outside, insects . . . frogs, the radio's distant Hawaiian music.

Pierce had gotten used to insect sounds, frog sounds, in Florida's summer—but now, listening, he heard their high chirping noises filling the night. And there was a deeper note, a soft grunting roar. . . . Big Louis, he supposed.

"Who did it?" Pierce said. "Who killed her?" —And when Horacio didn't answer right away, Pierce sprang onto him, rested a knee on his neck to hold him still, and put a thumb into the man's right eye . . . felt the softness giving way.

Horacio gave a little scream, like a child's—and talked so fast he was hard to understand. *"No oh no oh no it was Sequin!"*

"You sure of that?"

"Sí—yes! Take . . . take it out!"

Pierce lifted his thumb away. There were little broken veins in the man's eye.

"Go on."

Horacio was looking worse, as if the damage from the shotgun's butt was growing across his face like cancer. "That's what people *say*, man. People say Tomás put her down for skimmin'. Jim just took over, then—an' he was smarter than Nedlund, an' he caught on she was peelin'. So then, Tomás, he went right out and put her down quick."

"Like the Sweetwater . . ."

"That's right. That's right. So that fuckin' nut would get blamed, man."

"And why not just bury her, Horacio, or give her to the reptile?"

"They didn' want the cops lookin'. People lookin'. That way, it was all over, a done thing and the nut did it. . . . But man . . . I'm sick, man. I'm tellin' you that shit was all before my time."

"So, how many other girls—how many other mules went that way?"

"None of 'em . . . None of 'em. We use guys, man. Grove guys an' pickers." Horacio stopped talking, took more deep breaths, trying to breathe the pain away was what it looked like to Pierce. "Women are too fuckin' much trouble . . . an' picker trucks go all over the state, man." Horacio closed his eyes, and looked to be resting awhile. . . . Then he went to sleep, lying there on his side, snoring as if Pierce wasn't there. Man hadn't been so badly hurt, it would have been funny.

Pierce leaned over and gently shook him. Shook him again, and Horacio woke up and said, "Shit . . ."

"Who else?" Pierce said. "You people ever have a Coast Guard officer working for you—a lady? Have one of those working for you a few years ago? Maybe caused what's-his-name—Nedlund—some trouble back then?"

"Oh, are you kiddin' me? A *Coast Guard* officer? An' a *woman*? I never heard anybody dumb enough to trust that. . . . An' hey . . . an' hey, I feel bad. I'm sick, man. . . ."

"What about that ranger out at Manchineel Park? Didn't you people just have to put a lady ranger out of your way?"

". . . No, hell," Horacio said, and closed his eyes again. "We don' use that swamp last two years. No reason to fuck with those people." He opened his eyes, squinting in the light; even the soft light seemed to hurt his eyes. "—That's your girl. We didn' mess with your girl, man. . . ."

Pierce stood, switched off the overhead bulb, and yanked a length of the electric wire down and loose from the wall. Working by touch in near dark, he tied Horacio hard—wrists behind him, and ankles together. Horacio groaned every time Pierce moved him. . . . He tore Horacio's shirt, wadded a piece of cloth, and stuffed it into the man's mouth, used a cloth strip knotted to hold the gag in.

Pierce leaned down to be sure Horacio heard him. "If I see you again tonight, I'm going to kill you. So if you start feeling stronger, and you work loose? You still better stay right in here, and real quiet. . . ."

Horacio nodded. Hadn't gone back to sleep yet.

Pierce picked up the shotgun and went out into the night. A very cool night, for Florida. He supposed if they didn't have those hurricanes, the summer storms, the weather would get hotter and hotter and no relief from it. That would be more than people could stand. . . .

There was more light as he came into the yard. Light spilling over the fence from the parking lot. . . . The Hawaiian music—a regular guitar and some other instrument sounded like a mandolin—was still playing off a tape or radio past a storeyard of stacked lumber, fence wire, and rusted oil drums. Some of the barbed wire had popped loose from its spools, and was sprung and coiled in heaps in the moonlight—made a thorn scrub crueler than the Manchineel's.

Pierce moved past the storeyard very slowly, looking and listening, the shotgun resting easy in his hands. He looked for changes in the light as anything moved through it. . . . Listened through the insects singing, and the frogs, for any other sound but Hawaiian music. A man was singing with that music now. Sounded like slow yodeling . . .

The music was coming through two lit windows at the far end of a long building—opposite end of the building the people had come out of, greeting him first time he came.

Pierce drifted over . . . drifted over and found a plain wooden door around the other side, and it wasn't locked. —No question these people had had it peaceful for a while, to be so casual.

He opened the door quietly, let the shotgun lead into a short hall with beat-up tan linoleum on the floor. Old-time thick linoleum; not the new stuff.

Music was coming from down the way, an open door on the right. . . .

Probably because of the music—and being busy typing on a computer keyboard—Jim Clarence didn't hear Pierce step into the office doorway. Didn't realize he was there, until movement caught his eye.

"Holy *shit!*" Jim Clarence jumped as he sat, made his swivel chair squeak. He sat for a moment, his head turned to stare at Pierce, his soft dark hands still resting on the computer's keys. Jim Clarence was dressed up in tan slacks, white shirt, and a summer-weight brown sports coat; looked as if he'd been out somewhere for dinner. His shirt was pooched out in front by his belly.

". . . Well, well, *well*. You are a resilient old dude, aren't you?" His fingers played delicately on the computer keys, as if he was getting ready to write . . . enter something more when he turned back to his work. "I hope we're not going to have some bullshit revenge fantasy acted out here. I hope we're not going to get bizarre."

"You just stay sitting right there. You move, you better move slow."

"Oh, you can count on it, Pierce; I'm not a fast mover." As if demonstrating, he reached slowly across his desk, turned off the tape player. ". . . I expect you've renewed acquaintance with Horacio. He was *supposed* to be on security."

"He's not going to bother us."

". . . No, I bet not. Didn't kill the poor guy, I hope."

"No, I didn't. But he's hurt."

"Don't doubt that for a minute. So, if this isn't a you-fucked-with-me-so-I'll-fuck-with-you call—then what is it?"

Pierce saw himself dimly reflected in the lenses of Jim Clarence's glasses. "Start with, I'll take my wallet and ID."

"Okay . . . okay. No problem. I have that tucked away in a safe place. Not here. But it will be delivered to your motel. And I believe there was also a shirt, trousers. . . ."

"Toss 'em."

" 'Toss 'em'? Toss that shirt? I recall that shirt being a major shirt. Pineapples."

" 'I don't want the shirt."

"Okay. You don't have to have it. —But you do have my admiration. How the hell did you get out of there? You were in miles deep, man—and Olivia coming right on top of you."

"I was lucky."

"Sure . . . Well, I could use a man *that* lucky. If you don't turn me into a good Indian right here and now, how would you like to come work for me?"

Pierce, watching over the shotgun, saw in Jim Clarence the calm a criminal needed if he was to make any great profit at all. A considerable young Indian, and likable if you didn't have something he wanted. "No thanks."

"—Don't be hasty," Jim Clarence said. "You'd be surprised, the low level of help available these days. Be surprised what I've managed to do with an organization I found fucked up to the max."

Pierce shook his head.

"Well, think about it. Don't be so quick to say no to a major amount of money. —Unless, of course, you decide to shoot me with that big gun after all, do me to death. In that case, I withdraw the offer."

"I have some questions for you, Jim Clarence."

"Questions? That's all?"

"Long as you answer them."

"Oh . . . oh, I'll answer them. You've got the shotgun, and I'm a realist and a businessman." He folded his hands in his lap and settled into his swivel chair, brown, plump, and relaxed, apparently happy to answer questions.

"Your man, Seguin . . ."

"What about that handsome devil?"

"Know any of his old girlfriends?"

"Odd question . . . No, I don't. I came up here to work for Chuck Nedlund almost four years ago. And in that time, our dashing Tomás has been an old married man, and very useful. . . . As it happens, Chuck was not realizing the potential of the area, so I had to take over responsibility here." Jim Clarence pursed his lips, seemed regretful.

"Nedlund retired?"

"Yes. It was a . . . it was a retirement for the good of the business."

"Could I get in touch with him?"

". . . I wouldn't think so. No."

"I see."

"But what's all this about my executive officer? Tomás is a good friend of mine—and despite his looks, hasn't been a ladies' man as far as I know. His wife's a sweetie."

"Supposing he'd *had* a girlfriend—woman he'd been with for years—would you have let her work for you?"

"You bet not. Unhealthy relationship." Jim Clarence smiled and seemed patient, waiting for Pierce to get to the point.

"Tomás Seguin and Rue Long were together since high school here. Together for several years. —Kept quiet, but still known locally."

Jim Clarence sat silent and relaxed, but no longer smiling.

"—I understand you caught her skimming and selling on her own . . . supposedly on her own. You caught her, and when Seguin knew she was caught, he murdered her real quick. Used the Sweetwater's style."

Jim Clarence listened, still and silent as a stone. He looked more Indian than he had before.

"Tell me, Jim—does Tomás have any relatives?"

"Talks about two sisters," Jim Clarence said.

"Does he? And he hasn't mentioned a brother?"

"No. Hasn't mentioned him."

"Well, Jim, he has a brother. Older brother, man doing very well up in Jacksonville. *Very* well—in venture capital. Now, I wonder . . . I wonder where that venture capital has been coming from."

Jim Clarence took his glasses off, rubbed the bridge of his nose between thumb and forefinger. Without the glasses, his dark eyes looked softer and sadder.

"—Tell me, Jim . . . does Tomás go up to Jacksonville often? Maybe started going up there—little trips—when his girl was carrying for you?"

Jim Clarence put his glasses on. "Can't say it doesn't hurt," he said. "The foolish human heart will look for friendship at least. One area of trust . . ."

"I've been blessed that way," Pierce said. "Never had a friend turn me; never had a man I went robbing with, go bad."

"Well . . . it's the business," Jim Clarence said. "This is a morally equivocal business. Yours is more straightforward. . . ."

Pierce lowered the shotgun, and walked over to lean it against the wall.

"—And you dug this up because you thought we might have done your girl."

"That's right."

"Well, we didn't. The park got a little obvious some time ago. We scoot around out there now and then— keep their attention off the roads and groves. . . ."

"So I understand."

"Horacio going to need a doctor?"

"I'd have one see him," Pierce said, and went to the door. "So long."

"Take care, Pierce," Jim Clarence said.

Chapter 20

"And none of the other women?"

"None of the others. Rue Long was working for them—working for Tomás Seguin, really. He killed her to keep her mouth shut."

Naomi had insisted on meeting at the IHOP in Fort Talavera. "I have to have pancakes." She'd ordered the blueberry pancakes, sausage, and coffee, and said, "You're a bad influence, Tyler. We're always meeting for these breakfasts and they're making me fat. —Why can't we meet at the ballet?"

"Be all right with me," Pierce said. "I saw the *Nutcracker* ballet with Lisa in St. Louis when she was eight and I liked it."

"I'll check the paper . . . arts section. —And you think these drug dealers were telling the truth?"

"You bet. Man was hurting too bad to lie to me, and Jim Clarence is too careful to lie to me."

"And not even the Coast Guard girl? She couldn't be useful to them?" Naomi had gotten her blueberry pancakes, put maple syrup on them. Put some more on, now.

"It's a . . . you'd call it a macho trade—"

"Like bank robbing?"

"Like bank robbing. —People aren't going to bring women into it except for a little muling or small sales. People who try to use a lot of girls for the business, are going to have difficulty with them sooner or later. Have to have a real good reason to go to that much

trouble—and Jim Clarence's territory is transport in-
state, not over ocean, so the Coast Guard wouldn't be
his problem anyway."

"So—only Rue Long."

"That's right. Seguin brought her in."

"That shithead."

"Don't think old Tomás is going to be around to
worry about." Pierce had ordered eggs and bacon.
Hadn't felt like pancakes. The bacon wasn't bad, but it
was that thin restaurant bacon. Not like real
country . . .

Naomi put down her fork, and took a sip of coffee.
"You do know what this means, Tyler."

"Right. Yes, I do—it means we could have an excep-
tion that disproves the rule."

"That's exactly right. We have something the police
never had. We have a control, Tyler! A murder we
know the Sweetwater *didn't* commit. So, whatever's
true of all the other victims—but isn't true of Rue
Long—that's the Sweetwater's reason for doing what
he does!"

"Maybe."

"And Dr. Salcedo said, when we have the reason, the
why, we'll have the killer, standing clear in the sunlight." She had some more coffee, made a face, and
poured in another little package of sugar, stirred it. "I
never thought we'd do it, Tyler. But now, I think we
will. —What do you mean, 'maybe'?"

"I mean that his reason doesn't have to be a *why*. It
could be a *where*, or even a *when*. He might choose
them for stopping to look in a pet-shop window. He
might choose them for buying lamb chops on Friday."

"I suppose that's true. . . . He's so fucking crazy."

"And there's something else, Naomi. If Tomás
Seguin could use the Sweetwater's way of killing,
another man could too."

"I doubt it, Tyler."

"I know it isn't likely—but these were all young

women, two of them married, three single. And there's
bound to have been a lot of relationships there, a lot of
men."

"And the police checked all of them out!"

"Didn't check out Tomás Seguin." Pierce poured
Naomi more coffee. ". . . Cops have to *know* about
them—have a name, a face. Man they don't know
about, they can't check."

"But there could be someone like that for any one of
those girls. . . ."

"That's right, and what happens to our control case
then?"

". . . Okay, Tyler, I'll go back to that damn report,
and our notebook—the stuff you copied from those
newspapers—*and* what Jackie told us. I'll lay everything out in a chart. A big chart. I'll write in every
damn thing we know about each girl—and *where* and
when they were killed. I'll compare all that to Rue
Long's death, and we'll see what differences show up."

"We need to do that, or we're going to lose track."

Naomi wrote something down in the blue notebook.
"And can we get anything more from your cop? I'm
sorry—but for one thing, we should look at those
autopsy findings. The summary didn't have much in
there at all from the autopsies. Think they thought it
would upset the governor."

"I know it . . . I know that. Jim Clarence owes me
one, so I'll see if he'll push Burney to do that for us."
Pierce put some egg on the corner of a piece of toast,
ate that in a bite. "—And it's time I had a talk with
Jason the Diver. Little man who wasn't there . . ."

"Tyler, you're not going to threaten him or anything?"

"Wasn't planning to."

"Because you know, it wasn't his fault. He wasn't
there. There was no way he could protect her."

"I know that. That's right . . . if he wasn't there."

"Because you weren't there either, Tyler," Naomi
said. "—And that isn't *your* fault. It isn't something

you should be feeling so bad . . . so guilty about. It was the Sweetwater that killed your Lisa."

"Tell you something, Naomi. . . ." Pierce put down his coffee cup. Wasn't good coffee, anyway. "Tell you something. I'm paying you to help, and I know you mean well, but sometimes it would be a good idea to just mind your own business."

"Never," Naomi said. "Not when a friend's in trouble—so don't put on your bank robber's face for me, Tyler." She picked up her purse, and slid out of the booth. "—And by the way, you owe me three days' pay."

. . . Outside, as they walked to the parking lot, Pierce felt—for the first time in this state—the pleasures of Florida weather. A slight salt breeze, even inland, and still some morning coolness despite the sun's bright light. The hurricane had blown the summer heat away; it was coming back, but not yet with all its weight.

At the truck, Pierce went around to the passenger-side door, and unlocked that for Naomi first . . . put his hand on her elbow to help her climb in. It occurred to him as he walked back around to the driver's side, that he hadn't been doing her that courtesy.

He started the truck and said, "Haven't been treating you with the politeness I should have, Naomi. I'm sorry."

Naomi looked at him. "You don't have to open doors for me, Tyler. I can use the exercise. . . . And you have been polite. You've been very nice."

"My folks taught me manners. Daddy'd teach me real sudden, he caught me out. It was 'sir' an' 'mam' on our place."

"They sound like good people."

"Well, they were. My mom was real nice. And my daddy could be, too. Earl Pierce never hurt a woman. 'They're all queens' was what he'd say. '—And see you treat 'em that way.' " Pierce put the Ford in gear and turned out of the lot. "Daddy didn't qualify treating men that well. He had a real bad temper with any man crossed him. . . ."

"Was he good to you, Tyler?"

"Long as I didn't cross him. . . ." Pierce held the truck at the curb exit, waiting for a break in the avenue traffic.

"You go left."

"I know I go left. I've been studying the city maps. I know the towns pretty well now, Naomi."

"Pretty well," Naomi said, opened the blue notebook in her lap, and started writing in it.

"What are you writing?"

"Making notes what to ask Jackie. . . ."

"Ummm." Pierce pulled out onto the avenue.

"—Tell you what I'm going to do, Tyler. I'll make our big chart . . . and enter in there anything else she can come up with. She told us what her old ladies *know* about the women who were killed. Now, I want any damn thing they *heard*—rumors, gossip, stories people told at the time . . . whatever. It'll be mostly crap, but there may be one useful thing."

"Go to it. I'll drop you back at Montfort's. You can keep the Nissan."

"Jackie'll charge you again."

"We'll pay—for that 'one useful thing.' Meantime, I'll be over at Lisa's boyfriend's, the scuba shop. Then maybe look up another one, Marcie Tredenberg—the pizza girl. . . ."

"Her boyfriend?"

"Right."

"Ummm . . . Ecklin. Terry Ecklin."

"Ecklin, that's right. . . . What did it say in that bullshit report? 'Subject wept'? Well, I'm going to have a talk with a couple of 'subjects.' " Pierce drove for several blocks . . . saw the expressway sign, and turned right, staying in the right lane up to the on-ramp. Out of the corner of his eye, he saw Naomi glance up to see

which way he was going, then look back down at the
notebook.

No different from having a wife along.

. . . If the car had stayed in place back there, Pierce
wouldn't have noticed it. He'd been enjoying the day,
the coolness of it with the truck windows down—cool
compared to before the storm. Enjoying driving his
truck through such really fine weather. Didn't mind the
paint job so much, now; good truck deserved good
paint. . . . But the car back there, a car three or four
vehicles back, kept moving in and out of its lane.

Gray car. Smoke-gray Ford—and swinging out of
lane back there right now, swinging out just a little
way, then sliding back. Checking to see Pierce hadn't
ducked down an exit ramp.

He wouldn't have noticed that car, if it had stayed
where it belonged.

"What is it?"

"Nothing."

"What *is* it, Tyler?" Naomi turned in her seat to look
back. "Is it . . . is it that fucking car?"

"Looks to be."

"Oh, Christ. But how?"

"Probably parked back at one of the First Avenue
intersections—parked there early every morning, last
few days. Then just sat, waited. . . . Seen us heading
into that neighborhood, and figured we'd have to be
driving out sometime, come through there. . . . Whoever, they're real patient."

"Assholes. Who *is* it? Is it one person?"

"About to find out. —Look on that county map—
look for a dead-end road. Little road way out in the
boonies."

"Oh, for God's sake. . . ." Naomi opened the glove
compartment, sorted through Kleenex and several
Almond Joys misshapen by heat, melted in their blue
and white wrappers. She tugged the map out, unfolded

it into a big unwieldy sheet, and punched a crease out. "Now, we want a what?"

"Dead-end road. Little nothing dirt road way out in the county."

"I don't even know if they have that on the map, Tyler. . . ." Naomi studied the map for a minute, then turned around to look out the truck's back window. "Are you sure? Sure it's the same one?"

"You bet."

"Maybe it's that fucking cop. Or some other cop."

"Nope. Isn't Burney—he wouldn't come around me. —Isn't any other cop, either. They use unmarked Chevies in this county. . . . Car back there's a Ford. Taurus, same as last time."

"Shit."

"Find me that dead-end, Naomi."

"All right, I am. Give me a minute. . . ." She rattled the map, gave it another little punch to get a crease out.

Pierce checked his rearview. Saw a blue van just behind him. And a big car, maybe a Lincoln . . . then a smaller car—cream-colored—just behind that. All following center lane.

And right while he was watching, the gray Ford—a considerable distance back—moved out a little into the express lane . . . then eased back.

"I see you," Pierce said.

". . . All right now, Tyler. I have a road here, dotted line, probably a dirt road. You'll have to exit . . . you have four more exits, then you have to get off and take Whitemarsh."

"Whitemarsh."

"That's right. It's a county road. Take that exit, and then we're going to have to go a long way. Ten, fifteen miles—their mileage thing on this map is ridiculous! You have to measure the goddam miles by how many fingernails it is according to this line on the bottom. . . ."

"That's all right. Whitemarsh exit off this highway."

"—Then a long way to what looks like a Rural Route Fourteen. And your road is off that to the left; it's dotted for dirt road. Unimproved. And it seems to be a dead end. It trails off on this map . . . and I don't see a road crossing it. —Is he still behind us?"

"You bet."

The rural route was paved—or had been paved years ago. Now the sand had drifted over it in long white feathers from its shoulders, and tough little plants—very dark green—had broken through the heat-crumbled blacktop in little knots of stem and leaf.

"We go left off this road," Naomi said. "But I don't see a sign. . . ."

"Next left?"

"It will be the next left. That's right. —Are they still following us?"

"Way way back."

Naomi turned to look. "I don't see anybody."

"He's back there."

The day was getting hotter, the storm's coolness draining away. Pierce felt the heat in the air blowing in, and thought of closing the windows, turning the truck's air-conditioning on, but didn't do it. He didn't like the idea of window glass in his way, if something happened. . . .

"Listen to me, Naomi—"

"Here's the left! This is it. . . ."

"Looks like just a damn dirt driveway."

"This is it!"

"Okay. . . . All right." Pierce swung the truck left, rear wheels breaking loose a little in the sand.

It was barely a road. Pierce stayed on it, going slower so as not to slide into an old irrigation ditch running along the right. He looked in his door-side mirror . . . couldn't see the gray car coming. Must be way back. . . .

The track went straight back for a quarter mile—

nothing but sand, sand scrub, and a few stumpy fat little palm trees—date palms—on both sides. No shack. Nothing but an old dump passed on the left side of the road, rusted metal framing, a heap of bottles— clear glass turning colors from years under the sun. Two sets of mattress springs, rust-red.

Track went straight back—then took a sharp curve off to the right at a thick stand of palms. . . . And around the curve was just more of the same. Some more trees—palms, a good distance away.

Pierce drove a little farther after the curve . . . went down a hundred yards more, then pulled up, turned off the truck's engine.

"Now, listen to me, Naomi. I figure our friends, or whoever's back there, will follow on in. They'll drive the straight. —Then, when they get to that curve, it's going to make them nervous. So they'll pull up, take a careful look around the curve, checking to see where we're at."

"Okay." Naomi had her hands clenched in her lap.

"—And when they pull up at that curve, I'll be there. I'm going to cut back through the scrub."

"Do you have to? Couldn't we just keep driving?"

"Honey, it's a dead end." Pierce opened the driver-side door and climbed down. "Now listen to me. I want you out of this truck. I want you to go take a walk in that scrub and out of sight—and I mean out of sight. And you just stay there till I call you in. You understand me? —You don't come out of there for any reason, till I call."

"No. That isn't what—"

"You do as you're told! Do it right now. Something bad happens—I don't call for you—then you wait till dark and walk back down the road. Just keep going out on that route, till you get to a grove farm or whatever."

"Tyler—"

"Move," Pierce said. He shut the truck door, went

around to jump the irrigation ditch . . . and jogged off into the scrub.

. . . He wished he had a long gun. Wished he had a shotgun or rifle. —What he really would have liked, he would have liked big Freddy Simmons right here in this hot-sand shit to side him, to be solid as he'd been in that Michigan thing. Freddy'd be a hell of a comfort right about now, and no mistake. . . . Sand was hard to run in, and the scrub bushes and vines hard to run through, and keeping low as he could all the way. Nasty stuff had hooks and points on it every damn way you went. And all getting warmer with the day. Full heat or not, would be hot enough. . . .

Hot enough so he was sweating pretty good by the time he'd cut across and back to where the track curved right—could see the road there, just before it turned.

No gray car, not yet.

Two date palms were growing there, scrub side of the ditch—and Pierce had just stepped in behind them when he heard Naomi—had to be Naomi—struggling through the brush behind him. Trying to catch up.

Wasn't even time to be mad at her. Pierce saw the gray Ford turning in from the main road.

He ran back into the scrub—found Naomi struggling in a vine more like a snake than a plant, and tore the thorns off her.

"My dress . . ."

Pierce dragged her back to the palms, and in behind them. The gray car was coming fast . . . turkey tail of sand dust raised behind it.

"I couldn't stay—"

"Now you're here," Pierce said, "you be quiet and stand still."

The gray car came down the road . . . and slowed . . . slowed as it approached the curve. Didn't like driving through that blind turn. . . .

Pierce tried to see who was in there . . . how many

. . . but the sun was flashing off the windshield glass, blazing off that glass like it was a mirror.

The gray Ford slowed, went past him, and pulled over to the shoulder, tires crunching on white sand and small shells. . . . The engine was turned off.

Pierce felt that Naomi was too close to him, and on his right side. He reached out and gently pushed her back and away a little.

He heard the Ford's emergency brake being set. Then the driver's-side door swung open and Allen Mardanian got out of the car, walked a few steps to the curve, and stood looking down the road. The gun dealer was wearing shorts, and one of those fancy long white shirts Naomi was always trying to get Pierce to buy. He had a white baseball cap on to match. Close-cut gray-blond hair beneath that, and a thick, tanned neck.

He stood looking down the road. Looking at the truck parked way down there.

Pierce came out from beside the palm tree—took a long step over the ditch. "Foolish," he said.

Mardanian didn't start. He turned slowly, smoothly, and as he turned, he slid his right hand up under the side of his long shirt. These outside shirts were handy, no question. . . .

"Well, this is too bad," he said. And Pierce, looking into his eyes shaded by the baseball cap, saw he was a man who didn't mind trouble. . . . Had missed that in the bookstore office.

"I'd say too bad," Pierce said. "And you've been following after us—went through the lady's motel room—looking for what?"

"Why, for that nearly a million in gold, or the way to it, Mr. Pierce! Your share of the Michigan job." Mardanian seemed at ease as a man talking from a barbershop chair. "As I believe I told you, armed robbery and armed robbers are a hobby of mine. I'm a buff, a *fan*. It's proved profitable for me on several occasions." He shifted his shoulders just a little, to face Pierce

squarely. "—That express-company job had the
Iceman written all over it. . . . Three men. Always only
three men. And the plastic explosive as a threat to get
vaults open or whatever."

"What if you're wrong?"

Mardanian shrugged. "Then, Mr. Pierce, I've wasted
a week or two. . . . I've been hoping you'd circle in to
where you've been keeping it."

"And now?"

"Now," Mardanian said, and he seemed lit by special
light, standing in the road under bright sunshine. His
shadow stretched black as tar behind him. "—Now, I'll
have to persuade you in unpleasant ways."

"That so?"

"You—or your lady friend," Mardanian said,
crouched and drew his pistol.

He was quick—looked to Pierce like a man who'd
studied that kind of thing, practiced it. Weapon coming
out was a heavy revolver with a short barrel.

He was quick—made Pierce hurry his draw and no
mistake.

Pierce snaked the Smith & Wesson out from the
small of his back and shot Mardanian through the
right shoulder—had aimed to center him and missed
somewhat.

The Armenian was knocked sideways in a half turn,
and he lost his revolver in the air from the impact. Lost
his baseball cap, too. The revolver was bright, bright in
the air—and Mardanian did a fine thing. He reached
out with his left hand and caught the piece—got a grip,
and still off balance shot at Pierce once and twice. Two
heavy slamming sounds out of that weapon and quick
winks of white light. A round numbed Pierce's left ear.

Then Mardanian was back into that crouch he must
have practiced, set to fire an aimed round left-handed.

Pierce shot him in the stomach—saw the white shirt
flick as the slug went in. Mardanian seemed startled
and stepped back. His gun went off, very loud, and

Pierce shot him again, a little higher, and the Armenian tripped and fell straight back as if there was someone waiting there to catch him. He raised dust from the white sand as he struck.

". . . What happened?" Naomi said, though she was standing right there across the ditch and must have seen everything. Pierce could hardly hear her after the gunfire. "What happened . . . ?"

Pierce walked over to Mardanian, hoping the man was dead. But he wasn't. His eyes were open, squinting up into sunlight. He was hauling in slow breaths . . . looked to be concentrating on that. Too busy trying to breathe to talk, say anything. There was blood down the center front of his fancy shirt and up on his hurt right shoulder, and a spatter of bright scarlet drops across the Ford's trunk and back bumper.

The man was dying, and it sounded like harder and harder work. —Too hard. His breath caught in his throat with a click and he began to strangle.

Pierce stood off a yard, took a bead, and shot Mardanian through the head.

The shovel from the pickup's bed, that in Missouri dug Pierce's buried money up, had put Mardanian under.

Pierce had held one of Naomi's Kleenexes up to his left ear until the nick there stopped bleeding. She'd wanted to do that, but he hadn't let her. . . . He'd dragged Mardanian off almost two hundred feet into the scrub, left Naomi to pour iced tea from her thermos to soak his bandanna, then wash the blood off the sedan's trunk and back bumper.

"Do a good job," Pierce had said. And Naomi had nodded, stayed silent. She'd said nothing after she'd asked what happened. Seemed to Pierce it had been too fast and too noisy, too frightening for her.

He'd dug out in the scrub for quite a while, shoveling soft hot white sand that made for harder digging than it looked—loose stuff would slide back down into the hole every time. . . . But even without the sand, it would have been hard digging. Pierce felt the same weariness he had up in Michigan, as if he'd done all this many times before, and it was just wearing on him.

It had taken him almost an hour to dig deep enough—deep enough so no smell would come up, no animal dig down. Almost an hour to do that. . . . Then Pierce, making sure Naomi was still over on the road, had opened his pocket knife and sliced the dead man's fingertips away. —Had almost cut his own fingers doing it, with his hands shaking in a tremor like an old man's. He'd thought that might be from all the digging . . . then supposed not.

When he was done with it, he'd searched Mardanian's short pants . . . taken his wallet and what looked like a lucky piece—foreign coin with a little loop of silver chain on it—then rolled the dead man into the ground and begun to shovel the sand over him. The wallet, the lucky piece, and Mardanian's pistol all to go deep under different sand a way away from here. Revolver had been a Ruger. GP-100, and fine . . .

Naomi, still with nothing to say, had kept doing as she was told . . . had driven the truck to follow Pierce in the sedan. Driven back through one intersection off the rural route, then two miles farther, then a right turn onto another narrow country road.

Pierce had waited until there was no traffic at all, then pulled over to the side of the road and stopped. He'd sat for a minute, carefully smearing any prints he might have made on the door, steering wheel, and shift lever—careful to wipe no prints off clean, attract some smart detective's attention. . . .

He got out of the car, kneed the door shut, and came back to get in the truck. Naomi scooted over to let him drive. She seemed to be doing fine, except for not talking. Pierce thought she looked all right, but pale. Her lipstick stood out red as blood.

Naomi cleared her throat as they went down the road, left the gray sedan back there on the shoulder under the sun's hard heat. "The Michigan thing he mentioned. . . ."

"I did that robbery, Naomi."

"I see. . . Okay. Well, I suppose . . . I suppose this means I can go back to motel living. There's nobody to bother us, now. I mean except for the Sweetwater. And since we haven't found him yet, he probably hasn't found us."

"Probably not."

"—Because I have to tell you, Tyler, a move back to Manchineel and Motel 6 can't come too soon. Old Montfort is a nice man, but he's driving me crazy with fish stories. He comes to my room, knocks on my door every damn morning with a string of huge fish and waves them in my face and then tells me all about each one. Lures, spoons, bait, everything. —Remember all that about privacy, and how nobody was going to bother me?"

"He's lonely."

"I know. I know he's lonely, Tyler," Naomi said, and as if for that reason, brought her hands up to her face and began to weep.

"Oh, now . . . oh now, honey," Pierce said, reached over and patted her knee. "Don't you be upset now. Don't you be upset. —It's all over. All *over*. He didn't suffer any. . . ."

Naomi shook her head as if she didn't believe him, still weeping into her hands.

"Besides," Pierce said, "the son of a bitch asked for it."

And that seemed to help Naomi a little.

Pierce lay on the bed in his motel room, though it was only afternoon, and thought Naomi would be okay. She'd stopped crying after a while, then asked how his ear was and said she supposed she was an accessory to manslaughter, and had Pierce to thank for it. Said she was finished for the day, wouldn't want lunch or dinner—and also had he ever heard of a silencer, so as not to make so much fucking noise when he shot somebody?

"Not on revolvers," he'd said. But she didn't pay any attention.

So it seemed to Pierce she would be okay.

But all the while Naomi'd been talking, he'd thought, *Well, I've killed a man.* Thought, *Well, I've killed a man . . . and it had to be done and it can't be undone.*

That had turned over and over in his mind all the time Naomi was talking, so upset. Turned over and over until now, lying on the bed, he'd come to a conclusion about why killing people was absolutely a wrong thing. Worse than just hurting them, which he'd done many times. Even hurting people seriously, like that young black man up in Michigan.

Killing was different from hurting—and now, having killed Mr. Mardanian, Pierce could see why. The reason was that no man was good enough, big enough, a fine-enough person, to *deserve* to take another man's life. It was just that simple. . . . And even if it had to be done, like with Mardanian, or in a war—even if it *had* to be done, it was wrong, and nothing to be proud of.

All the killers he'd known—in the joint and out of the joint—he could see that none of them had understood that. They were like children, and never even thought about it.

. . . It was going to be a lonely rest-of-the-day. Mardanian's dying had filled the day up, and emptied it at the same time. Didn't feel right to be calling Carolyn, or going out on Lisa's business this afternoon, either. It was as if he might leave a mark on the women, the living and the dead, just by having to do with them today. . . . Seemed to Pierce it would be a good idea to get up off the bed, though, and get out of this room. Maybe buy two more Florida shirts—surprise Naomi.

"Oh, my God."

"What's the matter with it?"

"Tyler . . . Tyler . . . Tyler. It's a green shirt, with blue flamingoes."

"I think it's nice. Did a nice job on the birds."

"Oh, good birds—see the little circles in the water where they're dipping their beaks? But they're blue, Tyler. Blue and green clash."

"I don't . . . I don't see that at all."

"And it's huge. What is that, an extra-extra-large?"

"I like it."

Naomi gave him a look. ". . . Okay. If you like it, I'll learn to like it. The birds are good—those *are* well-done birds."

Pierce saw the shirt had helped after all, even being blue-and-green. It had helped Naomi, kept them from having to deal with the killing, first thing.

The only mention about that all morning was when Pierce was driving to a restaurant called May's, in Palmetto Lake. In the Palmetto paper the day before, that restaurant had advertised special breakfasts.

"No McDonald's?" Naomi said, when he drove into the restaurant parking lot. "Tyler, I'm all right. You don't have to baby me."

And when they finished breakfast—Western omelets with sausage on the side—she said, "Another breakfast, another pound."

"You're too thin, anyway."

Naomi seemed to like that, took it as a compliment. "And how's the ear, Tyler?"

"It's fine." Tyler put the last of his marmalade on a piece of toast, and ate it. Marmalade was the best jam that came in those tiny restaurant packages, but they almost never had it. Always had a lot of strawberry and mixed fruit. . . .

"You're going to have a little nick there."

". . . Naomi, now we know Mardanian was the one searched your room. Isn't any reason for you to be staying, get any deeper into this. You need to be going on home."

Naomi put down her coffee cup. "Can't afford me anymore, Tyler?"

"I can afford you. But also you could have got shot, yesterday."

"But I didn't."

"If I'd gone down, Mardanian would have dealt pretty hard with you. He'd have figured you knew something about the money."

"That's a laugh. You don't tell me anything about your money, Tyler. You're very tight about money."

"It's gotten way too rough—that's what I'm saying to you, Naomi. A man's been killed. . . . It's time for you to pull out, go on down to Miami. I mean it, now."

Naomi tried a smile. "Well, if you don't want me, you don't want me."

"It's not that. It'll probably take me more time without you helping. But I'd rather take more time, Naomi, than lose a friend. . . . My Lisa's dead. Doesn't have to be such a terrible hurry, finding the one killed her. I'll get it done."

"I don't want to lose a friend either, Tyler. If I go, who'll watch out for you? Keep you from driving to Tallahassee . . . ?"

"Naomi, you're out of it," Pierce said, finished his coffee, got up and went to pay the check. They'd been expensive breakfasts, ten dollars and eleven cents, and that was besides the tip. It was hard to understand what had happened to good two-dollar breakfasts. . . .

He paid, got his change—eighty-nine cents—and Naomi touched his shoulder. She was standing behind him, looking at newspapers stacked in a wire rack near the cash-register counter.

She picked up a paper and handed it to him. Under

the headline there was a picture of a woman in a stewardess uniform. Pretty woman, slight, with short hair. She was smiling.

"Tyler," Naomi said. "There *is* a terrible hurry."

He sat in his truck out in the restaurant parking lot. It seemed like too much work to start the engine. Way too much work . . . Naomi sat beside him, and had nothing to say for a while. Then she said, "It's not your fault."

"You bet it is," Pierce said. "I don't know what it was that I missed. Don't know the mistake I made—but it's my fault for sure, or I'd have caught the son of a bitch already. And that poor little lady would be fine."

"The police haven't—"

"Don't talk to me about cops."

"All right . . ."

"Mr. Big Mouth, coming down here saying he was going to get something done—and goddam well didn't do it! Wasting time . . . wasting time with those dealers and that Jackie. Your old Mr. Lombardi must think I'm the fool of the world. . . ."

"I'm sure he doesn't. And I don't. And I'm not going anywhere, Tyler—I don't care what you say."

"Yes, you are."

"No, Tyler. . . . I'm an aging prostitute living in a bad investment in Miami. These are women, and I'm a woman. Why should I run away while they're being murdered? Have I got something more important to do?"

Chapter 21

First time.

First time out on the ocean. Pierce balanced against the small boat's roll. That motion, and the salt wind, and sun flashing off the wavetops ... flashing and sliding like mirrors between the waves.

Pierce had seen TV and movies of people out on the sea many times—had fished lakes and rivers himself—but none of that had prepared him for such constant motion, constant bright changes of light. And also the wind.

It was a different world from the land.

Davis—Pierce didn't know if it was the boy's first name or last—spit in his mask, fitted it, then rolled off the rail backward into the sea. Big splash, all that equipment ...

"Lot of gear."

"Heavy in the air," Jason said. "Light under the water." He was standing beside Pierce by the low rail, looking down into the sea as Davis sank away out of sight.

Jason Schroeder was wearing only a dark-blue bathing suit; the rest of him—stocky, very strong-looking—was tanned the color of coffee with cream in it. He seemed to Pierce to be more of a person out here, where his business and pleasure were. More of a person than he'd appeared to be, sitting eating dinner at Margaret's.

"You want to go down, Mr. Pierce, I'll run you

through swimming-pool drills tomorrow, bring you out for shallow dives in the afternoon."

"I don't have the time—and it scares me, too."

Jason looked surprised to hear Pierce say that about being frightened. "That's smart. Safest thing you can be out here, is a little scared. I've had fools come diving that were just too dumb to worry. Can be a . . . a problem in the business."

"Well, it's just being all the way out in the sea like this. . . ."

"You can drown in a bathtub, Mr. Pierce. Out here, you just have more room—you can roam around down there."

"Sharks," Pierce said.

Jason smiled. "Got more chance of getting stung to death by killer bees. It's a big ocean."

"It's . . . I'd have to live beside this water for a while, before I felt right swimming out here," Pierce said. "Have to get to know it."

Jason looked down into the sea again, checking for Davis. "Lisa went right in," he said. "Did her drills and came out and went deep. Too deep, for first time out."

"She enjoyed this?"

"Loved it." Jason turned to lean against the rail, relaxed, swaying with the boat's movements. At home in his country . . . His big stainless-steel watch gleamed in sunlight on his wrist. "Truth is, that was a lot of being with me, for Lisa. You know, our relationship—a lot of it was diving."

"Where did getting married come in, Jason?"

"Mr. Pierce, that was something that was going to happen. It was just—it was just there were other things involved."

"Other things . . . ?"

Pierce had come down to Jason's store at the Fort Talavera marina early in the morning . . . been surprised by the size of it. Place looked prosperous, a real business, not just a half-assed kid's thing.

"Mr. Pierce . . ." Jason had been out back of the store, filling breathing tanks at some sort of compressor. "—We have to go out and reset some wreck markers . . . buoys. Hurricane blew them away. If you want to come out with us, we can talk."

So, first time out on the ocean . . .

"Well, when I say 'other things,' Mr. Pierce, I mean personal things between Lisa and me."

"If my daughter was alive, Jason, I'd say all that was none of my business. And I wouldn't ask about any of it." Sun was bright out here. Bright as brass—and very hot, too, under the sea wind. "But she isn't alive. She was butchered like a sheep. And I want to know every damn thing you can tell me."

Young businessman thought about that. . . . Seemed to Pierce the boy wasn't afraid of him. Part of that, of course, was being young and strong—not knowing what it was to be bad hurt, yet. Part of it was being out on the sea.

Jason looked at his watch . . . checking Davis's dive time. "We've got an old cabin cruiser down there. Wreck's been stripped to the max. Somebody even took the carpeting out of it. But it's at sixty feet, easy intermediate diving, and it's handy for us. People like to go down, look at something. . . ." He pushed a button on his watch. "Lisa and I went great together. You have a . . . you had a wonderful daughter. We loved to dive together. You don't know what that means, to have a . . . to be close that way and just about every way. And sex was great. Just . . . it was great. —*And* she had good business judgment too, which a lot of these beach girls around here have no idea about. They think you get money out of coconuts."

"No problems?"

"No serious problems, Mr. Pierce—except one. One problem. You want to hear all this, so I'll tell you. Lisa got pregnant last year. —And I didn't think anything about it, because we were going to get married and it

was just a fabulous thing and it was no problem at all."
He looked at his watch, and said, "Come on, Davis—it
isn't the fucking *Titanic* down there. —But, the problem was she didn't want the baby. Lisa wanted kids,
but not right away. She said she just wasn't ready to
play mama, and I . . . I saw her point. We were having
a lot of fun, and she was young—hell, we were both
really young. And I'm smart about business and I don't
mind working hard, but I guess I'm not all the way
grown up, either."

"So . . ."

"So, we had a serious disagreement. I saw her point,
and I saw the burden of the kid would fall on her,
mainly. . . ."

Pierce was surprised to see that this calm and
collected boy was crying. Tears just sliding down
out of cool blue no-nonsense eyes. No other sign of
grief at all.

"But, Mr. Pierce, I'm Catholic. My parents are
Catholic. And that would have been all right—I could
have handled that—but I just started expecting that
child. My child. I'd . . . I'd have dreams about him—
her. I mean, I'd think about teaching the baby to swim
and everything. . . ."

He wiped his eyes with the back of his hand. "—The
more time went by, the more the baby meant to me, as
if it was growing in my head the same time it was
growing in Lisa. It was just becoming more and more
of a person to me." Jason looked out over the sea as if
something might be out there. A ship, or a sailboat running with the wind. "—And that got to be really difficult after a while, that she was going to have the baby
killed." He smiled at Pierce. "Politically incorrect lan-
guage. I mean, exercise her personal choice, by having
the baby killed. . . ."

"Looks to me like you're still mad about it."

"Well, I am. We had bad fights. . . . And that's when
I found out I was on the hook with Lisa. Because I

couldn't get mad enough at her to let her go. And I gave it a try too, for a few weeks. You know, tried not to see her. . . ."

"Been my experience, a fight like that sours things pretty bad."

"It did. It wasn't the same after that. It wasn't ever going to be quite the same, but I still couldn't do without her. And she couldn't do without me."

"You got a good alibi, time she was killed."

"I don't need an alibi, Mr. Pierce. I would never be able to do to anybody, what happened to Lisa."

There was a *pop* and hiss off the boat's bow, and a small blaze-orange marker, the size of a child's balloon, floated tethered on the sea.

"About time." Jason went to the rail, looked over. "Davis would live down there if he could."

"This last year," Pierce said. The boat's motion, this constant slow rolling back and forth, was beginning to bother him. Fish smell, too. He thought of sitting down on one of the lockers, but doubted that would help. ". . . This last year, and back a little farther than that— tell me anything else that happened the least little bit out of the way. . . . Somebody bother her? Somebody make her nervous or scare her? —Just maybe a little incident you didn't think a thing of at the time. Maybe somebody new come into your lives. . . ."

"No. Nobody new came into our lives. We know— knew a lot of people, and I heard Lisa had a girlfriend she saw sometimes. I didn't know her; don't know who she was. . . . Lisa and I weren't doing much talking then. Well, we were split up is the fact of the matter, and I guess the chick was just some beachy to talk girl-talk with about being pregnant. —But nobody scared Lisa or threatened her. That was the first thing the police wanted to know, any threats, letters, or phone calls. But nobody did anything like that. Lisa was . . . pretty tough. She was sweet, she was very good-natured, but she didn't take any shit, if you know what I mean."

"Um-hmm." Pierce felt better looking way out over the ocean. Out to the horizon. There were clouds out there, pink and white along the edge of the sea. Looked like the clouds in a children's picture book. "So, no trouble at all? Not even just a passing thing—someone following her out to a parking lot? Somebody staring at her? Maybe one of your friends trying to get closer than he should have?"

"No. No trouble. And nobody bothered her—and I've been trying to think . . . trying to remember anything like that since she died."

"She have a boyfriend before you, Jason?"

"Two." Jason's watch buzzed, and he pushed a button on it to turn it off. "Guy at the university—he's married now, lives over in Tampa. And another man. Older guy, and that was almost three years ago. Ran an art gallery, and he's dead. He died of lymphoma. . . . Police checked all that out, I think."

"All right," Pierce said. "All right. But if you were to make a wild guess—just a far-out guess—what do you think happened?"

"Okay . . . What I think happened is that somebody has an authority thing about women. Can't stand to have them over him, or part of an organization like that. And he goes somewhere, and there's a police-woman, or a stewardess like the one that just happened. Or a ranger. I think whoever it is is a guy just too sick to handle women with any power at all."

"A little girl delivering pizzas . . . ?"

"I know. I know, but all that tells me, Mr. Pierce, is what a sicko this guy is. . . . I try to think it was all just an accident. Like a shark—you asked about sharks. Well, that's what I think it was. I think Lisa was swimming through life, and a tiger shark or great white— that one chance in a million—a shark just happened to come along."

"And no idea at all who that shark might have been?"

". . . You know, people say they'd give their right arms for something, and all that bullshit? Well, I'd *give* my right arm to know, and have that fucker caught or dead."

A splash in the sea on the boat's other side, and Davis, masked, a harness of double yellow tanks on his back, was floating in the waves.

"Hey, dude," Jason called to him. "About fucking time, and I'll bet with no decomp. We have two more buoys to set off Pelican, so do me a favor and get your ass on board." He looked at Pierce. "You feeling okay?"

"Not so's you'd notice."

"Listen, tell you what, Mr. Pierce. We can linger a little, twenty more minutes, half hour. I hate to have you ride back and never have gone in." He bent over a locker, rummaging through. "—We've got a snorkel set . . . mask and fins, and at least you can do some surface swimming, shallow-dive a little."

"No thanks," Pierce said.

"Tell you, you'll feel fine the minute you're in the water. Minute you're in, seasickness is *gone*."

"In that case, I'll do it," Pierce said. "And the sooner the better."

Davis came up the boarding ladder, heaved himself inboard with drips and splashes of ocean. . . .

Neither boy remarked it when Pierce took off his shoes, socks, and shirt—then drew the revolver from his belt and wrapped it in the shirt against salt spray before taking his trousers off. They noticed, but said nothing . . . just helped him fit on the fins and mask, demonstrated the snorkel as he stood in his boxer shorts.

Trying to blow through the snorkel made him feel sicker. Pierce had a vision of himself hanging over the boat's rail, vomiting his guts while the two boys stood swaying on their ocean, watching him.

. . . On the ocean. Then a climb down the boarding ladder, and into the ocean.

And great relief. Jason had been right; the sickness was gone in the sea. Pierce sank a little into living coolness and color, and turned slowly . . . turned again in a great blue-green room of light. He looked down and the blue-green went to blue . . . then darker blue that might have things traced through it, along the bottom there.

Only sixty feet deep. Only six stories deep. It was hard to see how a man could keep his courage swimming over the deepest ocean. Miles down beneath him, cold, and black. With whatever might be coming up from under. . . .

Pierce turned again, looking past the boat's smooth-straked white fiberglass. Peering this way and that through the mask to be sure this wonderful room of light was empty.

But the sickness was gone, and when the worry went with it, he began to use the fins as well as he could . . . went up to swim along the surface, and tried the snorkel. It worked pretty well.

He swam out from the boat . . . finning along, then swimming like a frog, the way he'd managed in the Manchineel. . . . What a blessing these fins would have been. Fins and mask and snorkel, all a blessing in the Manchineel. . . .

Pierce swam in oceanic light and felt just fine. It was very restful. The seawater was lively to swim through, rich and salty around the snorkel's mouthpiece. You could tell, swimming in it, that the Darwin people had an argument. It felt like the water where all things began. . . .

Karen, relieved the Angel had slid too low in her legs to trouble her, leaned against the tissue vault and wished, for the first time in years, for a cigarette.

A late partial-birth abortion—first thing in the morning—still troubled her. The Angel, preoccupied, remembering Moira, had been no help.

Torguson had scissored the head open, suctioned out the little boy's brains, and crushed the skull for removal. The partials unusual now, with a lot of referral paperwork to show necessity. . . .

Karen wanted to go out into the parking lot, into the light, so she could stand and wait to see if the Sun would speak to her. It was what she needed more and more as she grew sadder and happier at the same time. She'd felt those two feelings separate one afternoon, and start moving in her—the Angel bumping them, shoving them aside. She supposed that sometime—maybe in the grocery store while she was pushing her cart—one of those feelings would come out, tear her, and come out and fall on the floor for everyone to see.

Keep them inside, she said to the Angel, and it slid up her legs a little way and made her left knee ache. . . . D&Cs, D&Es the rest of the day, with only one second trimester at four o'clock, where the baby might be sent to the Sun. And if she hadn't gone into nursing. . . . if she'd become a teacher or office person, she would never have had the responsibility. . . .

And there was nothing at home for dinner. Canned tuna. Eggs. But it was a really bad habit to get into, eating out almost every night just because you were tired, and didn't want to shop and then cook something. Restaurant food always had some fat and salt sneaked in, for taste. They put it in the salad dressing, or cooked with some kind of fat, and then supposedly drained that away. Supposedly.

It was the worst thing about being big . . . big-boned. Put on just a little weight, and you looked fat. And that unhealthy food was what the Angel liked, was always making excuses for eating. . . .

"Karen?" Fran coming down the hall. . . . And there was an example of bad eating habits. Poor thing was five feet two inches tall—and just obese. It was sad, really.

"—Karen? Oh, honey, you look tired."

"Fran, I am tired."

"Well, come and sign for your check. I have to close the safe—I'm going to be gone this afternoon."

"Tarpon?"

"Karen, where else?" Fran led the way down the hall. "Going to do an overnight to see my Uncle Johnnie. He's *in* from Greece—he's going *back* to Greece. And I have to drive all the way across the state to say hello. He comes over every year, asks where the sponges went, and then he goes back to Athens."

"You could skip it."

"Don't I wish." Fran walked into the office, sat at her desk, and started going through envelopes. "It's in here somewhere. . . . Listen, my Uncle Johnnie has more money than the rest of the family put together. When he comes over, we go see him. Period."

Karen heard some people start to shout outside the Clinic. Only a few, two or three.

"Court order's working," Fran said. "First today, and not so many. —And *here* is your check. Give me a signature."

"Thanks, Fran."

"Go spend it. Have a ball. —Oh, and I love your hair."

"I haven't done anything to it."

"Well, it looks great. Windblown . . . curly—and short. I do everything to mine, and when they're finished it always looks just a little shittier. I think I have them do too much. . . ."

"Why don't you just brush it back into a ponytail, or up in a French knot? You have great hair."

"Karen, what I have is thick, very oily hair."

"A ponytail or a French knot with silver combs."

"I don't know. . . . Miss Irma—what a bitch; she

looks at me like I'm the dwarf of the world. She's always after me to have a big 'do.' "

"Tell her no."

"Then she'll give me the 'another dummy' look."

"It's your hair, Fran."

"Karen, I know *legally* it's mine. But it's a strength-of-character thing."

". . . What isn't?"

Jim Clarence was smaller than Naomi had thought he'd be.

And his voice on the phone last night had been lighter and younger than she'd expected. In her last few professional years, she'd gotten used to older, more bass-baritone hoodlums.

"I'm calling for a friend."

"What friend?"

"Ummm . . . Jesse James."

Jim Clarence had laughed at that, seemed to think that was pretty good. He didn't ask who she meant. Didn't ask who *she* was, either. "Okay, where are you?"

"I'm in a phone booth."

"All right, give me the number and hang around. I'll call in about twenty minutes."

It was twenty-five minutes.

". . . Hello?"

"Guess who. —And what does Mr. Pierce want with me? We already said good-bye."

"He'll be busy the next couple of days, and he asked me to call and say you owe him one."

Jim Clarence had sighed over the phone, sounding like a boy, someone too young to be taken seriously. ". . . Well, I suppose I might owe him one. —*Just* one."

"We want—Tyler wants copies of all the autopsy results in the Sweetwater cases. Not just the short summaries. Everything."

"Jumping Jesus, old dad is sure pushing the envelope.

My poor pet cop—who has already suffered at your guy's hands—is going to shit a brick."

"We need that material. We . . . we're getting somewhere, but we need that material as soon as possible."

"Um-hmm. Let me tell you something: we are talking about a real stretch, here. My man is going to have to get hold of that material, then copy it, then get those copies out of the sheriff's department. Three chances to fuck up—and I have to tell you, my dude *is* a fuckup."

"I know—Tyler knows it's a serious request. But he thinks you owe him."

"Do you realize . . . do you know how many of my people old dad has damaged physically? It's like a fucking hospital ward at my place!"

"I'm sure Tyler's sorry—"

"The hell he is!"

"Well . . . maybe he isn't sorry, but this is very important. What we're—what he's trying to do is very important."

"I know what he's trying to do. And that's one of the reasons—despite my better business judgment—that he's still walking around."

Jim Clarence hadn't said anything more. Silence on the line, until Naomi said, "Will you do it?"

". . . Do you know a restaurant called Cobbler's?"

"No."

"It's in Palmetto Lake, out on Third Avenue. Third Avenue and Croton."

"I'll find it."

"You park on the west side of Cobbler's tomorrow evening. Nine o'clock on."

"I'll be there. . . ."

Jim Clarence had hung up. —And now came walking across the restaurant's parking lot under yellow sulfur lights, looking smaller, looking even younger than Naomi had expected. A plump college student in khakis, sports shirt, and safari jacket. Native

American, or part Native American . . . He was wearing glasses, and carrying a shopping bag.

Naomi saw a man—an older white man, balding—standing down the lot beside a BMW sedan.

Jim Clarence came to the Nissan's passenger side, opened the door, and slid into the seat.

"So you're the Sancho Panza in this setup?"

"I suppose that's right."

"And you're . . . who? Naomi who?"

"Naomi Cohen. I'm from Miami."

"And you know who, in Miami?"

"I know Phil Lombardi."

"Only Lombardi I've heard of down there is about three generations out of it. Do better."

". . . Norm Lehman."

"Any trade people?"

"Jaime Ruiz, but he's dead."

"And one not dead, please."

"No."

"No you don't know, or no you won't say?"

"No I won't say."

Jim Clarence smiled at her, reached down between his legs into the shopping bag, and brought out a folded blue shirt patterned with pineapples. "I know dad doesn't want it back, but I thought this shirt was just *him*, you know, so I had it mended and cleaned."

"Thanks. He won't wear guayaberas."

"And . . ." Jim Clarence leaned down and brought up a big rectangular manila envelope, very thick, and sealed with shiny brown tape. "—And here are those autopsies, every one . . . including the last woman, Durchauer. I can tell you it was hairy shit getting this stuff, getting it so fast. My pet cop has grown old before my eyes. . . . So, your buddy and I are now definitely squared out. I hope that's understood."

"Right. He'd say that's fine."

"—*Because* . . . because I do not want to be troubled again. Is that clear?"

"Yes."

Jim Clarence reached down into the shopping bag and handed Naomi a wallet and a wristwatch. "Dad's. And the money's in there, and everything else. —Who did he get to do that paper for him? Really nice ID."

"I couldn't say."

"Won't say?" Jim Clarence said, and smiled at her. He looked like a teddy bear wearing glasses.

"That's right. —You can ask Tyler."

"Guess not. I'd wind up owing Dad again, and I can't afford it. —By the way, you can give him a message for me."

"All right."

"Tell him a certain handsome Hispanic said good-bye—and Big Louis says thanks." Jim Clarence opened the car door, started to get out, then turned back to her. "How are you two doing on this Sweetwater thing?"

"I think we're going to get him. I didn't think so at first, but now I do."

"And Pierce is letting you stay in the game?"

"No, he told me to go—but I won't."

"That so . . . ?" Jim Clarence sat looking at her. "Well, none of my business." He started to get out of the car, then stopped again. "You all right for bread, hunting this crazy motherfucker? Seems to me Mr. Pierce has been spending heavy. I could . . . I suppose I could contribute a modest amount."

"We're fine. We—Tyler has plenty of money."

"Does he?" Jim Clarence looked at Naomi as if he were a friend of hers. "—Has old dad been bad?"

"I suppose it's possible," Naomi said, and Jim Clarence laughed, got out, and closed the car door behind him.

Chapter 22

"—And Big Louis says thanks?"

"That's what he said."

". . . Okay."

They were sitting in Pierce's motel room, speaking softly as if after some terrific explosion, so the quietness was very restful. . . . Naomi thought that despite the pictures, Tyler looked better than he had since the Manchineel. Tired, though. A little sunburned.

"How's your ear? You keeping the bandage on? —Is that a Band-Aid? You took the bandage off?"

"Naomi, I didn't need the bandage. Just a notched ear, that's all."

" 'That's all.'. . ."

"It's all over—"

"Tyler, don't keep telling me it's all over with."

"Well, it is."

"So you say—and so I hope. He could have killed you. . . . And you were out on the water all day with no hat?"

"No. Just . . . not all day. I looked for the woman's husband in the afternoon. Jo-Ann Dailey."

"The crossing guard in the laundry room."

"That's right. But the neighbors said he left the state. He and the boy are out in California. . . ."

"No hat, and I'll bet no sunblock, either."

He wasn't paying attention; Pierce was looking down at the photographs spread neatly across the beds.

On the beds, and some on the chair and dresser. Each set of photographs had a nine- or ten-page printed report beside it.

The girls . . . women . . . all looked very much alike. Naked, their heads propped on the block at the end of a steel autopsy table, their eyes closed or barely open, their skin a light yellow-gray, they looked as if they were screaming in their sleep. Their mouths sagged open so the lower teeth showed, their hair—tied roughly back—was spattered and stiffly spiked with knotty threads of spoiled refrigerated blood.

Under their chins showed deep slices of complicated dark. In two of them, white bone peered out in back. In one, the tongue had retreated and fallen in.

Below, they lay spraddled as if at sex, sliced down the middle, then roughly sewn back up. Where their breasts had been were disks of crusted red. Bone plugs had been sawed from their foreheads, then partially replaced.

". . . Don't look at Lisa," Naomi had said. But Pierce had looked at her as he'd looked at all the others. Not for a longer time, and not for a shorter time, either.

He'd looked at every picture, studied it . . . then read the coroner's findings very carefully. Reread them. And Naomi had done the same. It had taken more than three hours.

Once, Naomi had said, "Excuse me," and gone into the bathroom to be sick. But she wasn't. She'd just sat on the toilet for a while. . . .

"Well," Pierce said, "what do we have?" He'd moved some pictures to sit on the edge of the bed near the window. He looked tired. His forehead was reddened with sunburn.

Naomi checked through the notebook. She'd stopped to make notes all the time she was looking . . . reading. "We have . . . several things. First, they were all fairly young women. Oldest was Moira Durchauer, and she was only in her thirties. So, we have young women, and there's no difference there with Rue Long. She was about the same age as the rest of them."

"Okay." Pierce looked tired, but very calm—and with a little shock, Naomi realized that of course it was how he'd looked planning his robberies. How he'd looked doing them. Tired, determined, and calm. Iceman . . .

She looked back at her notes. "They'd all been sexually active—including Rue Long—and the Coast Guard officer had had gonorrhea, some scarring from gonorrhea."

"That's right."

"And all of them were otherwise very healthy, well nourished. The . . . the police officer, Mercedes Calderón, she'd had TB at one time, but it was a minor lesion and inactive."

"So. All healthy young women." Pierce looked away from the photographs on the bed. "No old ladies—not even middle-aged ladies. Maybe excepting Durchauer."

"And we already know that except for the uniform thing—wearing some sort of uniform at work—they didn't have the same kind of jobs at all. Didn't have the same interests, hobbies. . . ." Naomi turned a notebook page. The notebook was almost filled; they'd need another notebook.

"Two had their appendixes out," Pierce said.

"—But the reports specify their personal medical people. And except for one dentist in Fort Talavera, none of them used the same doctor or dentist—"

"And that was only the pizza girl and the last one," Pierce said. "—The stewardess. And it was three years ago."

"Yes. —Okay. The sex thing," Naomi said, ". . . that part. Two had had repeated anal intercourse at some time."

"Marcie Tredenberg and Lisa."

Watching him, Naomi saw only interest, only determination. Everything else set aside. The criminal, the armed robber, was there to see in that detachment. . . .

"—And none had been injured or beaten or had any broken bones except for Rue Long, who hurt her knee doing gymnastics—and the Coast Guard officer. She broke a vertebra in her back, waterskiing."

"Pregnancies," Pierce said.

"Yes. . . . Two of the women had already had children. Police officer and Jo-Ann Dailey. But all of the women, including those two, had been pregnant within a year of being murdered. Except Rue Long."

"Except Rue Long."

"Tyler, that girl was the only one who'd never been pregnant—who wasn't pregnant within a time frame of about a year before they were killed. The shortest time was Moira Durchauer. —Recently pregnant. Her report said, 'Recently pregnant. Pregnancy terminated, apparent D&C.' "

" 'D&C.' Naomi, what is that, exactly?"

"Well, it's when they dilate the womb, and then scrape out the . . . tissue."

"I see. And they all had that done. . . ."

"That or some other method. D&E—that's evacuation, suction. Or saline injection or whatever. . . . All except Rue Long. And with only five murders altogether then, she would have been enough to break that pattern for the police. It's . . . you know, Tyler, it's really not unusual for young women to have had abortions down here. I'd guess almost one out of every two women that age has had an abortion."

"But not five out of six."

"No . . . Not five out of six."

"But is that a reason to kill a young woman, Naomi? That she's done that?" Naomi saw Pierce's hand lying relaxed on the bedspread beside photographs of Mercedes Calderón. There was a photograph of her face, and a photograph of her abdomen. Running for a few inches alongside the black sewn slice of the autopsy incision, was an older one, more delicate and healed. A cesarean scar . . . Pierce's hand lay relaxed beside the photographs. A big hand, weathered, calloused, and capable.

"A reason to kill them? Yes, Tyler, I think the abortions could be a reason. I think they are the reason."

"And how come you're so sure?"

"Because it's . . . important. They—these women did something important. All of them made a hard choice, and I think it made someone angry. I think it's a good reason."

"Okay. But is there anything else? Any other difference here, between Long and the others?"

"Drugs, Tyler. Long had evidence of two drugs in her system when she was killed. Cocaine, and another drug . . ." Naomi looked through the notebook. "This is full—it's getting full. . . . Cocaine and one of two possible barbiturates."

"And the pizza girl had smoked some pot."

"Pizza girl had smoked pot just before she was killed. And the Coast Guard officer had taken a tranquilizer. Umm . . . I can't remember. Some tranquilizer—it's in here." Naomi went through pages. "It's in the damn report here."

"It was Valium," Pierce said.

"Right. Valium."

"Still—as far as serious illegal drugs go, Long was the only one using."

"That's right."

"Naomi, you see anything else true of the others, that isn't true for her?"

"Except the abortions—unless we've missed something else, here—only one other thing that's different. Rue Long was hit, first. Hit on the temple and bruised there, before she was killed."

"Right. Know what that was? . . . They'd been together a long time. Tomás Seguin had to kill her, but he didn't want her to suffer, didn't want her to know what he was doing to her. . . ."

"But not enough of a difference to alert the police."

"No. —They'd figure, well, that time the Sweetwater had to subdue her a little and so forth. Everything else exactly the same."

"The same—except no pregnancy in the last year before she died. No pregnancies at all."

"That's right, Naomi. Except that."

". . . We have the *why*, Tyler?"

"Yes, I think we do. Too much of a coincidence, otherwise. Just too many pregnant ladies, and having those abortions. —And come to serious business, robbing banks or whatever, I never saw a coincidence didn't have a reason behind it."

"I agree."

"—Now, *who* could be tougher to find out."

"Also, I agree."

Pierce sat looking down at the photographs paving the bed. "Guess it cost me a grandchild," he said. "—Lisa doing that. Seems like a real sad thing to me . . . but then I wasn't the one carrying that baby."

"Sad but necessary, Tyler? —As in Allen Mardanian?"

". . . I'd say that depends on the 'necessary.' "

"Well," Naomi said, "next couple of days, while you check out more husbands and lovers, Tyler, I will go see Jackie on this for what I hope is the last time. The question now being only . . . *who*. Who did all those dead women—except Rue Long—meet? Who did they know, that she didn't?" She gathered the pictures, the printed report sheets scattered on the bed. "This is really so fucking grim. So fucking sad. It's worse than I thought it would be." She stacked the autopsy reports together. "You know, Tyler, I've had two abortions in *my* distinguished career. That's why no Joshua. No Rebecca. . . ." She got up and went into the bathroom.

When she came out, she said, "I'll be getting back to Talavera, and my lonely giant fisherman."

"It's late, Naomi—what time is it?"

"It's almost two."

"Too late to be driving all the way back," Pierce said. "Why don't you just stay here?"

Naomi stood in the bathroom door and looked at him. "I suppose I could. . . . But are we talking hanky-panky?"

"We're not talking hanky-panky. It's just late."

"All right . . ."

Pierce went into the bathroom . . . and when he came out in his boxer shorts, the room lights were off, Naomi a dim small heap in the bed away from the window.

Pierce got into bed and felt as odd as if he was dreaming. Felt he would surely wake, hear Mickey's voice at the door, and dress and go down in the dawn to get out on a job, nailing shingles. Feeling the pleasure of work guaranteed for decades of shedding rain and snow. Keeping people dry and warm long after they'd forgotten who'd hammered on their roof for a day or two. . . .

He lay in bed and thought of Lisa having sex . . . bearing the result of sex. *Poor sweetheart,* he thought. *Poor sweetheart* . . .

It was hard to imagine a person who could conceive such a hatred of young women, and murder them. . . . On the other hand, if he and Naomi were right, those young women had made a similar decision, and found it possible, for every good reason, to put an end to their babies' lives.

It was almost an hour, and still no sleep—Pierce had been imagining talking to his daughter as if she sat beside him, sat on the other bed, listening. Agreeing . . . Disagreeing.

A little later, Naomi got out of her bed, came and slid into his.

"No hanky-panky," she said, and lay beside him, her

skin cool . . . bare except for bra and panties. She was very thin. "Oh, Tyler," she said in the dark. "Oh, Tyler. What in God's name have we gotten into?"

"Bad cess," Pierce said. "Bad . . . luck."

"Oh, it's so strange," Naomi said. "Isn't it strange?"

"It is damn strange."

"All those young women, those pretty young women dead, and their lives over. And me—I cannot believe I spent my life as a whore. Now I can't *believe* it. It's as if this poor . . . this sick murderer has shone a flashlight on my life. I mean, what in God's name was I thinking of? Did I think I'd have another life to live— so I might as well be a . . . a whore in Miami for twenty years? *Twenty years* going up to strangers' hotel rooms."

"I understand that feeling real well."

"It's like a goddam dream."

"Isn't that the truth. . . ."

"Oh, shit," Naomi said, turned and hugged Pierce and held on to him. "I just want to . . . this is all I want to do," she said. "I know you don't feel that way about me. Is this all right?"

"Don't worry so much, honey." Pierce put his arm around her.

"I'm sorry," Naomi said. "But you know . . . and I know. Just let me do this, a goddam hug, and I won't say anything tomorrow. I'll just shut up."

". . . Listen to me, Naomi. I want you to do me a favor."

"What?"

"Tomorrow, I want you to go. —I'll come down and see you afterward, tell you all about it. But I want you to get on home. Get on home, tomorrow."

"No."

The Angel, discarding Karen in her sleep, dreamed of Moira Durchauer, her smallness, ignorance, and confusion . . . the tender white of her little belly, not yet risen, that had been full of a future. The vivid blood she'd gargled and spit scarlet before she fell . . . Then the Angel dreamed deep into the Sun's corridors of light, where things smaller than smallness stirred in storms for half a million miles.

Here, the Sun held the Angel to its heart, and showed Moira, still journeying through cold toward heat, through darkness to brightness, through emptiness to everything, the way all souls should go.

Then, at the star's broiling folding and unfolding edge—cooler than the perfect center, not quite so searing even in immense fires—the Angel was almost certain it saw Moira's daughter, waiting. Tiny light amid great light. Tiny spark of warmth amid battering heat titanic, the child rode seas of fire waiting for her mother where the Sun's border blazed into emptiness and silence.

This seeing in a dream was the Sun's thanks to its Angel. The Angel, honored, retired to rest as Karen woke, got up to pee and wash her hands and face. Then prepared a bowl of shredded wheat—and after breakfast, dressed for work.

"Well, you're a little late. You can forget breakfast."

"I had breakfast on the way over, Jackie."

"And sweetheart, you're looking sad . . . sad . . . *sad*. Being just a buddy seems to be uphill work. —Mr. Old-Fashioned still uninterested?" Jackie smiled from the lobby love seat behind the fountain's potted palm. She was wearing a long-skirted white summer dress with gauzy long sleeves. A white silk neckerchief was knotted at her throat. —Jackie noticed Naomi's glance. "Wattles. What can you do? I've had all the slicing I can stand. —And speaking of slicing, what's new with the great manhunt? Your frantic phone call for any gossip at all was not reassuring."

"Jackie, I think we're going to get him." Naomi sat in the armchair opposite.

"Oh, sure."

"Really."

". . . Really?"

"Yes. A good chance, anyway, if we can learn just a little more."

"And what was the big breakthrough?"

"Something you told us . . . about Rue Long's old boyfriend."

"Are you saying it was the *spic*?"

"He killed Rue. The Sweetwater killed the others."

"Well . . . well . . . *well*. You two have been busy. . . . And now you need whatever it was that all the other victims had in common—that the Long girl didn't."

"That's right."

"And my crony crones might provide it?"

"Have they?"

"Well . . . they've reminisced. They've muttered and recalled with what brain cells they have left. Whether it's anything worthwhile, God knows. Probably not."

The fountain's water was dyed bright green this morning. Naomi didn't ask why.

"—But, and I do hate to sound so ceaselessly commercial, I will expect some cash for even useless information at this point—for my patience, if for nothing else, listening to my sisters-in-decay."

"We'll pay you."

"Um-hmm. I would dearly *dearly* like to know who or what your friend robbed—and for how much. . . . Do you know?"

"I don't know what he did."

"Naomi, are you lying to me? I think you are—and I could always tell in the old days."

"No, I'm not."

"Well, *if* you don't know where his money comes from, then you are a very unenterprising woman."

"It's none of my business."

"Bullshit. It's every woman's business where a man

she's interested in—*even* . . . even if she has no hope of getting him—it's every woman's business where that man's money comes from. Period."

"Why don't we just drop it."

"—I mean, what else is there? Some flirting? Some fucking? Some amusing company? Get real, Naomi."

"It's none of my business. And it's none of your business, Jackie."

"So *stern*. Are we . . . could we be worried about what we might find out? That perhaps—in his last job, or the job before that—our hero tied some people up in a bank in Iowa, and then shot them in the head? Hmmm? Are we worried he's done something really nasty?"

"No. He never killed anybody before."

". . . *Before*? Oh, and you're red in the face. Do you . . . have you seen something upsetting, Naomi? Something like that time out on the Weisbrods' yacht?"

"Jackie, I don't think you have friends enough to throw one away."

". . . Oh, all right. I haven't said a word. And it's not that I don't like your stickup guy. I do like him. And if I hurt your *feelings*, I'm sorry."

"Listen, Jackie, let's get out of here." Naomi stood up. "I mean, you're always in The Palms. Isn't there someplace you'd like to go? We could talk there. . . ."

Jackie seemed to sink deeper into the love seat. "Go out? . . . I go out occasionally, not that Palmetto Lake's full of wonderful places."

"Well, would you like to go out this morning? Like . . . right now?"

A few moments' silence, then Jackie said, "Of course. We can go out. I just don't know what there is to go out *to*. . . ."

"Anywhere you like—let's just get the hell out from behind this palm tree."

". . . We could go to the Gallery, I suppose. It's an art store—I was there last year. I've been thinking of getting a print. It would have to be small. There's a space between the closet and the bathroom. Opposite the door to the bathroom . . . I suppose I could look for a print." Jackie stood up, smoothed her skirt.

"Good. Let's go."

"I'd have to run upstairs and get my hat and purse. . . ."

"So, go and get your hat and purse. I know you're not going to ask me up to see your room."

"My apartment. I have a very nice studio apartment, Naomi. —And no, I'm not going to invite you up, because it's the housekeeper's day. My apartment gets cleaned today."

"That's okay, Jackie. Go get your purse. . . . I'll buy lunch."

"My lunch here is already paid for. I pay the first of the month."

"Go get your purse, Jackie. . . ."

". . . Naomi, you are driving way too fast."

"Sorry. I'll slow down. Do I have a turn coming up to this place?"

"No, not yet. I'll tell you. . . ."

Coming out of The Palms' entrance into sunshine, Jackie had seemed to Naomi almost clearly an elderly man in drag, slightly dazed by light and heat. She'd come carefully down the steps to the drive in her white summer dress, dark glasses, and wide-brimmed straw hat—stilting along too tall, harsh-featured, ankles knobby above outsized white high-heeled sandals, veined wrists too thick and hands too large for the cuffs of the dress's delicate long sleeves.

". . . I think it's up ahead. Clematis and Vine."

"We're on Vine, but this one coming up isn't Clematis."

"Yes, it is."

"Jackie, read the street sign."

"Well . . . what is it?"

"Chinaberry. Who named these streets?"

"It should have been Clematis. . . ."

Naomi glanced over and saw only the wide brim of Jackie's straw hat, a slice of dark glasses lens, the Norman beak of her nose. There was a subtle nodding, slight and continuous, that Naomi hadn't noticed before, hadn't seen in The Palms when Jackie sat facing her.

"Are you sure about Clematis?"

Jackie's bony hands were folded tightly together in her lap. "Yes, I'm sure."

"—Because there's a Clematis in West Palm."

"I said I'm sure. —What's this one?"

"Chinchona."

"That's it!"

. . . The Gallery was part of a small one-story courtyard mall—*The Courtyard*—green and shaded with plantings, palms and jacaranda. Boutiques and small shops lined the white coral walks, all very upscale, *faux* Worth Avenue. Jewelers, interior decorators, an ice-cream parlor, a florist, a coffee shop, a bakery and café. The Gallery was at the end of the south row.

Naomi found herself walking slower to accommodate Jackie's unsteady stride. Jackie took long steps—a man's steps—but wavered slightly now and then on the walkway, as if only The Palms' carpets were familiar. This was a different Jackie, out of doors and her age upon her.

At a curb, Naomi took her arm, and Jackie said, "Christ," but didn't pull away.

Inside the Gallery's heavy clear-glass door, greeted by a breeze of air-conditioning, Jackie seemed to revive, took back her arm, and called, "Is anybody working here, or what?"

"Yes, anybody is and I'm it." A beautiful middle-aged woman, with reddish-brown hair cut short, came walking down a long display counter from the back. She wore glasses over tilted eyes a darker green than

Naomi's, and matching bronze blouse and slacks in Italian silk.

"You've got to be the owner," Jackie said.

"My casual air?"

"Your casual air—and the outfit."

"Well, I do own the place—own half of it, anyway."

"I'm looking for a print. A small print for a space opposite my bathroom."

"Pen-and-ink?"

"I don't give a damn how they did it, but I want something interesting—and I do not intend to be screwed on the price. I can get it framed very inexpensively—I won't need you people to do it."

"Too bad," the woman said. "We do make money framing. Listen, dear, why don't you come over here to this wall section, our print display, and see what we have up. If you don't find anything, I'll pull out some portfolios and we'll go through them. It's easier with prints—the quality's higher than original oils these days."

"People can't draw a fucking cow," Jackie said, and went over to the wall.

"Yes, isn't it sad?" the woman said. She was smiling, apparently appreciated Jackie.

Jackie stood at the wall, surveyed the artwork for a few moments, then took off her dark glasses and exchanged them for bifocals from her purse.

The owner stood beside Naomi, and they watched Jackie examine the prints.

"Is she your mother?"

"No, thank God," Naomi said, and Jackie called from across the room, *"I heard that."*

The woman murmured, much more quietly, "Is she your father?"

"No, thank God," Naomi said, also quietly.

"Well," Jackie said, "—this one isn't bad. I don't know what the hell it is, but it isn't bad."

The owner walked over. "That's a Koren. One of his

early ones, estate sale—and it really is interesting, isn't it? I don't know what it's supposed to be. It seems to me to be some tremendous complicated collapse."

"Hmmm. —Naomi, come look at this."

"I've got something to finish in the back," the woman said. "Framing, as a matter of fact. If you find anything you like, call and I'll come out and take your money. . . ."

"Naomi, what do you think?"

"Jackie, I just have my photographs up at home. This looks . . . it looks serious." The print was a pen drawing of a compacted structure of fine and shaded black lines. A small complicated cliff . . . that had just exploded, was falling away in the frame. "I like it. . . ."

"But?"

"Well, it's a little stark."

"So am I." Jackie stood bent and peering, large nose almost touching the print. "I wanted something smaller."

"You could look at something with color."

"Mmmm. But you get tired of that, Naomi. Color gets boring, but line stays fresh. Speaking of which, 'fresh' as in revelations—as I said, my companions in decay searched their failing memories on your murders, and came up with not very much new."

Jackie moved down the wall, examining prints, and Naomi sidestepped with her.

"—Basically, your all-too-female gynecological gossip. Oh, look at this, Naomi."

It was a little merry-go-round pony in colored inks. Small, gaudy, and beautiful, prancing impaled on a silver pole.

"There's your color," Jackie said, and moved on.

Naomi paused to study the little pony. "What gynecological gossip?"

"Remember our first victim—the possibly-dyke Coast Guard officer?"

"Tessler. Marie Tessler."

"Right, well, *Mama* Tessler's dear friend Eleanor Cernan—that great bridge player—said Marie was pregnant. Got rid of it?"

"Yes. I remember."

"Well, the news is that another one—the crossing guard who got chopped doing the laundry?"

"Jo-Ann Dailey."

"Right. And who *also*—according to Pauline Speckler, who's actually still pretty sharp—*also* was in the family way, and got rid of the kid a year before she was killed. Went to The Clinic out on Palm Way, south of town; it's the county's abortion mill. Pauline's husband—gone now, to her relief—was Mr. Dailey's boss, and Pauline's daughter knew Jo-Ann and was confided in."

"Any of the others?"

"As to positives—damned if I know. But as to negatives, I do have an interesting one. Her Auntie Myra let me know in no uncertain terms that our golden girl, Miss Snow-for-Sale Long, had never been pregnant. Would *certainly* have told Auntie—and, if she had been, would have absolutely kept the child. Our little drug dealer was very Catholic."

"Yes. . . ."

" 'Yes . . .'? And just what the fuck . . ." Jackie said softly, and turned from the art. "What the fuck are you trying to pull?" Jackie Keith looking like Jack Keith now, makeup and all. "You already *knew* this shit, didn't you? I see through you like glass, Naomi; I always did. —And nobody chumps me out!"

"All right, Jackie, we knew about it. All the women—except Rue Long—were pregnant and had abortions before they were killed. Usually a year before they were killed."

"Well, haven't you been cute. . . . And how did you find all this out?"

"Autopsy reports. The Long girl must have broken the pattern for the police—apparently another Sweetwater killing, but with no previous pregnancy and abortion."

"And where did you two get the autopsy reports?"

"Jackie, what difference does it make?"

"Finding anything you like?" The owner, calling from the door to the back of the gallery.

"Not yet," Naomi said. "Still looking."

"Well, let me know. . . ."

"I asked where you got those reports."

"Why?"

"Because I want to know, Naomi!" Not speaking as softly, now. "You two—you and your bank robber—come here, and all of a sudden you have a confidential copy of the Sweetwater task force summary. And now, *now*, you just happen to have the official autopsies." Jackie loomed over Naomi like the Wicked Witch of the West, but larger. "—And what I'd like to know is, is your aw-shucks Mr. Midwest just another fucking undercover *cop*? . . . Because thanks to you, Naomi, he's been enjoying my cooperation."

"No."

"No what?"

"No, he's not a cop."

"You say."

"That's right. *I* say, Jackie! And you are really . . . you have really slipped if you think he *is*."

"Keep your voice down. . . ."

"You keep *your* voice down."

Jackie sighed and stepped back, seemed to grow slightly smaller. "So . . . how did you get all that shit?"

". . . He got hold of a crooked cop up here."

" 'Got hold' of him. . . ."

"Got his name downstate . . . came up and leaned on him. Paid him money, too. —And that's where those things came from."

Jackie turned away, examined a green-ink holly shrub set in a small silver frame. "Is that true?"

"Yes, it is."

Jackie moved down the wall. "Well, why didn't you tell me?"

"Because it's none of your business, Jackie! I only told you now so you wouldn't have a senile fit."

"Mmmm. I just have this ... extreme dislike of being taken for a fool."

"Then don't act like one. —That holly's nice."

"I'm not looking for a Christmas decoration, Naomi. I am trying to find something that won't bore me to tears on my *wall*."

"So, what's he out of? Manchineel or the sheriff's office?"

"He who?"

"The bent cop."

"Jackie, you wanted a sundae? —So eat your sundae."

"All right. Be that way. . . ."

Finished shopping the Gallery, the Koren print wrapped and tucked into a small shopping bag, Jackie had steered down the mall into Rainbow Cream Ices. She'd ordered a double butterscotch sundae with vanilla ice cream. "I don't know," she said, "how people can go mad for chocolate. It tastes like burned rubber to me—always has. Even as a boy, I liked vanilla better. And with butterscotch—perfect."

"You've mentioned that before." Naomi had ordered the hot fudge classic.

"Still true," Jackie said. "Look at that. Looks like a cat shit on your plate." She put a swift spoonful of butterscotch in her mouth to demonstrate goodness, and two light-brown drops of syrup fell down her front.

Naomi was tempted to let them lie on the white linen bosom, stain the hell out of it.

"Jackie, you spilled on your dress."

"Oh . . . Jesus."

"Here." Naomi dipped a corner of her paper napkin in her glass of water and passed it over. "Two spots."

"Well, what a pain in the ass. . . ." Jackie looked down, dabbed at butterscotch and vanilla. "I don't know what it is, but more and more of my food never gets into my mouth! Did I get it?"

"More water—and don't rub, just sort of sponge it."

"It's infuriating—well, the whole goddam getting-old thing is just infuriating. . . . This isn't going to come out."

"It is out. You got it out pretty well. Just . . . more water. You need to really wet it."

Jackie, head bent to see down her front, and still holding her sundae spoon in one hand, dabbed with the other. "What about that?"

"It's . . . it really looks pretty good. It's just mainly water stain, now. When you get home, you can soak it in the sink. Cold water."

Jackie sighed and relaxed, put the wet napkin down. "I'll tell you, if you wear something really nice it's just asking for trouble. I could have come out with my old blue cotton that makes me look like some retired Kansas schoolteacher—and I could have eaten two orders of fucking spareribs with my fingers and not spilled anything on that dress."

"True," Naomi said, and went back to her sundae.

"And you're not going to stain that so-called outfit you've got on, either. What is that, a chino pantsuit or something?"

"That's what it is, Jackie."

"Well, you're not going to stain it. It's already ugly."

"Thank you."

"Well, it is." Jackie finished her butterscotch and vanilla in four careful spoonfuls. "Girlfriends."

"What?"

"Girlfriends."

"Us?"

"No, Naomi; don't flatter yourself. . . . Another item from the senile set: the Coast Guard girl had a close beach-bunny buddy about a year before she cashed in—"

"I remember that."

"And . . . *and* so did our crossing guard."

"Jo-Ann."

"That's right. According to still-sharp Pauline, her daughter, whose name escapes me—something floral—saw the two of them together a couple of times. Big buddies, at least for a while. And Jo-Ann wanted them all to get together sometime, shop or lunch or whatever, but Pauline's daughter worked and this other woman worked and they somehow never met."

"I don't think that does us much good. A lot of women have women friends."

"Not short-term—and only while pregnant."

"Could I talk to Pauline's daughter?"

"If you can find her. She and her second husband are in Greece for the summer. Pooping around the islands."

"Great . . ."

"Do the stains still show?"

"Barely."

"Well, I'm not wearing white again. I won't do it."

"It looks good on you, Jackie. Very elegant."

"Oh, please. I know what I look like. But—and here's why I mention it after your exception-proves-the-rule stuff about our victims. But . . . guess who *didn't* have a real close lady pal come into her life about a year before she died. Guess who *never* had a female buddy because she just didn't like other women—and since she was such a Miss America perfect piece of ass, other women didn't like her, either."

"Rue Long."

"So her Auntie Myra says."

"Well . . ."

"Well?"

"I guess it could be something. . . . If it's true of the others."

"Whether it's 'something' or not, Naomi, I expect money for the possibility. It's no fun, you know, trying to go down memory lane with my fellow hags. It's like following parade horses with a shovel. —Once, they knew everything unpleasant about everybody. Now they only remember little lumps. . . . It's not fun." Jackie patted her lips with her napkin, careful not to smear her lipstick. "—And you owe me for the abortion shit too, even if you knew it before, because you didn't *tell* me you knew it before."

"We'll pay you, Jackie."

"Damn right you will. Though if I were ten years younger—fifteen years younger—I'd take it out with Mr. Midwest in trade." Jackie winked, apparently on a slight sugar high.

"You finished, Jackie?"

"Yes, I am finished—and I assume you're going to get this check."

"I'll get the check. You leave the tip. . . ."

. . . Coming back to the table, Naomi glanced down as Jackie got up, and saw that she'd left two dimes.

"For God's sake . . ." Naomi took a dollar from her wallet and put it on the table.

"If you're trying to shame me with that dollar, Naomi," Jackie heading for the door, Gallery shopping bag in hand, "—you're wasting your time. That waitress is a kid, and she's got her whole life ahead of her to make money in. —I don't."

Chapter 23

Mr. Montfort came to the door glittering in the sunshine, his work shirt and overalls spangled with fish scales.

"Afternoon. Been fishing?"

"I know, and I'm going to clean up. And yes, I have been fishing big-time, Mr. Boyce. Fished past noon. . . . Come on in. Your sis is helping me clean seven of the prettiest mackerel you ever saw. Trolled 'em right off San Isobel Inlet."

"Spoon?" Pierce said, and stepped into the hall past a fish-stained wall of Montfort.

"Hell, no. Mullet. Mullet's the only summer bait for mackerel." He lumbered down the hall after Pierce, floorboards creaking under him. "—Though there are newspaper fishermen and radio-program fishermen will tell you different."

"You have sportfishing limits down here, Mr. Montfort?"

"I wouldn't know," Montfort said above and behind him. "—And I never cared to ask. If the Disciples could fish their boat full, then so can I. . . ."

"Hi, Gil. Want to help?" Naomi at the sink in a sunny kitchen, its air conditioner roaring and dripping under a window. She was wearing green dishwashing gloves and a yellow-and-white-striped apron over her dress. The apron was oversized; it came down past her knees. "—We've got plenty of knives and a scraper."

Several large handsome dead fish lay piled, soft silver, along the counter.

"No, thanks," Pierce said. "I'll watch."

"Two left to do."

"I cleaned three of those beauties," Montfort said, and hulked over to the refrigerator to put wrapped mackerel away. "—And damn if my hands didn't seize up on me. I have arthritis in these hands. . . ."

"I can fillet these for you, Charlie."

"No, no, honey. Don't bother doing that. We'll just clean 'em and scale 'em and put 'em up."

"All right."

Pierce leaned against the narrow white door of a floor-to-ceiling cabinet, and watched Naomi work. She had a blue bandanna knotted to hold back her hair, and was bent over the sink, concentrating in that sweet serious way women had with a task. She might have been a country woman working cleaning fish, except for her arms being so thin, her wrists too delicate to have done farm work—that, and the cleverness and sadness in her face. . . . Alone, and no family to do for—though the wanting was there, the heart and competence were there. But something had been lacking in the will.

Same thing, Pierce supposed, that had been missing in him for all his wasted years. A reasonable opinion of themselves had likely been lacking in both of them, so they saw themselves either too good to live as other people did—or too bad.

As he'd thought himself too proud a young man to mind any will but his own—certainly too heroic a fellow to heed the law—so Naomi, softer and shy, must have thought herself worthless. And had acted on that notion for money in many hotel rooms.

Naked in strange hotel rooms, or running armed in banks. Poor places for people to be acting out their lives . . .

"I hate cutting off the heads," Naomi said.

"Oh, I can do that." Montfort searched a counter drawer and took out a cleaver.

"I'll do it." Pierce went over, took the cleaver and balanced it . . . then put it back in the drawer and picked up a fillet knife with a good edge. He stood beside Naomi, slid his left hand under a fish to lift it slightly, position it, then put the point of the knife in just behind the gill. He thrust through, cut once up, once down, drew the blade back hard, and the big shining silver head, its eyes almost intelligent, came free.

"That was quick," Montfort said. "Where'd you learn to cut so neat?"

"School of hard knocks," Pierce said.

. . . Finished with fish, Naomi took Pierce down the hall to her room, and said, "What do you think?"

"What do I think of what . . . ?" The room's air conditioner was rumbling, working hard.

"This," she said. *"This."* And went to the wall between her two tall windows, and pointed to a little picture of a circus horse . . . merry-go-round horse.

"Well," Pierce said, "it's real nice."

"Do you like it?"

"I sure do. It's . . . very pretty." And it was; looked like a horse on a Christmas card.

"I think it's beautiful," Naomi said. "It's kitschy, but really gorgeous. Jackie hated it."

"I wouldn't pay any attention to Jackie. I think it's a very nice little picture."

"Two hundred and twenty dollars, Tyler."

". . . Well . . . well, that's worth every penny. Fact is, I'm going to give you that money extra, Naomi. Because I want you to have the picture of that little horse as a present from me."

"Thanks, Tyler, that's very sweet. But no thanks. For luxuries, I only spend *my* money."

"Now listen—you're getting that cash and it's a present and that's all there is to it, Naomi. I owe you a lot more than you've been paid."

"No, you don't."

"Yes, I do. What we got done together, I couldn't have done alone. ... And you've been real good company."

" 'Good company'. . ." Naomi said.

"Now I'm heading over to the beach, talk to a fellow. Remember Terry Ecklin?"

"Marcie Tredenberg's boyfriend."

"That's right. I called his mother—she told me where he was at. So, if you want to come along, we can catch up as we go."

". . . I wanted to go out to The Clinic this afternoon—the local abortion clinic. See if anybody there has noticed they've been losing a few old clients through the years."

"Right. Time that was done. —This thing with Ecklin won't take long, though."

"Sunglasses and purse and I'm with you."

"And Naomi, if you're tired of cleaning fish, we can move you out of here back to the motel."

"Oh, the hell with it." She was going through her dresser. "I'm used to Charlie—I'll stay." The sunglasses were found in the top left drawer.

"Because he's lonely?"

"Because he's alone, Tyler. —Are we going, or what?"

Pierce parked far up the esplanade, and turned the truck engine off. He and Naomi rolled their windows down to let a warm sea wind blow through. The surf was low along the beach, pressed down and lit a translucent green by the sun's furious heat. The concrete of the walkway was burned white.

"So the two victims the ladies told Jackie about, confirm the autopsies?"

"Yes, word was that both Marie Tessler and Jo-Ann

Dailey were pregnant. And they both aborted within a year of the time they were killed."

"And all the rest, too, except Rue Long. . . ."

"That's right. Jackie doesn't know about the others. But the autopsies say yes."

"Well," Pierce said. "We have the Sweetwater's reason, for sure."

"For sure. And you know, people have killed people over this abortion thing before now."

"But not the women." Pierce took a cigar out of his shirt pocket, then put it back.

"Oh, smoke the damn thing, Tyler. . . . No, nobody's killed the women who've *had* abortions. Not until now."

Pierce took the cigar out of his pocket again. "Sure you don't mind?"

"Just smoke the cigar."

Pierce reached to the dash for a book of matches. "So, how does the Sweetwater find out these women are pregnant? And then, how does he know they got rid of their babies? . . . He's a friend? . . . A doctor? . . . One of the people who picket those places, make a fuss?"

"Friend? A friend to all those girls? —Only friends Jackie heard about were women. Marie Tessler and Jo-Ann Dailey both had women as short-time buddies when they were pregnant."

"No names come with those women?" Pierce lit his cigar, began puffing on it with such satisfaction that Naomi decided to keep quiet about the smell.

"No. No names Jackie heard of. Passing friendships . . . and this is all old secondhand, thirdhand stuff."

"And Rue Long didn't have a special lady friend like that?"

"No, Tyler. Apparently she didn't. Didn't like women much."

"Right. No lady friend for her. She wasn't pregnant . . . wasn't a Sweetwater girl." Pierce blew a slow smoke ring. "But here's a funny thing: when I talked to Jason, he told me he'd heard there was a woman friend came around when Lisa was carrying *her* baby. Said he believed they were close for a while—but he and Lisa were having a serious disagreement at the time, so he never got to meet this lady. Never got her name."

". . . That's . . . that's three of them."

"You bet. Three lady friends came around when those girls were pregnant. And I wonder if maybe all three of those ladies . . . weren't just one lady after all."

"My God . . ."

"Now," Pierce said, opened his door and got out of the truck, "—let's go talk to my man Terry. See if that little pizza girl had a lady friend too, when she was expecting."

It was a beautiful morning, even so hot. And walking with Pierce in the sea breeze, walking down the long curving esplanade under the shifting feathered shade of the palms, Naomi couldn't help but make a private fool of herself . . . pretend she and Tyler were walking together to be together. Then pretended deeper, that they lived in a small bungalow off the beach, a small stucco house resting behind jasmine and hibiscus— with a barrel-tile roof, to please Tyler. . . . And all the rest: his Carolyn waiting in Missouri, and this murderer—this man or woman—that and all the rest somehow solved and over, done with and gone, so they could be together.

Naomi imagined herself happy as they walked along, and supposed it would feel very strange. . . .

Halfway down the long arc of the esplanade, there was a cluster of buildings on the beach. A restaurant— Googy's—and shops, and public rest rooms. There was a stand of rental beach umbrellas out on the walkway just past a shop called the Conch Shell.

"There we go," Pierce said, and walked to the umbrella stand. A very thin young man, in a Bad Band sleeveless T-shirt and long baggy purple shorts, was furling bright-striped umbrellas, tucking them neatly into a long two-tier wire rack. He was balding early, his fragile sandy hair braided into several skimpy dreadlocks.

"How's business, Terry?" Pierce said.

"Hey, business is great." Terry Ecklin had a fine gold ring through his left nostril, and another through the tip of his tongue. "Do I know you, man?"

"Not yet. Like to talk to you about something, Terry. It's a personal thing. This is Naomi. Naomi—Terry Ecklin."

"Hi."

"Hi, Terry."

"So . . . hey. This is a business, you know, man. And I'm busy."

"Just take a minute. Personal questions."

"Well . . . I don't know, man."

"For instance, let me ask you a question right now. First thing I'd like to know is, why would people come to a beautiful beach like this to get some sun—then rent a big umbrella for the shade?"

"Hey, I'll tell you. They do that because of my partner. Okay?"

"Your partner . . ."

"That's right, lady. You ever hear of malignant melanoma? Black skin cancer? Well, that's my partner—and I saw it comin' years ago and I got this concession license and there's not a fuckin' thing the city can do about it and believe me they'd like to. They want me to comb my hair and wear slacks and a sports shirt!"

"Wrong," Naomi said. "You look like *you*. And that's how a man should look."

"Hey, right on. So, if that was your question, man . . ."

Two plump teenage girls in bathing suits came over to the stand. They looked enough alike to be sisters. "Terry, do you have a yellow-an'-green?"

"Yes, I do, Elizabeth—are you two renting or fooling around?"

"We're renting."

"Okay. Two dollars an hour. Ten-dollar deposit."

"Ten *dollars*?"

"These umbrellas are made in England, Elizabeth. They cost almost fifty dollars. So that's a major cheap deposit, and don't complain about it."

"You are so weird, Terry."

"Ten *dollars . . .*"

When the girls were gone, Terry put the money in a narrow olive-green tin box beneath his umbrella racks. "See, man—I'm extremely busy here."

"I can see you are," Pierce said. "But I need to know something, and I'm sorry to have to ask you. I need to know if Marcie Tredenberg made any new friends while she was carrying her baby."

"Oh . . . oh fuck you, man! What are you, a cop?"

"No."

"I told the cops all about Marcie when that happened, and I'm not saying shit to anybody about it."

"Terry, my name's Pierce. The Sweetwater killed my daughter, Lisa—and Miss Naomi and I are looking into that. The police aren't having any luck, so we're looking into it for my daughter's sake, and the other young women too. So, Terry, I need you to answer my questions. You understand? I'll pay you, if that's what it takes. . . ."

"Look, Mr. . . . Pierce, I'm just . . . I'm trying to do some business here. Okay? How did you know where I am?"

"Found your mom in the phone book. Called her and she told me."

"Great . . ."

"Tell us about your girlfriend, Terry," Naomi said. "Can you tell us if anybody new came into her life when she was pregnant?"

"Marcie was not my girlfriend. She was not my *girlfriend*! I told the cops that and they didn't pay any attention. Apparently it was just beyond their dull minds to imagine that Marcie and I could be best friends without fucking each other." Terry went back to adjusting his umbrellas, straightening them in the racks. "Marcie and I went to school together, okay? We were friends from the sixth grade. She wasn't pretty, and I was the class weirdo, and we were friends when nobody—and I mean nobody—was interested in being friends with us. Nobody liked our music or anything."

"You must miss her, Terry."

"No shit, lady. Yes, I miss her. —You know what the other kids called her in school? They called her Miss Toad. And Marcie was *nice*. She was gentle and intelligent and nice. And they just didn't care. They hurt her anyway."

"So," Naomi said, "it wasn't your baby, Terry."

"I told you we didn't have that kind of relationship. We had a . . . a karmic relationship. We listened to music—we went to concerts together—Dump, Pork Queen, all the really creative bands. Creep who managed the pizza place got her pregnant—and then he took off for Tampa. Then she came to me and I said, 'I'll marry you,' and she said, 'No, you're my Spirit friend, and that would be taking advantage.'" Terry saw a blue-and-red-striped umbrella out of position on the upper row, and carefully adjusted it.

"—That's the kind of person she was. She wanted to keep her baby, she wanted to have it, but she had to take care of her father and she didn't have any goddam money and I didn't have any money then, either. Now, I'm making money at last—and don't think those fascists in city hall wouldn't like to cancel my permit. Now, I have some money, and it's too late because some fucking maniac killed her! —And just because she was dressed up in that stupid uniform. It was a soldier's uniform, a Roman soldier's uniform, and Marcie would never have hurt anybody."

"Terry," Pierce said, "we don't think it was mainly the uniform. We think it was something else. . . . Did Marcie make any new friends while she was pregnant—before she had the abortion?"

"Marcie didn't have any friends except me and the girls at the pizza place. And she had . . . an older chick was nice to her then, but I guess she dropped her. A sun freak, doesn't rent an umbrella. I see her around every now and then."

"Terry," Naomi said, "what was the woman's name?"

"Damn . . . I don't know. It was some ordinary name. . . . I see her on the beach maybe once every month or two. Last time a couple of weeks ago. She has never rented an umbrella, tell you that."

"What does she look like?"

"Well, Mr. . . . Pierce?"

"Pierce."

"Hey, I couldn't describe her in detail, you know? She's always down on the sand, and I'm taking care of business. She looks like a . . . you know, an older in-shape beach chick. Looks like a surfer, volleyballer—you know? Dark hair." He started down the row of umbrellas again, turning some of them slightly to show their stripes better.

"Terry." Naomi put her hand on his arm to hold him still. "—Think a minute. Can you tell us anything else about her? Anything at all?"

"Why? I mean, what does she have to do with anything?"

"Maybe a lot. Are you sure there's nothing else about her . . . nothing at all?"

"Hey, she's not—I never even *met* her."

"Okay," Naomi said. "Okay . . . But listen, Terry. This is very very important. We'll come by in a day or two, just to check in with you. *Please* be thinking about this."

"All right . . . sure. Why? Is she supposed to know something about what happened?"

"That's right," Pierce said. "So, we'll stop by, maybe tomorrow."

"We appreciate your help, Terry," Naomi said.

"Oh, hey, it's cool. . . ."

Pierce and Naomi walked away back up the esplanade. Neither of them said anything. They'd walked past the Conch Shell . . . past Googy's . . . when Terry Ecklin called *"Hey!"* and came trotting after them. He was a clumsy runner. His feet flew a little out to the sides as he ran; the meager dreadlocks flopped up and down.

"Hey," he said, and glanced back over his shoulder to check on his umbrellas. "—Her name began with a K. Kristen . . . Kathy . . . something like that."

"Thank you, Terry!" Naomi said. "That could be really helpful. —And can I ask you something personal?"

"I guess so." Terry was still out of breath.

"Do those rings . . . that ring in your tongue, doesn't it hurt?"

"No. No, it doesn't hurt." He stuck his tongue out.

Pierce leaned to look. "Can you eat with that?"

"Yeah, I can eat with it. You just . . . you just learn to chew around it, you know? I'm Mr. Rings, I've got rings all over me."

"Well, they're very decorative," Naomi said. "And I think you'd look ridiculous in slacks and a sports shirt."

"Right on," said Terry Ecklin.

. . . The beach sand was very hot, almost too hot to walk on, and Naomi sighed with relief to get down to the damp sand along the surf line. They'd rolled their pant cuffs up, and were carrying their shoes. The waves curled, paused, then fell and seemed to fan the sea air to them. The packed sand trembled slightly under their feet.

"Tyler, we could go to the police with this. Your friend, Sheriff Macksie." Naomi had to raise her voice over the ocean's sound. "—We have enough that I think they'd believe us, at least look into it and try to find this Kathy or Kristen or whoever. The police must be desperate."

"No."

"Just . . . 'no'?"

"That's right." Pierce bent to pick up a small curled shell . . . held it up to his ear.

It seemed to Naomi a touching thing to do—try to hear the sea in a shell, over the sea's noise. "It has to be bigger."

"What?"

"Has to be bigger, Tyler. Conch shell, something like that."

"Oh . . ." He bent and put the shell back.

"You're just interested in blowing his head off? *Her* head off? Blowing whoever's head off?"

"Tell you what I'm not interested in," Pierce said. "Not interested in a real long trial, and then whoever it is going to some fancy hospital and having appointments with the doctors and sitting in the rec room watching TV and waiting for lunch. Giving out interviews . . . maybe writing a book. That sure doesn't interest me at all."

"You'd rather blow whoever's head off."

"You bet." Pierce strode away, bare feet splashing through the wave runners sliding onto the sand, and Naomi had to hurry to keep up.

"Do you think a woman could do that? Kill those girls?"

"I think a lady can do just about anything she sets her mind to, she figures she's got reason. —Was a

woman robbed banks around Omaha a few years ago—
did you know that?"

"No."

"Well, there was. And I'm not talking about going in
with a note and claiming to have this or that, and give
me the money or something terrible will happen. I'm
talking about going in planned-out, with three men
back of her and her with a pistol in her hand."

"I think I'll pass."

"Took four banks in three years, and took well over
half a million out of them."

"What happened to her?"

"Not a damn thing. Never caught her. She just made
her money, and quit. —So, I figure a woman can do
what she sets her mind to."

"But she didn't shoot anybody."

"Hell she didn't. She shot a meter maid tried to
ticket their getaway. Shot her in the butt."

"Are you—is that a true story?"

"Yes. But not the meter-maid part."

"Ha, ha . . . But you think a woman could have done
these crimes?"

"I believe so. Or a man and a woman—with the
woman the Judas goat luring those girls in, befriending
them when they were in trouble. You'd be surprised
what a woman will do when she's with a bad man."

". . . Or vice versa."

"That's right, or vice versa too. Also, could be it's a
group. People punishing those girls for what they did,
and the woman the only one we know about."

"A group?"

"Possible."

"But Tyler, a *group*. My God . . ."

The sun was straight over their heads, so their
shadows as they walked clung to their legs like shy
children. The sun's heat came down and stung them,
then the sea wind blew it away.

Walking beside Pierce, Naomi noticed what she'd

noticed before—that barefoot men seemed to stay as tall, while barefoot women grew shorter. She thought of taking his hand, then decided better not.

Chapter 24

The Clinic was on South Palm Way, at the edge of town. Miles into the country, Palm Way would become Palmetto County Secondary, the old two-lane going straight south, running down through Palm Beach County to Dade, and metropolitan Miami.

It was the way she and Pierce had come up, and reminded Naomi of their moonlit drive when, embarrassed at having talked too much—out of loneliness, she supposed—she'd pretended to fall asleep in the truck.

There were lots still vacant down the block from The Clinic's neat shallow lawn, its carefully kept coconut palms. Built out here on cheaper real estate to keep costs down, it was white clapboard single-story and designed to look like a suburban bank, with miniature plantation pillars on either side of its front glass double doors. The parking lot was in back.

Naomi turned right down the side street, then left into the lot. There were several cars there, baking on blacktop in the afternoon's heat, nests of sun glare dazzling off their paint.

When Naomi got out of the Nissan, she heard someone calling. "Yours . . . *yours*!" She looked around the parking lot, then heard the same voice. "Don't do it. Don't *do* it!" And saw, across the side street, three people standing at the curb beside a white van. Two young women and an older man with a beard.

The man was holding up a large white sign. DON'T

MURDER YOUR LITTLE BOY was printed in black block
letters. The man saw Naomi watching, and turned the
sign to show the other side. DON'T MURDER YOUR
LITTLE GIRL.

"Yours . . . yours . . . *yours*!" The two women
chanted together as if they were singing. They looked
like sisters . . . looked like college swimmers, big,
healthy, and handsome in summer dresses.

"Don't kill your little baby!" All three of them
chanted that.

Naomi started around to the front of the building,
and the three of them walked along the sidewalk—
staying across the street, but following her.

"It's *murder*. . . !" One of the young women was
screaming. *"YOU'RE KILLING A LITTLE CHILD!"*

All three of them chanted, then. *"Don't do it; don't
do it; don't do it; don't kill your little baby. . . ."*

Naomi saw a young woman, a girl, coming around
the building toward her. She looked Hispanic, and she
was walking with her head bent as if it were raining, as
if the screaming were rain she had to walk through.

*"OH, LOOK! LOOK WHAT SHE'S DONE! SHE
MURDERED HER BABY!"* One of the women came
out into the street, pointing at the Hispanic girl and
screaming, "Oh my God, oh my God, how could you
do that? Killer killer killer, she murdered her little
baby. . . !"

The Hispanic girl passed Naomi, head down, thin
brown face wet with tears.

Naomi told herself to be quiet, then she yelled,
"Why don't you fucking shut *up*!" at the woman in the
street. And the woman stopped screaming, and came
over to her and said, "Please. Please, don't be hurt."
The woman was taller than Naomi, and much younger.
She had gray eyes. "Please, we don't mean to hurt you.
We know how terrible these choices are—"

"It's private," Naomi said. "It's none of your

damned business! Screaming in the street like some lunatic!"

"There can't be privacy for a crime, can there? Can there be? It's not private to murder little children when they're helpless inside you . . . when they're growing in love and trust for you. —That's the worst betrayal of all. It is unforgivable. God will never forgive it, and soon no man or woman will forgive it, because it's an act of vile selfishness. Doesn't the murder of children *call* for the raising of voices?"

"It's not for you to *say*." Naomi wished she hadn't started this, yelled back at these people.

"If not us, then who?" the young woman said. "Now I can see that you don't have a baby growing in you. I know, I can tell—we can all tell when we're close enough. —What's your name? You're Jewish, aren't you? Do you know what Rabbi Schneerson, God's chosen teacher, said about abortion? Are you aware of God's wishes, his commandments concerning these disgusting acts?"

"Oh, give me a break, whatever your name is," Naomi said, "—and don't try to speak for God. We're talking about a scrap of tissue here! A lump of tissue *you* wouldn't touch with a Kleenex. And you say a woman has to carry that around for months until— maybe—it turns into a *child*?"

"It's a child from the beginning."

"Bullshit. It's snot with a possible future. —And you're telling women what they have to *do* with that? They have to keep it inside them? They have to wait and see if it develops? And *if* it develops, they have to be slaves to it for twenty years? . . . Lady, that's a lot of 'have to's'—and who the fuck are you to tell women what to do with their lives? Let me tell you something; women are *tired* of being told what to do with their lives. . . . Now, get out of my way."

". . . Sorry about that." The woman in The Clinic's registration office was plump and plain in a flowered summer print. She seemed harassed, as if the yelling outside, the anger, had leaked in through the walls. "They have to stay across the street—it's a court order. But they sneak over and we call the police and they run back."

"Is it always just those people? Same people?"

"You've got to be kidding! We get every nut on the Coast coming through here. Some days there's nobody, and then there'll be thirty of them out there. And they know everybody that works here—don't think they don't."

"Hard on your patients . . ."

"Oh, it's terrible. . . . How can we help you?"

"My name's Naomi Cohen . . . and I'm a freelance writer. I contract to do magazine articles, mainly. Right now, I'm doing a series—"

"Go ahead, sit down."

"Thanks . . . Right now, I'm doing a series—I hope for *Redbook*—on how the staffs at clinics like this cope with the pressures of their jobs."

"Pressures like those nuts outside?"

"That's right." There was a nameplate on the desk— FRAN. "That's exactly right, Fran. I don't see how you do it." Naomi put her purse on the floor beside her chair, opened the notebook.

"We just . . . put up with it—and if it gets too bad, we call the police. And like I said, there's a court order they're supposed to stay across the street. But they sort of creep over. . . ."

"One crept over on me, when I was walking around from the parking lot."

"Oh, it's really terrible." Fran had a very elaborate hairdo. It didn't suit her. "I've already been here longer than a lot of girls doing reception and registration. They come and they stay a little while, and then it just gets to be too much."

"I can understand that," Naomi said, took out her pen and made an entry.

"Oh-oh," Fran said. "—are you writing this down?"

"No. Just general notes. I could never quote anybody unless they said it was okay. I'd never embarrass anybody, Fran. I don't do those kind of articles."

"Because I just work here. . . ." Fran's hair looked as though she'd started a permanent, then abandoned it.

"I understand," Naomi said. "So, what I'd like to do—and I know you're busy—"

"Actually, this afternoon's been pretty slow."

"—What I'd like to do is talk to your director, or one of the doctors . . . you know, see how they cope?"

"Well, Ms. Cohen—"

"Naomi."

"Naomi, I have to tell you, interviews here would be really tough. . . ."

"Impossible." A tall nurse in operating-room greens stood smiling in the office's rear doorway. A corridor ran through back there. "—That'll be the day, that Torguson talks to a reporter."

"I'm not a reporter," Naomi said. "Just freelance."

"She's doing an article," Fran said, "on the joys of working at an abortion clinic."

"Oh, God," the tall nurse said. "—we'd need a war correspondent for that." She was smiling at Naomi, a tanned handsome woman with dark-blue eyes. "Anyway, Torguson will never go for it. He thinks any publicity is bad publicity."

"And Torguson is . . . ?"

"Dr. Torguson. He's one of the owners."

"No." Fran shook her head. "He won't do it."

Naomi sighed and closed her notebook. "That's really bad news—because I wanted to ask your director, or your owner or whoever, about something else too—and I know your records are kept very private."

"Oh, we have to do that," Fran said.

"I understand, but I wondered if you people had noticed something really weird."

"What weird?" the tall nurse said. "—I mean weirder than usual around here."

"Well," Naomi said, "while I was doing some research in Palmetto Lake, at the courthouse, I started talking to a man who has some information out of the medical examiner's office. And he told me—confidentially—that the Sweetwater's last victim, Moira Durchauer, had had an abortion just a week or two before she was killed."

"Oh, we know that! We all remembered her name when that happened." Fran made a fear-face. "That was scary—and I guess it's not a privacy thing, since she's dead."

"So, she did have it done here."

"Yes, and that *was* weird," the tall nurse said. "But we run a lot of women through here, and I suppose bad things are going to happen to some of them."

"Um-hmm." Naomi opened her notebook again, made an entry. "Well, that just confirms it—but you know that may not be all? My friend—this man—has information that all of the Sweetwater's victims, *all* of them, when they were autopsied, and their boyfriends and so forth were interviewed? —All of them had had abortions within a year of their deaths."

"Perfect," the nurse said. "That's all we need."

"Are you kidding me?" Fran sat with her mouth open. She had good teeth; her best feature.

"And that isn't what my article was supposed to be about," Naomi said, "—but it's so strange. . . . I just wondered if they all had had their abortion procedures here, and I thought I'd ask Dr. . . . Torguson?"

"Good luck," the nurse said. "He wouldn't touch that with a ten-foot pole. —And what it sounds like to me, is that so many women are having abortions on the quiet, you're going to get a lot in any group you pick. We do a land-office business here, I can tell you that. —And speaking of business, I have a prep to do." She stepped back into the corridor. "Oh, Fran. We're expecting those two women from yesterday?"

"Yes, I got 'em."

"You can tell them we don't appreciate last-minute cancellations." The nurse nodded good-bye to Naomi, and walked away down the hall.

"She may be right," Naomi said. "But you know, just for example, those people out there—"

"Those aren't the worst," Fran said.

"I believe it. But they seemed pretty serious about it to me. Pretty committed."

"You think they could be doing that? Killing women who came here?"

"Oh, probably not." Naomi closed the notebook, and bent to pick up her purse. "We could be all wrong, but I'd really like to speak with Dr. Torguson. It would just be a regular interview—but I could mention this other thing too, because he might have noticed something unusual."

"Oh, I don't know. . . ."

"If I could just have a few minutes of his time."

"Well, not today," Fran said. "For sure, not today, because he has surgery right through the afternoon."

"Tomorrow?"

"I don't know, Ms. Cohen—"

"Naomi."

"Naomi, I *really* don't know—I'll have to check with him. If I say something—that it's all right—he'll just get mad."

"Should I call you?"

"Okay. You call, and I'll ask him tomorrow morning. That's the best time."

"All right. I appreciate it, Fran."

"I can't believe those women who were killed were all from here. . . ."

"One way to find out for sure, Fran." Naomi stood up. "Just check your client list for the last few years."

"Oh, that wouldn't help; all the names are number-coded right away. Nobody would remember them after a while. And the real names are kept in the business safe-deposit at the bank. They are *very* confidential. We could get sued big-time!"

The front door buzzer sounded, and Fran looked out to see who was there. "We have to be careful who we let in. . . ."

She pushed her desk button, and two blond women—mother and daughter—walked into the lobby. They were arguing in whispers.

"Well, you've been very helpful, Fran." Naomi went to the door as the women came into the office. "I appreciate it. . . . I'll give you a call tomorrow, and you can tell me if Dr. Torguson can see me."

"I'll ask him. . . ."

"Bye-bye."

"Bye-bye . . ."

The demonstrators and their white van were gone when Naomi came out of the entrance and walked around the side of the building. The sunlight was very bright; she took her dark glasses out of her purse and put them on.

When she reached the parking lot, a heavy white door marked SERVICE opened at the back of the clinic. The tall nurse stood there in her O.R. greens and beckoned Naomi to her.

"Listen, *are* you a reporter, or what?"

"I'm freelance. I do articles."

The nurse stood looking at Naomi for a moment. There was an oddity . . . a small slice of white in the blue of her right eye. "What's your name?"

"Naomi. Naomi Cohen."

"Listen . . . listen, Naomi, the Durchauer thing did make me think. —And this has to be fast—I'm with a patient now. But you can just forget about Fran—she's sweet but not tremendously bright—and I have to tell you, no way, no *way* is Torguson or any of the partners going to talk to you about women being murdered by people picketing us or whatever. . . . That would be very bad for business. Know what I mean?"

"Yes, I can see that." Naomi could smell a faint odor of soap and disinfectant from the nurse. Hospital smells . . .

"But the Durchauer thing made me think. . . . And you say you have this guy who knows *all* the victims had been pregnant and had this procedure, and maybe right here?"

"All the *Sweetwater's* victims. That's right."

"I see. . . . Well," the nurse took a deep breath, smiled at Naomi, "this is definitely going to cost me my job. But definitely . . . Listen, if you come back tonight—and I mean late, say twelve o'clock tonight—I'll come back too, and be here. I have a key and the alarm code. It just so happens that Torguson's attorney told him years ago to take pictures. So, in his office, we have a file full of pictures and license numbers for just about every wacko that ever picketed the place. . . . And believe me, some of those people *could* kill. I'm talking really scary, screaming and following our clients and taking down their license numbers and everything."

"That would be so helpful! It would be fantastic. . . ."

"No, it's probably really stupid of me to do this."

"It isn't," Naomi said. "Believe me. What's your name?"

"Oh, listen—forget names. You don't know me at all, and we *never* had this little talk. Okay?"

"Okay."

"All right. . . . All right, I'm going to do it—but you promise whatever happens, you will absolutely *not* say where this information came from. And that's important, because it could mean more than my job. I mean, I could lose a career over this. We're talking about a career-breaker. . . ."

"No," Naomi said. "I promise. I absolutely promise."

"All right. Twelve o'clock. Now I have a patient—I

have to go." The nurse closed the door; Naomi heard her lock it.

Naomi walked to the Nissan through shimmering heat and light. She remembered that Tyler had never bought a hat . . . was wandering around in this, just asking for heatstroke. . . .

She unlocked the Nissan, opened the driver-side door, and stood waiting for a little of the oven temperature inside to dissipate. "My God, Tyler," she said aloud. "We're going to *get* whoever they are. Is this bizarre, or what . . . ?"

Pierce called Margaret from a drugstore pay phone on Third Avenue, and her phone rang for a while before she answered it.

"Hello . . ."

"Margaret, it's Tyler."

"Oh, for God's sake I haven't *heard* from you. I was out in the yard. —Are you still down here?"

"I'm still down here. I'm in Palmetto Lake."

"Well, for God's sake . . . You know, Tyler—and I know we're not married anymore. But you could have just called."

"I could have, and I should have, Margaret. I apologize for that, but we've been busy."

"Who's 'we'?"

"A woman named Naomi has been helping me. She grew up here, knows the state very well."

"I see. . . ."

"It's not a . . . it's not that kind of relationship, Margaret. She's just helping me."

"It's none of my business, Tyler. Did you tell Carolyn?"

"Yes, Margaret, I told Carolyn. She knows all about it. She talked to Naomi on the phone."

"Well, it's none of my business. . . . Tyler, have you found out anything?"

"One of the reasons I'm calling you. Yes, we have.

We found out a lot. We were very lucky, and came on something the cops had no way of knowing."

"From some of your nasty friends?"

"That's right—from nasty friends, Margaret. And I think we're going to get whoever—and damn soon."

"Oh, God. Oh *God*, Tyler, are you telling me the truth?"

"That's right."

"And if you do get him—I just can't believe it! You finding that bastard and all those policemen couldn't?"

"Luck, and nasty friends."

"And if you do get him—"

"May be a her. Or a couple of people."

"I don't care, Tyler; I don't *give* a shit. . . . What are you going to do then?"

"I'll take care of it."

"Oh, Tyler. Why in the world I ever . . . If I could have both you *and* Carl Hubbard, I would have been the happiest woman in the world. And I guess I sound like some crazy person."

"No, you don't. We had good times when we were kids, and I hold nothing against you, honey. The fault with us, was my fault."

"No, it wasn't."

"Yes. It was. —Now, I want to come out and talk to you, Margaret. We need to talk about Lisa, what was happening from last year to the time she died. We need to talk about it."

"Oh, I don't want to do that, Tyler."

"I know, but it's important."

"Well . . . all right. We're going out on Paul Nolan's boat this afternoon. We're supposed to leave right now—and we wouldn't be back until this evening late. Should I—should I just cancel that?"

"No, you don't have to. Tonight'll be soon enough. . . . Just some things I have to know."

"All right, then, Tyler. We'll be home about eleven.

Maybe a little after eleven—is that going to be too late?"

"That'll be fine. I'll come over then."

"Okay . . . I just can't believe it. Are you sure about this, Tyler? That you're going to get him? Or are you just wishing?"

"I'm sure as taxes."

"Good heavens," Margaret said. "Good heavens . . ."

Pierce hung up, then looked through the phone book for florists. There was one on Second and Poinsettia, and Pierce knew how to get over there. Had learned the city map pretty well. . . .

". . . Choice is, you're going to go either flown-in, hothouse, or delivered-today—and that would be tropicals or roses or wildflowers. Wildflowers won't last, be past it in a day or two."

"They don't have to last," Pierce said. The shop was air-conditioned nearly cold. It was a pleasure to be in it.

"Excuse me. . . ." The florist was an older man, stocky and balding, with a Navy tattoo on his left forearm. "Excuse me, but could I ask what the flowers are for? For example, is it love or regret or celebration or what?" The florist was wearing a white short-sleeved shirt with lace down the front. Like Mardanian's.

". . . I guess it's really all three of those things."

"Well . . . okay. All right. And this is for a lady?"

"Young lady."

"If they don't have to last—if that's not important—then personally, with a young lady involved, I'd recommend the wildflowers. Not as expensive, not as fancy, but they're pretty and have a sweet variety of color to them."

"I'll take the wildflowers."

"You can have roses. I can give you white roses."

"Wildflowers."

"Good, can't go wrong—but they won't last."

"That's all right."

"Nice bouquet, with fern and assorted greens," the florist said, and went to a wall of glass-doored coolers to make it up. . . .

. . . The cemetery was on Laurel—and not in Palmetto Lake, but just outside it. North, in the county.

Pierce found it with no wrong turns—remembered the last stretch from the funeral. The country out here was as pretty as south Florida country seemed to get. Fair-sized trees instead of just scrub and palms. And nice houses—big houses set back from the road.

The truck passed a stretch of white horse-fencing, and at the end of a long rolling pasture, Pierce saw the stock—looked like quarter horses, and good ones. Big butts on them . . . neat fined-down legs. It seemed to him the heat down here must be hard on horses, hard on all animals. Vermin and worms never killed by a real winter. . . .

The Glades was the name of the cemetery, and it was landscaped with small trees and shrubs, planted so as not to interfere with mowing the lawns. During the funeral, Pierce had noticed how well it was kept. Fancy landscaping . . . a section just in grass went down to a small lake. There were no tombstones, only bronze plaques set into the grass.

Pierce parked just inside the second entrance gate, got out of the truck with the bouquet, and walked through the heat up a long mild rise to the left . . . walking between rows of plaques with people's names on them. He knew the way to go, remembered the way the undertaker's blue limousine had gone. It had stopped on the other side of the slope, near a tree Carl Hubbard had said was a royal palm. —Best kind of palm tree Pierce had seen down here. Prettiest.

He knew the way to get there, and walked straight down to it past a flowering hedge of some kind. Little orange flowers with no smell to them. The thick little shiny leaves plants had down here . . . Past that, and on across the access road . . . then straight out over the lawn.

The royal palm was off to the right. It was as pretty as he'd remembered it. He'd watched it sometimes, while they were praying over the coffin.

Pierce walked across the grass past many plaques, and down to hers. Her name, and two dates—dates twenty-two years apart.

Lisa's grass was still new turf—slightly greener, in the Florida yellow-green way. And it was as hard to bear now as it had been at the funeral, that she should be buried here in the dirt to rot . . . the little girl who had come to him, come to hug him in that courthouse all those years ago while he was standing there, the fool of the world, in handcuffs with a deputy beside him. It was hard to bear. . . . Better, it seemed to Pierce, to have burned her to ashes, than this. He knelt beside the new grass, and untied the white ribbon that held green paper around the bouquet of flowers.

They didn't allow any vases here, because of the mowing.

"Hello, honey," Pierce said. "See what I brought you?" He took off the green paper and folded it up, and tucked it and the ribbon in his trouser pocket. Then he separated the flowers and fronds of greenery, and set them out, spread them like a lady's afghan coverlet over Lisa's new grass—little flowers, most blue or white, several bright yellow, and one small one almost red as a rose.

"Won't last long," Pierce said. "But aren't they pretty. . . ."

Chapter 25

Margaret looked tired, was the first thing Pierce thought, walking into the house. She looked as if she'd gotten too much sun on the boat.

She came and hugged him. "I still don't believe this. . . . It's so fantastic. Are you really sure?"

"Damn sure," Tyler said. "Damn sure of what we know now."

"Well, I'm sorry we were so late getting back."

"That's all right."

"—And you had to wait parked out in the street. . . ."

"It's all right. I had some dinner, and then I walked around."

"People start showing off their ridiculous boats, and they just want you to hang around and drink. —Come on out back. Carl's in the shower and he takes forever. . . ."

. . . And they were sitting where they'd sat before; this night hotter than the other had been. And darker, the moon not yet risen above the hedge, the low palms. The odors were the same. Tropical flowers, night flowers. And those swift night birds—insect catchers flickering past above them.

All the same, really. And Margaret sitting by him, her dress lighter than the dark.

"You want a drink, Tyler? Something to eat?"

"No, I guess not."

"That's good—about the drink—because I certainly could not join you. We spent the whole evening after

dinner drinking our fool heads off on that boat. . . . I
don't know what it is about those power squadron
people that they have to drink so much. You go out on
those boats and you just make yourself sick—and I'll
tell you, Carl really cannot do that anymore."

"Margaret, you mentioned, last time, that you and
Lisa had a fight. You know . . . before she died."

"Tyler, I'm not proud of it, but she was very strong-
willed. And I guess I am, too. So . . . you better believe
we had fights."

"I mean . . . I'm talking about something important,
Margaret." One of the insect-catching birds swooped
lower. Small darkness on darkness, flying by.

"What important?"

"Something serious, is what I mean."

"Tyler . . ."

"What is it?"

"I don't want to hurt you."

"You just forget about that, and tell me what I want
to know."

". . . We did have a bad fight last year. And we had
trouble between us all the time afterward, and I think it
was because of that. . . . Tyler, Lisa was going to have
a baby. She was going to have Jason's baby. —And
he's a nice boy. He wanted that child."

"Go on. . . ."

"He wanted it and I wanted her to have it, too—but
she was just . . . she was so stubborn she wouldn't
listen. Tyler, I honestly think if I had said, 'You get rid
of it,' if Jason had said, 'Get rid of it,' I honestly think
she would have kept that baby, she was that stubborn.
—And don't get angry with me, Tyler, but I think it was
your blood coming out in her, that . . . well, *recalci-
trance* is really the word I want. —And all she talked
about was having more time and her freedom—which is
just a lot of crap, pardon my French. Women don't have
any damn freedom, and that's the truth. We always lose

something no matter what we do. And that's a fact you don't understand and no man understands. . . ."

"So, she wanted the abortion and had it."

"Yes, she did, and we had . . . we had a terrible fight about it. I think I was more upset even than Jason. And she said it was her business and not my business."

"I see."

". . . And you *knew* all this, didn't you, Tyler? You knew it before I even started talking."

"Yes, I did. I knew it, or pretty near, but I'm checking and then I'm checking again. —And there's something else. Did Lisa have a friend while she was carrying that child? Somebody new come into her life then?"

"Somebody new? No. . . . There was a woman went around with her for a few weeks, back then. I wouldn't say a friend. They'd have lunch or shop or something I suppose. Carl saw them. But I don't think it was a friendship. I never met her."

"What was her name?"

"Oh, I don't know what her name was. Lisa never bothered to introduce her to me. —Which, I will say, was pretty typical at the time."

"Margie. . . ." Carl Hubbard turned a light on at the door, and came out onto the patio. He was barefoot and wearing a gray cotton bathrobe. "Why are you sitting out here in the dark? There's a phone call for Tyler. Hi, Tyler—it's some woman. Phone's in the hall."

"Hi, Carl. . . ." Pierce got up and went inside.

"Tyler?"

"Hi, Naomi. What's up?"

"I'm sorry to bother you there. I tried to catch you at the motel. . . . I'm sure your ex will not be pleased."

"Naomi, don't worry about it. What have you got?"

"First, what have *you* got?"

"Lisa exactly the same as all the others. —And that exact same friendly lady, too."

"All *right*. Well, I did The Clinic—and Tyler, I met

some very scary people going into the place. Not . . . you know, not toughies or anything. But very *very* serious people."

"I believe it."

"And I had some real luck. Tyler—they keep records there of all the people who harass their patients! That . . . you know, have come around the clinic."

"Do they now . . . ? What kind of records?"

"Photographs. And license numbers, Tyler. —And there's a nurse out there that's going to let me look at it now, tonight! She agreed there might—just *might* be something strange about a few of their clients being murdered."

"Will she let you copy all that?"

"If they have an office copier, I'll do it all right there. We'll have everything, Tyler. We'll have pictures to show Terry Ecklin."

"That's right. . . ."

"My God. It's just so *odd* to be succeeding in this. Do you feel strange?"

"Yes. I do."

"Okay. Okay . . . Why don't we meet for breakfast? I suppose another pound of fat won't make any difference. We'll meet for a celebration McDonald's breakfast, the McDonald's here in Palmetto Lake. There's one on Papaya, off Third; I saw it a couple of days ago."

"Eight o'clock?"

"Tyler—nine, please. I'm going to be up half the night."

"Nine o'clock. See you then."

"Bye-bye."

"Bye-bye."

Margaret came in from the patio with Carl, and said, "Carl, why don't you put something on your feet? . . . Walk around barefooted as if you never heard of spiders and scorpions. . . . Was that your lady friend down here, Tyler?"

"It was Naomi. . . . Listen, Margaret, are you sure Lisa never mentioned that woman's name? —Person we were just talking about, from last year."

"What woman?"

"Nobody, Carl," Margaret said. "That girl or whoever Lisa went around with for a little while last year. I don't— Tyler, I don't think I ever heard her name. Why is it so important?"

"It's important."

"'Well, I can't imagine why, and I don't know her name, anyway."

"What woman?"

"Oh, *Carl*. That woman Lisa was so buddy-buddy with for a few weeks last year. . . . She never brought her over."

"Hell," Carl said, "I remember her. Long time ago. I saw them downtown and they were going in the Peninsula to shop. Big girl. And I asked Lisa and she said that was a friend of hers and told me her name. . . . Can't remember the first name. Big girl. . . . Can't remember her first name, but her last name was the same as the pilot's."

"Pilot's? —Pilot's?"

"Tyler, let Carl think."

"—That's right," Carl said. "I was struck by that at the time. The pilot. . . . Fast pilot."

"Fast *pilot*?"

"That's right. I know *his* first name," Carl said. "Chuck."

". . . You mean Chuck Yeager?"

And Carl said, "That's it."

The Clinic's lights were off. Even the lights for the parking lot were off, and Naomi left the Nissan there and walked through darkness—the moon barely risen—to the back door, where the nurse had spoken to her.

She went up the steps, tried to see a bell, and the

heavy door swung open. The nurse was standing in shadow, with no lights on behind her. Her white uniform top and slacks shone in the darkness.

"Come in. . . ."

"I cannot tell you," Naomi said, and the nurse reached to close the door behind her, and lock it, "—I can't tell you how much we appreciate this."

" 'We'? Your friend?"

"We've been working on this very hard, last few weeks. I'm just—frankly I'm forgetting about the *Redbook* article. I think this is really important."

"Come on in," the nurse said, turned on the hall light and led the way down to the left. A striking woman, with those eyes, and her height.

"And I do think," Naomi said, "—and I know this sounds off the wall—but I do think the Sweetwater is probably one of your people that's been picketing out there. Been picketing for years, I'd say. Maybe more than one person—because a woman is definitely involved. No doubt about that."

"I guess it's possible," the nurse said. "The last one—Durchauer. That was *really* strange, so soon after her procedure. So I suppose it's worth it, reason enough to be sticking my neck out." She turned to switch off the hall light behind them. "I don't want a lot of lights showing outside. We're supposed to be closed, alarm on and everything."

"I really thank you," Naomi said, "for doing this."

The nurse turned a corner to the right, switched on a room light. It was a large supply room, cans and bottles of what seemed to be disinfectant . . . cleaners, and a powdered material in clear plastic. There were stacks of green sheets and white sheets, green pillowcases and white, on shelves almost to the ceiling. "—Isn't your friend going to meet you here?"

"No. He had something else to do."

"Okay . . ." The nurse walked through the supply room, waited for Naomi, then turned that light off and walked down a short dark corridor. To Naomi, the changes from dark to light to dark seemed almost dreamlike, as if she might follow the nurse for years through endless rooms—each dark, then lit, then dark again. . . .

"I already took the photograph file out. It's in the office."

"Could I copy things here?"

"Sure. We have a machine." The nurse went through a door to the right. "Come in. . . . There's something I need to do here, before we do anything else, Naomi." She turned on that room light as Naomi walked in. It was a utility room, with two sinks along one wall, and a coffee urn and cups on the counter between them. There was a white refrigerator and a big stainless double-doored freezer on the opposite wall.

The nurse opened the freezer's left-side door, slid a tray out of a stack of trays, and carried that over to the counter, set it down by the coffee urn. "I just need to finish this . . . take me a minute . . . and we'll go to the office." She lifted four packages—small heavy-duty plastic freezer bags—from the tray, then opened a counter drawer and took a clipboard out.

"—Torguson's so scared of legal trouble, we keep redundant records on all tissue. We enter stuff, then enter it again so there's always a double check on the fetal material. State doesn't require it, but he does it. Tissue used to go right down the disposal. . . ."

Naomi went to stand beside her, and saw in a freezer bag held in the nurse's hand, a frosted miniature. A fetal baby three or four inches long. It rested on its side, and its visible eye, its left eye, was open and a soft violet blue.

Naomi stepped back.

"Does this upset you?" the nurse said, and made her entry on the clipboard. "Most of them are just tissue, just scraps." She set that freezer bag back into the tray, picked up another one. "—What I do is fill the coded bag with those pieces, and put it in the freezer and make sure the entries are accurate. Occasionally we lose one . . . miscoded or whatever. Two other nurses coming in on shifts here, and sometimes they miss an entry. We get pretty busy. . . . But finally it's all red-bagged, and picked up every thirty days by the medical waste people."

Naomi stood back from the counter, and waited until the nurse was finished.

"—There we go. All done." The nurse picked up the tray. "Could you open the freezer for me? Left-side door."

Naomi opened the freezer door, and the nurse bent to slide the tray back in. ". . . All done." She straightened, really a tall woman, and smiled at Naomi. "You okay?"

"I'm fine."

"Okay. We'll go to the office." She reached out, switched off the room light, and walked away into the dark. Naomi followed her, and in the dark the nurse said, "Wait, one last stop," and stepped through a doorway.

When Naomi came in behind her, there was a sudden blaze of light, so bright it hurt her eyes. . . . It was a small operating room, tiled and very clean. The operating table was covered in plastic and white cloth. The table's examining stirrups, the machinery, wall cabinets, and trays of instruments were all stainless steel, shining under brilliant light.

"This is as close to sunlight as I get on work days," the nurse said. "This is OR One. We have another OR, and Dr. Bessler comes in sometimes if we have a rush."

"Let me ask you," Naomi said, "—and please tell me your name—I promise I won't use it or even write it down anywhere."

"Karen . . . Karen Yeager."

"Karen, what do you think of all this? I mean, it's your *profession*—and I don't mean to sound snotty.

I've had two abortions, myself. But I just wondered what you felt about all this. And if you want me to shut up, I will."

"No. No, that's all right, Naomi. I think you should understand what I feel about it. . . . Well, I know some women have reasons not to carry a fetus to term. I know that there are women who *shouldn't* carry to term, and they come here and I don't mind, because sometimes the child's spirit can still be saved."

"A religious thing . . ."

"It's a very personal belief." Karen Yeager smiled shyly, as if Naomi might make fun of her. "—But . . . but, what I was saying: in some cases I do feel that it's an improper separation. That mother and child should *not* be apart. And I'm—I feel tremendously lucky to be able to do something about that. Honored to do something at least in cases where you have a Must-be Mother who's aware of order, but still separates improperly."

"I don't . . . I don't understand, Karen. You mean when they shouldn't have the abortion at all, under any circumstances?"

"That's right."

"But what can you do about it? I mean, once it's over."

"I couldn't do anything about it, and it was really disturbing me. I mean bothering me a *lot*. But the Sun said some things . . . and the Angel grew—I think just by my being out in His light, and not being afraid of it. My feeling is, it's a plant inside me, that it's a growing thing. But I'm not sure. . . . It used to scare me half to death."

It was the oddest feeling. It was as if the dream of light and dark were continuing and making Naomi feel sick, as if this bright bright room were moving, swinging from side to side. "I'm afraid I . . ."

"That's what *I* said—'*afraid*'—but the Sun said, 'You will.' And the Angel grew."

Naomi's heart was hammering . . . hammering. She saw Terry Ecklin running after them, running so awkwardly through the warm wind from the sea. *"K,"* he'd called to them. *"First name begins with a K. . . ."*

"I think," Naomi said, and had been hearing a high humming sound, maybe from the lights. "Karen . . . I think I'd better go."

"No."

"Yes, I . . . have to go."

"No," the nurse said. *"Watch.* It's awake. It sleeps in my stomach. . . ." And the tall woman, tanned and beautiful, stood smiling down at Naomi. "It says . . ." And her mouth slowly opened wide, then wider as if her jaw would break, and her tongue curled and a voice came out, softly buzzing, as if a bee were speaking. "Hello, Naomi," it said. "I am meeting you. . . ."

Naomi ducked to the right to pick up a tray of bright instruments from a metal cart, threw them at Karen Yeager, and ran for the door.

And out of that shower of shining steel, out of the clatter and ringing of steel raining down onto tile, the Angel stepped, stretched out its left arm and caught Naomi's right arm as she ran, and stopped her running.

It was the strangest feeling. So odd that Naomi couldn't make sense of it as she kicked and struggled. . . . She'd been beaten by men a few times, had wrestled with one or two men in play. And this strength was no greater than any very strong man's. —But it was different. There was a sudden hard energy to it, like a machine's that would never tire, a machine that ignored her punching and kicking—though she kicked very hard—and ignored being bitten, too.

The Angel held her, paid no attention to her biting. It gathered in her flailing arms and hugged her very hard, so her bones ached.

"You fuck you *fuck*!" Naomi yelled, and still was kicking. Then the Angel hugged harder and broke two of Naomi's ribs. Naomi felt them break down her left

side; they broke like rungs in a ladder and stuck into
something inside her and she screamed *"Tyler . . . !"*
and still kept kicking.

"Shhh," the Angel said, held her a little away, and
hit her in the head.

There'd been four Yeagers in the Palmetto County
phone book. One K. Yeager.

Pierce found Cassava Street on the city map, and had
to go around the block once before he found the
number, 217, on a mailbox. He pulled into the curb,
climbed out of the truck from air conditioning into the
warmth and dampness of the night, and reached back
under his shirttail to check the Smith & Wesson.

The house was small and dark under a rising moon,
tucked back into palms and hedges. Seemed to have an
old tile roof. . . .

Pierce went down the front walk, then cut across the
lawn through a clump of low palms . . . fronds rustling,
stroking him as he passed. Insects . . . tree frogs sang
and rattled softly around him. No lights showed in the
house at all. There was no car in the drive.

Pierce went around to the back—pushed through
more plants as quietly as he could. Their leaves were a
deep green in the moonlight. British racing green. . . .
It was even warmer back here than out on the street.
The closeness of the palms and other plants made it
warmer. And the scent of tropical flowers, night-
blooming flowers, was very strong. The odors hung
still in the air, so Pierce moved through them across a
small yard to the house's back door.

All silent, except for the frogs . . . the insects. All dark.

Naomi woke naked, and lying down on a narrow
bed. Her forehead hurt so much it had wakened her.
There was too much light in her eyes, but when she
tried to bring her hand up to shield them, she couldn't.
Something held both her hands back up over her head.

Her feet. She couldn't move her feet either.

She looked down, and saw through yellow-white glare that her legs were raised and spread, her feet propped in steel examination stirrups, tied there at the ankles with strips of white cloth. She'd felt she was naked; now she saw she was.

"How do you feel?" The nurse, Karen . . . Yeager. The nurse bent over her. She had beautiful eyes, but her voice was the second voice, soft and peculiar, as if she were humming, as if something was wrong with her tongue. "How do you feel?"

"I—" Naomi cleared her throat. "I . . . feel naked and tied up. And my head hurts and my side hurts and I want to get up and get the fuck out of here." She was proud of herself for saying all that . . . for not crying and starting to beg. *Be careful, oh be careful,* she said to herself. *Don't beg.*

"Naomi, I want you to understand what's happening here." Soft . . . buzzing voice. "The person I possess is a daughter of the Sun, and we have a duty you were going to interfere with."

"You . . . are fucking crazy . . . !" *Not being careful . . . not being careful.*

The Angel smiled. "Sounds like it, doesn't it? And she thought so herself, for a while. But she's heard the voice of the Sun, and *that* voice, believe me, Naomi— may I call you Naomi?—that voice is beyond any madness. It is a fact, and it's the only fact. I wish he would speak to you—then you'd know and you'd help me, not try to prevent the reunion of mothers and their children in the Light."

"Listen to me . . . listen to me, Karen. You are murdering people." Naomi felt she would be fine, would be much braver if she weren't naked, and her legs held apart this way.

"Wrong. We're not murdering people." The Angel bent over Naomi, looked into her eyes, apparently wanted this to be made clear. "—You think that's so, out of ignorance." Soft, singing voice. "If you could have visited the Sun, if you could have rested in that endless, oh . . . oceans, oceans of endless light—and I *have*, I have been allowed to do that—then you'd know I'm only a messenger, an angel to arrange passage for them."

". . . I understand," Naomi said. "I understand and if you would just let me up, we can talk about it. I know you have an important message—"

"I don't have a message, Naomi. I wouldn't know what to say to people." The Angel shook its head. "I only have work to do—and you and your friend are interfering with it."

The Angel had an odd thing in its hand. It pushed with its thumb, and a long blade came clicking out. "You have no child inside you—but you do have the truth inside you. You can give birth to the truth for me, Naomi." Then it reached down between Naomi's thighs, where Naomi couldn't raise her head enough to see. In an instant there was a quick agony at her vagina so savage that Naomi lost her breath and jerked and thrashed on the table. She'd felt it while the blade was doing something there, and it was bad. It was very bad. A terrible pain and a sliding. . . .

"Now, you're open," the Angel said, and the blade of its odd knife clicked softly in and out. "And the truth should come out like a baby. . . . Where can I find your friend, the one you called for. *Tyler?* Was that his name? Is that his first name or his last name? . . . Tell me who he is, Naomi. Tell me where I can find him."

Naomi tried to take a breath; the pain was taking her breath away faster than she could breathe it. She tried, and was able to say, "You . . . kiss my ass." *Not . . . being careful.*

"Naomi, you're wasting the Sun's time." The Angel bent and did something, and Naomi felt it, but it didn't hurt as much as before. It was like a heavy line being drawn down her belly. The heaviest line being drawn. . . . But since it was the second time, something being done a second time, she supposed she was going to be killed. And that was so surprising. And so stupid. It seemed the wrong *time* to be killed. . . . and Tyler would blame himself.

"Open enough now, for the truth-child," the Angel said.

And there was something wrong in Naomi's mind, besides being killed and feeling so cold. She felt tired and she was remembering an afternoon from years ago, that couldn't have happened. Her father and Tyler were standing on a street corner outside the Rexall in Miami Beach, talking. Both of them so young . . . young men. She wondered if they were talking about her.

"This man who's with you, where can I find him? What is he?" asked the Angel, its clicking knife now bright red in its bright red hand. "Is he a police officer? What *is* he?"

"Good . . . company," Naomi said. Then, when the Angel bent and gave her close attention, she shouted in agony, but never said another word.

Pierce, at the house's back door, had stood listening. Bud Remburg, in the pen for breaking and entering, and a rape, had said, "Your B-an'-E is a cautious kind of business. Man don't look an' listen, he's goin' to fuck up."

"Guess you fucked up then, Bud." Freddy Simmons, in the weight room.

"Yes I did, Freddy," Remburg had said. "That's how come I know better, now. You need to look an' listen. . . ."

Pierce waited in an oleander's complicated moon shadow. . . . A car went past on the street in front. A dog barked several houses away. . . .

Then Pierce went up one step to the house's back door, found it locked, leaned back and kicked the door just above the lock. The wood split away with a hard crack, broke from the jamb, and the door swung open.

Only partly open. Something held it. Pierce stepped in, felt a soft thick fall of some dark cloth, gripped it and tore it down.

A blaze of light struck him—so bright it blinded him for a moment, seared his eyes so he stood squinting as they adjusted. And with the light, the soft thumping vibration of a muffled generator in a square closed porch to the left.

Down a short hallway, a small kitchen opened on the right. All the hall lights were on—and more than those. There were lamps and worklights, and bright reflector bulbs strung on extension cords along the walls. It was a space of light, still bright enough to hurt his eyes.

When he could see despite the glare, Pierce moved down the hall and into the kitchen ... through the kitchen, the Smith & Wesson weaving in front of him as he went.

The narrow living room was molten gold. Lightbulbs hung in rows from cords across the ceiling; floor lamps were ranked along the walls. There were strands of Christmas twinkle-lights woven over the furniture so the room pulsed with light, flashed and strobed with light. There were no shadows in the house.

The bulbs' heat stung Pierce's face as he went through. There were paintings on the living-room walls—all big paintings of the sun, flaming in bright yellow. And where there were no paintings, there were mirrors giving back the light. Pierce saw himself in them with his shining gun, and seemed to be standing in fire.

He went through and checked the bedroom—just as bright. A big tabby cat lay on the bed, sleepy, eyes slitted against the light. ... Pierce checked the bathroom, dazzling white and hot.

No one in the house.

He paused coming out, to check the bedroom closet.

A floor lamp stood shining there amid the hanging clothes. A woman's clothes. . . . And uniforms. White. And white shoes on the closet floor beneath them.

Pierce stood for a moment listening to Naomi's voice, clear as anything. "A nurse out here is going to help us. . . ."

He turned and ran out to the living room, through to the kitchen, toppling lamps, smashing their bright bulbs—running through a lake of heat and light that seemed to slow him like syrup. There wasn't time for 911, wasn't time to persuade the cops to move. . . .

Then he was out the back door and running fast through plants—shoving through—and on down the walk and out into the street.

Pierce got to the truck and was in it—door slammed shut, pistol put on the seat beside him—and he started the engine and pulled away . . . the city map, the route to Palm Way, coming clear into his mind as a favor from God.

He drove as fast as the truck would go and take the corners—and supposed if a cop came on him, he'd just lead him and keep going. Or kill him, if he had to. . . . There was some traffic, a few traffic lights—and Pierce paid no attention to any of it. He drove past and through as if he and his truck were roaring alone through a world of night. The truck got up to sixty on cross streets. Ninety on the avenue straights.

Cassava to Fourth Avenue. Sunnyside . . . to Banyan . . . to Third Avenue, leaving angry car horns behind him. Then down Third almost a mile . . . and right one street over to Palm Way. The Clinic was in the six hundred block, on the edge of town. . . .

Pierce saw it on the right, and pulled in to the curb—picked up his pistol, swung the truck door open and lit running. Around the truck and up the walk to the double glass front doors. He went up the steps and tried the doors just once. Locked.

He stepped back and fired three deliberate shots into

the right-side door—and the thick glass starred and frosted, then blew in with a crash, and Pierce stepped through into darkness.

"Naomi . . . !" He hunted for a light switch, found it by the door, and the lobby lights came on.

There was an open office past the small lobby, and he ran back through it to a corridor . . . couldn't find a light switch there, and ran to the left, trying doors. He found a switch beside a doorway. Another office, empty.

He shoved open the door at the end, clicked on the light of a big supply room—and turned and ran back down the hall the other way. *"Naomi . . . !"*

There were two doors at the other end of the corridor, and he kicked the first one open, found the light switch, and saw a counter and sink. Then turned, went down the hall to an open doorway . . . and through into a space filled with bright moonlight streaming down through skylights.

"Honey . . . ?" An operating room, machinery and cabinets along one wall.

There was a narrow white table at the center, and a salty smell. The table was mottled white and shadowed black in the shape of a woman—white and black and naked—knees up, bare feet tied into bright steel stirrups with white strips of cloth.

And Pierce knew.

He found a light switch by a cabinet that brought down a single beam, bright as gold, onto the table—and Naomi flashed into color with gloom around her. All her moonlit black became bright red in wet runs and streaks across her. In long stains down the table sheet. She lay spraddled, her bent legs propped wide, her arms tied back above her head. Her thighs were stained, her groin sliced open as if she'd given the most difficult birth.

"Oh . . . oh, sweetheart," Pierce said. And she was so thin. Paler than he remembered, and small, fragile under her scarlet decoration. "Oh . . . sweetheart," he said. And Naomi, dead, her face set in stern resolution, looked up at him with eyes deeper and darker than before.

Pierce felt he couldn't leave her tied like that. The pistol hindering, he fumbled at the knots that held her ankles. Got one loose and then the other. "Oh, Naomi," he said. "Oh, my *God*," as if he'd never seen anyone hurt or dead before. —And the light went off, and something swift came out of the dark and struck him as he turned. Struck him—muttering, humming—and was stronger than he was for a moment. It lifted him and threw him sideways across the operating table. There was a clicking sound.

Pierce felt Naomi's soft skin, still warm, damp against his arm as he twisted back and hit out with his other hand, his left fist—hit something that didn't seem to mind, and ice came sliding down his wrist.

Pierce had been cut before, and knew better than to heed it. Up off the table, he raised the revolver and fired into shadow—and saw in that blast and flash of light a tall woman dressed in white . . . calm, sad, certain as God Almighty. She reached out, knocked the gun aside, then suddenly stooped—and Pierce felt a blade run up his left leg and he leaned far back as the quickest breeze came up and just missed his belly. He saw the bright steel in moonlight and fired over it at what moved away so fast it blurred from the blast into dark, and out of the room and gone.

Pierce stood in ringing silence for a moment—listened, heard nothing—then went after her. He ran through the dark rooms as fast as he could, limping. Blood was sliding down into his shoe. . . . In the hallway, he heard a door slam shut, and limped through a back hall toward the sound.

A car's engine started as he came through the back door into moonlight, and a white Toyota pulled out of

the parking lot into the street, took a right turn with
squealing tires . . . then turned right again. South.

Pierce ran to the side of the building, and around to
the front . . . running with a good right leg, a bad left
leg that seemed filled with hot water, heavy, making
wet sounds in his shoe.

He limped down the front lawn, got to his truck and
climbed in, set the revolver aside, started the engine
and drove away. Drove away south. It was his good leg
on the accelerator, and he stamped the pedal to the
floor and didn't lift it. —And as he went, Pierce
thought he heard a squad car's warble faint in the distance behind him. Faint and far back, chasing a
reported speeder in a roofing truck. . . .

The truck rolled south in moonlight, down an empty
Palm Way. Almost empty. Nearly a mile ahead, tiny
taillights winked red. . . . She'd be going down the
same road he and Naomi had driven up. Down the long
backcountry blacktop, heading south to Miami to hide
among all those millions. Go to cover and hide, until
time to do again what she'd done before.

Pierce thanked God for his truck, its big engine and
solid weight. . . . Would be a chore for a little car to
stay out front all that way, on a country road.

He thought of Naomi for a moment, imagined her
sitting beside him. . . . No doubt would have something
to say about his driving.

"I see you're doing ninety miles an hour, Tyler—on
a narrow county road in the middle of the night. And
. . . *and* we have a canal running right alongside
here. . . ."

"I know that, Naomi." That's what he'd say to her.
"Why don't you just let me drive, and you reload that
revolver."

". . . You have one bullet left, Tyler—that's all you
have in this gun and in this truck. Don't tell me the
Iceman can't handle a tragic nut case with one round.
—And by the way, what was all that shooting back

there, to no avail? I'm surprised those Midwest bankers took you seriously. . . ."

Later, she would say, "Tyler, are you hurt? Did she hurt you?"

"Didn't hurt me enough," Pierce said out loud. "Not near what I deserve."

"Oh, bullshit," Naomi said. *"Drive."*

The truck hurled itself through moonlit night, its windshield speckled and spotted with killed bugs. Pierce rode it hard, his foot down all the way—and sometimes, over gentle rises in the blacktop, the truck would lift . . . lift away, and sail a few yards free of the pavement as if it were some huge and ugly baby bird, almost ready for flight. Then thump back down, springs humming, and tear along faster, jolting, out-running its headlights down the road.

Pierce, feeling slightly sick from his left arm and leg being cut, from losing blood, set that feeling aside. It seemed to him Naomi's being dead was the cause of those injuries, his left side paying for his carelessness with her . . . his fault.

When his attention wandered after a while, even only a little as the truck thundered on—chasing as if it didn't need Pierce with it at all—there would appear now and then those distant tiny red sparks of light before him, and Pierce would come alert to those lights, and drive hard. His right leg was sore from pressing the accelerator down; his left leg didn't hurt at all. And sometimes then, he thought he heard cops far behind him. Coming along far back, as they'd come from way across town to the bank in Wichita.

. . . The little red lights were slowly growing clearer, no matter how he felt. Growing clearer as time passed so slowly. Growing a little larger.

Sometime later, a car came toward him going north—and swerved away to the left, almost off the road, as the truck tore past.

. . . Now, Pierce could see the white Toyota. Far, far

ahead, a chip of ivory running on a ribbon of black. The moon was huge off to the west, a hot full red-gold summer moon. Its light seemed warmer than silver across the landscape of groves, scrub, and distant palms.

Pierce glanced too long; the truck's right tires ran off pavement onto the road's narrow shoulder and the vehicle thumped and shuddered at speed, and Pierce said, *"No,"* and turned the big wheel a sudden three inches to the left. The truck heaved and jolted back onto the blacktop and ran smooth again, slightly rising and falling in its speed with the rise and fall of the road.

... Now the red taillights, the small white car, showed very clear—and nowhere for it to turn. Any rutted road, any gravel or dirt road would slow it, give the truck's weight so much more advantage.

A mile ... more than a mile farther on, the moonlight brighter than the truck's dash lights, the Toyota seemed to tire as the truck grew stronger, and the car was now close enough to see very clearly. A hundred yards ahead, no more than that.

Pierce sat up straighter, tried to move his left leg— lift it, set it back down on the floorboards. He moved his hurt left arm ... raised it up, clenched and unclenched his fist, to be ready.

In the distance, he saw the line of a lesser road cutting across. There was a blinker at that crossroad. Amber ... amber ... amber. Pierce exercised his bad leg, tried to make a fist with his left hand.

The truck's moonshadow almost reached the Toyota's trunk, coming up ... coming up. ...

As they drove into the crossroads, the white car swerved and swerved hard left, trying for the turn—and Pierce braked and steered tilting after it, the truck's left-side tires lifting off the road. The Toyota stayed upright, but skidded and sailed ... sailed off the crossroad at a slant past a long shed—struck a high curb, then slid down a gravel drive to a tall hurricane-fence gate and smashed through it. It went through in a cloud of sand and dust and didn't slow but began to burn as it went, gasoline exploding out of its ruptured tank so it trailed fire out into scrub and wilderness.

Pierce followed fast, jouncing past a splintered sign, hanging, that read MAINTENANCE ACCESS. The truck broke through that damaged half of the gate, tore the rest of the structure away, and Pierce thought of Ronald Fiala for an instant . . . the paint job.

Then the truck was through, and following a trail of fire. Pierce saw the car burning and slewing sideways in soft sand a way away. And in the fire's light, he saw her come out of the car in white, away from the spreading fire—and she was fast out of it and away running into the night.

He steered to follow her, and had to gear down in the soft sand there. Passed the burning car on the left and kept driving. Now, he could see her by moonlight, the fire behind him, and he drove along behind.

The truck's engine lugged, and Pierce geared down again and in the headlights saw pools of water amid low scrub. The hurricane had left remnant ponds and puddles in these swales; the soil was softened to mud.

The truck ground through another quarter mile behind her, then sank to its hubs and stalled.

Pierced picked up the revolver, opened the door and climbed down. He could see the woman ahead, no longer running quite so fast—perhaps injured in her crash, perhaps one of the pistol rounds had touched her after all. Pierce went after her, but couldn't run—he tried it and fell down. . . . He couldn't run, but he would walk, hitch along pretty well. He felt he could do that until hell froze over.

The ground was wet mud almost knee-deep for a stretch, then began to rise slightly, and dry, and Pierce could see her very clearly . . . the moonlight was that bright. Could see her ahead—and staying ahead of him.

Just too far for a handgun shot. He could see the moon-shadow she cast. She was trotting . . . jogging as if she was out for exercise, moving—hurt or not—as if no man could ever catch her.

Pierce learned a new way of going—using his left leg like a crutch. Swinging along on that dead leg, and getting by that way. He was working at that, working at it . . . and saw a shadow away to the left. It was moving past . . . going past, very big. And there were other shadows after it. He thought for a moment it was a rail-road train, powered by electricity to be so silent, rolling through the nighttime country.

Then he saw it wasn't a train.

Dark . . . dark under moonlight, and silent, elephants were drifting through the scrub.

Pierce stood still. Stood still and almost called out to the woman running from him. Almost shouted out to her . . . then decided not.

The elephants had moved on . . . moved on past.

This was becoming higher ground, drier sand and rough high grasses. It was easier to travel through, easier to swing his leg along. Pierce had stopped trying to clench his left hand. That hand was useless to him. If his left leg was as bad as that left hand, he would be crawling. . . .

Karen Yeager trotted a distance before him, but he came after. And Pierce felt sorry for her, more and more. She had no chance at all, however fast or far she ran. He came after, and watched her shadow dance across deep grass.

She jogged ahead, and over a mild rise—and Pierce hitched along and hitched along, and climbed that fairly well. He came over the rise as she ran away deep into a great shallow bowl of high grass and moonlight, and he caught his breath and began to hobble down.

There was a sound. There was a sound. . . .

A cough and deep grunt as if a giant woke and cleared his throat. A cough again.

Out of the grass as the woman ran along, great figures rose and stretched and watched her come. —And Karen Yeager stood still. Lions rose from the grass before her, and the silver moonlight made them gold.

"Come back ...!" Pierce raised the Smith & Wesson, its single round. He called, *"Come back to me ...!"* And supposed he was doing this because it was what Naomi would have expected of him.

He called, "Listen to me! *Listen* ... to me. I won't hurt you. Just slowly ... slowly walk back to me. I promise I won't hurt you. Nobody will hurt you."

The woman stood still in the bowl of light. The lions watched.

"Please," Pierce called to her. "... Please. Slowly now, come on back to me."

Karen Yeager turned where she stood, and stared at him. And he saw her face in moonlight, and there was nothing human in it.

Then she turned and walked away toward the lions. A great maned male watched her. ... Then, off to the side, a female—gold and cream in moonlit grass—crouched and came running in her crouch, reached Karen Yeager and knocked her down.

Pierce saw no struggle at all. Saw none of the woman's savage strength and quickness, no last flash of sharp steel. Struck, she lay quiet beneath the lioness. Lay quiet as the others came to her. ...

Pierce turned and limped away. Hard going. He thought he heard cops' sirens in the distance. ... It would be hard going with so bad a leg.

The Angel lay in soft grass, content, its back broken. The clever knife, that still could slice, it allowed to rest quiet in its hand as a great cat stood innocent over the steel. The moonlight, so poor an imitation of the Sun's, was obscured at last. And golden eyes, like smaller suns, burned over the Angel as beasts bent to set it free.

* * *

"Ted, you remember Macksie?" Agent Hildebrandt at the office door, and looking pleased.

"I remember Sheriff Macksie," Gottfried said. That Florida law officer had, in the summer, sent several furious faxes to the FBI's office in Jefferson City, complaining about previously insufficient information concerning a major felon. A felon who, it was true, had—with another individual, deceased—stumbled on the probable perpetrator of several highly publicized homicides. With more publicity then following. . . .

"Well," Hildebrandt said, "here's a little item just came in. Wonder if Macksie'd like to see it. Union Sentinel Insurance just reported to Washington that a certain amount of money—almost seven hundred thousand dollars—has been deposited in a trust account in the name of Presley Robbins, currently resident at Hibbing Rehab."

"The Trans-Con Company guard. One was shot up."

"You got it. Deposited in that young man's name out of a Lesser Cayman bank by person or persons unknown—and, according to Washington, unknowable."

"Are you kidding me?"

"Ted, I would never do that. —Deposited in young Robbins's name. And I would say represents just about exactly all that would be left of a one-third share from the Trans-Con robbery, after cover-and-concealment expenses . . . and miscellaneous."

". . . I'd say that's about right."

"Insurance company claims it should be *their* money. But can't prove it."

"Can't prove it. . . . And we can't prove it, George. But I will bet you one dollar to one doughnut that it will be years before a certain small-time roofing contractor can afford a new truck. . . ."

. . . There are few places less comfortable than a high roof in a hard winter. Mickey was down to get another bundle of shingles—fiberglass stuff, and not the best fiberglass, either—and Pierce was taking the opportunity to pull several shingles the boy had nailed off the pattern. Mickey just could not read a pattern.

They'd swept the snow off in the morning, and that was a mistake, since it left slick ice and worse footing, so they'd had to set battens across the roof for safety.

You would think . . . a person would think that a man who owned a hardware store could plan putting a new roof on it in the summer. Wouldn't wait for winter leaks to convince him, and then make an emergency call to the poor roofer. . . .

Mickey called from below, and Pierce went over to the edge. "What is it?"

"Miz Pierce," Mickey said, and Carolyn was climbing out of her car into the snow piled along the sidewalk.

She called up, "I brought you two a hot lunch!" and held up a big paper sack.

"Get back home, damn it," Pierce said. "Mickey, you take that stuff from her."

"I'm fine, Tyler. . . ." Carolyn handed over the lunches, and stepped carefully back through the snow to her car. —She was doing very well, though she'd quit working at Snip N' Style, since that was so many hours standing on her feet. —Working at the library didn't bother her, though, and that wasn't big money but it was a help. She'd had amnio in Independence, and they'd said the child was just fine, a healthy little baby girl. . . .

Naomi would be born in the spring.

TERROR ... TO THE LAST DROP

SIGNET   **ONYX**

TALES OF TERROR

☐ **THE WEATHERMAN by Steve Thayer.** When Andrea Labore, a beautiful, ambitious Twin Cities TV newscaster, goes after the story of a serial killer of pretty women, it soon becomes clear that the monstrous murderer is after her. As the clouds of suspicion darken, the only sure forecast is that death will strike like lightning again and again ... closer and closer.... (184386—$6.50)

☐ **SAINT MUDD by Steve Thayer.** The gruesome double murder was not unusual for St. Paul, wallowing in the Great Depression. Even a hard, seasoned reporter like Grover Mudd couldn't get used to dead bodies. With the reluctant help of the F.B.I., the conflicted loyalty of a beautiful blond moll, and the hesitant encouragement of his own gentle mistress, Mudd targets the sociopathic killers with his own brand of terror. (176820—$6.50)

☐ **BONE DEEP by Darian North.** A beautiful woman runs for her life in a vortex of passion, lies, betrayal, and death ... all intertwine in this stunning novel of knife-edged suspense. (185501—$6.99)

☐ **FLAWLESS by Adam Barrow.** A woman is found brutally murdered, the pattern all too familiar. Her killer, long gone from the scene of the crime, is Michael Woodrow, a flawlessly handsome and intelligent thirty-year-old. He is a man who cannot control his compulsion to kill and kill again. "A nail-bitter."—*People* (188497—$5.99)

*Prices slightly higher in Canada

FEAR IS ONLY THE BEGINNING

☐ **PRECIPICE by Tom Savage.** The house is named Cliffhanger, a bit of heaven perched high on a hill in a Caribbean paradise. It is the home of the perfect family—until bright and beautiful Diana arrives, the ideal secretary-au pair. Now suddenly, everyone in this house is on the edge of a hell where nothing is what it seems, and no one is who they pretend to be. (183339—$5.99)

☐ **THICKER THAN WATER by Linda Barlow and William G. Tapply.** A precocious teenager's abduction leads to a seductive voyage of danger and self-discovery as he and his family must at last confront the very essence of evil.
(406028—$5.99)

☐ **JUST BEFORE DAWN by Donna Ball.** When Carol Dennison received the call after midnight, she knew without a doubt that the voice pleading for help was her teenage daughter's. Though the police had written her off as a runaway teen, Kelly's mother, Carol, had always suspected far worse. Now one parent's most fervent prayer has been answered. And her greatest nightmare is about to begin.
(187342—$5.99)

☐ **EXPOSURE by Donna Ball.** Jessamine Cray, Philadelphia's most poised and glamourous TV talk show host is being stalked. The police think she's faking the campaign of terror out of a twisted hunger for public sympathy. But her tormentor is using her own darkly buried secrets as a cunning weapon to destroy Jess's peace of mind—before destroying her. (187334—$5.99)

☐ **GAME RUNNING by Bruce Jones.** A stranger comes to your door, claiming he once knew you. You invite him in, and he drugs you. You wake the next morning to find your home has been stripped clean and your wife has been kidnapped. Your life has suddenly spiraled out of control. (184068—$5.99)

*Prices slightly higher in Canada

Buy them at your local bookstore or use this convenient coupon for ordering.

PENGUIN USA
P.O. Box 999 — Dept. #17109
Bergenfield, New Jersey 07621

Please send me the books I have checked above.
I am enclosing $_____ (please add $2.00 to cover postage and handling). Send check or money order (no cash or C.O.D.'s) or charge by Mastercard or VISA (with a $15.00 minimum). Prices and numbers are subject to change without notice.

Card #_____ Exp. Date _____
Signature_____
Name_____
Address_____
City _____ State _____ Zip Code _____

For faster service when ordering by credit card call **1-800-253-6476**

Allow a minimum of 4–6 weeks for delivery. This offer is subject to change without notice.